The Billionaire's Obsession

THE COMPLETE COLLECTION

Mine For Tonight

Mine For Now

Mine Forever

Mine Completely

Mine for Christmas

J. S. SCOTT

The Billionaire's Obsession

Cover by lorijacksondesign.com

ISBN 978-1718906518

Contents

Mine For Tonight

BOOK ONE

The Billionaire's Obsession

Chapter 1

S imon Hudson stood silently in the shadows of the opulent lobby, his hands in the pockets of his jeans and one shoulder propped against the frame of a large window that faced the street. His whole body was tense, his dark brown eyes scanning the sidewalk with the intense and total focus of a madman.

Where in the hell is she? It's ten forty-five.

He knew Kara was working tonight. She had called in sick for the last two evenings, but was back to work at Helen's Place, waiting tables on the swing shift. He had checked. His mother owned the bistro where Kara worked and was generally pretty forthcoming with information when Simon wanted it, but he was careful. If he wasn't, his only parent would be hounding him to find out why he wanted information on Kara. His wonderful but inquisitive mom would be like a bloodhound after a scent if she thought that Simon's interest was anything but casual. He would be nagged to death, his mother wanting to know exactly what his intentions were with Kara.

Simon frowned. Like he had any intentions? He had fantasies and all of them involved Kara spread out on his bed, screaming his name as he made her come, over and over.

Simon took a deep breath and slowly blew it back out, trying to get his body to relax and telling himself that he must be insane to take exactly the same position, night after night, for some woman who he had never officially met. But here he was…again, his back to the curious doorman, leering out the window like an unbalanced stalker, waiting to get a glimpse of Kara Foster. Something about the woman brought out strange, territorial, and protective instincts that kept him here, keeping watch, waiting for her to walk by his condo building on her way home from work.

And then, when he spotted her, he'd do the same thing he always did. He'd follow her at a distance, trying not to alarm her, and wait until she had let herself into her apartment safely before he turned around and walked back home.

He wouldn't talk to her, or even get close to her. He never did. It wasn't that he didn't want to, but Kara was going to nursing school and working full-time at his mother's restaurant. According to his mom, Kara adamantly refused to date because she didn't have the time or energy to put into a relationship. She was probably right about that. The insane woman didn't sleep enough, eat enough. She had no one who even worried about her except for his mother…and Simon. Hell, in the last year, Simon had probably cared more about Kara's well-being than a dozen family members would have, and he couldn't even call her a friend. Problem was…he wasn't a family member, and his feelings were far from brotherly.

God, she was sweet!

Simon had to bite back a groan of frustration as he thought about the first time he had seen Kara, her blue eyes flashing with humor, black tendrils of silky hair escaping from her ever-present ponytail and her lithe body moving gracefully from table to table at his mom's restaurant. At the age of twenty-eight, she still retained a look of innocence and vulnerability that had Simon caught in her unintentional web. He'd been a prisoner there ever since.

His mother spoke about Kara as if she were her daughter, and Simon knew that Kara and his mother had a special bond: one not formed by blood, but by a special friendship. Shit…if Kara were younger, Simon was pretty sure his mother would adopt her. Lips twitching slightly, Simon hoped his mother never expected him to be like a brother to Kara. It wasn't happening. His cock stood at attention, rock-hard and ready, every time he saw her. What in the hell was it about this particular woman that made him so edgy and restless?

Simon had fucked women who were more attractive or more sophisticated, and not a single one of them had ever touched any of his emotions. He was a loner, preferring to spend his time with his computer rather than attending social functions, but there were times when he needed a woman's company for physical relief. Occasionally taking himself in hand just wasn't getting it done. Simon had certain female acquaintances for those occasions, women who gave him the control he needed and had to have in the bedroom, without a lot of demands or questions. Damn it! That had been enough for him... until he had seen Kara.

Grimacing, his eyes never leaving the street, Simon shoved his hands deeper into his pockets and adjusted his position, giving his shoulder a break by resting his hip against the wall. God, he was getting pathetic. How long would he moon over a woman who had never even acknowledged him? Until she finished nursing school and moved away? Until she got married?

He nearly growled at the thought of another man putting his hands on Kara's delectable body. Simon fought a purely feral instinct that rose up at the thought of another man touching his woman.

She's not your woman, asshole. Get a grip.

For once in his life, Simon wished he were more like his older brother Sam, the other half of the Hudson Corporation. Sam would have no problem putting the moves on Kara. *Charm, conquer, and discard* had always been his brother's style and Sam wouldn't have given a thought to the possibility of rejection. Probably because Sam never failed! His only sibling went through the female population like a person with a nasty cold went through tissues. Sam would have broken down Kara's defenses, charmed her out of her panties and then discarded her for his next conquest.

Oh, hell no. Simon loved his brother, but he'd be damned if he'd ever let Sam seduce Kara. He didn't even want the two of them in the same room together.

Because she's mine.

Simon shook his head, surprised at his own behavior. Yeah…he liked control, actually needed control, but he had never wanted one woman in particular. Now, he could think of little else but the pretty waitress who had snagged his attention a year ago.

You're afraid of her.

Simon scowled at the thought. Like hell he was! He wasn't afraid of anything, and he definitely didn't fear Kara Foster. She just…was not a likely lover. Why bother?

He fucked.

He didn't date.

And he liked it that way.

His brother Sam was the face of the company, the marketer. Simon was a computer geek, happy to stay in the background. What did he know about seducing a woman? He'd never needed to coerce a woman to his bed. The females he fucked were only with him for personal gain. He was known as a generous lover. He wasn't fool enough to believe they had any personal feelings for him. That, he understood. That, he could handle.

Maybe I need to find a way to fuck her and get over this crazy obsession.

Would it be enough? Could he actually get free from his fixation with this woman if he could find a way to have her?

Christ! He had to do something. His irrational preoccupation with Kara had grown worse and worse over the last year, causing him to want no other woman except her. He hadn't gotten off with anyone except himself in well over a year, and he really needed to scratch that itch. Yet…he couldn't. If he tried to take action, to make a move to call another woman, he would see Kara's pretty girl-next-door face and hang up the phone.

I'm just that fucking obsessed with her.

Simon glanced at an approaching figure, his mind almost immediately starting to dismiss the dark-haired woman who was dressed in a short, black, leather mini-skirt and a bright red sweater. He'd never seen Kara dressed in anything other than jeans and a t-shirt that sported the restaurant's logo, standard casual dress for employees of his mom's restaurant.

He did a surprised double-take as the woman got closer, gaping when her face came into view. Holy Christ! It was Kara. She was close enough that he could see her features, the same face that haunted his wet dreams every damn night, but the outfit....

What in hell is she wearing?

Simon could see almost every inch of her long, slender, shapely legs in the ultra-short mini and the whole outfit molded over her breasts, torso, and ass like a glove. His cock was instantly standing at full attention and he pulled his hands out of his pockets. They curled into tight fists as a bead of sweat rolled down his face. Followed by another. And another.

Goddamnit! What was she thinking? Dressed that way, she was practically begging for some man to come and snatch her up off the street.

And, by God, he was going to be that man. He wasn't leaving that opportunity to another male, someone who might do her harm.

Didn't she realize that this was Tampa? A major city! It wasn't some tiny town where she could walk the streets at night and not be noticed or accosted.

Simon unclenched one fist and gripped the window frame for support, his eyes never leaving the approaching female. Gritting his teeth, Simon knew that today was the day he was going to have to get close to her, closer than he'd ever been before. He couldn't handle these animalistic and rampant emotions anymore. He didn't like them, wasn't used to them. All he wanted was his sanity back, to return to his computer and work on his passion for developing computer games without erotic thoughts of Kara taking over his brain.

Sense. Reason. Control. That was how he functioned and what he needed in order to be himself again, and dammit, he'd get back to his normal state of mind, no matter what drastic measures he had to take to achieve it. Somehow, he would purge himself of this incredibly stupid and raging desire for Kara Foster.

His mind made up, Simon pushed off the window frame and stood up straight, lowering his "mask" until his face was devoid of emotion. He was good at that. He'd been raised in an area of Los Angeles where most normal people would never even enter, a place where being weak, slow-witted, or fragile in any way meant being destroyed.

If nothing else, Simon Hudson was a survivor. His guise firmly in place, he ripped his gaze from the window, turned sharply and strode purposefully toward the door.

Kara Foster was having a seriously bad day!

She hefted her backpack to make it sit more solidly on her shoulder and reached for the hem of her ridiculously short skirt, yanking it down hard to cover her ass. The clothes looked great on her classmate, Lisa, who was several inches shorter and seven years younger than Kara. Unfortunately, they didn't look quite the same on Kara's taller, fuller body. The sweater hugged her generous breasts and the skirt was too damn short, barely concealing the cheeks of her ass.

She was a street-smart woman, having grown up in one of the worst areas of Tampa and coming through the experience intact. Kara knew how to protect herself, how to avoid any unwanted attention. So what in the hell was she doing in an outfit that was bound to get her in trouble? *Stupid, Kara. Really, really stupid!*

Frowning, Kara forced herself to keep walking. No big deal. She was in a decent area. So what if she looked like a sex kitten in sneakers? Eight more blocks and she would be home, free to finally strip off the ludicrous outfit and put on her own comfortable jeans and t-shirt.

Kara heaved a sigh as she focused solely on arriving at the tiny apartment that she shared with another student. Her legs were cold and she shivered, walking faster to get her body warm. It was January in Tampa, and while the daytime hours were pleasant, it got chilly at night. She should have brought her jacket, but she had been running late this morning.

She hadn't planned to have her legs bare and her behind flapping in the breeze.

The day is almost over.

Thank God!

She had spilled coffee on her own jeans and t-shirt earlier in the day. With no time to go home and change before she had to get to work, Kara had gratefully accepted the offer of clean clothes from Lisa, a classmate who was never without a change of clothing in her car. It wasn't that Kara didn't appreciate the kindness of her classmate. She definitely did. Kara just wished she could wear the clothing with the same attitude as Lisa. But…she couldn't. She was used to keeping a low profile, and she was mortified that she probably resembled a call girl with bad shoes, functioning the entire day and evening with a hint of red on her cheeks and trying desperately not to bend over.

When she had arrived at the restaurant for her shift, her kind boss, Helen Hudson, had taken pity on her and dug in the drawers for an apron that reached Kara's knees and covered her exposed backside.

Wishing she had worn the apron home, she jerked again at the bottom of the snug skirt with more than a hint of frustration, hoping she wasn't flashing anything more than some bare thigh.

Exhaustion tugged at Kara's body and her stomach rumbled. She had gotten so busy at work that she hadn't taken the time to eat. The small, cozy restaurant had been busy, much busier than usual because it was Friday night. She had actually been grateful for the customers. The tip money she had in her backpack was all that stood between her and a completely empty bank account. Maybe she could buy a few groceries now that she had a few bucks from tips. Her cupboards at home were bare and her roommate seemed to be in even worse financial shape than Kara. Lydia never bought food and whatever Kara bought disappeared quickly.

Last semester! You can make it.

Damn...it had been a long four years, and Kara felt much older than her actual age of twenty-eight years. Actually, she just felt old. Period! Most of her classmates were barely legal drinking age and were all about college partying, while Kara could only think about making it through each day, getting one step closer to graduation.

Kara had lost her parents in an auto accident at the age of eighteen and was pretty much alone. After working for several years as a waitress, barely surviving, she knew she had to either go to college or resign herself to struggling through life with no end to poverty in sight.

She didn't regret the decision to go to college, but it had been difficult, an arduous and lonely road that she could only be grateful was almost over.

You'll make it. Almost there!

Kara stopped abruptly as the sidewalk started to tilt and her vision blurred. Oh, shit. Her hand reached out to grip the post of a street-light to steady herself as her brain whirled and her body trembled. Dizziness made it impossible to function, to advance any farther. *Damn it. I should have taken the time to eat.*

"Kara!" She heard the low, no-nonsense baritone filter through to her foggy brain. The voice was abrupt, but it was reassuring to know that someone who knew her, who recognized her, was here.

Shaking her head, trying to clear her vision, Kara tightened her grip on the metal post and willed herself not to pass out on the cold stone pavement as her body swayed precariously, preparing itself for the fall.

Chapter 2

"Christ, you look like hell!" The same voice, impatient and husky, broke through her hazy mind, and she felt a pair of solid, muscular arms come around her as she was lifted against a solid, rock-hard chest.

Warm...so warm. Instinctively, she snuggled into the heat of the sturdy, heat-producing form, trying to use the body heat to unlock her chilled muscles.

She rested her spinning head against a very broad, very solid shoulder and sighed as the mystery man passed through a set of doors and into a warm building. Somewhere inside her mind, she knew she should be fighting him, trying to break away from the strange man whose voice she didn't recognize, but she didn't have the strength.

Kara acknowledged the *ping* of an elevator bell and her stomach rebelled as the steel chamber lurched, moving upward at what seemed like a lightning-fast, head-spinning speed.

Moments later, she was gently lowered to a comfortable bed and covered in a warm comforter that eased the chill from her body. Her shoes were removed roughly and dropped to the floor. She opened her eyes and tried to focus. Struggling to sit up, she found herself pushed back down onto the pillows by strong hands on her shoulders. "Don't move. Not one inch."

"I'm fine. I've had a little bug. I thought I was over it. It was just a little dizziness," she argued as she tried to sit up again.

"You're not fine," the voice barked. "The doctor is here to see you. He lives in the building. He saw you nearly take a nosedive into the pavement."

"Doctor?" Alarmed, Kara focused on another man who lurked behind the bossy one. "I don't need a doctor." She couldn't afford a doctor.

"Too late. He's here. And you are being checked."

"I can refuse," she answered hesitantly, her gaze finally meeting the dark eyes of her rescuer.

"You won't," he told her in a warning voice.

His perilous appearance kept a sharp retort from exiting her mouth. God, he was huge. Broad shoulders filled her vision as he crouched beside the bed. She had felt his muscular body while he was carrying her, but now she could visually appreciate the strength of those arms and his solid bulk as her sight cleared and the dizziness began to subside.

Big. Dark. Dangerous. Kara's blue eyes clashed with his dark brown stare, his look so ferocious that it was almost frightening. He ran his hand impatiently through his short black hair, his expression grim. He wasn't handsome in any conventional way, his features too sharp and his olive complexion marred by a small scar to his right temple and another on his left cheek. But damn…he was appealing in a carnal, sensual sort of way. Kara could feel the intensity vibrating from his body and entering hers, making her nipples hard and sensitive. "Who are you?" she asked him softly, remembering that he had called her by name.

"Simon Hudson. Helen Hudson's son." He stood and backed up to let the older man behind him step forward.

Helen's son? Simon. She had never met Sam or Simon, but she had heard all about them from her boss, a woman who had become a very close friend over the years. Simon was the youngest. In his early thirties. A computer genius, he developed computer games that had started the Hudson Corporation on its way to becoming a company worth billions.

"Young lady, I heard you've been sick. I'm Dr. Simms. Let me take a quick look at you." A kind, middle-aged face replaced Mr. Tall, Dark and Unhappy. Kara let out a relieved breath and gave the jovial doctor a small smile.

"I'm fine. A virus. Maybe I wasn't quite over it and it's been a long day. Just a little residual fatigue," she assured the physician, wanting to put on her well-worn sneakers and run away from this humbling situation as soon as possible.

Simon stood behind the good doctor, his arms crossed and his face formidable. Geez…the man was fierce. It wasn't that she hadn't seen plenty of scary men in her life, but there was something about Simon that had her heart thumping and her body on high alert.

Kara let the doctor do his exam. Dr. Simms was kind and efficient with a bedside manner that had her smiling as he chatted absently during his evaluation. He gave her commands and asked the standard questions. She answered his questions as briefly as possible, wanting to get the exam finished and get out of Simon Hudson's constrained presence.

Dr. Simms stood with a congenial smile as he completed his exam. "You need rest, food, and more time to get over this virus. You might have been feeling slightly better for a day because your fever broke, but the fever is back and the virus isn't completely through your system. You're already run down and it doesn't sound like you sleep or eat properly." The doctor's smile broadened. "Typical of us medical folks. It may have been a while ago, but I still remember medical school." After a pause, the doctor asked professionally, "Any chance you could be pregnant?"

Kara's eyes shot to Simon's face, her cheeks burning with embarrassment. Did Simon really need to be hearing all of this? His eyes locked with hers and his body seemed visibly tense as he waited for her answer.

"No. Absolutely no possibility," she answered with a timidity that was usually not part of her personality. There wasn't a chance in hell that she was pregnant, unless a vibrator could knock her up, and lately, she was even too tired to use that. Her sex drive was dead from eighty-hour weeks of work and school. The only action her bed got was Kara, alone, sleeping for the few hours of rest that she got every night after her late-night study sessions.

The doctor breezed over the subject, instructing her to rest and treat the symptoms with over-the-counter fever medications.

Kara thanked him and gave him a tremulous smile before he turned to Simon, the two men talking quietly as they left the bedroom.

She sat up quickly, too quickly, and the room rotated for a minute before her head cleared. God, she was as weak as a kitten from the return of the fever and lack of food. She bent slowly and snatched her shoes from the floor, sitting on the bed to cram her feet into them without even untying the laces.

"What in the hell do you think you're doing?" Kara jerked up at the sound of the booming voice, her foot only halfway into her second shoe.

"I need to get home," she answered, uncomfortable now that she was alone with Simon. He was too big, too gruff, too demanding, too much of everything. There was something about him that made her feel off-balance, and it had nothing to do with her virus.

He swung her legs back onto the bed and pulled her shoes off. Damn. All of that hard work gone in seconds. Putting on those shoes had been an effort and she didn't appreciate having to do it again.

"You're sick and you're staying here," Simon told her sternly as his dark eyes swept over her and he grimaced.

"I can't. I'm working tomorrow. I need to get some sleep."

"You're not working for at least the next week. I already called Mom and told her to replace you." His expression was disapproving as he covered her body with the comforter and sat on top of it, effectively trapping her. "I also took the liberty of grabbing your keys from your backpack so that my assistant can go to your place and get you some clothes in case your roommate isn't home."

"But I-"

"Don't argue! This discussion is over. I'm going to make you something to eat and you will eat it. Then you'll go to sleep." He stood and exited, the orders still reverberating through the rather impressive space of the bedroom.

Fuming, Kara sat up and debated whether she dared to spring out of bed and through the door of what looked like a condo. A very nice condo! The bedroom was spacious and decorated in shades of tan and black. Tan, plush carpet and masculine dark furniture dominated the room. The bed was enormous and sat on a frame of intricate black ironwork that supported a canopy of what looked to be tan silk with woven black and brown designs. It was a beautiful room, bold and dark, just like the man who owned it.

Did he really expect her to stay here? Yes, his mother was her boss and friend, but she didn't know Simon and she wasn't sure she liked him. He was bossy, impatient, and expected people to jump when he said jump. Or stay when he said stay-sort of like a well-trained dog. Unfortunately for him, Kara didn't take orders well. She had made her own decisions since her parents had passed away and the last thing she needed was a domineering billionaire calling the shots in her life. The only thing money meant to Kara was security. Other than that, she couldn't care less about what money could buy; it was hard to miss material things that she had never had.

He called Helen to replace me? There was no way she could miss a week of work. Missing two days this week had already stretched her empty bank account. She relied on her tips to survive, and she didn't get tips by sitting on her butt at home. She had missed two evenings because she had no choice. The virus had eaten her up and spit her out, leaving her prostrate on her bed and sicker than she had been since she was a child.

She sighed and leaned back against the pillows. She was so tired and so damned weak right now. All she really wanted to do was bury herself in this warm, comfortable bed and sleep until she wasn't tired anymore. What would that be like? She couldn't remember a time that she wasn't exhausted. It had become normal for her to feel drained during the last four years; she only slept a few hours a night and her meals were sporadic, depending on what she could afford.

Kara looked up as she heard the *clink* of glass-on-glass and saw Simon coming into the room, juggling dishes. She bit back a smile, thinking that it was a good thing that he was a computer geek, because he would never make it as a waiter. He had a glass in one hand and a plate in the other. A bowl was balanced precariously between his elbow and chest. She wanted to tell him it would be easier if he just put the bowl on the plate, but she bit back the suggestion.

"I don't know what you like," he grumbled as he put the glass on the bedside table and handed her the bowl. He sounded cantankerous over the fact that there was something he didn't know. "Soup. Eat."

Talk about a man of few words. He issued commands like a drill sergeant. "Simon, I can't stay here," she told him softly as she accepted the bowl of steaming soup. Chicken noodle. Her favorite. Stomach rumbling from the tempting aroma coming from the bowl, she lifted the spoon and took a cautious bite. She could tell that it had come out of a can, but it tasted delicious and her rumbling stomach made her shovel it in like a starving woman.

"You are staying. Take these." He scowled at her as he held up a hand and dropped two pills into her open palm.

Extra-Strength Tylenol. She popped them into her mouth gratefully and reached for the glass. Simon handed it to her before she could reach it. She swallowed and handed the juice back to Simon's waiting hand before replying, "I have to work. I can't afford to be off. I already took two days because I was sick. I'm sure I'll feel better by tomorrow."

"You bet your sweet, exposed ass you will. I'll make sure that you do," he replied, his voice irascible.

Kara continued to eat her soup as she eyed his expression. He was serious. Dead serious. How did a sweet woman like Helen end up with a crabby-ass son like Simon? "You're not my boss, Simon."

"No, but my mother is and she agrees that you aren't working. She didn't realize you were still ill," he told her, his expression surly. "Hell…I don't know how she missed it. You have black circles under your eyes that make you look like a raccoon and you look dead on your feet. Mom's definitely slipping. She can usually dig out any problem. Painfully, if necessary," he rumbled, as though he were remembering a few of those painful experiences.

"I was feeling better earlier. And she was trying to help me find something to wear over my skirt," she told him calmly as she finished off the soup.

"Where in the hell did you get that outfit? I've never seen you in anything but jeans," he queried softly, dangerously. Kara quivered as his eyes roamed over the quilt, as though he could see her scantily-clad body through the material.

"It was a loan," she said, accepting the plate that held a yummy-looking sandwich as he took away the bowl. "Like a complete idiot, I spilled coffee down the front of my clothes today and didn't have time to run home before work."

"You are not an idiot," he stated curtly.

Swallowing a bite of the delicious egg salad sandwich, Kara's eyes jerked up to his face in surprise. "We've never met. How did you recognize me? How do you know what I usually wear?"

He shrugged and diverted his eyes. "I've seen you around the restaurant."

"I've never seen you at the restaurant."

"I stop by to see Mom. I usually don't go out front."

Helen's office was in the back, so it made sense. Kara was silent while she wolfed down the rest of the sandwich. God…she was hungry…and grateful for the meal.

"Thank you," she told him sincerely as she handed the plate back to him and he set it on the bedside table.

"You need to eat. And sleep." He touched the dark patches under her eyes softly with his index finger. "I've never been close enough to see how tired you look."

"The virus kicked my rear," she murmured lightly, feeling warmed not only by the food, but by the concerned frown on Simon's face. "I'll feel well enough to work tomorrow."

He handed her the glass of juice. "Don't even think about it. Finish that and sleep."

Too tired to argue, Kara downed the juice and gave up the glass to his waiting hand. She'd deal with everything later. Her eyes were drooping and exhaustion pressed on her body like weights. She needed to close her eyes.

Snuggling under the quilt, Kara sighed and rested her head on the pillow. For the first time in years, she felt full, comfortable and...safe. Simon might be cranky, but he had apparently appointed himself her protector. It was somehow...comforting.

With that strange thought rolling around in her mind, she slept.

Chapter 3

Kara woke late the next day, feeling completely rested and wondering where in the hell she was until she remembered the episode on the sidewalk and her subsequent rescue by Simon Hudson.

Was he here, or had he left for the day?

Slipping silently out of the massive bed, Kara popped her head out of the bedroom door, hearing nothing but silence. Scooping up a black silk robe that probably belonged to Simon, she pulled open a door at the other end of the bedroom, relieved to find the master bathroom. She locked the door and stripped quickly, pulling her hair completely free of its confining clip, and letting her clothes lie in a puddle at her feet.

She needed a shower. And coffee!

Feeling more like herself after finishing in the shower, clean and wrapped in Simon's robe, she hesitated as she looked longingly at a toothbrush and toothpaste on the marble counter next to the dual sinks. Not wanting to intrude, but desperate for a toothbrush, Kara opened a few of the cupboards and almost giggled with happiness as she found a brand-new toothbrush still wrapped in plastic. She put it to good use and tried to tame her wet hair with one of Simon's hairbrushes. Belatedly, she hoped he wouldn't mind. *Make yourself right at home, Kara.*

Like she would ever own a place like this one? The sheer decadence all around her nearly blew her away and she stared at the large garden bathtub with a heavy sigh. What she wouldn't give for an hour or so in that tub.

She wasn't a material girl, but still, she could appreciate a phenomenal bathtub. Her apartment only had a tiny shower and a good, long soak was something that would have to wait until she graduated from school and could get her own place. *And it will have a bathtub.* She decided right then and there that she would make it a requirement.

Turning away from the temptation of the huge oval tub, Kara tightened the robe around her and picked up her clothes and towel, trying not to picture Simon's muscular, naked body reclining in the water.

Stupid woman! Stop thinking about your boss's son and find your damn backpack so you can get the hell away from here.

Exiting the bedroom, she hesitated, not sure exactly where to go. The condo was huge. There were spare bedrooms, tastefully decorated, at the other end of the long hallway that led to the master bedroom. She almost gasped as she stepped out of the corridor and into a spacious living room with cathedral ceilings and beautiful, tan leather furniture.

Holy crap! Had she ever seen a television that big? The screen dominated one wall, making it look almost like a movie theater screen.

I soooo don't belong here!

Her bare feet left the plush carpet and landed on smooth tile as she walked slowly into a kitchen that would be any chef's dream. Decorated in forest green and cream, it had every convenience a person could ever want and several that she couldn't even identify.

Kara spied her backpack on the island table and unzipped it to stuff the borrowed clothing in the large center pocket, still clutching the wet towel because she wasn't quite certain what to do with it.

"How are you feeling?" She jumped as the low, inquiring voice spoke in the soundless kitchen. She covered her chest with a shaky hand as her heart accelerated and she turned to Simon, who was watching her silently, one arm propped casually against the door-frame. His dark hair was wet, as if he had just showered, and he had on a pair of jeans that hugged his muscular lower body lovingly. A green fleece pullover shirt stretched to accommodate his massive shoulders and broad chest. The man was seriously…ripped.

His liquid brown eyes raked over her body, growing warmer with each pass. Up and down. Up and down. Kara pulled the robe tighter. "I'm sorry. I didn't have anything else to wear."

He shrugged as he pushed away from the door. "It looks a hell of a lot better on you than it ever did on me," he answered in a husky voice as he sauntered over to the far cupboard. "Coffee?"

Oh, hell yes. He might as well have asked her if she wanted to finish nursing school. She was a complete addict. "Yes, please. If you don't mind."

"Sit. You're supposed to be resting." He motioned toward the island and she sat on one of the high stools.

She watched as he popped a cup into the coffee maker, dropped a coffee into a slot and closed it. The machine sputtered and came to life. Her coffee was done within seconds.

"Every coffee lover's dream," she sighed as he set the steaming cup in front of her.

"I hope you like it bold," he commented as he pulled creamer from the refrigerator and placed the sugar bowl and the cream in front of her. "It's a stronger blend."

Kara breathed in the delicious aroma coming from the steaming cup and her mouth watered. "It smells fabulous." He held out a spoon and she took it, their fingers brushing as she grasped the utensil. Her hand tingled from the light touch and warmth spread through her body. He was standing close, so close that she could breathe in his clean, masculine scent as his hand reached toward her silk-covered legs. Her breath caught as his fingers brushed against the silk, sending heat straight to her core.

"I'll take this." He lifted the wet towel from her lap, his knuckles sliding slowly along her thighs as he relieved her of the wet linen she had been holding.

She was trembling. Actually shivering, just from his light, casual touch. Dear God, she needed to move away. Somewhere she couldn't smell him, couldn't feel his heat and unsettling vibrations of sexual energy. "Thank you." Her voice was weak as she let go of the towel.

She breathed a sigh of relief as he strolled into a side room off the kitchen and returned without the towel. "You didn't answer my question. How are you feeling?"

She diverted her eyes from his tempting body and dumped cream and sugar into her coffee. "I feel great. Fever's gone. Thank you for helping me, but I need to get moving." Her eyes closed and she nearly moaned as the rich taste of premium coffee hit her palate.

"You can't leave. Not today. Not tomorrow." Simon's voice was neutral as he moved to the coffee maker and slammed another coffee into the machine, lowering the lid with more force than necessary.

"Why?" Her eyes popped open to give him a surprised look.

His eyes glued to his steaming mug of coffee, he sat across from her on another stool, lifted the spoon from the table and added a small amount of cream to his coffee. "You've been evicted."

Coffee sloshed over her fingers as she jolted in shock, her eyes flying to his face, momentarily stunned. "That's not possible. Lydia pays the rent. She gets my share every month." She reached automatically for a napkin in the center of the island to clean her fingers, the pain of the superficial burn not even registering because she was too shocked by his statement. Was it a joke? Was his sense of humor completely twisted? Didn't he know that it wasn't nice to tease a near-destitute woman over that sort of thing?

He finally met her gaze, his eyes grim and holding a touch of sympathy. "I'm afraid your roommate has fled. All that were in the apartment late last night was a few boxes that contained some of your school documents, birth certificate, and other paper items."

Kara's hands started to shake and she twisted them together on the marble counter. It couldn't be true. It wasn't true. "There has to be some mistake."

"It's no mistake. My assistant checked with the landlord early this morning. Your roommate was evicted, has been going through the eviction process for some time. Yesterday was the last day." Simon took a sip of his coffee, his eyes never leaving hers.

OhmyGod, ohmyGod, ohmyGod! Kara's mind raced as she took in the implications of his revelation. No place to live. No possessions. What the hell?

"There has to be some mistake," she whispered, her gaze landing on the coffee mug. *Please let it be a mistake.* There was no way she could catch up the rent or replace her possessions. "What about my things, my clothes?"

"Your roommate was thorough. There was nothing there except a few boxes."

"It had to be the wrong place."

"It's the right place, Kara. I'm sorry."

Simon rattled off the address and the name of her landlord and roommate. "Everything correct?"

Tears filled her blue eyes as she nodded, unable to speak past the knot in her throat. Dear God…she had been balancing on a tightrope for years, without a net, and now she was plunging to her death just as she neared the end of the rope.

She rarely communicated with Lydia, but she never thought her roommate was capable of something like this. They were cordial to each other, but Kara was only home at night to study and sleep, making her encounters with Lydia sporadic. She left her portion of the rent and utilities on the tiny kitchen table every month, never doubting that her roommate used it to pay their bills. Apparently, she hadn't. "This is not happening," she choked out, feeling as if her whole world had just shattered. And actually, it had. Just a few words-one disaster, one betrayal-was all it took to bring her life falling down around her.

"You okay?" Simon asked hesitantly, sipping his coffee and watching her cautiously.

"Yes. No. I don't know," she breathed incredulously. "I have to think." What to do. Where to live! How to survive? She pushed the coffee cup away and buried her head in her arms in front of her. Dear God…she was destroyed. *Think, Kara. Think.* "I didn't know. How could I not know?" she asked Simon, but mostly herself really, as she tried to understand how this could happen.

"Your roommate dropped out of school last semester. Apparently, she hid everything so that she could still collect your money up until she had to leave," Simon answered, his voice edged with anger. "I'm sorry, Kara. You have enough on your plate without this happening."

She raised her head and her confused, fear-filled gaze met his angry eyes with surprise. He was angry. At Lydia. At the circumstances. Simon obviously did have a heart. "E-everything is gone? The furniture, my bedroom stuff, my other belongings?" she stammered, tears choking her throat.

"The only boxes left were brought here by my assistant, Nina. They're on the bed in the guest room," he said gravely. "I checked everything out, Kara. It was legal. Your roommate took everything on the very last day. If you had gone home last night, you would have found an empty apartment. I'm glad you were spared that particular late-night surprise. Nina gave the key back to the landlord. The locks were due to be changed. You can't go back there."

No home. No bed. No place to go.

Despair and loss welled up inside her and she suddenly couldn't breathe, couldn't think. Silent tears rolled from her eyes and all she could think about was the last four years of struggle and hardship. For nothing. All for nothing. She'd end up in a shelter, if she could find an available spot. School would have to wait until she could get back on her feet.

"No. Oh, God, no." She sucked in a deep breath, trying to squelch her panic, but she couldn't.

Her body heaving, her hands over her face, Kara Foster did something she hadn't done since the death of her parents.

She wept.

Chapter 4

T he ice around Simon's heart cracked just a little as he watched the totally despondent, forlorn woman in front of him break down in tears, her hopeless sobs twisting in his gut.

Fuck! If he could locate her worthless roommate, he'd make her pay for every bit of pain Kara was suffering right now.

Unable to stop himself, Simon went to her and gathered her body against his own, lifting her into his arms with careful tugs until she came to her feet and put her arms around his neck, turning her face against his chest. He could feel her body quivering, her smaller form plastered against his own, keening her misery against his shoulder.

"Shhh...Kara. It will all be okay. I'll take care of you." Simon ran a hand down her silky black hair, knowing that he meant every word. It wasn't just something he was saying to quiet her, take away her pain. He wanted to take care of this woman who had seen more than her share of bad luck and hardship, bearing it with admirable strength. She was special, and her tears nearly undid him.

He took a deep breath and tightened his arms around her waist, splaying one hand along her slender back, moving the hand in soothing circles to calm her. She felt so good, so right in his arms. His cock twitched as he breathed in her alluring scent. She smelled like spring and Kara—a natural, enticing smell that made his mouth water.

He cursed his twitching cock as he held her pliant, soft body against his. Now was not the time to get hard, but he wasn't sure he could be within a mile of Kara and *not* get a raging erection. A warm sigh left his mouth, making a few tendrils of her hair flutter.

Simon wanted to make all of her problems go away, banish them like they had never existed. "We'll deal with it, Kara. I'll help you."

She pulled away from him, swiping tears away with the fingers of both hands. "I got you all wet." She hiccupped as she brushed at the front of his damp shirt.

Simon wanted to whine as she pulled herself completely from his arms. "It doesn't matter."

"I can't bawl like a baby all day. I have to see if I can find a shelter. This has put me over the financial edge." Her face was composed now, her expression lifeless.

"No shelter. You can stay here. I have plenty of space." He tried to keep his voice calm, but he was ready to wrestle her to the ground if needed. She wasn't going to a shelter. She might be broken at the moment, but she would recover. "Think reasonably, Kara. You need help. I'm willing to help you. You can finish your last semester and live here."

"Why? Why would you want me here? I'm a complete stranger to you."

He wanted to tell her that she had never been a stranger, not since the first moment he saw her. Something had clicked inside him, something raw, and something elemental. "You need help. Everybody needs help sometimes. I had my brother. I was lucky."

"Simon, I can't just take advantage of you."

Oh yeah, you can. Anytime you want to. Simon plopped back into his chair to hide his growing erection. Thankfully, she sat and pulled her coffee cup toward her. "You aren't taking advantage. You're just accepting a little assistance."

She snorted before taking a sip of her lukewarm beverage. "It's more than a little. I still have more than four months of school left. No money. No clothing. Nothing."

Even though he wanted to tell her to feel free to walk around naked, he answered, "Nina is getting you some clothes. No worries." He took a deep breath before continuing, "I only have one condition. Otherwise, my assistance is unconditional."

"What is it?" She looked at him cautiously over her mug.

"I want you to stop working while you're in school." He had to bite back a smile as her face turned up in a stubborn, implacable expression. This was going to be a sore subject, but he wasn't going to lose.

"I can't stop working. I need to live. I have nothing," she told him adamantly.

"No work. I'll help you financially. You already do forty hours a week at school and that doesn't include study time. My offer, take it or leave it." He wasn't about to watch her continue to fade away. After just one night of decent sleep, the dark circles under her eyes had decreased. It would be nice to see them gone altogether and watch her eat decent meals. She might have an inner core made of steel, but damn it, her body was fragile.

"But, I-"

"That's the deal. Take it or leave it?"

He watched her face turn red and her eyes clashed with his in a disgusted stare. Simon's breath caught silently, and his heart began to race. It was a risky move, but where else could she go? What could she do? But for a moment, for an instant that felt like an eternity, he watched her face, certain that she was going to tell him to go screw himself.

He was dictating to her, telling her how to run her life, and instinctively, she wanted to rebel. Kara let go of a frustrated breath. His gaze was immovable and inflexible. No compromise, then. It was his way or the freeway. Did she really have a choice? She could look for a shelter, but it would mean giving up school for now and messing up the whole program. "What about my insurance, my benefits? What about the restaurant?"

"Mom's place will be fine. She has waitresses who want to be full-time."

Kara flinched as he made the statement, knowing it was true. There were other employees who would be only too happy to step into her full-time position.

"And I'll make sure that you stay on COBRA. You won't lose your insurance."

She searched his eyes, trying to read him, but Simon was a mystery to her. Why was he doing this? Did she trust him? She hardly knew him. She trusted Helen, and Helen adored her sons. "Okay. I'll do it. But you need to keep track of the funds and I'll pay you back."

"No deal."

"You said you only had that one condition." She drained her coffee, trying to keep her hands steady by grasping both sides of the mug.

He shrugged. "It's an add-on since you tried to change the original terms."

"What are you getting out of all of this? I'm going to disrupt your privacy, take your money, and you get nothing?" She gaped at him, baffled by the whole arrangement.

"I don't want your money. Can't you just take the help without questioning my motives? I want to help," he balked in an uneasy voice, finishing the last of his coffee, slamming the cup back to the table with an impatient *whack*.

"I want to do something, give you something for your trouble. I've always paid my own way." Agitated, she stood and collected the cups. She took them to the sink and rinsed them before putting them in the dishwasher. Honestly, she should be kissing his feet in gratitude, but being in his debt somehow bothered her. She wasn't used to taking. From anyone! She was a survivor, doing what she needed to do just to stay one step ahead of poverty. This was so foreign, so freaking confusing.

Kara turned around and slammed into Simon's powerful body, a force that easily kept her body from advancing. The man was like concrete, fixed and immobile. She put her hands on his solid, muscular biceps to steady herself. "Sorry," she mumbled, but he didn't move away.

"There's only one thing I want from you, Kara." His voice was low and husky and he bent down and inhaled, as though he were breathing in her scent. He slapped a hand on each side of the counter, pinning her.

The man was like a seething kettle of testosterone, and every female hormone in her body was rising to happily meet the masculine lure. He surrounded her, holding her body in thrall, making her want to surrender to his dominance. Something inside her melted, wanting to sway into his powerful arms. "W-What?" What could he possibly want from her?

She shivered as he crowded her, feeling the heat radiating from his body. Kara was five foot eight barefoot, but Simon towered over her in height, strength, and power. He leaned his head down, his lips nuzzling her ear. "You. In my bed. One night. Anything I want, anything I need." His sultry, low whisper sent fire careening through her entire body.

"Me?" She squeaked as his hungry lips trailed down the side of her neck, making her core clench tightly with need and her pussy moist.

"You. One night," he repeated as his hands moved to her hips and stroked against the silk robe, exploring her body greedily.

Her head dropped to one side, giving him free access to let him explore the sensitive skin at the side of her neck. Oh Lord, he felt good, smelled good. She couldn't think as his mouth descended on hers.

Simon didn't ask; he demanded. His tongue pushed against the seam of her lips insistently and she gave way, letting him take her, his tongue owning her mouth with demanding strokes. She released an involuntary moan into his kiss, feeling ravished and overwhelmed, her response automatic and wanting. Pushing back, she entwined his tongue with hers, exploring him, tasting him.

Without releasing her from his impassioned embrace, his hands came up to spread her robe, running possessive fingers over the responsive flesh, the hardened nipples. He alternately pinched and stroked, heightening her desire until she was out of control. A strong, jean-clad thigh thrust between her legs and she pushed against it, desperate for the friction. Her hands plowed into his coarse dark hair, fisting as she rode a wave of erotic pleasure.

He pulled his mouth from hers, panting as though he had run a marathon. "God, you are so hot, Kara. So responsive." Her body was pulsating as his hand moved over her stomach. "I want one night."

She jerked as his fingers reached her saturated pussy, stimulating the pink, ripe flesh, moving his thigh back to explore her more thoroughly.

"So wet, so ready," he husked as he circled her clit. "I can smell your arousal and it's making me crazy. I want to taste you."

"Oh, God. Please." Kara was caught up in sensation, heat sizzling over every nerve ending in her body. Her hands went to his shoulders, needing the support to keep standing.

"So sweet," he murmured in her ear before his tongue trailed over the side of her neck, flicking in a rhythm that mimicked what he wanted to do elsewhere, overwhelming her with white-hot desire to feel it there, making her want that velvet tongue between her thighs.

Her hips flexed, needing more contact, more of those talented, teasing fingers. "Simon, I need-"

"I know what you need. The same thing that I need! But for now, I can give you this." His fingers zeroed in on her needy bud, slipping through her moist folds, finding where she needed to be touched.

She moaned as he increased the pace, the intensity. She was mindless with raw need and a whimper escaped from her lips as one hand continued his erotic torture of her breasts, while the other kept up a relentless assault on her inflamed clit. "Yes. Oh, yes." Kara knew the passionate, hot voice was her own, but she barely recognized it. It was high-pitched, keening, begging for relief.

His mouth swallowed her moan, as though he wanted every bit of her pleasure. She responded, nipping at his lip, opening for his possession, surrendering completely.

Her channel clenched and she could feel the impending climax all the way to her toes. Ripping her mouth from his, she threw her head back and let out a long groan as a powerful orgasm took her over, making her ride on waves of pleasure that she had never experienced before.

Her head dropped against his shoulder as ripples continued to make her body shudder. "Oh, God. What in the hell was that?" She panted as Simon closed her robe and pulled her sagging body against his.

"Pleasure. Just a taste of what we could have in bed," he replied quietly, his large body rocking her slightly as she recovered. "I'd like one night, Kara. Not because you have to, but because you want it, too. I'll help you regardless. It's your choice whether or not to give me what I want. But be warned…I like control."

Still shattered, her mind in chaos, she asked haltingly, "What does that mean exactly?"

"Total surrender," he answered in a low, hoarse voice that vibrated with barely-controlled passion. "Think about it. Say the word and I'll give you every ounce of pleasure that I'm capable of giving."

"I'm not really that experienced. I-I…you'd be disappointed." She hadn't had sex in more than five years and even then, only with one boyfriend. It had been her only sexual relationship, one that had lasted five years and ended badly.

"I don't want sexual expertise. I just want you," he replied abruptly as he moved back, giving her space.

Kara noticed the tense look on his face, the grooves around his mouth. Eyes dropping to his groin, she could see his large shaft straining against the denim.

He leaned forward and gently kissed her forehead. "Decide later. You've been through a lot today and you need to get over your illness. Rest. Eat. Relax. I'll be in my computer lab upstairs if you need anything. Nina will be here soon with your clothes. Feel free to keep the robe. It looks good on you. But just so you know…I'll have a raging erection every time you wear it. I'll remember every sweet sound, every delicious response from you while you were coming in my arms."

Kara grasped the counter behind her, her knuckles white from the strength of her grip as he turned and sauntered away, muscles rippling in his perfectly formed ass and back as he casually left the kitchen.

"Did that really just happen?" she whispered in an astounded voice, hoping that this whole day was just a bad dream and she would wake up in her own bed, in her own tiny apartment.

Simon Hudson was a danger to her sanity, and she needed to stay as far away from him as possible.

Four months. Could she do it? She straightened her spine and wrapped the robe tighter around her body. She was a survivor; she would survive. Simon had mentioned that sleeping with him wasn't a requirement. It didn't have to happen.

Kara took a deep breath, trying to relax her body. She'd do whatever she could to help Simon *except* sleep with him. She could cook, clean, help him out with whatever he needed to have done. Not having a job was going to leave her restless. There had to be other things she could do to repay him.

You want to. You know you want him.

She shook her head, trying to silence her wayward thoughts. Getting involved with Simon Hudson was not a good idea. The billionaire genius was the type who would leave her devastated after one night of passion. He had just proved it by rocking her world, and she hadn't even had sex with him.

But now you know it would be a one incredible night that you'd never forget.

And it would. That was her fear. It would be much too memorable.

Shaking her head, she suddenly remembered the clinic. She should have been there this morning.

Oh, shit. I have to call Maddie. How could I have forgotten?

Kara spent every Saturday morning volunteering at the free children's clinic with Dr. Madeline Reynolds. It was something Kara had been doing every Saturday morning for the last year and although she wasn't yet licensed as a nurse, she helped out by taking on every task she was capable of so that Maddie could see as many children as possible on clinic day.

Kara snatched up a cordless phone from the kitchen counter and hastily dialed the clinic number, explaining to Maddie what had happened and that she was sorry she didn't make it.

"It's not like you're a paid employee, Kara, even though I appreciate the fact that you keep showing up to help. I'm fine for today. Are you okay? Do you need a place to stay?" Maddie's voice was concerned and Kara's heart lifted. Maddie was so generous, so caring… but she couldn't impose on her friend. Kara knew that Maddie put every extra penny she had into the free clinic and she was fairly fresh out of medical school. Kara had heard Maddie say jokingly, more than once, that she would still be paying back student loans when she retired.

"Nope. I'm good. I have a…friend helping me out," she replied, hoping her voice sounded normal.

There was a pause before Maddie told her sternly, "You call me if you need help, Kara. You will, won't you?"

"I will. I promise. I'll see you next Saturday."

"Stay safe. If you ever find that bitch of an ex-roommate, feel free to call me. I'll beat the shit out of her," Maddie said, her voice indignant.

Kara laughed. "You'll have to get in line. I'm pissed enough to do it myself."

With a few more assurances to Maddie that she would be fine, Kara hung up with a sigh and headed through the condo, wanting to see what was left of her belongings.

You'll make it. You've made it this far. Four months will be easy. Someday, you can replace whatever was taken.

A tingle went down her spine as she searched for the guest room that housed her meager belongings, sensing that the next four months would be more challenging than anything she'd ever faced before.

Poverty!

Loneliness!

Rejection!

Insecurity!

Fear!

They all looked like a piece of cake compared to several months with Simon Hudson.

Temptation was going to be a real bitch.

Chapter 5

Over the next six days, Kara discovered that living with Simon was easy...as long as he got his way. She caught herself grumbling, more than once, about his overbearing attitude and take-charge tactics. Without question, the man was generous and she had already had several conniption fits over how much money he spent on her. Clothes, laptop, iPhone, iPod, iPad-Simon loved gadgets that began with an *i*-and anything he thought was essential to her well-being. She had tried to patiently explain that she had lived well enough without those things before, but Simon simply grunted and soon gave her another so-called essential item, all of which were definitely not necessities.

The only fight that she had actually won was the argument about him buying her a car. Kara had put her foot down and refused, telling him that she preferred to take the bus. Honestly, she hadn't really won that argument either. The only reason he had relented was because he had his driver, a delightful man named James, take her to school every day and pick her up again after class or clinicals. James seemed to be at Simon's beck and call, even though Simon drove himself to the office every morning in a Bugatti Veyron. Kara had almost choked the first time she saw the outrageously expensive sleek automobile, a car that she actually had only seen previously in photos. Simon shrugged, telling her that Sam had one too, only Sam's was newer, a fact that seemed to irritate Simon whenever his precious vehicle was mentioned. Kara had rolled her eyes at him and walked away. Honestly, he was just like a boy...only richer-a lot richer-and his toys a hell of a lot more expensive.

Nina, Simon's personal assistant and another employee to whom she'd taken an instant liking, delivered Kara's new clothes early the previous Saturday morning. And she hadn't come alone. It had taken a string of strong, able-bodied men to trail in with a whole new wardrobe that definitely hadn't come from Walmart or a normal discount store. Kara now had a huge walk-in closet filled with expensive designer clothing, most of which she would probably never wear. For God's sake, even the jeans were designer and expensive. Every item fit perfectly. Simon had checked the soiled clothes in her backpack to get her size. The clothing incident had been the first experience of many that was teaching Kara that Simon never did anything in a small way.

She had really balked when she saw how much money he had deposited into her checking account. How in the hell had the man found out her checking account number? He had just raised his shoulders again and told her to let him know when she needed additional funds and he would take care of it. Additional funds? He had transferred one hundred thousand dollars to her account, a fact that had nearly sent her into heart failure when she had checked her balance. An account that usually sat in the single digits had suddenly become an endless source of cash. How could anyone spend that much money in a few months? Kara had tried to get him to take most of it back. Having that much money in her account was actually a bit daunting and her needs were simple. She already had everything she needed and more, thanks to Santa Simon. Simon had just mumbled a curse and some statement about her being a stubborn woman and ignored her request. She had finally thrown her hands in the air and stomped away, muttering something about inflexible, arrogant men. A quiet chuckle had followed her out of the room and she had forced herself not to look back to see if Simon was smiling.

Actually, she was happy that she could provide him with some amusement, because she couldn't seem to find anything else to do to help him. She felt swamped by guilt most of the time for taking advantage of his generous nature.

He had laundry and cleaning staff who came in once a week, so it left little for Kara to do except cook, and she had plenty of extra time to do that. Baking and cooking were about the only useful things she could do to help, but Simon seemed to think it was some monumental task akin to saving his life when she fixed a meal. It seemed that Simon didn't cook and existed mostly on sandwiches when he was at home because he had never really wanted to employ a full-time chef. Of course, his personal assistant bought his groceries, a task that Kara had taken over from a grateful Nina. Simon's assistant said that she was tired of seeing Simon live on the microwave dinners and the sandwich fixings that he requested every week. The tiny, well-kept woman, probably somewhere in her sixties, had just uttered an emphatic, "Hallelujah, he'll finally eat," and handed Kara his usual grocery list quite joyfully.

Kara closed her nursing book, her studying complete, and stretched out on her back, rolling on the huge king-sized bed in the guest room until she was staring at the ceiling.

She should ask Simon what he wanted for dinner, although she already knew how he would reply.

Anything that I don't have to cook!

He usually spent the morning in his office and the afternoon and evening in his computer lab upstairs. The condo was enormous, and Kara wondered if she would ever find her way around without making a few wrong turns.

Hopping off the bed, she walked through the gorgeous living room, admiring the view from a large picture window. Simon lived in the penthouse, the largest condo in the building, and every twinkling light of Tampa was spread out in front of her in breathtaking splendor. How incredible to have this splendid view every single night. She wished Simon would take a moment to enjoy it. He seemed to be obsessed with a project right now and only came down for a brief time for dinner before returning to his lab.

Kara wondered if he was avoiding her and felt guilty that he might be hiding in his own home. They had never spoken about what had occurred in the kitchen six days ago. They circled around each other politely, making superficial conversation at dinner.

As she turned and mounted the black spiral staircase, she admitted to herself that she actually wanted his company. Working and going to school had kept her busy and her loneliness at bay. Now, she had too much time with nothing to do in the evenings except watch Simon's enormous television or read after she had finished studying. Solitude was all well and good, but it got lonesome night after night. At least when she was working, she had the company of customers and the other employees.

Disgusted with herself, she turned left after she reached the top of the staircase, making her way to Simon's lab. What did she have to complain about? She had every luxury, every convenience. She lived in a home most people only dreamed about and never had to worry about funds. Still, she wanted a little more of Simon's company when she should just be damned glad she had a roof over her head and an endless amount of food to eat.

Stopping outside the door to his lab, she tapped lightly.

"Come in." The abrupt, distracted reply made her smile. He was definitely consumed with some sort of project.

Usually she just poked her head in, but curious about Simon's lab, she entered and closed the door behind her. Computers were everywhere and Simon had a chair on rollers that slid from one computer to the other, making it easy due to the plastic that covered the floor under the circle of computers. She padded across the plush carpet until her feet met the smooth plastic and peeked at the computer screens. Gaping, she realized she recognized the picture on the largest screen.

Squinting, she asked quietly, "Hey. Is that Myth World?"

His head popped up and he met her eyes with a surprised look. "Yeah! You know the game?"

"Know it? I'm at expert level," she answered, slightly insulted that he thought she wouldn't be familiar with such a popular game. "Lydia had it and I was hooked after trying it the first time."

She loved the game and always got some time in whenever she could on Lydia's computer, even if it was late at night. It was her one indulgence. She couldn't resist letting the computer take her to a whole new world when she played the game, challenging her to find out its secrets and battle mythological figures.

Simon's lips started to curl and kept going until he was wearing a shit-eating grin that made her heart skip a beat. It was the first honest, completely brilliant smile that she had ever seen from Simon. He rolled his chair over to the computer screen with the familiar figures as he answered, "It's my game. This is Myth World II."

"Oh, my God. Let me see." She pushed in front of him in her excitement. She hadn't seen the original game in a week, and here was the newest edition. Right here in the home she lived in. "Is it done? Can I play it? I really miss that little bit of escapism."

"I just have the demo. It's not on the market yet. You can try it if you like," Simon answered in an indulgent and boyish voice. He went through the controls and stood, allowing her to plop her rear in the available chair and focus on the new game.

It was similar, yet completely different, and Kara worried her bottom lip as she tried to figure out all of the intricate details of the game. "You made it harder," she accused in a laughing voice.

"Was the original version easy?" he asked her with a smile in his voice.

"No. But it wasn't this hard," she answered, her eyes concentrating on the busy screen.

"It was. You just aren't used to this one yet." His eyes scanning her face, he asked, "What do you like about the game?"

"The strategy, the challenge of figuring out secrets, the make-believe world. It's like being catapulted into another dimension for a short time." She tipped her eyes to his as she got completely destroyed on screen. "You are a genius, Simon," she told him with complete honesty. "I never realized that this was a Hudson game."

Kara could almost swear he was blushing as he turned his head, replying diffidently, "It's just computer stuff. Nothing exciting."

She pulled her hands from the desk and folded them neatly on her lap as she told him emphatically, "It's incredibly creative, Simon. It takes more than programming to come up with something like this."

"I'll put them on your laptop," he told her quietly.

"Oh, Lord, no. I'd never get my studying done." Her eyes laughed up into his, her tone playful.

"I think you can control yourself," he returned, sounding disappointed.

"Absolutely not. I have no control when it comes to Myth World. Do you have other games that you've designed?"

"Of course, dozens of them."

"Would you mind putting them on the PC in the den?" she asked hesitantly.

"You can come up here. Play on the usage computer." He pointed to a large computer and chair in the corner. "All of my games are on it. Actually, just about any game you can think of is on there."

She put her hand to her heart in mock astonishment. "Oh, horrors! You actually have other people's games on that computer?"

He moved closer to her, towering over her with a mischievous grin. "Sometimes I find it necessary to...check out the competition."

"And are they good?" She looked up at him, loving this boyish side of Simon.

"Nah...but I have to keep up with what's selling," he told her, his tone impertinent.

God, the man was so hot when he was joking around. Oh shit, he was always hot. She could smell his masculine scent with a hint of sandalwood. It was a warm, rich aroma that made her squirm and her body tingle. "If you don't mind, I'll take you up on that offer. I'm used to being busy and I'm not up on all the recent television shows. I get a little lonely sometimes. This place is so big." Why had she admitted that? "Just don't be upset when I don't get dinner ready on time. I get lost in your games," she told him in a mock warning voice, an attempt at levity.

He came down on one knee, his eyes level with hers. "Are you lonely here, Kara?" His tone sounded concerned, dumbfounded, as his dark eyes met hers. "You don't like it here?"

"No. Oh, no. Simon, it's lovely here. How could I not be happy?" She sighed, trying to explain. "I'm just so used to not having much time to think, much time to myself. It takes getting used to after the crazy pace I had before."

"Suicidal, you mean," he said, his tone edgy. "That lifestyle was draining you dry, Kara."

"I know. And I'm grateful. Really, I am. This is just different," she assured him, not wanting him to think she was ungrateful. Shit, she'd be on the streets if not for his generosity, but still… "I'll be happier up here with you."

"You want my company?" He searched her face, sounding baffled.

"Of course. But I know you're busy. And I thought maybe you were avoiding me after...well, after…"

"After I told you that I wanted to fuck you?" he asked bluntly, his eyes holding hers prisoner.

"Yes," she breathed softly, startled by his brusque statement, but glad that it was out in the open. It had been simmering, making her anxious.

"I wasn't avoiding you, Kara. I want to see you, be with you, whether you want to fuck me or not," he stated, his voice adamant.

"You do?" she asked with a hint of wonder. "Why?"

"I get lonely sometimes, too. I enjoy your company."

She took a deep breath, willing her racing heart to slow.

I want you to fuck me. I want you to take me a hundred different ways and then do it again.

The breath left her body as her eyes roamed over him. Just thinking about that large, solid, dominant body over her, in her, made her fidget in her chair. Her fingers itched to touch the face so close to her own, to stroke the sexy, rough jaw with the sensual five o'clock shadow that made his scars nearly invisible. Strangely, those small scars added to his sex appeal, making him more masculine, more irresistible.

No, Kara. Don't think about it. Dinner. You came to ask him about dinner. Simon Hudson is way out of your league.

"I-I actually came to ask you what you wanted for dinner." Her voice was unsteady and she was practically stumbling over her words. Simon's close proximity was getting to her, making her want much more than just his company. She scooted her chair back and stood, nervously wiping her sweaty palms on her jeans.

It didn't help. Simon towered over her as he rose to his feet. "I'll help you. I'm done here for now."

Kara gulped, wondering if the massive kitchen was big enough for both of them. She wanted to be near him, but not so close that the longing that she felt overwhelmed her. "Okay. Let's go see what we can round up." Her strides were long and quick as she led the way to the kitchen, happy that she would have Simon's company, but not quite sure how to deal with her treacherous body and its reaction to him.

Total surrender.

What exactly had he meant by that…and did she really want to find out?

Chapter 6

Simon knew he was slowly, silently becoming completely unglued. His mind was wandering to places it shouldn't go, and he'd had to work extra hours the last several days just because he couldn't think of anything except the fact that Kara was here, in his home, driving him closer and closer to insanity.

If I don't fuck her soon, I'm going to become unhinged.

Glad he was following behind her so that she couldn't see his obvious erection, he watched her hips sway in a pair of ass-hugging jeans as he followed her to the kitchen. Her fresh, alluring scent wafted from her body and he breathed it in like a man deprived of oxygen, hungry for her fragrance. He smelled her everywhere, even his bedroom. Her aroma seemed to cling to every portion of his house, reminding him of her presence. Like he could forget it?

What was it about her that fascinated him so much? It wasn't as if she tried to make herself irresistible. She wore very little make-up and he had yet to see her in anything except jeans-minus the heart-stopping night that she had appeared in that tight mini and sweater-but he was completely enthralled.

"Why don't you have a boyfriend?" he asked curiously. "Wouldn't it have been easier to go to school if you had a man in your life?"

They had reached the kitchen and Kara was pulling lettuce, peppers, and other vegetables from the refrigerator. "Do you want to help cut the vegetables for a salad? I'll put in some steaks." She pulled meat from the refrigerator before adding, "Why would I want a boyfriend when I'm going to school?" Giving him a perplexed look, she pulled out a cutting board and handed him a knife from the block.

"Someone to help. Wouldn't it be easier?" he replied as he washed the vegetables and started cutting awkwardly. Cooking was not one of his best skills.

He almost sliced through his finger as she burst out laughing before answering, "In my experience, boyfriends aren't exactly helpful."

She was amused, but Simon could hear a touch of hurt in her voice. "Bad experience?"

"Yes."

"What happened?"

She put the steaks in the broiler and bumped him out of the way. She opened the refrigerator and pulled out a beer. Twisting the top off, she handed it to him and shooed him away to the island sitting area. "I'll cut. You're likely to amputate a digit or two."

Simon frowned as he took a seat and watched her profile as she sliced and diced like a professional. "So, what happened?"

She sighed. "I dated Chris for five years. I thought we would end up married. Unfortunately, I came home from work early one day and caught him in bed with the person I thought was my best friend."

Was the guy totally insane? He had Kara in his bed every night and he wanted someone else? "He was an idiot."

"It wasn't meant to be. I'm actually thankful that I wasn't married to him."

"It still hurt you."

She shrugged. "It was a long time ago."

"Bastard." Simon couldn't help himself. He wanted to hurt the asshole.

"What about you?" She glanced toward him as she scraped sliced green peppers into the salad bowl.

"What about me?"

"Girlfriend? I feel like I might be cramping your style. Me living here, I mean." She didn't look at him as she started on the tomatoes.

He shrugged. "I've never had one."

She stopped slicing and gaped at him with a look of astonishment. "Seriously?"

Simon didn't include the one woman who had changed his life forever, at the age of sixteen. He hadn't spoken her name or talked about her in years. Not to anyone.

"Nope. I'm not exactly a social kind of guy. Sam is the compulsive dater. He's got the looks for it," he replied dryly, taking a swig of his beer.

She mumbled something that Simon didn't quite catch.

"What was that?" he asked, wondering why her face was turning beet red.

"I said that you're better looking."

Simon almost dropped his beer, barely catching it before it fell into his lap. "Have you seen Sam?"

She breezed out to the dining room to put the salad on the table, calling out behind her. "Sure. You have pictures of him and Helen everywhere."

His jaw dropped and he waited until she came back to check the steaks before replying roughly, "Then you know that's not true."

"In my opinion, it is," she told him stubbornly. "Just don't get a fat head over it."

Simon grinned. Only Kara could throw out a compliment and then immediately deflate him. Still, he couldn't believe she actually found him attractive. "What about my scars? Sam is a movie-star-handsome blond with green eyes. Women seem to love that." Women loved Sam…and Sam loved women. All of them! He charmed women of all ages. Too bad that he couldn't seem to keep that adoration after they started dating him.

"I guess I prefer my men tall, dark, and grouchy," she told him lightly as she pulled the steaks from the oven.

He grabbed a potholder, his grin broadening as he took the sizzling steaks from her, dropping one on each of the two plates that she had set out. He watched her from hooded eyes, trying to figure out if she was actually flirting with him. He didn't have a clue. Maybe she was just being nice. After all, she didn't know Sam and she was living in his house. Still, her comment warmed him, made him feel special. No one had ever considered him handsome when compared to Sam, except possibly his mother. The women who had sex with him did so for financial gain. A mutual agreement that had suited him just fine…with those women!

Kara was an altogether different story. Instinctively, Simon knew an arrangement with Kara that was similar to his previous ones would destroy him.

As they settled at the dining room table, Simon suddenly remembered what he had managed to obtain for her earlier. "I have something for you."

He nearly laughed as she frowned at him, shaking her head as she said, "Simon, I'm not taking one more thing. You've done enough. Way too much."

He didn't think he had done nearly enough, but he replied, "You'll take this."

"No…I won't."

God, he loved that stubborn look on her face. He tipped the dining room chair back and reached into the front pocket of his jeans. He held out his hand, but Kara was still shaking her head tenaciously, so he dropped the object on the table.

"Oh, my God," Kara breathed softly, her voice filled with awe and delight. She reached for the ring with trembling fingers, sliding it on her finger slowly. "My mother's ring. I didn't think I would ever see it again. How did you find it?"

"Pawn shop," he replied, glad that he had made some of his employees troll all of the area stores for the ring. "I knew it was the one thing that you were sad to lose."

"It's not expensive, but it means a great deal to me. It's the only thing I have left that belonged to my mom," she choked, her voice wobbling with emotion.

Simon would never tell her that her roommate only got a few dollars for the piece of jewelry on her finger. It was an inexpensive ring shaped like a butterfly with a tiny amethyst chip in the center, but Simon had seen Kara's sorrow over losing it.

"I'm glad we could find it."

Simon never saw her coming. She flew from her chair, her delicious ass landing in his lap and her arms flung around his neck. His arms tightened around her waist to keep her from sliding as she peppered him with kisses. On his face, on his hair, everywhere that she could reach. He could feel the excitement radiating from her body, joy oozing from every pore. "Thank you, Simon. You're the most wonderful man on earth."

Oh, Christ! As much as he loved her enthusiasm and treasured her happiness, if she didn't stop bouncing that luscious rear end against him, he was going to come in his pants. Her ample breasts were rubbing against his chest and her scent was making him want to devour her. Every delightful inch of her. "I think I deserve a real kiss. I told you that you would accept it," he mentioned softly, his voice sultry.

She threaded her fingers through his hair and their eyes collided as she tipped his head back. Simon's heart stuttered as he saw the hungry, passionate glow of her gaze.

Her lids lowered slowly as her mouth descended to his. Simon closed his eyes and moved one hand up to the back of her head, sighing as his fingers sifted through her silky mass of dark hair. She tasted like woman and need, and he responded with an uncontrolled desire that nearly pushed him over the edge. Her tongue teased his between little nibbles on his lips and it made him want more, need more. Putting pressure to the back of her head, he crushed her mouth to his, wanting to plunder and explore every inch of the sweet cavern. The hand on her waist slid to her ass, bringing her almost fully against him, making him groan into her mouth as their tongues dueled and tasted.

She was so responsive, so eager, that Simon lost himself to her in that moment, not caring if he was ever found. *Kara. Kara.* Her name pounded against his brain as he tried to consume her, own her. Feral possessiveness drove him as his marauding tongue swept into her mouth, over and over, sliding sensuously against hers.

She pulled her mouth away, panting as she buried her face in his neck. Simon could feel her hot breath against his ear as she delivered small licks and nips down the side of his neck.

"Kara, I'm not a saint." Jesus Christ, he couldn't take much more of this. His cock was hard enough to pound nails and every instinct was screaming at him to take her.

"I want you, Simon. Desperately." Her fuck-me-breathless voice saying those particular words made Simon groan, desperate to be inside her. Still…

"Don't do this out of gratitude," he growled.

She pulled back to look at him, her eyes shining with need. "I would never do this out of gratitude. I'm tired of trying to fight this attraction between us, Simon. I want my one night. The one that you offered."

One night. Simon's heart was thundering. "Total surrender?"

"I'm not sure what that means…but yes…total surrender. I know you would never hurt me."

Her trust and faith in him nearly brought him to his knees. She had no idea what lie ahead, but she wanted him enough to agree to his request. He nuzzled her ear as he whispered harshly, "It means that I need control. I want to tie you to my bed, blindfold you, and fuck you until neither of us is able to move."

Simon felt her shiver in his arms, but she answered softly, "Then do it. Take me to bed, Simon."

Barely able to believe she was in his arms and willing, Simon stood and carried her toward his bedroom, hoping he wasn't in the middle of the best wet dream he had ever had.

Chapter 7

Kara trembled as Simon swept her up in his strong, muscular arms and cradled her gently against his powerful body. Had she really just told him to take her to bed and do anything he wanted to her? Yes…she had…and she was shaking with anticipation. What she had told him was true. She was tired of fighting her attraction to him, an attraction that was so much more than a tiny bit of chemistry. Drawn to him as she had never been to another man, the struggle was futile, the outcome inevitable. Her body burned to be taken by him, and only him.

A smart, street-wise woman should probably fight the temptation. But Kara had never been enticed by a man like Simon Hudson. He was an enigma, a mystery that she hadn't yet solved. Gruff, abrupt, brilliant…but also considerate, kind, and every now and then she caught a vulnerability that made her want to hold him close and soothe his battered soul. Kara had no doubt that at some point in his life, Simon Hudson had been hurt. Badly! How could she resist the yearning she had for him? She had to have one night with him, one chance to experience true desire. If she didn't grasp this opportunity, Kara knew she would regret it for the rest of her life. It was gut instinct, but she had grown up tough and had learned to go with her intuition.

It had been screaming at her tonight, beating at her to accept Simon's earlier proposition, telling her that she should take the chance to experience a passion and desire unlike anything she had ever experienced before and that might never come along again.

She felt her feet hit the plush carpet in Simon's bedroom as he lowered her slowly to the ground, their bodies sliding together until she found her footing. His expression was volatile, his eyes dark with hunger and desire as his mouth came down on hers. Raw need ripped through her and she tightened her arms around his neck as he plundered her mouth, pulling the clip from her hair and burying his fingers, pulling her mouth tighter against his. One hand came down and gripped her ass tightly, pulling her up and against his hard erection, making her moan into his mouth with her desire for him to be inside her. She was already wet, ripe for his possession.

Needing some skin to skin contact, she reached for his shirt, desperate to touch his bare skin.

"No," he barked as he ripped his mouth from hers and grasped her wrist.

"I just needed to touch you," she panted, confused by his complete change of attitude.

"I need you naked. This has to go my way, Kara," he told her quietly. "I told you what I wanted. I was completely serious."

His voice was demanding, but Kara could hear a tinge of vulnerability in his statement. Wanting his possession more than she wanted her next breath, she stood back and pulled her t-shirt over her head. Popping open the button of her jeans, she lowered the zipper as she met his eyes with no shyness or hesitation. Shimmying out of the tight designer jeans, she let them drop to the floor, kicking out of them as they stopped at her ankles. She stood, her eyes never leaving his, in a very flimsy black silk bra and matching thong.

"Holy Christ. You're the most beautiful woman I've ever seen," he breathed reverently as he cupped her cheek and let his finger slide slowly over her face and down the side of her neck, until he reached the swell of her breasts, accentuated by the barely-there bra.

"It's the expensive lingerie," she told him softly, her breath hitching as he caressed the tops of her breasts lightly, making her shiver with desire.

"It's you," he answered, his fingers reaching for the front clasp of the bra. It gave way easily, spilling her breasts into his waiting hands. "You're perfection."

Kara shook her arms and the material dropped to the floor silently. She hissed as his hands roamed over her body, cupping the tender flesh of her breasts, his thumbs teasing her sensitive nipples. His fingers branded, leaving trails of heat wherever he touched.

"Although I love those panties, they need to go," he insisted in a husky voice, a mere whisper, as his mouth nipped at the lobe of her ear.

They were gone in seconds, her desire to have him inside her intense, her core screaming for relief.

Longing and apprehension warred in her mind as she stood in front of Simon, completely naked. "Simon, I haven't been with anyone for a long time."

"How long?" he growled, his hand cupping her ass possessively.

"Five years. And even then I wasn't very good in bed. There was only Chris, and I wasn't enough to satisfy him," she answered softly, trying not to let the insecurities of the past hammer against her brain.

"Did he fucking tell you that?" He insisted on knowing, his breath hot against her neck.

"Yes. He said that's why he needed another woman," she choked out, humiliated. She had believed Chris. Even though he was her first and only, she knew something had been seriously lacking.

"He was a complete idiot, Kara. You're all the woman any man could want or dream about. Exactly what I need. It was his issue, not yours," he grunted, placing his hands on both sides of her head and pulling her away from his body until his eyes met hers.

"I want this. I really do. I want you. I'm just a little nervous," she admitted, her body still singing with arousal. "I don't want to disappoint you."

"Listen to me," he grumbled as his hands fisted in her hair. "You could never, ever disappoint me. I want you so badly I'm ready to lose my mind. I have you. I have control. I make the decisions. You have nothing to do except to come, as loud and as long as you want to. You please me just by being here and wanting me. As long as I can make you come, I'll be ecstatic."

She sighed, her body relaxing. Simon would make it good. She already knew that. "Then make me come, Simon. Take me to bed."

Simon picked her up and placed her in the middle of the bed, pulling the bedding down roughly until it lay crumpled at the end of the bed. Her ass was stroked by the black silk fitted sheet that still remained under her as she scooted up on the bed.

Simon sat on the edge of the bed, his hand reaching for the drawer beside the bed. He yanked four fur-lined handcuffs, complete with attached hardware, from the drawer, followed by a long strip of black silk.

"Complete surrender," she murmured softly as she leaned back against the silk-covered pillows.

"Yes," he answered softly, his eyes raking her body hungrily as he reached for her arm to attach the first cuff.

She had no doubt that Simon had done this many times before. He had her secured to the bed, spread-eagled, in less than a minute. She watched him, his eyes ravenous on her body as he went through the motions.

She was surprised by her own reaction. The more helpless he made her, as he attached each limb to the bed, the more aroused she became. Being spread out for his pleasure gave her a freedom she had never experienced. No decisions to make, no wondering what would please him. He was the master and all she had to do was wait for her pleasure. There was something so erotic about being bound to his bed that her hips rotated and she moaned softly as she yanked on the cuffs, feeling almost no give, but no pain.

"Are you going to gag me?" she asked curiously, but not afraid.

"Oh, hell no. I want to hear every little cry of pleasure, every sweet little sound that you make as you come for me."

The heat flowing over her body spiked to boiling at his growling, sexy words. She closed her eyes, so desperate for release that she whimpered softly.

Opening her eyes again, she saw his face, fierce and ravenous, before he blocked her vision with a swatch of black silk, obliterating all of her sight, leaving everything pitch black. A moment of panic seized her, but she felt Simon's hot breath hit her ear, his tongue tracing the edges as he whispered, "Being sightless will heighten every sensation, Kara. Every touch of my tongue will be sharper, more acute. Everything more arousing."

"I'm aroused enough, Simon. For God's sake, touch me before I die of longing," she whined, waiting in the darkness to feel him.

She heard a low, rumbling chuckle as he left the bed, his clothes rustling as they hit the ground. The bed dipped with his weight as he returned. "You look so incredibly beautiful it's hard to decide where to start. I've imagined this for so long. I can't believe you're really here with me. In my bed." His voice was rough, graveled.

Kara was about to open her mouth to tell him to pick any spot, *just please start now*, when his mouth covered hers. His kiss was voracious and filled with longing. He was naked and she sighed into the embrace as she felt his blazing hot skin against hers. His marauding tongue and mouth claimed her over and over, while a wandering hand stroked her body, teasing her nipples, sliding over her hip, slipping between her bound, spread legs and into her wet folds.

She broke her mouth from his, panting as his fingers slipped into her tender flesh, brushing over her swollen, sensitive clit. "Please, Simon. Oh, God." She needed him. Her whole body burned and she jerked at her bindings, desperate for more contact.

His lips moved down over her breasts, his tongue stroking and gently biting at one nipple, and then the other. He slid one finger into her channel, and then another, stretching her, opening her, making her wish he would fill her with his cock.

"Jesus, Kara. You're so wet, so tight," he murmured hotly against her nipple, his body tense against hers.

With her sight gone and her limbs bound, all Kara could do was feel, and Simon was playing her body like it was a musical instrument. It was heightening her senses…to an almost unbearable level. "I need you. Please."

"Soon, sweetheart," he crooned as that wicked tongue trailed down her abdomen, flicking into her bellybutton, before it finally laved the lips of her pussy, making her cry out and shudder with fierce, aching lust. His fingers sifted through the well-trimmed hair on her mound as that talented tongue slid along her slick folds, delving deeper and deeper as she released a series of short, incoherent, puling noises.

Her back arched, straining against her bindings, as his firm, insistent mouth circled her needy bud, before finally latching over the nub, clamping it lightly with his teeth. White-hot need hit her like lightning, her body sizzling as he positioned the naked nub for his flicking, relentless tongue.

"Oh, God, Simon." Her voice was hoarse and needy, begging him to let her climax. Every nerve in her body was alive and tingling, her core clenching with longing as the pressure built to an almost unbearable level.

His large hands slid under her ass, bringing her pussy tight against his mouth. The pressure increased on her clit and Kara could feel her climax rip through her, every inch of her body shaking as spasms gripped and released. Over and over. "Yes. Oh, yes." Her head fell back and she moaned with abandon as her entire body went up in flames. Simon lapped at the juices that flowed from her, murmuring his enjoyment of every drop.

She shuddered, feeling his exquisite, burning, naked flesh against hers as he slid up and over her.

His mouth covered hers and she sighed into his kiss, tasting her own essence on his mouth. Dear God, she had never experienced an orgasm so strong, so intense. She returned the kiss, trying to make Simon understand the significance of what had just happened, of what she had experienced, by pouring every ounce of passion she felt into the embrace.

"That was incredible," she breathed as she pulled her mouth away. Feeling his hard cock against her thigh, she squirmed, more than ready for him to take her, knowing it would fill more than one empty place inside her. Primitive and wild, she bucked against him, begging for his untamed possession.

"You taste like fine wine, Kara. I could have stayed there all day," he mumbled in a ravenous, yearning voice. "You're so beautiful. So very beautiful."

"So are you, Simon. Please fuck me," she groaned, her body pleading for him.

"Tell me that you want me, that you need me," he demanded, his tone raw and harsh.

She could feel the head of his member nudging against her tight opening.

"Oh, shit. Condom," Simon groaned painfully.

She lifted her hips, needing him inside her so badly that she was ready to scream. "I'm on the pill to regulate my periods. I'm covered. I'm clean."

"I'm clean, too, and this would be my first time without a condom. I won't last, but I want you this way. Nothing between us," he warned her, his breath heavy and hot against her neck.

"I don't care. Come inside me, Simon. I want you so much. I need you so badly," she begged with a slight sob, completely out of control.

His hips thrust forward and she was instantly filled. He was big and she hadn't had a man inside her for so long. Simon stretched her, forcing her walls to expand and accept him. Her slick, wet flesh gave way, allowing him entrance as his massive member lodged completely inside her.

"God, sweetheart, you're so tight," Simon choked, almost as if he were in pain. "So hot. You feel so damn good, so incredible."

"Yes," she panted, completely filled, completely taken by Simon. His big body consumed her, dominated her as he pulled back and entered her again, rubbing against her g-spot, driving her higher and higher as he increased his pace. His hips pistoned into her, one hand sliding under her ass to pull her up to meet him, making their skin slap together in a satisfying, forceful meeting.

In the dark, Kara absorbed every sensation, every thrust. Simon was making her body sing with pleasure and she grasped the chains on the cuffs, her fingers digging into the metal as she cried out his name. His body slammed into hers and she relished each thrust, every pump of his hips. Their bodies were both slick with sweat and they moved against each other in an erotic slide. A dusting of hair on Simon's chest abraded her nipples as he moved, adding to her arousal, making her moan as she moved her head from side to side, not sure if she could bear the sensation overload.

"Come for me, Kara. Come. I want to watch your pleasure." His low, seductive voice whispered to her, coaxed her, as his cock filled her again and again. Faster and faster.

When his hand moved between their bodies and boldly stroked her clit, she exploded as ecstasy seized her, seeing brilliant colors flash through the darkness as her body pulsed and her channel spasmed around his cock, milking him.

"Oh, Jesus, Kara," Simon groaned. "You're so sweet. And so damned hot." His mouth came down on hers as he entered her one last time, as though he wanted to possess every part of her, spilling himself deep inside her with a harsh, tortured groan.

They both came back to reality slowly. Simon pulled away from her and rolled to her side, his head resting on her shoulder, his arms around her body, squeezing her possessively. Her lips searched, kissing the top of his head as she tried to catch her breath.

Her heart was thundering and she wished she could see Simon right now, his hair mussed, his eyes still smoky with spent passion. She was nearly destroyed by the depths of her feelings. Scared. Exhilarated. Confused. She was a jumbled-up mess at the moment, not quite sure how to feel or how to react. Sex had never been so all-consuming for her. What in the hell had happened?

Simon. Simon had happened. And she would never be the same.

She felt his kiss, a light caress to her lips, before he rolled out of bed. She heard the zipper of his jeans close and knew that he was getting dressed. It was only moments before she was free and the blindfold was being removed.

His hair was adorably mussed and his eyes were raking her nude body as though he was ready to have her again. Kara shivered, not only from her nakedness, but from the tortured look she saw in his eyes.

He scooped her up and carried her down the hall to her room. He pulled the covers back and deposited her in the middle of her bed, pulling the covers over her nude form. The room was dark, the only illumination coming from the window and the brightness of the moon, but she could see his frown.

Did he regret what happened? Was he upset that he had just slept with a woman he barely knew? So upset that he wanted to get rid of her, put her back in her own bed and forget their cataclysmic joining had ever happened?

Or perhaps, it had only been life-changing for her.

Leaning forward, he kissed her forehead lightly and whispered in a low husky voice, "Thank you, Kara. I'll never forget tonight."

Tears choked her, jamming the back of her throat. She couldn't answer, couldn't ask any of the questions she so desperately wanted to ask.

He exited the room, closing the door softly behind him.

Gone. Just like that. He hadn't even wanted to sleep with her.

Kara let go of her tears, letting them slide down her cheeks as she rested her head against the pillow, wondering what had just happened. Having Simon dump her back in her room after the most incredible sexual encounter of her life was like being slapped in the face. With a heavy dose of reality.

He's a billionaire, Kara. Wake up. Did you think he wanted anything more than a casual screw?

She had to remind herself that she was a big girl. She had gone into the encounter with her eyes wide open, knowing it was nothing more than one night.

Then why does this hurt so damn much?

Sliding quietly out of bed, Kara opened one of the drawers of her dresser and slipped into a nightgown before returning to her bed. She drew the covers tightly around her as her body quaked. Simon had been so hot, so warm. Now all she felt was cold and empty.

Pushing aside his rejection and her hurt feelings, Kara tried to reason out the situation. Regardless of what he felt for her, Simon had some issues. The restraints, the blindfold, not wanting her to see him when they had sex. Maybe he liked a little kink—she had certainly discovered that she liked it—but something more was going on in his head.

Something deeper.

Something darker.

He'd never had a girlfriend? That, in itself, was strange. He certainly didn't lack sexual prowess. He was incredibly rich and as handsome as sin. Why had he never had a long-term relationship?

Kara rolled to her back, her mind racing. Simon's problems were really none of her business and she doubted if he would appreciate her poking her nose into his life. But she wanted to help him. It wasn't his fault that he couldn't care for her. He'd been nothing but generous and kind. If she could help him, maybe he could fall in love and have a relationship with a woman he could love some day.

Her gut twisted and her chest squeezed tightly at the thought, but she tried to ignore it. Simon deserved to be happy. She needed to be a friend and try to get to the bottom of his issues.

You want to be more than his friend, and you know it.

"Shut the hell up," she whispered furiously to the dark room, flopping onto her stomach and pulling a pillow over her head, as though her actions would silence her treacherous thoughts.

It didn't. And it took Kara quite some time to finally fall into a troubled, restless sleep that brought disturbing dreams of a handsome, dark-haired, dark-eyed man with an expression filled with anguish and misery, trying to fight demons that he couldn't truly see. In the dream, Kara was an observer, trying desperately to reach the man in agony, holding her hand out to him, begging him to latch onto her, to let her help him. He started to slowly lift one hand, still stabbing at the dark with the other, trying to vanquish the clawing, dark shadows that threatened him. Finally, his hand met hers, his grip firm and she tugged with every ounce of strength she had, trying to bring him to her.

In the end, she couldn't. The man yanked her into the darkness and she let out a terrified, blood-curdling scream as he pulled her to him, taking her into a deep, dark, whirling vortex.

He fell, and she went with him, knowing neither of them would ever escape.

Mine For Now

BOOK TWO

The Billionaire's Obsession

Chapter 1

Simon woke the morning after his incredible sexual encounter surrounded by the tantalizing scent of Kara and feeling like something was missing from his bed.

He rolled to his back, his cock hard and swollen, trying not to think about the heart-stopping events of the night before. He pulled a pillow over his face and breathed in her fragrance, a scent that would likely haunt him forever. And every time he imagined her scent, he would think about her taste. Her smile. Her moans. Her absolutely beautiful nude body. Her cries as she came for him, her flesh tightening around him until he found release.

Oh, fuck. He was so screwed.

Last night had been a life-changing event for him. Never again would he be able to settle for just any woman in his bed, an unemotional fuck to satisfy his body.

He wasn't sure whether to be completely pissed off or in awe of the woman who made him feel this way. Sure, he only had one woman at a time. He was monogamous in a fucked-up sort of way, always calling the same woman until he went on to the next one, but not because one was really any better than the one before. Or the one before that. There just came a time, and he could always sense it, when he thought he should move on to avoid any entanglements. Not that any woman had ever really wanted *him*, but they began to want more and more of what his wealth could provide.

He pulled the pillow from his face, but it didn't relieve the bone-deep ache that he had for Kara. Taking her back to her own bed had been one of the hardest things he had ever done. But she had only offered one night, and he had never been able to sleep with a woman. He wasn't capable of it and had never wanted to…until last night. He had wanted to fall asleep with Kara in his arms, her body draped around his, her warm breath on his face.

He had returned to his room, but he hadn't been able to sleep. He had tossed and turned in a bed that smelled of hot, smoldering sex and Kara. Frustrated as hell, he had gone to his gym and worked out, hoping to exhaust himself, desperate to escape into latent unconsciousness. Unfortunately, he didn't. Instead, he had ended up tired and defeated…and still unable to sleep.

What time had he finally given in and passed out? His eyes went to the clock, realizing with shock that it was almost noon. Generally an early riser, he had never slept this late, even on the weekend. He slid out of the bed and went straight to the shower.

He showered quickly, hating the fact that he was washing away *her* scent, and made his way to the kitchen, wondering if Kara was still asleep. The kitchen was spotless, the remains of their unfinished dinner from last night gone. He grabbed a cup of freshly brewed coffee and walked around the condo. Her bedroom door was open, the bed made. Obviously she was up, but where in the hell was she?

He shot up the stairs, thinking that maybe she was in his lab, playing computer games.

She wasn't.

She's not here.

Simon felt a chill crawl slowly down his spine and experienced a brief moment of panic.

He went back down the stairs two at a time, his heart racing. Rationally, he knew she wouldn't leave. She had no reason to go.

They had both agreed to satisfy their sexual urges by spending just one night together.

One night.

One night, my ass. One night will never be enough. She's mine.

Simon had known it last night and he knew it now. He would never get enough of Kara. She was an obsession that he couldn't get over with one night of incredible sex. He wasn't sure what it was going to take, but it hadn't been relieved by screwing her brains out. If anything, it was worse. Now that he had possessed her once, he wanted her again and again.

The coffee he was drinking churned in his gut. Truth was, he goddamn hated feeling so possessive of a female. Giving a shit about anyone other than his family meant trouble. Hadn't he learned that lesson painfully a long time ago? Apparently it hadn't stuck, because he cared more about Kara than he wanted to…and it scared the ever-loving crap out of him.

Simon snatched his phone from a coffee table in the living room and sent a text message to her phone.

U ok?

He tapped his finger against the plastic cover of the phone, impatient. Hell, he didn't even know if she had her phone, but he'd be pissed if she didn't. How many times had he asked her to always carry it for her own safety?

A snort escaped his mouth as he carried the phone and his coffee to the kitchen. Like she really listened to him? She patted him on the head and went on her merry way, doing whatever the hell she pleased. Secretly, he loved her independence, but it also drove him insane. There were just too many instances where she was nonchalant about her safety.

The phone beeped, startling Simon enough for him to spill his coffee onto the pristine tile. *Fuck, I'm on edge this morning.* Cursing, he read the return text.

Police Station. Tell u about it later.

What. The. Fuck. His fingers flew as he typed another text.

Where? Why?

She answered briefly, giving him the location of the station and another infuriatingly vague explanation and a promise to tell him about it later.

Later, my ass. Nobody goes to the police station on a Saturday morning for shits and giggles. Something's wrong.

Simon ran a frustrated hand through his hair, nearly yanking a few locks from his head. Jesus! At this rate, he'd be fucking bald within a week. He sent her a brief text telling her he was on his way and crammed his cell phone into his pocket. The phone beeped again a moment later, but he ignored it. He already knew it was Kara, probably telling him not to come.

Snatching up his keys, he slammed his feet into the nearest pair of casual shoes and exited the door of the condo, not even flinching when it slammed violently behind him.

Kara sighed softly as she took a sip from the foam cup, hoping the coffee would help her focus. Swallowing hard to get the strong, burnt-tasting liquid down her throat, she looked up at Maddie with a weak smile. "I think we're almost done."

She had already identified the two suspects from mug shots, the angry gunmen who had stormed the clinic that morning, demanding drugs. Maddie had been in an exam room and hadn't seen the men, but Kara had gotten an up close and personal look. Grimacing, she wished to hell that she hadn't. Alone in the waiting room, watching over a child whose sibling and mother were in the exam room with Maddie, Kara would probably never forget the dead look in the men's eyes and their haggard faces that told the story of years of drug abuse. She knew the look, had seen it often in her youth, but she hadn't had a gun in her face at the time. That moment, that terrifying instance of not knowing whether the next few seconds would be her last, had been enough to scare the bejesus out of her.

She had scooped up the child and raced around the corner, hitting the alarm button under the desk as she tucked the child behind her. The alarm wasn't silent and the ruckus had been enough to bring Maddie running out and the men to scatter.

One of the men had a twitchy trigger finger and his firearm had exploded at the sound of the alarm, the path of the bullet coming so close to Kara's head that she had felt the air ripple at the side of her face.

Shuddering, she wrapped her arms around herself, not really cold, but remembering with more than a touch of unease the faces of the men and their final brutal comment as they escaped through the clinic door.

"We'll get you later, bitch!"

Maddie had only seen their exit, arriving seconds after they had turned to run. Thankfully, everyone had escaped unharmed.

"The nice detective should be back soon and we can affirm the police reports and get the hell out of here," Maddie responded grimly, her eyes focused on Kara. "Are you sure you're okay? You look a little pale."

Kara shrugged, trying to look unaffected. "A little shaken up is all. I'm...good." *Terrified. Scared shitless. But otherwise, just fine.*

The last thing she wanted was to alarm her friend, knowing Maddie already felt responsible for Kara nearly getting shot.

Maddie reached across the table and grabbed her hand, squeezing it until almost all of the blood left the extremity. "They shot at you. It's normal to be upset. That was a damn close call. I'm so sorry, Kara."

"Maddie, it isn't your fault-"

"Who the hell shot at her!" A bellowing male voice came from the door, and Kara didn't even have to turn around to know exactly who stood there. She recognized Simon's blustering tone immediately. The man might not yell often, but he made up for it in quality. No one could roar more ferociously than Simon when his temper flared.

"What in the fuck is going on? The police said you got attacked at some clinic-"

"My clinic," Maddie interrupted, standing to confront Simon. "Who the hell are you?"

Uh-oh.

Kara stood, ready to jump into the fight. Maddie might have the face of an angel, with fiery red corkscrew curls that surrounded her perfect features, but she could be a furious foe when she wanted to be. Not that people saw that side of her often. Her patients, young and old, adored her and her usually sunny personality. But when Maddie was fighting for a cause or something she believed in, she could be a dangerous enemy.

Kara watched as her friend threw back her shoulders, her white physician's coat floating around generous curves that complemented her angelic features. She forced back a grin as Maddie straightened to try to compensate for her five foot three height, in preparation for battle.

"I'm Kara's..." Simon stopped abruptly, as though not quite sure what to say, before finishing hesitantly, "friend. And I want to know why the hell someone shot at her."

"Helloooo. I'm right here, Simon." Reaching out her hand, she gripped his jaw, forcing him to look at her. "I am able to answer for myself."

His face transformed, the anger draining from his features as his still-hot eyes met hers. Reaching out to grasp her shoulders, he demanded, "What happened? Are you okay? Did they hurt you?" His hands ran over her arms before landing again on her shoulders.

Explaining what happened turned into an exhausting event. Simon interrupted, swearing like a sailor and asking what felt like a million freaking questions. Kara tried to answer them patiently to calm him down.

They all took a seat on the flimsy, uncomfortable chairs at the enormous table. Kara talked, first introducing Simon and Maddie, and then going on to answer more questions that were flowing from the furious man in front of her, almost faster than she could answer them.

Simon cursed throughout her explanation.

And Maddie just watched with a dumbfounded, perplexed expression.

"Did they catch them?" Simon asked, his voice rough, as though he had been through hell himself.

"No. And Kara needs to be careful since they threatened her." Maddie finally jumped in, her voice protective.

"You neglected to mention that." Simon shot Kara a dark look.

Their conversation was interrupted by a plainclothes detective, a very nice, youngish blond man who had identified himself as Detective Harris. He dropped papers in front of both Kara and Maddie, asking quietly, "Can you look at the reports and see if you have anything to add?" He put a casual hand on the back of Kara's chair and leaned over her shoulder, perusing the report with her.

A low, reverberating sound came from Simon's throat and she pulled her eyes away from the report to look at him. But he wasn't looking at her. His eyes were shooting fire at Detective Harris, a threatening look that startled her.

Obviously, the detective wasn't the least bit intimidated. "Boyfriend?" he asked quietly, quietly enough that Simon couldn't detect the words.

"Friend," she mumbled back, hating herself for wishing she could confirm the question with a simple "yes" answer.

She read the report quickly, with enough haste to get through it fast, but not so rapidly that she wasn't accurate. After the official paperwork was finished, she stood, stretching her back as she got to her feet, feeling slightly unsteady.

"Careful!" The detective took her arm to steady her slightly swaying body. "You've had a tough day," he stated kindly. Reaching into his pocket, he pulled out two business cards and handed one to both her and Maddie. "My card. Call me anytime. My cell phone number is on the back just in case you need it."

"Is that really necessary?" Simon snarled, his arm curling around Kara's waist, pulling her body against him protectively.

The detective shrugged. "Yeah. It is. Kara was threatened. I want these ladies to be able to reach me any time."

"Thank you, Detective Harris. You've been very kind." Smiling softly, Kara shook the detective's hand. Maddie did the same, before all three of them exited the building together.

Kara took a deep breath, letting the crisp, refreshing air of the outdoors enter her lungs. "It's a good day to be alive," she muttered to herself, thankful to just be among the living and healthy.

As the three of them descended the stairs, approaching the sidewalk, Maddie asked Simon quietly, "You wouldn't happen to be related to Sam Hudson? I know the last name is pretty common, but I was just wondering."

Stopping at the bottom of the stairs, Simon looked at Maddie with surprise. "Yeah...he's my brother. Why do you ask? Do you know him?"

Maddie frowned. "Oh, God." She let out a heavy breath. "Uh... yeah...I did. A long time ago."

"Were you friends?" Simon asked curiously, looking at Maddie expectantly.

"No! Not really!" Maddie answered abruptly, her face turning as red as her hair.

"Ah...I see," Simon answered. Not ready to let the subject drop, he added, "Bad experience with my brother?"

"He's a complete and total snake." Maddie reached up to rake the curls from her face. The wind was brisk and errant spirals were whipping around her head.

Kara jumped as a harsh bark of laughter escaped from Simon's mouth. "Believe me, you aren't the first woman to feel that way. I'm sorry."

"It's not your fault that your brother is a slimy reptile. I just hope the two of you aren't similar in some regards," she replied awkwardly. "Take care of Kara."

"With pleasure, Maddie," he replied smoothly, reaching out his available hand. "Bad circumstances, but nice to meet you."

"You too. I think," she answered as she grudgingly shook Simon's outstretched hand. "I know I can't judge one brother by the other, but I hate anything that reminds me of Sam Hudson." Shuddering, she released his hand and hugged Kara. "Take care of yourself. I'll call you. Don't do anything stupid," she warned Kara fiercely in a whisper low enough that only Kara could catch her adamant advice.

Kara threw herself into Maddie's arms and hugged her tightly, well aware of the danger that both she and her friend had been in and how easily things could have turned out differently. She loved Maddie to death. Although she could be prickly on the outside at times, her friend was a complete marshmallow on the inside. "You too. I'll talk to you soon."

Simon reclaimed her, slipping his arm around her waist and leading her to his car as Maddie crossed the parking lot to her own vehicle.

God, what a horrible day.

Tired, shaken, her mind on the events of the day, she didn't even balk as Simon led her to his ridiculously expensive Veyron and seated her in the passenger side before climbing behind the wheel himself.

They were both silent, lost in their own thoughts, as they made the journey home.

Chapter 2

S imon didn't take them straight back to the condo. He pulled into a parking lot close to home and whipped the small sports car into a vacant parking space.

"We need to eat. This place has the best Italian food in the area, but it's nothing fancy." He hopped out and jogged to the other side of the car, opening her door and taking her hand to pull her out of the vehicle.

"Uh...I'm not exactly dressed for fancy." Still in her jeans and sweater that she wore for the clinic, she knew that she was a mess. Both physically and emotionally.

"You look beautiful. But I know it's been a tough day. Is that okay?"

"It's great. I love Italian and I'm starving."

Surprisingly enough, what she told him was true. She had skipped breakfast because she had gotten up late, and lunch had come and gone while they were at the police station.

Simon held the door for her, guiding her through it with a hand at the small of her back. God, the man had great manners. She'd have to remember to compliment Helen later for raising her son to be polite. Kara couldn't remember the last time a guy had actually run to open her door. Probably...never.

The interior of the restaurant was dim, each table lighted with a large, fat candle in the middle. It wasn't fancy, but it wasn't exactly a dive either.

"Mr. Hudson. How lovely to see you again." The leggy, beautiful blonde who greeted them showed them to a corner table, gracing Simon with a smile straight from a toothpaste commercial.

After they were seated, Simon ordered a beer on tap and Kara asked for an iced tea. She breathed a sigh of relief when the fawning female finally left to get their drinks.

"Flirty woman." Kara wanted to bite her tongue immediately. What business was it of hers if a woman flirted with Simon? Maybe he liked it.

"You mean Kate?" Simon's expression was puzzled as he closed his menu, obviously already decided on what he wanted.

"Is that her name? She didn't introduce herself to me. She seemed much more interested in you." *Shut the hell up, Kara. You sound like a jealous girlfriend.*

"She wasn't flirting. I'm a regular customer. She has to be nice." Simon shrugged.

Oh Lord, the man was clueless. She studied the menu, trying to let the subject drop. "You've been here before. Any recommendations?"

"It's all good. I'm having the chicken parmesan."

Kara looked at the menu like a kid in a candy store. It had been so long since she'd had so many choices or eaten in a restaurant as an actual customer. "It's so hard to decide."

Simon was grinning when she finally looked up from the menu. "You look like you're trying to solve a major problem."

"Do I look like I don't get out much?" she asked with a light, self-mocking laugh.

His eyes grew stormy as he shot her a look so intense, she could feel heat wash over every inch of her body. "You are the loveliest woman I've ever seen sitting across a table from me. No one else even comes close."

She blushed, actually flushing rose-red from the I-want-to-fuck-you look in his eyes and the heat of his gaze. No man could drive her crazy like Simon did. One word, one statement, one look…and she was flustered like a freaking teenage girl.

Kara was actually grateful to see an older, dark-haired waitress coming to deliver their drinks and take their food order. She decided to make things easy and have the same thing Simon was having. As the waitress left, Kara picked up her drink, puzzled. "I think they made me an alcoholic iced tea."

Simon chuckled as he glanced at the beverage in her hand. "It's definitely an alcoholic iced tea. I didn't know you wanted the real thing."

"What's in this?" she asked, staring at the glass of liquid that was actually pretty close to the same color as conventional iced tea, but it was in a stout drink glass and topped with a cherry. None of the restaurants where she had worked were equipped with a full bar and she wasn't really an expert on drinks.

Simon grinned wickedly. "Rum, gin, tequila, vodka, triple sec… and a splash of cola and sour mix."

Oh, crap. She'd be doing a happy dance on the table. A glass of wine made her tipsy. Holding her alcohol well wasn't a talent she had ever perfected, probably because she seldom imbibed. "Promise you won't let me dance naked on the table when I'm done." She cocked a brow at Simon, waiting for his agreement.

She glared at him as he burst into a full belly laugh, gasping for breath as he answered, "Seriously? From a drink or two?"

"It's not funny. I don't drink much," she told him defensively, suddenly feeling pretty damn unworldly and out of place sitting across from a billionaire who had been around the block a time or two. Or three.

Simon grinned at her. "I know. Try it. If you don't like it, I'll get you something else." His expression sobered, his eyes alight with heat and something else that she couldn't quite define. "And I definitely promise that you will not dance naked on the table, unless it's at home in a private performance." His voice was gruff, his expression heated, as though he were imagining exactly that scenario and was looking forward to it.

She refused to meet his eyes, the lump in her throat feeling as big as a baseball. Hell, why not? She could use a drink after the morning she had just been through. Sipping cautiously, she let the liquid flow over her tongue and down her throat, swallowing hard to get by the knot that had formed from Simon's sexy comment. "Not bad." She licked her lips. "It doesn't really taste all that strong."

He shot her a wicked smile. "It's deceiving. They're pretty potent."

They enjoyed their drinks and dinner with companionable conversation. Simon talked about his family and told her about some of his projects. Kara shared funny stories from her career as a waitress, and a few from her years in nursing school.

Simon destroyed his entire plate of chicken parmesan and finished hers when she couldn't eat another bite. He ordered them each a tiramisu and a second drink. The dessert was delicious, but she couldn't finish it. Of course, he was willing to polish that off for her, too. The man could put away a lot of food. Maybe he needed it to fuel that big, sinewy, sculpted body that never failed to leave her panting like a dog after a tempting treat.

"How do you maintain such an incredible body when you eat like that?" she asked him, wanting to kick herself for wording it quite that way, knowing that it was the alcohol that was twisting her words.

Note to self: Do not drink more than a watered down glass of wine from now on.

His eyes shot to her face, his expression mischievous. "Incredible, huh?"

She shrugged. What was the point in denying it? His body was incredible. "Well, it is." *Incredible. Rock-hard and sexy as hell. The hottest body on the planet.*

"I work out in the gym at home every day. If you think I look good, I guess it's worth it," his incredulous voice informed her.

Oh, hell yeah. Way worth it.

"It shows," she choked out, trying not to be obvious about the fact that she wanted to jump his bones in about a hundred different ways.

"It's one of the reasons that women like Kate fall all over you. Not the only reason, but one of them." *Oh, shit. Had she really said that out loud? Damn alcohol! She needed to bite her tongue.*

"Women don't admire my body, my personality, or anything else about me except my money," Simon told her in a matter-of-fact tone.

Kara looked at him, flabbergasted. Did he really believe that? "Oh, so it doesn't matter that you're insanely handsome, a genius, funny, and extremely kind? Women just want the cash?" God, he really was infuriating. Didn't he know? Didn't he realize that he had so much more to offer than just his money?

"Yes."

Her heart ached, knowing that he really did think that money was his only asset. Hard to believe, especially when she had been on the receiving end of his generous nature so many times. Also difficult to comprehend as she glanced yearningly across the table at the most handsome, desirable man she had ever laid eyes on. "I do." He looked at her with a bewildered expression as the words slipped from her mouth in a heated rush. "I want you. And it has nothing to do with your money." The words spilled from her lips without pause, uncensored. She looked away from him, slightly mortified at what she had revealed, but his constant refusal to realize his own value made her insane. "I don't give a shit about your money."

"Yeah…I noticed that," he said in a graveled voice.

Finally, she looked up at him and his expression was unreadable. Confusion? Disbelief? Distrust? Hope? They were all there, but she had a hard time figuring out which one took priority.

She tipped up her glass, finishing the last of her second iced tea. "I'm done." If she had another drink, she'd be stripping off her clothes and begging him to take her. Right now.

Kara wondered if she would regret her spontaneous outburst later, and decided she most likely wouldn't. Somehow, she needed to get through to Simon, even if it was uncomfortably humbling. He was so self-contained, so controlled, but there was an underlying vulnerability lurking beneath the surface. That self-doubt that she occasionally spotted in those gorgeous eyes should never linger there. No man as handsome, kind, and generous should ever know a moment of uncertainty.

Simon was, without question, an alpha male, but she had to question if his need to have a woman helpless and blindfolded during sex was a domination issue. Certainly, that type of domination was erotic, so hot that she creamed her panties every time she thought back to the night before, but she hated to think that Simon was constrained to only one type of sex because of distrust. Unfortunately, that was her suspicion. Gut instinct was clawing at her insides, telling her that his issue had nothing to do with domination and everything to do with some type of trust issue.

They stood and Simon pulled out his wallet, dropping some cash on top of the check. She sighed as he grasped her hand tightly, tugging her gently through the door. It was early evening and the cooler air helped clear her foggy head. She couldn't remember every one of the ingredients in the drinks, but they had certainly loosened her tongue.

The drive back to the condo was only a few blocks, but it left Kara squirming in her seat. Simon was too close and smelled way too tempting, and she was still embarrassed about the fact that she had basically spilled her soul to him. Oh, maybe not everything, but admitting how much she wanted him and getting no real response was pretty deflating.

What did I want him to say? I want to help him and that means expecting nothing back. He never promised anything except for mind-blowing sex. And he gave me that. In spades!

Really, she hadn't expected anything, but having him say that he wanted her too would have been nice. She felt raw, exposed. And being in his company was anything but comfortable at the moment.

I don't understand him. I don't know what motivates his behavior.

But she wanted to. There was nothing she wanted more than to understand every one of Simon Hudson's secrets.

She breathed a sigh of relief as they entered the condo. Wandering through the kitchen, she headed for her room to take a shower. She was about to call a brief goodnight to Simon when a large, muscular arm wrapped around her waist, pulling her against an equally large, masculine body.

"Don't go. Not yet." Simon's husky voice against her ear sent a shiver of need through her body, momentarily stunning her into silence.

He lifted her, cradling her against his chest as he strode into the living room and sat on the couch, her body sprawled on his lap. "What's wrong?" she questioned softly, feeling the restless tension in his body. His muscles were bunched tightly as she fanned her hands over his shoulders.

"I need to hold you for a while. Please. You took twenty years off my life today, Kara. I'm going to end up old, bald, and crazy if you keep having incidents like this." He wrapped his arms around her, plastering her body tightly against his.

"I'm sorry." She laid her head on his shoulder, relishing the abrasive feel of his whiskers against her cheek, trying not to let her spirits soar because he was hinting at a future for them.

"I can't take it. I can't stand the thought of anything happening to you," he said in a strangled voice.

The living room was dim, lit only by residual light from the kitchen. Her heart raced as she pulled back to stroke his rough jaw. He was afraid for her safety. She couldn't help but be touched by it. There had been very few people in her life who had really cared about her in that way, and certainly never a male, except for her father. Her ex probably would have shrugged it off and told her that it was her own fault for volunteering in that part of the city. He hadn't exactly been the nurturing type.

Capturing her hand, he drew it to his lips, dropping light, soft kisses to her palm. "I had a very hard time not going for your cop's throat today."

"Why?"

"For God's sake, Kara, the man was eye-fucking you right there in the station." His answer was harsh.

"He was just being nice-"

"He was imagining what it would be like to fuck you," he informed her in a raspy voice. "I'm a guy. Believe me. I know. And I fucking hated it. I don't like to share."

Gulp. Was he insinuating that…

"I didn't know that I was yours." *Was she?*

"You are now."

"Since when?"

"Probably since the first moment I saw you. Definitely since the moment I touched you. And absolutely since last night." His hand moved to the back of her neck, guiding her mouth to his.

He flipped her in one smooth motion, his mouth never leaving hers. One moment she was on his lap, and the next, she was spread out on the massive sofa beneath him. He kissed her until she couldn't breathe, couldn't think; she could only feel. Legs parting to accept his body, she wrapped her arms around his muscular back, trying to get as close to him as she possibly could.

She needed this, needed him. She slid her tongue along his, desperate to get closer, wanting to crawl inside him. Her hips shifted longingly against his groin, whimpering into his mouth when she felt the hard erection straining against his jeans, pushing against her mound, making her crazy to feel him inside her.

Pulling her mouth away from his she gasped, "I need you to fuck me, Simon. Please."

He buried his face in her neck with a guttural sound. "Bedroom."

"No. Here. Now. Right now," she panted. She didn't want to move, didn't want to be blindfolded and tied this time. Wrapping her legs around his waist in silent entreaty, she brought her hands to his ass, pulling him against her as she undulated her hips. "Fuck! I can't think when you do that. I don't want to wait," he rasped, his hands sliding beneath her ass, pulling her tightly against his raging erection with a low, tormented groan.

"Don't wait. Please." Her body was igniting like tinder on a raging forest fire.

"You know I can't." His voice was angry and frustrated, but he didn't release his hold on her ass.

"You can." She wanted him like this, spontaneous and needy. Unwrapping her legs from his waist, she bucked and slipped her hands between their bodies, unsnapping her jeans and ripping at the zipper to get them undone. She wriggled, making Simon lift up while she lowered her jeans and panties enough to kick them off her legs. "Touch me."

Simon groaned as his hand slipped between them, his fingers sliding into her drenched pussy. "Oh Jesus, you're so fucking wet."

"For you," she answered fiercely. "So don't tell me that no woman wants you for anything other than your money. I want you so damn desperately that I'm begging you to fuck me," she told him furiously, trying to make him understand that what she felt was far from monetary.

She couldn't tell him the depths of her need. She wasn't ready to strip her soul and Simon wasn't ready to hear it. And maybe she wasn't ready to deal with it. But, damn it, he'd take *this*. He'd take *her*. Now.

Her body shuddered as his fingers glided through her tender, wet flesh, zeroing in on her throbbing clit. "Yes. Touch me." She was lost, her body reacting to every sensation, every brush of his fingers. Her head tossed wildly as she abandoned herself to his bold, undaunted stroking.

"You're so hot. So damn responsive. It's so hard to believe that you want me like this. Tell me. Again," he demanded, his strokes becoming harder, more demanding.

"I need you, Simon. Fuck me."

"Only me?"

"Only you. You're the only one who makes me feel like this." And he was the only man who could make her this crazy with a simple touch. She knew it was a weakness, but at the moment, she couldn't bring herself to care.

He reared up and tore open his jeans, yanking them down until his cock was liberated, springing out throbbing, hard and needy. "I want you so fucking much, Kara, but I'm not sure I can do this." His voice was both passionate and angry.

She recognized his need to dominate. The cause wasn't clear, but she knew he needed to be in control. "Hold my hands, Simon. Take control. Fuck me how you need to. I don't care, as long as you do it now."

She wanted to grasp that beautiful cock and put it where she most needed it, but reached her hands up and grasped both of his. Both of his hands were clenched in a tight fist, but they opened slowly and wrapped around hers. He entwined their fingers and lowered their joined hands over her head.

"Yes. You have control. I'm exactly where you want me. Now take me," she pleaded, needing him to take her this way. She had enjoyed last night, but she wanted him to bind her and blindfold her because it was erotic and sexy, not because he needed to. Instinctively, she knew it was critical that he learn to trust in small steps, make love instead of just fuck.

Nearly ready to weep as he lowered his powerful body over hers, she moaned at the feel of his cock poised against her tight opening. She swirled her hips until they were in position.

And then, miraculously, he entered her with one strong thrust.

She hissed as his cock slammed into her, stretched her, possessed her completely. "Yes. You feel so good." She wrapped her legs around him, wanting to savor the feel of him.

"Shit. You're so wet. Nothing between you and my cock. There's no fucking better feeling than this," Simon panted against her neck, his chest heaving against her breasts, abrading her swollen nipples.

Hands entwined, his fingers squeezing hers until they were nearly numb, Simon pumped his hips as she answered him by grinding up against him, meeting him halfway.

Her heart ached as her body joined again and again with Simon's, knowing that this moment was pivotal, extraordinary and special.

Her heels dug into his rock-hard ass, urging him deeper, faster. His strokes became powerful, forceful. In and out. Over and over.

His mouth covered hers, his kiss almost violent as he ravaged her mouth, owning it, as his velvet-soft tongue swept through every inch of her mouth, thrusting in the same rhythm as his cock.

Overwhelmed by his strength, absorbed in the cadence of pum-meling cock and thrusting tongue, Kara lost herself in Simon. Completely. Utterly. Willingly.

Tears rolled down her cheeks as she whimpered into his mouth, her body trembling, pulsating, in the most incredible climax she had ever experienced.

Her channel clenched, her flesh tightening and releasing around Simon's cock as he pounded in and out of her body with furious abandon.

He groaned into her mouth, entwining his marauding tongue with hers, as he buried himself one last time deep inside her, his big body trembling above her as he came, flooding her womb with heat.

Dragging his mouth away from her lips, his face fell against her neck. "Holy fuck. Holy fuck. Holy fuck," he chanted breathlessly against her skin.

She yanked on her hands, needing the return of her blood circula-tion. She freed herself and wrapped her arms around him, threading her hands through his sweat-soaked hair, cradling his head against her neck. His weight was heavy on top of her, his body relaxed and sated, but she wasn't ready for him to move.

"I think I just died," he huffed, still breathing hard.

"I guess I must be dead right along with you then. I was there," she answered with a gasp, her hands still sifting through his hair.

Later, she would wonder how long she and Simon had laid there in a world of their own, stunned and astonished by what had occurred, but at that moment she just absorbed the peace that came after the turbulent storm.

After an unknown amount of time, Simon rolled off her. "I'm heavy. I'm sorry."

Curling into his side, she sighed heavily. "It was fine."

"It was beyond fine," he growled, playfully and intentionally mis-understanding her.

"Thank you, Simon," she whispered softly.

"For what?" he asked, puzzled, as he wrapped one arm around her protectively and stroked the hair from her face with another.

"For what just happened." *For trusting me. For letting go of a few ghosts. For giving me what I needed. For giving yourself what you needed.*

She couldn't see his face, but she didn't need to. She could hear the grin in his voice. "Sweetheart, don't thank me. I should be worshipping at your feet."

"Ah...well...if you must...go ahead." She answered like a queen addressing one of her subjects, trying to lighten the mood.

Small steps.

He snorted. "Can't right now. You wore me out."

"Ungrateful cad." She swatted his shoulder with a smile.

"I don't need to be at your feet. I already worship you," he whispered gently as his lips brushed over hers and he released her to tuck himself back into his jeans.

She sat up, groping for her own jeans and panties. "Yeah, yeah... men will say anything after a decent orgasm." Denim brushed her fingers and she hopped up, quickly pulling the panties and jeans over her hips.

Simon snagged her hips as she turned to leave. "It was a lot more than a good fuck. You were crying. Just tell me if they were good tears or bad tears," he asked, his voice warm with concern.

"Good. Definitely good." Unwilling to say anything more, she brushed her lips against his and forced herself to walk away. She knew how Simon felt about sleeping with someone. She'd have to be content with what had just happened for now. "I need to shower. Someone made me all...wet."

Laughing at the low growl she heard behind her, she slipped away to her own room to shower and crawl into bed, falling into an exhausted but contented sleep.

Chapter 3

*E*verything ok?

Kara smiled down at the text message from Simon as James drove sedately toward Helen's Place. She hadn't talked to Helen in several days and they had made arrangements to have coffee. Since Helen couldn't stand to tear herself away from the restaurant, Kara usually popped in after school during the slower hours to chat.

She sent a return text. *Yes Daddy. All's well.*

It was Friday, almost a week since the incident at the clinic. Simon checked in with her every day, usually several times a day, to make sure everything was okay. She might joke with him about being like an overprotective father, but she secretly found it touching that he cared about her safety.

They hadn't gotten physical since the night of the incident at the clinic. They joked, they talked, but they didn't screw. It was almost as if they were both afraid that what happened couldn't be repeated. Or maybe it had just scared the shit out of both of them. It had certainly frightened the hell out of her. She had never experienced anything quite that intense.

Her phone beeped again.

Be careful. Let me know when u leave. RU there yet?

She replied. *Pulling up now. Will obey orders, sir.*

The car pulled in front of Helen's restaurant as her phone beeped again.

I wish. Only in my dreams do you ever obey orders.

She snickered as she put the phone in her front pocket, almost able to hear Simon speaking those words out loud in a disgruntled voice. "Thank you, James. I'll see you in a little bit." She smiled at the kind, elderly man as she reached for the door handle.

He grinned broadly at her. "Have a nice visit, Ms. Kara. I'll be here waiting for you. Give Helen my best."

James had worked for the family for several years and knew everyone.

"Will do." She slid from the vehicle, lifting her hand in a wave to James as she reached the door.

Even during the slower hours, Helen's Place wasn't lacking customers. The place was well known in the area for having reasonable prices and great food. Kara made her way to a corner booth and was about to seat herself when Helen came rushing from the back doors, a wide smile on her face and her arms open wide.

Kara hugged the older woman fiercely as she arrived beside the booth, breathing deeply, taking in the welcoming scent of vanilla that always seemed to radiate from Helen.

Helen pulled back and grasped Kara by the shoulders. "How is my son treating you? You look good. Rested."

"Let me get us some coffee." Kara went behind the counter and snatched two mugs, filling them with steaming coffee, before making her way back to the table, grabbing a bowl of creamer on her way. "I'm doing well. Classes are good. It's getting to crunch time." She slid a mug in front of Helen before seating herself in front of her own.

"Honey, you don't have to serve coffee. You aren't an employee anymore." Helen shot her a grin, one so similar to Simon's that Kara was momentarily distracted.

Leaning back, she studied Helen for a moment, trying to find other similarities to Simon. There really weren't many. After viewing tons of photos of the two brothers with their mother, Kara had come to the conclusion that Simon must take after his dad, even though she had never seen a photo of his father. Helen looked like Sam, with her short, wavy, blonde hair and green eyes. Her friend had always dressed with casual elegance. Today, it was a paisley calf-length skirt with a button-down pink sweater. Large, pink, dangling earrings fell from her delicate ears, bumping against the side of her neck every time she moved her head. Helen's rather flamboyant earrings were the only ostentatious thing about her. She was a truly kind, gentle soul.

Kara smiled. "I need my caffeine fix." She dumped liquid creamer into the steaming brew. "I just got you some at the same time." She added sugar and picked up her spoon to stir the mixture. "And Simon is treating me fine. More than fine. He's a wonderful...friend." Kara nearly choked on the last word. Well, Simon was a friend.

Helen sighed. "He sounds happy. I talk to him almost every day. I haven't heard him so upbeat in a long time. He sounds completely smitten."

"He's not," Kara answered quickly, nearly choking on a sip of coffee. "We're not. I mean, we're friends." God, she couldn't lead Helen to believe there was anything permanent in her relationship with Simon.

"Uh huh. And Simon talks about you every day, nonstop for an hour because...why?" Helen shot her a teasing look over the rim of her mug.

Kara shrugged. He did? Really? "I live in his home. He's helping me. It's only natural that he talks about a roommate. We see each other every day."

Helen snorted. "Sweetie, he and Sam see each other every day, too, and he certainly doesn't ramble on about his brother. And he's never talked about a woman before."

Kara tried to get her hopeful heart under control. Just because Simon mentioned her in his conversations with his mom didn't mean anything. "He and Sam don't live in the same home."

"You like him. And he likes you. A lot."

Her shoulders slumped as she set her mug back on the table and toyed with a napkin. She had never been able to hide much from

Helen. "I do. I just don't want to expect too much. Simon isn't into commitments. I get that." Sort of. "He's never even had a steady girlfriend."

Helen reached out her hand, resting it over the fingers that Kara was using to slowly rip up a paper napkin. "It doesn't mean that he can't or won't." Helen let out a heavy breath. "Something happened to Simon when he was sixteen and he's never been the same, Kara. He's always been quiet, my intelligent little boy with his face firmly planted in a book and as studious as any parent could ever wish for. But he was also humane, the type of child that would rescue any stray. I remember how badly Sam used to tease him about his bleeding heart. There was hardly a day that went by that Simon wasn't dragging home a lost animal or trying to right some wrong." Helen squirmed uncomfortably on the bench seat. "But I think he lost that when he was sixteen."

Kara squeezed Helen's hand. "He didn't lose it. It's still there. Look at how he's helping me. I know something happened. I don't know the specifics, Helen, but he's still as kind as he's always been."

"That's just it. He wasn't before he met you. You're the first person outside the family who he's cared about in a whole lot of years. It gives me hope."

Kara flinched. "Please, don't get your hopes up. We're friends. That's it. Just consider me a stray that he's rescuing."

Helen beamed as she pulled her hand away and grasped her coffee mug, shooting Kara a knowing look. "Yeah, well, then you're the first stray he's taken in for about sixteen years. I'd say that's kind of significant."

Kara did the math, her heart pumping. Of course, the party. *Simon's turning thirty-two tomorrow.*

"I'm sure that's not true. He probably just didn't tell you." Certainly, she couldn't be the first person he had helped since the unknown incident that had changed him at the age of sixteen.

Helen laughed and said cryptically, "I'm his mother. I have eyes in the back of my head. Ask my boys. It irritates the hell out of them that I know things even when they haven't told me."

Do you know that Simon can only have sex with women if they're blindfolded and tied? Kara was pretty sure that Helen wasn't privy to that information, and she sure as hell wasn't telling her. There were just some things that mothers shouldn't know. Still, she wondered about Simon's supposed years of isolation, of containing his rescuer tendencies. It made her chest tight to think about what had happened to Simon, what had changed him from that sweet young boy to an isolated, detached adult.

Was he really changing? He was aloof at times, and a little bit insular, but Kara didn't think she could ever imagine him as uncaring or completely solitary. There were some things that were just…Simon.

Gruff…check.

Cranky…check.

Bossy…check.

Controlling…sometimes.

Kind…definitely check! Beneath his rough exterior, he had a very good heart.

Sexy…check, check, check.

He was also witty, smart, and completely irresistible in more ways than she could count.

"Hopefully, he'll tell me what happened someday," Kara whispered to herself.

"I hope he does. He needs to talk about it and leave it in the past," Helen replied quietly.

Oh, hell. Simon's mother had heard her comment. In addition to eyes in the back of her head, Helen must also have supersonic hearing.

"Do you know what happened?" Kara asked her friend curiously.

Looking uncomfortable, Helen replied, "I know the event. He nearly died. But I don't think I know everything." Helen's expression was grim.

"It's a painful memory for you. I'm sorry." Kara vowed to never take her friend down this road again. She hated seeing the woman who was like a second mother to her looking so forlorn.

"There are a lot of memories in the distant past that are painful. I can't always avoid them. My boys went through a childhood that they never should have had. That no child should ever experience. I should have done more, protected them better." Helen's eyes were filled with pain, as though remembering that painful past and the toll it had taken on them all.

"Stop. Right now. Simon and Sam both turned out fine. They're sons to be proud of, Helen. You did your best and it shows." Kara hated that mournful expression on Helen's face. "You don't have to have a perfect childhood to grow into a terrific adult. Look at me." She smiled broadly, trying to cheer Helen up with humor.

Helen smiled weakly. "Sometimes I forget how hard you've had it, sweetie. Your parents left you alone too young, but they raised you right."

"And you raised your boys right. I don't know Sam, but I do know Simon. He's a wonderful man," Kara told her friend honestly. Hoping to change the subject and see Helen smile again, she was determined to change the topic. No good could come out of Helen wishing that she had raised her children differently. Kara knew Helen, and that her friend had done her best to raise her two boys, whatever the circumstances might have been. "Simon invited me to Sam's party tomorrow."

Helen laughed. "Simon's annual birthday bash, hosted by none other than his brother, Sam. You are going to go, aren't you?"

"Yep. Simon wants me to go. Are there going to be a lot of people there?" Kara couldn't keep the apprehension from her voice. How in the world was she going to blend in with a bunch of wealthy guests at Simon's birthday party?

She had been surprised when Simon asked her attend the event. Not only had she not known that he had a birthday coming up, but her own birthday was the day after Simon's.

"Are you nervous?" Helen lifted her brow, giving Kara an inquiring look.

Damn. Was there anything that Helen couldn't get out of her? "A little. It's not exactly a crowd that I'm used to mingling with."

That was an understatement. Things done for pleasure or relaxation weren't events she attended at all. Between work and school, she had never had the time.

Helen's delighted chortle filled the air around them. "One thing I've learned over the years is that rich people aren't really that much different than normal folks. Some are nice. Some are not so nice. You'll be fine. Having money doesn't make any of them better than you are, sweetie."

Rationally, Kara knew that. Still, she was nervous. Her anxiety wasn't caused so much by the wealth as the idea that she didn't want to disappoint Simon in front of his friends, business acquaintances, and family. Her social skills were sadly lacking from years of neglect, her only practice her customers at the restaurant and very young college classmates.

Kara's phone beeped, startling her back into reality. She pulled the phone from her pocket. "Simon," she informed Helen with a smile as she glanced at the text message.

RU done talking about me yet?

Really? Like she and Helen had nothing better to do than talk about him? Her fingers flew as she flipped back a message.

Your name hasn't even come up. Arrogant much?

A reply came almost instantly.

No. But I know my mom. If you don't come home soon, I'm cooking dinner.

"Oh my God, I have to leave." She gave Helen a grin and an expression of mock horror.

"Why?" Helen asked, her expression perplexed.

"Simon's threatening to cook if I don't get back to the condo."

Helen's tinkling laugh shimmered around Kara, making her chuckle along with the older woman. Helen sucked in an amused breath and replied, "An ominous threat coming from Simon. He's likely to hurt himself."

"Yep. He's a culinary disaster if he tries anything except sandwiches or microwave dinners," Kara answered Helen as she typed.

I'll head that way soon. Please, do not cook.

"Sneaky, manipulative man," Kara whispered fondly as she slid out of the booth.

"He's obviously missing you. It's romantic." Helen sighed, a dreamy look in her eyes as she stood up beside Kara. "Just don't let him get away with too much."

Kara hugged her friend with an amused expression. It was more likely that Simon was hungry and didn't want a sandwich, but she didn't want to squash Helen's lofty ideals about her son. "I'll see you tomorrow night," Kara answered, heading for the door.

She searched for James and the Mercedes with eager eyes, ready to be back at the condo with Simon. He might not be truly missing her, but *she* missed *Simon*. The best part of her day was evening, spending time with him, talking about what had happened during their day, throwing around opinions and ideas. They could talk about important things, or just little things. It never seemed to matter.

Oh God, I'm pitiful.

Spotting James, she picked up her pace to get to the car, realizing with shock that she had been incredibly lonesome before she had met Simon. Strange, but she had never felt alone. Every day, she had been surrounded by people, customers, students, crowds. Yet, the loneliness had been there, buried deep inside her, shoved beneath exhaustion, hunger, and the need to survive. Waiting.

Pulling the car door open, she slid into the front seat beside James, still wondering why she had never recognized her yearning for the company of a male.

Because it wasn't there. Not until I met Simon. It's him. I don't want just any male.

Damn it, it was true. She knew it. There was something about Simon that called to her, beckoned her to bring him closer, so close that she may very well get burned. Nevertheless, the lure was there and it was seductive; Simon's come-hither vibrations were enticing and impossible to ignore.

Why am I so drawn to him? We're nothing alike.

Shaking her head against the supple leather of the seat, Kara admitted to herself that in some superficial likes and dislikes...they were different. But in many ways...they were so very similar.

After being burned by Chris, she was wary...just like Simon. The causes might be different and she was fairly certain that Simon's were much more traumatic, but the two of them circled each other like frightened children, not quite sure if they wanted to be friend or foe, whether they wanted to trust or not.

She knew Simon had given her a valuable gift when he had trusted her enough to take her without his usual procedure of bondage and blindness. She just wished she knew what caused his distrust. And why the blindfold? The man had a body to drool over.

She shivered and shot a weak smile at James as he pulled the vehicle into traffic, weaving his way slowly toward the condo.

She blew out a long, shaky breath, desperately hoping that she wasn't inadvertently putting her head on the chopping block by getting so involved with a man like Simon.

Just go with it. Relax. Enjoy what you have while you have it.

She bit back a self-deprecating laugh. She didn't relax, she didn't roll with the flow, and she had never, ever lived in the moment. Those were all difficult things to do for a woman who needed to worry about where her next meal was coming from and if she could scrounge up enough money to pay her rent every month.

But you don't need to worry about that now.

No...she didn't. It might not last very long, but for a brief time, she knew she had a bed to sleep in, a roof over her head, and plenty of food to eat. Because of Simon, she had time and space to actually breathe.

Her heart stuttered as she pictured him, as he was last week on the couch, vulnerable, yet so very strong. How could she not admire that strength and determination to beat whatever phantoms of the past were haunting him?

He did it for me. Because I wanted it.

Drawing power from her memories, Kara gathered her backpack. She was home. James had delivered her to the front of the massive building. "Thank you, James." She gave him a sheepish grin, suddenly noticing that she hadn't spoken a word to the driver on the short trip home.

"You're most welcome, Ms. Kara. As always. Have a nice evening."

"You, too." Sliding out of the seat, backpack in hand, she closed the door and jogged toward the entrance.

She would have a nice evening. How could she not? She had a dark, sexy, handsome man waiting for her. He might want dinner, but she was determined to give him something more than just food. It was time to give back to Simon. After all, he had trusted her, sheltered her, made her feel like she was someone special.

She hoped he was hungry, and not just for food.

Waving at the watchful doorman, she slipped silently into the elevator that went to the penthouse.

Live in the moment. Don't think about the future.

It might feel totally alien to her, but she was going to try.

Chapter 4

S imon cursed as he wrapped a white towel around his waist, pissed off at himself for forgetting to bring clean clothes. After his workout, he had headed straight for the shower that was attached to his gym, completely forgetting to grab something to wear from his bedroom. The damn towel barely covered his family jewels.

He scowled at his sweaty, stinking workout clothing. There was no way he was putting them back on after he had just washed the stench from his body.

Kara wasn't home yet. He should have time to make it to his room. Finger-combing his wet hair, he opened the bathroom door, ready to sprint down the stairs and to the master bedroom.

Cold air blasted him as he left the steamy bathroom behind. Shit. The gym was freezing. He'd cranked the temperature down for his workout, and he was feeling the chill.

"Simon, are you-"

The light, feminine voice startled him. Halfway across the gym, he froze, his heart thundering as Kara came breezing into the room.

He flinched as her eyes roamed over him, ready for her look of distaste…or worse. The scars on his chest and abdomen were glaring, something that he went to great lengths to hide from the world… especially from women.

He tried to get his feet to move, to turn around and take him back to the bathroom. But as his eyes met Kara's, he was paralyzed.

She advanced slowly, her eyes huge and round, but she didn't look appalled. She looked…hungry. Her tongue darted out to lick her lips as she said reverently, "God, you're huge. Muscular. I knew you were ripped, but you make male strippers look like a joke."

Simon swallowed hard as she reached him and dropped her back-pack on the floor. "I'm scarred." *Fucking brilliant, Hudson.* Like she hadn't noticed?

She was close enough that Simon could smell her sweet scent. He inhaled, his cock rising as she craned her neck to glance up at him with a look of longing that slammed into his gut like a freight train.

Her voice trembled as she said in a breathy whisper, "Please don't ask me not to touch you, Simon. I need to touch you. I think I'll die if you don't let me."

He'd expected any number of reactions from her, but not this. His whole body flooded with heat, with the need to feel her small, capable hands on his body. How could she look at him with this sort of need?

"I don't like to be touched," he said, his voice husky.

"Don't like it, or aren't used to it?" she queried softly.

Fuck. He was such a liar. There was nothing he wanted more than Kara's hands on his body right now. Right. Fucking. Now. "I don't know," he answered honestly, shaken by her reaction to him.

"You have a beautiful body, Simon," she told him as she lifted her hands to his chest.

He braced himself as her hands caressed his chest lovingly, glid-ing over his skin, setting his whole being on fire. The contact felt like pure sex, so erotic, so sensual. Gritting his teeth, he willed his body to relax…but it wasn't listening. Her fingers slid slowly over his abdomen and he heard her breath catch.

"You're so hard, Simon."

Yeah. He was hard. Everywhere. "Fuck! Kara." His breath started coming in hard pants as her moist, warm lips joined her roaming fingers, her tongue lapping at his chest.

"Mmmm…you smell so good. Taste even better."

He nearly came in the towel as her teeth latched onto one of his flat nipples, followed by a soothing lave of her tongue.

Holy Christ! His whole body was trembling, ready to go up in flames. "Stop," he groaned. *No, don't stop.*

She grasped the towel around his waist and tugged. The material gave way easily and she dropped the towel to the floor. "You feel so good, Simon. Don't make me stop," she crooned as she palmed his engorged member in her small hand. "I want to taste you." Seriously? Did she mean-

"Everywhere."

Oh yeah, she did.

Her blue eyes darkened as she looked up at him with a pleading glance. Dear God, he couldn't turn away. He wanted those luscious lips on his cock more than he wanted to take his next breath. "Kara…I haven't. I don't-" He'd always needed to dominate, to tie women up. He had never wanted to shove his cock in their mouths while they were lying helplessly beneath him. And none of them had ever wanted him to.

"Good. Then you won't know if I don't do it well." Her look of vulnerability floored him, making him forget his own insecurities about his scarred body, and he had the sudden urge to pound her ex into the ground.

"Not possible that it wouldn't be incredible with you," he told her harshly, his voice graveled with rampant desire. He snaked his hand behind her neck and brought her mouth to his, his other hand splaying over her ass to tug her closer to him.

She doesn't care about my scars. She still wants me. There's no woman on this earth who could fake her reaction.

He took her mouth over and over, wanting to somehow show her how much her acceptance meant to him.

She returned his kiss with a fire that heated his blood. Her tongue entwined with his and she moaned one of her sweet little noises into his mouth, a needy sound that nearly made him lose it.

She pulled her mouth from his and slowly lowered herself to her knees, trailing her tongue along his chest and over his abdomen as she went. Jesus Christ! He wasn't sure he was going to live through this.

Sweat beaded on his forehead, dripping slowly down his face. Blood pounded through his ears, the swooshing noise of his heartbeat deafening him. All he could do was feel.

The first touch of her tongue was sublime. It twirled over his sensitive tip, licking a drop of pre-cum like it was her favorite candy.

"Shit. Kara." He pulled the clip from her hair and buried his fingers into the silken mass, shuddering as the soft waves flowed over his hands.

He inhaled sharply as she closed her mouth over his cock, taking him into the moist, hot clasp of her lips, pulling the swollen shaft as far as she could possibly take it, bumping the back of her throat.

Fuck. Fuck. Heaven. Hell. Bliss. Agony. He'd never experienced anything like the exquisite sensation of that talented tongue sliding over him, tasting him with an erotic pleasure that was about to make the top of his head explode. She sucked and glided, twirled and tugged, until Simon thought he was losing his mind.

"Oh, Christ." The words exploded in a tortured voice that he could barely recognize as he looked down at her, watching her devour his cock with obvious enjoyment. Her eyes opened, her look scorching as their gazes met and locked.

Simon felt his balls tighten and the gathering pressure at the base of his shaft. He was going to come…hard. Their eyes lost contact as he threw his head back, his hands guiding her head in a rapid rhythm along his pulsating shaft.

Her hands cupped his ass, her nails scoring over his sensitized skin. "Oh, hell yeah. I'm gonna come," he grunted, unable to verbalize anything else, knowing he needed to give Kara a warning that he was about to erupt like a fucking nuclear explosion.

She didn't move away. She moaned around him, the vibration sending him over the edge. Her nails dug into his ass and she practically swallowed his cock as he released himself with an agonized cry, his muscles screaming as they tensed and released from his violent orgasm.

Simon panted heavily as Kara continued to lave his cock, licking every drop sensually, languidly.

He wanted to kiss her, needed to kiss her, but his pants were coming so heavily that he couldn't catch his breath. Hauling Kara up and into his arms, he simply held her, his arms wrapping around her body, her face in his neck.

He gulped, trying to force air into his burning lungs as he molded her sweet body against his.

"Was it good?" she asked him quietly as her mouth nuzzled his neck.

Simon laughed, wheezing as he replied, "Sweetheart, if it was any better it would have killed me." God, this woman was special. So sweet, so sexy. So...his.

Mine.

A hard wave of possessiveness swept over him and his arms tightened around her.

"I actually was coming up to ask you what you wanted for dinner," she informed him in a matter-of-fact voice, her apparent nervousness about not performing well seeming to have vanished. "But seeing you gloriously nude took away my appetite for food. I wanted to take a bite out of you."

Her hands swept over his body and his chest ached with the realization that she really did lust for his body, scars and all. "I wasn't nude until you stripped me of my towel," he reminded her.

"How do you expect me to resist? You're a walking temptation. A testosterone menace in a tiny little towel," she sniffed, but there was humor in her voice.

Simon chuckled softly against her hair. He couldn't help it. Kara was a fucking miracle. His miracle. "How about I take a bite out of you, now?" he murmured warmly, his body more than ready to start rising to the occasion.

She broke away from him and picked up his towel, snapping his abdomen with it as she demanded, "Oh no, you don't, mister. I'm starving now. Put that thing away. It's dangerous." She tossed the towel at him with a delighted giggle that struck him right in the chest. Catching the towel in mid-air, he wrapped it around his waist, his cock already half hard again for her.

It was strange, how comfortable he was with his body exposed around her. He was still shaking his head over her obvious delight in seeing him nude, but he wasn't going to question something that had him happier than he had been in…well…ever. "Come on, sweet thing. Just a tiny nibble," he growled as he stalked her.

"Nope. No way. Put it away. I need food." She laughed out loud as she scampered for the door.

He roared and lunged, chasing her down the stairs and into the kitchen, her laughter ringing through every corner of his empty house.

And filling every inch of his empty heart.

What in the hell am I doing in this dress?

The next evening, Kara stood in front of a full-length mirror in her room, contemplating her appearance.

Simon didn't want to go to this party, had admitted that he hated Sam's annual birthday bash.

Who hated birthday parties?

Kara frowned at herself in the mirror as she turned one way and then the other, trying to decide if she was overdressed. Or underdressed. The burgundy dress was beautiful, but the clingy silk material draped every curve, ending at mid-thigh and leaving a considerable amount of her legs on display. The nude silk stockings that ended in delicate lace at the tops of her thighs did little to warm her long legs and the drape across only one shoulder left the other one completely bare.

She had flinched when she pulled the dress from the closet, shocked by the price tag still attached to the garment. Holy crap! Who wore a dress that cost as much as her previous grocery allowance for six months? Seeing the outrageous price had been enough to make her want to shove it back in the closet. The only reason she hadn't was because she had nothing appropriate to wear.

She slipped her feet into a pair of matching shoes, the stiletto heels high enough to ensure that she would be as tall as some of the male guests.

Except Simon. No shoes would ever put her eye-to-eye with Simon.

Nervous, she shoved her long hair over her shoulder. Leaving it loose might not have been the best plan, but she had no idea how to do fancy styles. Her long, dark hair was generally more of a nuisance than anything else, making her think about cutting it short more than once over the last several years.

Staring back at herself in the mirror, her eyes looked enormous. She had added make-up, something she rarely bothered with because of the cost and time involved, the result not something that she was sure she liked. Was the red lipstick a little too much? Oh hell, she just didn't know. It wasn't like she attended parties or gatherings of this type. Actually, she hadn't been to a party of any type for more years than she could remember; probably the last one had been when her parents were still alive. After that, her life had been a constant cycle of work and survival.

She shoved her sagging shoulders back, trying to tell herself that she would not be intimidated. Simon had asked her to go, wanted her to be there, and she wouldn't let him down. It would be so much easier to play chicken and tell Simon she wasn't feeling well and couldn't go, but she couldn't do it. Simon was good to her, had literally saved her life.

Taking one last look in the mirror, Kara scooped a small black bag from the bed and headed for the kitchen. She shifted one hand to her belly, trying to quiet the swarm of butterflies that seemed to have invaded her stomach.

Calm down, Kara. It's just a birthday party. No big deal.

Stopping at the entrance to the kitchen, she saw Simon dressed, ready and none too happy. He was standing near the cupboard, handsome as sin in brown dress pants and a gorgeous cream-colored fisherman's sweater. Hair neatly groomed, his evening dark whiskers already showing, he looked good enough to eat.

You already did that. Yesterday.

Kara flushed, the room suddenly way too warm, as she remembered the day before. Her behavior had been so out of character. So brazen. But it had been difficult to see Simon, in all his glory, looking slightly insecure and trapped. It had kicked in a protective instinct, a bold and audacious behavior that had surprised her. When had she become such a bold seductress? She was sexually repressed, totally not the type of woman to come on to a man like Simon. His look of uncertainty had spurred her on, made her determined to show him how incredibly sexy he looked, how tempting he really was. And he was tempting. Sure, he had some scars on his chest and abdomen, some small, some not so small, all white from age and standing out on his olive complexion. But Lord, it had been impossible to walk away, to not touch that ripped, muscular body. The scars did nothing to detract from his sex appeal. Simon was simply...splendid.

"Oh good. You're here. I was just-" Simon stopped in mid-sentence as he looked up at her.

"I'm ready," she told him, trying to sound confident as she stepped into the kitchen.

His eyes turned dark, his gaze roaming her body. She wanted to squirm when his perusal continued, his jaw firming as his eyes lingered on her exposed lower limbs.

"D-Do I look all right?" Oh, shit. Maybe she was dressed all wrong.

"You're stunning," he answered in a husky voice, his eyes finally landing on her face. "But you're showing way too much skin. And your hair is down."

She tilted her head quizzically. "Is that bad?"

"I'm not sure that I want other men to see you this way." He prowled forward, stopping in front of her. One hand on her naked shoulder, he slowly caressed the exposed skin, making her shudder from his light, sensual touch. "You're way too much of a temptation."

Kara let out a breath that she hadn't realized she was holding, relieved that he thought she looked acceptable. "I think you're the only one who thinks so, Simon. I think you need your eyes checked," she told him lightly.

"You're so fucking beautiful that it almost hurts to look at you," he rumbled as his lips grazed her temple. "My cock got hard the minute you walked into the room." He grasped her hand, bringing it to his arousal. He was so firm and erect that her panties dampened and her stomach clenched.

God, he smells so good.

Kara kissed his whiskered jaw, breathing deeply, loving his masculine smell. Her fingers spread over his engorged member, totally unable to stop herself from copping a feel.

"Kara, you drive me insane," Simon ground out as he trapped her wandering hand and lifted it to his lips, placing a warm, lingering kiss to her palm. "If we start this, we'll never get to the party. Not that I mind," he growled.

"It's your party," she answered with amusement. "You can't blow it off."

"Kiss me and see," he answered provocatively, his arm sliding around her waist.

She could feel his warm breath on the side of her face. His tempting mouth was close, so close, and slipping away from him was almost torture. "Your mom would never forgive me. Let's go, party-boy."

He pouted like an infant whose favorite toy had been taken away, but the curse that sprang from his mouth was anything but boyish.

"You need a coat," he told her, his tone protective and demanding.

"I have one. I'll grab it. And I'm sure Sam's house is warm," she mused quietly.

She went to her room, returning quickly to the kitchen with a black tailored jacket in hand.

Simon held his hand out, pulling the jacket from her grasp. He held it out and she slipped her arms into the garment, appreciating the luxurious feel of the silk lining.

Turning her around, he did up the large buttons on the front, every single one of them.

He frowned. "Do you think that will be warm enough?"

"Yes. It's fine. We only have to get in and out of the car. I probably wouldn't have even worn a jacket if you hadn't mentioned it."

Kara sighed lightly as she pulled her hair from the jacket, surprised by her delight in Simon's little gestures that made her feel cared for. It had been so long since anyone had cared about her wellbeing that his actions were alluring and heady for a street-smart woman who had been so alone for so long.

"I'm still not sure I like you showing that much skin," he grunted as she picked up her handbag and headed for the door.

Kara bit her lip as shivers ran down her spine. His sexy voice was so possessive, as though he were claiming her.

Don't even think about it. He doesn't mean anything by it.

"It's not that sexy," she told him wryly, wishing she were as irresistible as he made her feel.

"It's way too sexy. Every man there will be thinking the same thing as I'm thinking," he told her, his expression unhappy as he ushered her out the door and locked it.

She pushed the button with the down symbol for the elevator and turned to him. "And what is that?"

"That I want to fuck you," he answered bluntly, his hand coming to rest at the small of her back.

Her breath hitched as the elevator bell rang, the doors swooshing open in front of them. Would she ever get used to Simon's blunt remarks? Her cheeks flushed and her body was way too warm. Hot, actually. Extremely hot. "Simon!"

He shrugged as he entered the elevator behind her. "It's true."

"You're terrible," she admonished him in her best teacher-like voice.

"Oh, I can be bad. Very, very bad," he told her in a seductive, low whisper, his hands trapping her against the elevator wall, one on each side of her head. "Kiss me and I might behave. For now."

Kara looked up into his glowing eyes that presently resembled hot melted chocolate. Oh hell, she loved chocolate, so she did what any self-respecting chocolate lover would do.

She kissed him just as the elevator doors closed, locking them briefly in a silent little world all their own.

Chapter 5

Kara released a startled squeak as Simon's hand reached out and slapped the stop button on the elevator. She'd been lost in his kiss, oblivious of the motion of the elevator as he kissed her into a coma. But the loud, smacking noise of his palm hitting the button and the lurch of the moving elevator car coming to an abrupt halt yanked her out of her alternate reality. Damn it.

"What in the hell are you wearing underneath this dress?" Simon growled against her lips as his wandering fingers stroked lightly over her ass.

"Stockings, panties." She nipped at his bottom lip as she answered.

His hand reached for the hem of the short dress, lifting it and spinning her around. Momentarily confused, she let him.

"Christ. Those aren't underwear. Your ass is showing." His tone was low and husky, his hands exploring the supple cheeks of her exposed backside.

Her cheeks flushed as she remembered pulling on the tiny black thong and matching bra. The wardrobe that Simon's assistant had purchased for her contained mostly racy lingerie. "You bought it. Matching sets. All very similar to this one."

"It's not that I don't appreciate it," he answered in a slow, sexy utterance as his fingers slid underneath the tiny back strap.

"I thought you said you were going to behave," she answered breathlessly, her conscious mind slipping away as his fingers slid lower and lower.

"I lied. That was before I felt these panties and had to see them. Now I want to see the matched set."

Oh, God. She groaned as he turned her to face him, his fingers nimbly unbuttoning her coat and dropping it on the plush carpet in the elevator.

"Simon, we're in the elevator. We can't do this here," she replied with a combination of mortification and desire.

The zipper of her dress gave way under his searching hands and she could feel the light brush of his fingers down her spine as he pulled it down in one smooth jerk.

"Private elevator for the penthouse. It's not like someone is waiting to use it." His breath hitched as he exposed her upper body, letting the dress catch at her waist. "You're so beautiful."

She sucked in a trembling breath as he trailed a finger from her cheek, down her neck, and along the exposed swell of her breasts over the top of the lacy bra. Heat pooled between her legs, soaking the tiny scrap of material between her thighs. His thumbs rubbed lightly over her thinly covered nipples as his mouth lowered to trail over the hot flesh above them. His whiskers abraded her seductively as he licked, nipped, and suckled, driving her half mad to have him inside her.

"I can smell your need and it's making my mouth water for a taste of you." He lifted his head, his dark eyes appearing almost black with hunger.

His hand trailed down her quaking belly and underneath the dress pooled at her hips. She hissed as his blunt fingertips slipped beneath the saturated silk of her panties. Suddenly, she didn't care if she was half naked in an elevator. All she wanted was Simon.

Knees weak, she steadied herself by putting her hands on his shoulders and took whatever he was offering. As he pulled his midnight gaze from hers and kissed his way down her taut stomach, she knew that what he was offering was pure bliss, and she wasn't about to fight it.

He ripped the delicate material of her panties, pulling the garment forcefully from her body. Her naked pussy tingled as it was exposed to the ambient air. She gripped Simon's shoulders tightly as he dropped to his knees in front of her, the sight of his dark head dipping under the hem of her dress making her legs unsteady and her whole body shiver with hot need.

Scorching hands ran from her knees to the tops of her thighs, gliding smoothly over her thin stockings. She held her breath as his hot tongue explored the sensitive flesh of her thighs at the top of the lace before finally parting the folds of her pussy slowly, exploring the flesh of the protective lips.

"Oh, God. Simon." She moaned as her head fell back and her eyes closed, wanting to watch him devour her, but unable to tolerate the intensity of her desire.

Heat snaked through her belly, slithering over every inch of her skin as he pushed his tongue deeper. And deeper. She wanted to grasp his head, pull his mouth harder against her needy flesh, but she didn't. It was one small step at a time with Simon. She didn't want to push any buttons that might cause him to stop. Curling her nails into the heavy sweater on his shoulders, she clutched the fabric like it was a lifeline, her body whirling as Simon's sizzling tongue found her clit, flicking over it with bold, fast strokes.

Whimpering, she thrust her hips forward, silently begging for more. And he gave it to her. His big hands cupped her ass, bringing her forward, jerking her tightly against his plundering mouth, the sound of him lapping at her plentiful juices erotic and hot.

She exploded in his mouth with a long moan, her body quaking, her pussy flooding with welcome relief. Simon continued to lave, drawing out her climax until she was a quivering mess, before he drew himself up and kissed her.

Her arms tightened around his neck. She stretched and yanked his head down, frantic for contact. The taste of herself on his lips as he kissed her senseless made her undulate her hips, feeling his rock-hard erection rubbing between her thighs. She needed him inside her. Desperately.

"Fuck me, Simon. Please." She begged without any shame, feeling the emptiness that only he could fill.

"Upstairs." He groaned as his mouth pulled away from hers. He gripped her ass, grinding himself against her.

"Here. Now," she insisted as she turned and faced the wall of the elevator. Placing her hands on the wall, she bent at the waist and opened her legs wide and told him, "My hands will stay on the wall. Please. Just do it. I need you now."

"Fuck!" His curse was frustrated, but so passionate that Kara wasn't surprised to hear the zipper of his pants lowering.

Yes. Another victory.

"I need you." Simon's hoarse whisper was almost inaudible. Kara knew he hadn't meant for her to hear him, but she did. The quiet, harshly uttered words echoed in her mind, drawing forth an answering primal response that nearly brought her to her knees.

The air in the elevator was steamy and the only sound in the small, cramped space was the ragged, uneven breaths coming from their mouths, as she waited for him to impale her, to feel him filling up the lonely places inside her. "Please, Simon. Now."

Kara nearly sobbed with relief as she felt the blunt head of his cock brush the needy flesh between her spread legs. His large hands gripped her hips with an almost savage strength, pulling her back against him, his cock slamming into her slick channel with one powerful, hard stroke.

She gasped from the pure elation of Simon's possession. "Did I hurt you?" Simon rasped as she felt his body tense. "You're so tight."

"No. No. It just feels so good." She pushed back against him, urging him to move.

"Jesus, Kara. You deserve better than getting fucked in a damn elevator." Simon groaned as he pulled back, tightened his grip on her hips and buried himself to the root inside her again. "But I can't stop. Never want to stop."

"You can't stop. I couldn't take it if you stopped. Harder, Simon. Give me more." Her head fell back as Simon started an even, deep rhythm that threatened to drive her insane. The coarse wool of his sweater abraded her spine as he leaned forward, his body curling around her protectively as he kept up a hard, punishing thrust with his hips. In and out. Over and over. She quivered as his hot, uncontrolled breath hit the side of her face as he nipped at the tender flesh of her neck.

Never had she experienced a need so volatile and untamed. Yearning to hold him as he pounded into her, she gripped the metal balance bar and shoved her pelvis back, meeting Simon stroke for stroke, needing the contact of skin on skin wherever she could get it.

One of his hands left her hip and slid down the front of her, between her thighs. He caressed the springy curls before his fingers slipped lower, so very close to the swollen bud of flesh right above his pounding cock.

"Oh, God!" Every nerve in her body throbbed as Simon's fingers circled her clit, making her hips slam back on his cock with a strength that she didn't know she had. "Touch me. Please."

"Come for me," Simon's deep voice commanded as his fingers zeroed in on the tiny bud of flesh that was aching for his touch.

Whimpering, her head fell forward and she was blinded by the curtain of hair that was swinging wildly from Simon's brutal thrusts. She closed her eyes, nearly unable to bear the waves of pleasure that coursed through her body as his fingers stroked relentlessly over her clit while his cock possessed her channel, owning her, taking her, melding their bodies together until she wasn't sure whether the ruthless desire belonged to her or to Simon.

Her climax hit with a jarring explosion that had her crying out his name as spasms wracked her body, a body that was held in helpless thrall, unable to do anything except ride out the sharp, endless orgasm that was rocking her body.

"Fuck!" Simon's hand returned to her hip, both hands gripping her firmly, tightly as his cock cleaved into her faster, deeper. A groan that held both agony and anguish sprang from his throat as he buried himself to the hilt, flooding Kara with the heat of his release.

She would have sunk to the floor, her legs unable to hold her up, had Simon not wound a steely arm around her waist, keeping her upright. He turned her gently and wrapped his strong arms around her utterly limp body. Their breathing was heavy and labored.

She lifted her arms around his neck, resting her head against his shoulder, unable to think.

Simon supported her weight, stroking her hair gently as his breathing slowed.

It took her several minutes to speak. "I'm a mess. I need to go back to the condo for a few minutes." Looking at the remnants of her underwear lying on the floor, she added, "I guess I need to get a new pair of panties, too."

Simon's shoulders shook with suppressed laughter. "Did you lose them?"

She pulled back, her heart melting at the naughty, amused look in his eyes. "No. Some caveman ripped them off me."

He raised an eyebrow. "Must have been some lusty encounter." He pushed her hair back from her eyes, draping it softly over her shoulder. "I'll buy you more."

She rolled her eyes. "I don't need more. I have several drawers filled with lingerie. I could go without doing laundry for a month. I've never owned so much lingerie in my entire life."

"I'll still get you more. If what you have is as sexy as the pair I just destroyed, it won't last long." His voice was hoarse with a touch of warning flowing through his words.

His warm gaze caressed her partially clad body, lingering on every inch of bared skin.

She shuddered, imagining Simon ripping off various articles of lingerie in a fit of passion. "You can't ruin all my lingerie. Those things are expensive."

"I didn't hear you complaining a few minutes ago." His voice was hot, sultry and filled with a promise of things to come. "I'd buy lingerie for you every day if what just happened is the result. Hell, I'd buy it for you just to see you smile."

Kara's heart skipped a beat, her chest aching from unexpressed emotion. How much longer could she do this? How much longer could she hide the powerful and sometimes painful emotions that Simon wrung from her with just a casual comment or a simple touch? Her brain, which had always ruled her life, and her heart were in conflict. She knew that nothing more than a casual sexual relationship and friendship would ever exist between her and this incredible man who was holding her as if she was the most important person in his life. Still, she wanted him. How pathetic was that?

Backing away, she slipped her arms back into her dress. "Can you zip me?" She hoped she sounded casual as she gave him her back.

"Do I have to? We could skip the party."

"Yes." She bit her lip to keep from smiling. He had sounded so hopeful that she couldn't help being amused.

He didn't answer, but she felt his finger sliding lazily over her spine before he slid the zipper up with a masculine sigh.

Turning her around, he placed one hand on her shoulder and tipped her chin up with the other, searching her face with a frown. "Did I hurt you? I was a little rough."

Kara knew she would probably have a few bruises on her hips from his strong grip, but his rough, raw possession was something she had been begging for, something she needed. The intensity of her passion for Simon wouldn't have been satisfied with anything less. She lifted a hand to his rough jaw. "I was there, Simon. I think I was begging for it. No, you didn't hurt me." Her orgasm had been intense, but the fact that he cared about whether or not she minded his gritty, feral possession made her care just a little bit more.

I can't believe I just had some of the hottest sex I've ever had in an elevator.

"Oh God, I hope nobody heard me." She groaned as she picked up her purse and jacket, snatching her shredded panties from the floor and shoving them quickly into her handbag.

"I doubt anyone heard you, although I'm surprised"-the red phone on the elevator panel rang, interrupting Simon in mid-sentence, piercing the silent space with a noise so shrill that Kara jumped- "that nobody called." Simon smirked as he finished the comment.

"Oh, God." Kara slumped back against the wall, mortified. While she was in the grip of ecstasy, she hadn't thought about the fact that others would question the sudden stop of the elevator.

Simon snickered and snatched the phone from the wall. "Hudson." His voice was instantly professional and impatient.

She couldn't hear the conversation at the other end, but she could tell that the voice was male.

Simon shifted as he zipped his pants, his hip leaning against the balance bar, his expression serene as he listened. How in the hell did he do that? No one would ever know that she and Simon had been screwing like their lives depended on it only a few moments ago. He looked cool and calm; she was sure she looked like she had just been thoroughly ravaged.

"No. Everything is fine. I needed something and I stopped the elevator to look for it." Simon's voice was nonchalant, but he shot her a dark, wicked look, his eyes hooded, a half smile forming on his lips.

Her face heated and she shot him back a murderous glance.

"Yes. I'm quite ecstatic that I found it. Thanks for checking. Have a good night." Simon dropped the phone back on the hook and slapped the button to return to the condo.

She punched his shoulder. "How can you tell such a whopper without blinking an eye?"

Simon shrugged and pulled her into his arms. "I'm quite sure I probably blinked since the average person blinks every ten seconds. And what I said is absolutely true." He kissed her lightly on the forehead before continuing. "I needed something. I found it here in the elevator. And I was definitely ecstatic."

She laughed. She couldn't help it. "And I was orgasmic."

The elevator lurched, stopping at the penthouse. "I know. That's why I was ecstatic," he answered in a husky, quiet voice. "Hearing you come is the sweetest sound I've ever heard."

She swallowed, trying to push down the lump that formed in her throat. Her nipples hardened as Simon reached around her body to unlock the door of the condo. His words were dripping with blunt, raw honesty.

Uncertain how to answer his comment, she made a beeline for her room as soon as he opened the door. "I'll be out in a minute. Try not to get my new pair of panties wet this time."

She heard a satisfied, male chuckle behind her. "Getting your panties wet is becoming my main goal in life."

She smiled as she entered her room and pulled out a fresh pair of underwear, trying to push her own jumbled emotions aside.

Simon had trusted her enough to fuck her without binding her. Again. Maybe some day…

Small steps, Kara. Don't expect too much. Whatever is eating at Simon has been there for a very long time. It could take years to gain his trust.

And she wouldn't be here for years. She grimaced, her scalp crying out in protest as she ran a brush ruthlessly through her disheveled hair.

Do what you can. Enjoy what you have while you have it. And for God's sake, don't take all of this too seriously.

Enjoying her time with Simon was not the issue. She cherished every moment in his company because being with him filled her lonely places in a way that she had never experienced before.

I'm poor. I'm pragmatic. I am not a woman who believes in soul mates: one man and one woman who complete each other and are meant to be together.

Problem was, her parents had been like that. Poor as they had been, they had also been completely happy. In many ways, it was almost a blessing that they had gone together because Kara was almost certain that one would not have survived without the other. They had been so connected that either of her parents would have been tormented and miserable without the other. It was hard not to believe in real, soul-binding love after watching her parents for eighteen years.

She heaved a sigh and set her brush back on the vanity. Okay... maybe she did believe that love could be that intense, that consuming. But not with Simon. Never with Simon. The man was heartbreak waiting to happen. He didn't do committed relationships and she was already on emotional overload with him.

The only way to survive her relationship with Simon was to keep it casual, not let her heart get involved.

Scooping up her jacket and purse, she sauntered toward the kitchen, hearing only two words running over and over in her head and her own self-deprecating laugh echo through her mind.

Too late. Too late.

Chapter 6

Samuel Hudson had a lavish mansion in South Tampa, an area so affluent that Kara had never been there before, even though she had grown up in the city. She had to force her open mouth to close as James pulled the car around the circular driveway, letting them out in the front of the palatial residence.

"This is…spectacular," she whispered to Simon as he took her hand to help her out of the car.

"You see why I decided not to drive?" he said in a lazy voice, his eyes scanning the expensive vehicles lining the long driveway.

"You draw quite a crowd, Mr. Hudson," she told him softly, her eyes roving over his handsome face. "Happy Birthday. I have a present for you, but I'll give it to you later."

His face lit up in a wicked, wicked grin as their eyes locked in a heated gaze. "I thought you gave it to me last night. And tonight."

"Simon!" She refused to blush again. She wouldn't. Absolutely not. She was a mature, adult woman and she didn't blush over a simple sexual comment. She was an almost-nurse for God's sake, used to seeing the human body in all states of dress. It wasn't like she was a young girl, but it was an infuriating fact that Simon could make her feel like one sometimes.

"Well...just saying. But I won't argue if you want to do it again. In fact, we could go home right now-"

"In the house, birthday boy." She laughed as he slipped his arm around her waist and led her to the door, a small, satisfied smirk still present on his lips.

"Tomorrow night we're going out alone," he muttered, his arm tightening around her body as he led her to the front door.

"Tomorrow?" she said, confused.

"For your birthday. I'm taking you out. Alone."

She turned to face him after they had climbed the marble steps, stopping at the huge double doors. "You aren't taking me out. You've done enough. It's not necessary."

"It's very necessary," he answered, his voice harsh. "I want to. It's your birthday."

The door swung open before she could answer.

"Hey, bro! Glad you finally decided to join your own party."

Kara immediately recognized Sam Hudson. Simon had been right. He was movie-star handsome. Dressed similar to Simon, his sweater was an emerald green that nearly matched his eyes. He looked like an enormous, blond, mythological god...but in Kara's opinion, he lacked Simon's sex appeal. Although she could aesthetically appreciate Sam's handsome face and gorgeous body...he had nothing on his younger brother.

Sam stood back and motioned for them to enter. Kara could feel Sam's eyes studying her, his brain working furiously to figure her out, put her in a box. As she entered the marbled entryway, she wondered what Simon had told his brother about her.

"Kara, this is my brother Sam," Simon introduced them casually, his hand reaching out to take the jacket she was discarding. An elderly man, obviously an employee, took the coat from Simon's arm.

"Well, bro, no need to ask why I haven't seen much of you lately," Sam said softly, his tone mocking.

Kara extended her hand politely. "It's nice to meet you, Sam. I've heard a lot about you from your mother."

"A pleasure." His hand engulfed her smaller one in a firm grip, holding it a little longer than necessary. "Mom's talked about you a lot, too. All of it good, of course," Sam answered, his smile brilliant and his manner persuasive.

He's good. I see why Helen says he can charm anyone. It's really too bad that his smile doesn't quite reach his eyes.

Kara reclaimed her hand by pulling it out of his grip and letting it drop to her side.

"Eat, get a drink, have a good time," Sam suggested jovially, slapping Simon on the back. "Happy birthday, little brother."

"Yeah, thanks for the party," Simon grumbled, shooting his brother an I'll-get-you-for-this look that only brothers could exchange as he nudged Kara toward a cluster of guests and the food in the living room.

"You love me. You know you do." Sam smiled, his voice teasing and arrogant at the same time.

"Not today," Simon snarled back.

Sam laughed wickedly as he moved away, advancing toward a group of people who were motioning for him to come over.

"Bastard," Simon said in a low, irritated voice.

Kara rolled her eyes, keeping her amusement to herself. "He's your brother, Simon."

"Not today," he repeated, his hand sliding across her back as he led her to the lavish food and drink tables.

Sam's home was stunning, surprisingly decorated in white, light, airy décor that made the already-spacious mansion appear even more enormous and grand. Well-dressed guests chatted in groups, their wealth and status obvious by their dress and their ease with the sumptuous surroundings.

Kara tried not to gawk like the penniless woman she really was, but it was difficult to keep her gaping mouth closed. The women were dripping with diamonds and gems and their expressions were cool. The men smelled of money and power, gathering in groups, probably discussing business or golf scores.

Simon filled their plates from a large buffet that was bursting with elegant-looking appetizers that were being continually replenished by silent employees. She picked up two napkins that were folded so precisely that she almost felt guilty about messing them up. The dishes were obviously fine china and Kara frowned. Crap...she'd hate to have to clean all of these dishes and wondered how many servants it took to clean up the mess after the party was over. Hadn't the wealthy ever heard of paper plates and napkins?

She didn't have any idea what she was eating, but she downed every morsel on her plate after she and Simon had found a quiet corner to eat. Every bite melted in her mouth and she licked her lips as she consumed the last delicate treat, hoping she hadn't left crumbs on her face.

"God, that was delicious," she uttered appreciatively as she handed her empty plate to a roaming waiter.

"May I get you anything else, madam?" the older waiter asked politely.

"No, thank you. I'm full." She smiled as the little man gave her a polite bow and moved away.

Simon had discarded his plate and snatched two full champagne flutes from a passing waitress. "I love that about you," he said quietly as he handed her a glass.

"What?" She gave him a confused look as she accepted the glass, sipping slowly at the drink, trying to decide if she liked champagne. It was dry, but not bad.

"You enjoy your food. You don't pick away at it or eat like a bird. I'm almost jealous when I watch your face. If it's good, you look well-pleasured," he answered before taking a healthy sip from his glass. "Watching you eat is almost an erotic experience."

She shrugged as she lowered the glass from her face. "If you don't have an endless supply and you're never sure when your next meal will be, you appreciate the taste of good food."

"Will food always be an orgasmic experience for you?" he asked casually, but his eyes were full of mirth.

She tried not to smile, she really did, but her lips twitched as her eyes met his. "Probably."

"Simon!"

The male tenor voice carried across the room and both of them turned to see a middle-aged man raising his arm, trying to get Simon's attention.

"You better circulate, birthday boy. You *are* the guest of honor," she told him with a smile. "I'm going over to talk with your mom for a while."

He didn't look happy, but he left her side and went to greet the man waving frantically for his attention. She sipped her drink and watched as Simon moved around the room, greeting people, his smile charming. While he might not have quite the charisma that Sam had, Simon could work the room. Not for one second did he look uncomfortable with these people. He was able to chat and make small talk, taking total command of himself, moving in and out of the crowds as if he belonged here.

Because he does. He may not always like socializing, but he plays the game well.

Her gaze stayed riveted on him, marveling over this part of Simon that she had never seen before. The man had so many layers, so many facets to his personality.

Forcing herself to stop staring like a complete idiot, Kara looked around for Helen, finding her at the buffet table.

She chatted for quite some time with Helen, until her friend was pulled away by another acquaintance. Not wanting to appear as though she knew no one else-which she didn't-she strolled to a set of ornate doors, fairly certain that they led outside, knowing the view would probably be spectacular.

There were more people outside, seated at small, intimate tables. Not all of them were occupied. It was getting later and the air was brisk, but it felt good to Kara after being inside the crowded house for so long.

She took a deep breath as she stepped outside. There was a lighted path in front her, a cobbled walkway that appeared to lead down to a boat dock. Before she could follow the path, a conversation right next to her stopped her in her tracks.

"I thought we could spend some time together, Simon. I saw this divine diamond bracelet that I'd love to have." The female voice was artificial and simpering.

Kara drew a deep, bracing breath, hoping that she wouldn't see the Simon that had, just a short time ago, left her breathless in an elevator.

She turned her head slowly, knowing that she had to know. Her breath caught as she took in the broad shoulders, the dark hair and the sweater that she knew were Simon's. He was no more than five feet away, his back to her, a slim set of arms around his neck and perfectly manicured fingers resting casually against the nape of his neck.

"I've heard about your…arrangements. I was hoping we could come to an agreement." The sugary voice was seductive and the woman's hands wandered over Simon's shoulders like she owned him.

Nausea began to rise in Kara's throat and she moved soundlessly away from the couple to creep to the steps. She didn't want Simon to see her and she didn't want the nameless woman to think that she was spying on them. Not that blondie would probably care. The woman looked like a cat with its claws solidly imbedded into something it wanted and wasn't about to be distracted.

The light wasn't as bright as it was inside, but it took only a brief glance back at the couple to see that the woman in Simon's arms was everything that Kara was not. She was blonde, thin, her make-up and hair perfect. In other words…sickeningly gorgeous.

Kara couldn't move, couldn't function; her eyes were riveted on the couple and her feet felt like they were embedded in cement. She could hear the woman murmur something softly, but she couldn't make out the words. Cherry-red lips curved into a calculating smile before the blonde grasped the back of Simon's head, pulling his lips down to hers.

Her heart thundering, Kara took the steps leading down to the path faster than she should have in thin, delicate heels, needing desperately to get away from the scene that had been playing out in front of her like a horror movie. Her heels got caught up in the cobbles on the path and she kicked her shoes off, scooping them up with barely a pause.

Breathe. Just breathe.

She reached the dock, panting and nauseated. She gripped the wooden railing on the dock to steady herself, trying desperately to calm her ragged breathing.

Breathe. In. Out. In. Out.

It doesn't matter. It doesn't matter. The sex life of Simon Hudson was none of her business. She wasn't committed to Simon and he certainly wasn't committed to her. They had sex with no strings attached.

In. Out. In. Out again.

Her breathing settled, but the nausea refused to go away. No wonder Simon had never had a girlfriend. There was obviously an endless supply of women to entertain him…for a price. An arrangement? Really? No wonder Simon had never had a real relationship. Women used him and he used women. Her stomach rolled and she gripped the wood harder.

Forget about it. It doesn't matter.

It shouldn't…but it did. It hurt that Simon could be making a casual agreement to screw another woman while he was still making time with her. They had nearly fucked each other to death a few hours ago. Or so she thought. Maybe it had only been earth-shattering for her. Maybe he missed tying up his women, having them helpless and blindfolded. Maybe he needed it.

Did you think you were someone special, the person who was going to help Simon break free of some of his past insecurities? Maybe he really doesn't have any. Maybe he likes his life exactly as it is. Maybe you're just a complete bonehead who can't comprehend a billionaire playboy who can buy any woman he wants.

Her thoughts grated, ground her down until she wondered if everything she had convinced herself was true about Simon was actually a big fat lie, a self-created falsehood, a man she only imagined.

You don't really believe that.

"The problem is...I don't really know anymore," she whispered softly to herself, her voice trembling.

Her illusions were shattered, and she had no idea what to believe in anymore. She had trusted Simon, had thought he was a decent but troubled man, and his actions left her confused, raw, and completely devastated.

She stared numbly at the lights that were blinking over the rolling water and wrapped her arms around her shivering body. How would she ever erase the memory of Simon kissing a blonde bombshell, a woman so perfect that it made Kara wonder what Simon had ever been doing with her?

She blinked and a lone tear slid silently down her cheek. Most likely, she wouldn't forget. The memory, the sense of betrayal, and the crushing pain were likely to hang around for quite some time.

Lost in her thoughts, Kara stood on the dock like a shadow, unmoving, no longer feeling the chill, wishing that she never had to go back and face reality.

She would. She had to. But she would avoid it as long as possible.

Chapter 7

"Whatever my brother is giving you, I'll give you more if you come to me when he's finished with you." The sultry male voice pierced the silence right next to her ear, startling her so badly that she would have toppled over the dock railing if a strong male hand hadn't gripped her waist. "Whoa. Steady."

She whipped around to face the voice, already recognizing it as Sam's. He crowded her, resting one hand on each side of her, keeping her from escape.

"W-What did you say?" The man left her cold and she didn't appreciate his familiarity.

"I'll pay. Whatever you want. However much you want." His eyes were cold and she shuddered.

Oh, God. She was going to be sick. Gulping, she stared up at Sam's deity-like appearance, barely able to believe that he was actually propositioning her.

Like a harlot.
Like a prostitute.
Like a whore.

Anger rose inside her like a phoenix, climbing higher and higher, stronger and stronger. She could barely see through the haze of red that clouded her vision as her body trembled.

"Simon won't mind," Sam assured her as his hand moved to her bare shoulder.

His comment resonated through her, making her snap. What the hell was with the Hudson men? Did they think they could buy any woman they wanted to fuck? She drew her hand back and let it fly... hard. It connected with his smirking face with a satisfying *smack* that exploded in the near-silent evening, cracking through the peace of the night.

"Maddie was right. You are a complete snake," she hissed, her body shaking with rage.

"Maddie? Maddie Reynolds?" Sam's expression was complete astonishment and shock. She wasn't sure if it was the slap or the mention of Maddie's name, but she didn't wait to find out.

She pushed his arm out of the way and ran, deviating from the path to run across the well-manicured lawn to the front of the house.

She tore down the driveway and ran until she found James waiting patiently in the Mercedes. Tearing the front door of the car open, she dove into the front seat. "Please take me home," she choked out, tears clogging her throat and making her voice raspy. "Please."

"Ms. Kara. Are you all right?" She couldn't see his face in the dark, but the concern in the driver's voice was evident.

"I'm not feeling well. I need to go home," she stated, not able to keep a pleading note from her request.

"Is there anything I can do?"

"Yes. Take me home. I'll be fine."

She wouldn't be fine. Not now. Not tomorrow. Probably not for a very long time. But she didn't tell him that.

James, bless him, didn't ask any more questions. He started the vehicle and headed directly toward the condo.

Kara knotted her shaking hands around the soles of the shoes in her lap, trying not to let the tears flooding her eyes fall. She couldn't cry. There wasn't anything to really cry about. The Hudson men were just doing what they normally did. She was the one with the problem.

Somehow, she had done an incredibly foolish thing. She had allowed herself to fall in love with Simon Hudson. Deeply, passionately, completely in love. It wasn't like the love she had harbored for her ex. This was a confusing, soul-shredding, rip-your-guts out love that was going to hurt. Big time.

Swallowing down a bitter sob by biting her lip until it bled, she turned her head to the right, watching the city fly by as James drove her competently toward home.

You've gotten through loss before, Kara. You'll get through this.

Since the death of her parents, she had used encouraging words and pep talks to get herself through her toughest battles. They had always worked before. Hadn't she made it this far?

You'll forget him. It will just take time.

An uncomfortable weight settled on her chest-hard, heavy and totally crushing.

For the first time in her life, Kara Foster felt like she was lying to herself.

"Kara!" Simon bellowed loudly as he slammed the door of his condo behind him, tossing his keys carelessly on the kitchen counter.

There was a small, neatly wrapped present on the counter with a card, but he ignored it and raced through the condo like a man possessed.

"Kara!"

He yelled her name until he was hoarse, but every single room was empty. Her room looked basically untouched, except that her backpack was missing.

"Shit!"

He went to the kitchen and lifted the gaily wrapped package, finding a personal check from Kara in the amount of ninety thousand dollars and a single sheet of paper under the card and gift.

> *I'll repay the rest as soon as I get a job. I left all of the things you gave me except for a few pairs of jeans and a couple of shirts. Thanks for everything. I'll always be grateful.*
>
> *Kara*

What. The. Fuck. He didn't want her damn gratitude. He wanted... her.

He crumpled the paper in a tight fist, his knuckles white from the effort.

She had left him?

No explanation.

No goodbye.

Just...gone.

He scooped up the gift and the sealed card, carrying them both to the living room while he poured himself a stiff drink. After knocking back a whiskey in one gulp, he poured himself another and dropped into a leather chair, setting the drink on the coffee table beside him.

He leaned his head back and closed his eyes, wishing he could get a do-over on the evening, starting with the part where he and Kara had left the condo for the party. If he could have a do-over, they would never have left the condo.

He had nearly killed his own brother tonight, had happily beat the shit out of him after he had found out that Sam had hit on Kara. It hadn't been hard to figure out. Kara had been missing and Sam had a tell-tale handprint on his face, an obvious souvenir from a pissed-off female. Furthermore, Sam had led Kara to believe that Simon wouldn't mind if Sam fucked his woman.

Granted, Sam had been two sheets to the wind, but Simon had been so out of control when his brother had made his drunken confessions that he didn't care. He had pounded his brother into the ground, stopping only when his mother got between the two of them.

It was the only physical fight that he and his brother had ever had. Sam had never laid a finger on him, and Simon would have never imagined punching his brother. Until tonight. Until Kara. The thought of any other man touching Kara made Simon completely insane.

It hadn't made Simon feel any better to know that Kara had rebuffed Sam, bitch-slapping him hard enough to leave a mark. She had probably been scared, confused. And she had left him. It made him want to lay into his stupid-ass brother all over again.

He opened his eyes, noticing that he had crumpled the card in his lap. Smoothing it out, he opened it.

> *Simon,*
>
> *Happy Birthday! I wanted to give you something that I didn't have to buy with your money, something special. I know you collect coins, so I thought of this gift.*
>
> *This belonged to my father. It was his lucky penny. He found it on the exact same day that he met my mother. He swore it was only moments before he saw her for the first time. He always said it brought him the luckiest event of his life.*
>
> *I've always carried it with me. I've made it this far, so I guess it has been lucky.*
>
> *I know it's not much, but I want you to have it. I know you don't really need luck, but I'll feel better knowing you have it. I hope it always keeps you safe.*
>
> *Kara*

Simon tore open the package and stared long and hard at the small, worn plastic case. He finally popped it open, and glanced at the lucky coin.

Astonished, he flipped it over and then over again. Hell, it was a 1955 Double Die Obverse. And in very nice condition. He wasn't a professional grader, but he was willing to bet that it would grade high.

Did the crazy woman realize that she had been carrying around such a rare coin? A coin that would probably feed her for several months if she sold it?

Probably not. And he knew that Kara would probably rather die than sell something so sentimental, something that belonged to her dad.

But she had given it to him. She had parted with something extremely dear to her to give him a birthday present.

He closed the case and gripped the coin hard, placing it over his heart as pain ripped through his sternum. Why had she parted with this? Why had she given it to him? Instinctively, he knew it was special to her, so special that she always kept it close.

Simon knocked back his second drink and put the coin in his front pocket. It wouldn't leave his possession until he could give it back to her. Personally.

Grabbing his cell phone, Simon dialed his security manager, Hoffman. He answered on the second ring.

"Are you tailing her?" he asked his security chief gruffly, not bothering with niceties.

"Of course. I wasn't sure what was going on, but she seems settled for the night. Good neighborhood, decent house. Belongs to a Dr. Reynolds," Hoffman informed him.

"She left. Keep a team on her twenty-four-seven. I want to know if she sneezes."

"Okay, boss. Will do."

Simon disconnected with a sigh. Obviously she had gone to stay with her friend, Maddie. She'd be okay there. For now.

He had never told Kara, but she had been guarded every moment of every day since the incident at the clinic had occurred. Hoffman's team ran in shifts, always watching, always ready. The police had never caught the junkies who had shot at her and robbed the clinic, and Simon wasn't willing to take any chances. Kara had seen their faces, had helped with composite drawings. Until the assholes were caught, she needed to be safe. Simon needed to know that she would be okay.

Every instinct, every cell in his body was screaming at him to go after her, to drag her back over his shoulder if necessary. He wanted to, but he couldn't win her over that way. The incident with Sam had obviously upset her. Giving her some time would help. Hauling her back would only settle the problem for a short time, and Simon wasn't in this for the short haul. He needed Kara, had to have her forever. Anything less was unthinkable.

If someone had told him several weeks ago that he would meet a woman he couldn't live without, he would have laughed until his ribs hurt. But he wasn't laughing now. Kara had become his life, and he couldn't even think about going on without her.

What kind of life had he lived before her? As he thought about all of the women he had fucked in the past, he frowned. Women who had to get half-drunk and be offered expensive gifts, just to give their bodies to him. They had been empty experiences, women who tolerated him for his money. They may have temporarily satisfied his urge to get off, but they had left him with a huge emptiness that he had never even thought about before he met Kara. Now that he knew what it felt like to be with a woman who actually wanted *him*, he acknowledged that he could never go back. He needed Kara as much as he needed the air that he breathed. God knew, he didn't deserve her, but he would have her.

Forcing himself to his bedroom, he stripped out of his clothes and headed for the bed. Turning around abruptly, he headed back to the pile of clothing on the floor and fished in the pocket of his pants. Pulling out the coin that Kara had given him, he kept it in his grasp and slid into bed, not sure if he could even sleep, but longing for some sort of oblivion.

Having Kara gone was the ultimate torture. The house was too quiet, too empty. Her presence had been palpable since she had first arrived and now he could feel only the ghost of her essence, echoes of her laugh.

Sliding the coin under his pillow, Simon flopped onto his back, already restless. He prayed for sleep to take him away...but God must have been busy because he lay awake most of the night, trying to decide the best way to get Kara back.

He would get her back. That was the only option. It was just a matter of figuring out how to accomplish his goal.

Dawn was breaking before he slipped into a troubled sleep, visions of Kara tormenting him in his dreams.

Chapter 8

Kara pulled the heavy wooden door of the restaurant manager's office closed behind her and leaned against it with a heavy, broken sigh. It was her eleventh interview in the last ten days, all of which had been a complete waste of time, and this one hadn't gone any better. No one wanted to hire a student who was only a few months away from graduation. No restaurant wanted a waitress who was likely to leave within six months for a position in her chosen profession. While Kara couldn't blame the prospective employers for their judgment, she really needed a freaking job.

The familiar sounds of clanging dishes, barking cooks, and sharp-tongued servers filtered through her mind as she took yet another walk of shame through the back halls of another restaurant that wasn't willing to take her on as even a part-time employee.

Okay, it wasn't as if she would starve. She still had ten grand in her bank account, the loan she had given herself from Simon. Biting her lip as the pain of thinking about him crashed over her, she exited the main door of the restaurant, letting herself lean against the cool brick exterior to gather her thoughts after the disastrous interview.

Actually, she had more than ten thousand dollars in her account. Nine days ago, on her birthday, Simon had sent several delivery men and a messenger to Maddie's home with all of the items that she had left behind. The delivery guys had been loaded with her belongings, all of which had been purchased by Simon, and the messenger came bearing several dozen red roses and an envelope with a note.

> *Kara,*
>
> *I am returning your check. Please accept the money as a birthday present from me and don't fight with the delivery people. They have been instructed to put the items wherever you want them or leave them on the doorstep. As they work for me, they will follow instructions.*
>
> *I'm sorry about what happened with Sam. Please come home.*
>
> *Happy Birthday. I wish we could spend it together.*
>
> *Yours,*
> *Simon*

Kara choked back a sob and rubbed unconsciously at her upper thigh, feeling the stiff paper of his note that was resting in her front pocket.

I'm going to have to talk to him.

Kara had hoped that giving herself a little time might help her feel more grounded, less mired in depression. But it wasn't working. Every day she didn't see Simon seemed like an eternity, and she was just fooling herself if she thought that a week or two would help her get over her longing for him. If anything, she sank deeper into the darkness as each day passed.

I have to talk to him. Make him take my check. Work out terms to repay what I borrowed. Return the things he bought.

She had bawled like a baby when she had turned on the laptop he had given her and realized that Simon had downloaded every game that she had ever played on his computer lab. Myth World-both games-had been first on the list.

Wiping furiously at an escaped tear rolling down her cheek, Kara knew she had to stop mooning over Simon Hudson; she just wasn't sure how to do it. The silly, thoughtful things that he did, such as taking the time to download all of those games, tugged at her heart. Then, she would remember the sight of the blonde supermodel on Sam's porch pulling Simon's lips to hers and she'd be pissed all over again. How could any man be so thoughtful, yet be such a dog when it came to women?

"Hello, Kara." A deep, rumbling voice sounded right next to her. Her eyes jerked up to discover Sam Hudson leaning a shoulder against the wall next to her. Instinctively, she backed up several steps, putting distance between her and a man she didn't like or trust.

Sam advanced, but left space between the two of them.

"What do you want?" Her tone was sharp and she put her hand up to stop him from coming any closer.

He raised his eyebrow at her defensive move. "I just want to talk." He looked as arrogant as he had at the party, even dressed in casual jeans and a black t-shirt, but there was a thread of remorse running through his words, and his green eyes were clear and bright. "Please." That addition actually sounded painful coming from Sam, as though he had to force it from his throat.

"I don't know you and I have nothing to say," she snipped at him, eager to get away. The last thing she wanted was to chat with Sam Hudson.

"I'm not going away until you talk to me, so you might as well do it now."

Kara wanted to stomp her foot in frustration, but she wouldn't give Sam the satisfaction. "Just say whatever it is you have to say and leave."

He motioned toward the restaurant door. "I could use a cup of coffee. It's been a long day."

She shook her head. "I just interviewed there. I really don't want to go back in there."

He waved to the eatery across the street. "We can go there."

Rolling her eyes, she answered, "Been there, done that one, too. There isn't a place in this neighborhood where I haven't interviewed."

Taking her arm lightly, Sam led her into the fast-food place next door. She jerked her arm out of his hold, but followed behind him. It was obvious that she needed to let him have his say or he wouldn't leave her alone. He had the same stubborn, Hudson male look that Simon got whenever he wasn't going to budge until she relented or compromised.

They both ordered a coffee from the front counter and Sam took a small booth in the corner. She stalled, loading her coffee at a side table with cream and sugar before joining him. Fingering the disposable cup, she finally looked up to find Sam watching her with the intensity of a hawk ready to swoop down on its prey. Squirming and uncomfortable, she still refused to look away. Sam's gaze wasn't sexual. It was as though he was trying to examine a perplexing microbe underneath a magnifying glass. If he wanted to do some intensive search of her personality...so be it. It wasn't as if she had done anything wrong, except fall in love with Simon Hudson.

Interestingly enough, Sam caved in first. "I'm sorry." He diverted his eyes as he muttered the statement. It was sincere, but she could tell it wasn't something this man said very often. "That was a shitty thing I did at Simon's birthday party. I was so drunk I could barely stand, but that isn't an excuse. A man needs to be responsible for his actions, drunk or not."

"Why did you do it? Why are you doing this? Did Helen send you to apologize? I didn't mention a word about what you did. I'm not sure how she would know." Kara had only spoken to Helen once, and she hadn't mentioned Sam's appalling behavior that night to his mother.

Sam shot her a dark look. "My mother knows everything, and I appreciate the fact that you didn't mention it. You didn't have to. Simon figured it out and beat the hell out of me when I confessed. Our barroom brawl ended the party rather abruptly, soon after I came inside and you left." He hesitated, taking a swig of coffee. "And no, my mother didn't send me here. I'm here because I want to be. Because Simon is miserable and I was wrong. He doesn't know I'm here and would probably smash my face in again if he knew I'd approached you." He stared out the window beside them.

Kara searched Sam's face, noticing the faint bruises above his left eye and his right cheek. Simon must have done a job on his brother. Ten days after the event, Sam still had a faint bruising to his face that she hadn't looked close enough to see before. "Why? Why would Simon do that? He was already in the process of lining up another woman. I saw him kissing her on the terrace when I walked outside. It makes no sense."

Sam's head jerked back to her. "He didn't line up anyone. What did she look like?"

"Tall, thin, blonde, perfect make-up but she'd probably look just as good without it." Kara frowned at Sam. "Beautiful."

His head nodded once. "Constance. I saw her march in as I was stepping outside. I saw you go out on the terrace, but I got caught up by a client for a few minutes before I could follow you. If it makes you feel any better, he didn't take her up on her offer. Connie was coming in angry, and Simon was already gone." Sam's gaze dropped to his cup, fidgeting with the half-empty container. "Simon would never fuck Connie. She's married to a man old enough to be her grandfather, but her husband isn't exactly generous with his money. My brother doesn't do married women. And if he was fu...uhh... having a relationship with you, he certainly wouldn't be arranging another one. Simon may not get emotionally involved, but he only has one woman at a time."

Kara sputtered, nearly choking on her coffee. Sam's comment about Simon not getting emotionally involved hit her hard. She could believe that Simon wasn't having an affair with a married woman. For some reason, she believed that just wasn't something that he would do. Simon might not believe in relationships or marriage for himself, but he just didn't seem like the type of man to step over that line. But really, did it matter? Maybe it made her feel better to know that Simon wasn't tying up, blindfolding, and screwing the centerfold woman who had been kissing him at his party, but the fact that Simon didn't do relationships hadn't changed. She was so connected to Simon that she could barely breathe. In the long run, she would end up completely shattered when he moved on. "Thanks for telling me all of this. And for apologizing." She tried to keep her voice flat, free from emotion.

Sam looked concerned, his eyebrows drawing together as he looked at her. "He cares about you. I didn't know or I would never have made you an offer."

"Why did you? I'm sure there are plenty of women who throw themselves at you every day."

"Because I'm a billionaire," he answered, his tone disgusted, his expression harsh. "I saw how happy Simon was after you came to live with him. I've heard my mother talk about you. I guess I thought that once you and Simon split, that I could grab a little happiness for myself. I was drunk. Feeling sorry for myself. I'm an asshole. You're the first woman my brother has ever cared about and I betrayed him. And I insulted you. You didn't deserve that."

Kara leaned back against the hard plastic of the tiny booth seat, stunned. "Simon doesn't care about me that way. But I admit, I was insulted. You can't buy any woman you want, Sam. And I don't believe it was really me you wanted."

Sam released a ragged sigh. "I wanted…something. I guess in my drunken pity party, I was ready to try anything. And there's only one woman who cared about anything except my money in the past. And I blew it." His voice was filled with an aching sadness and remorse. "Are you going to accept my apology?"

The charming smile was back, lighting up his face, bringing back the Adonis she had seen at the party. Strangely, it didn't bother her now. Sam Hudson was troubled and the radiant smile that he was throwing her way was nothing more than a cover for a man who wanted much more than monetary gain in his life. She had seen a small crack in his unemotional façade. "Yes, I accept. I guess we all say and do things that we wouldn't normally do when we drink." Her words brought back the day that she had told Simon he had an incredible body and that she wanted him after she had had a few drinks at the restaurant. "But I'm not sure why it matters to you."

Sam's eyes grew stormy and he grasped her wrist as she went to slide out of the booth and make her escape. "Kara, Simon cares. He's had a rough time and he may not know how to express it. But he does. Please don't judge my brother because I was an asshole."

His detaining hold was gentle. She tugged lightly and he released her, a pleading look in his eyes. Dammit. She couldn't leave Sam thinking that this was all his fault. It wasn't. She was in love with Simon Hudson and it would have ended up a disaster even if Sam hadn't caused things to fall apart. His actions had only hastened the bad ending. "It isn't you, Sam. It isn't what you did." Shaking her head, she reached for her backpack.

"What is it? Tell me. I'll fix it." He sounded desperate.

She barked a short, humorless laugh. Maybe the brothers weren't so different after all. He sounded just like Simon. Did they both think they could fix anything with money? "You can't. Just know that it isn't your fault."

Nope. It's my fault for being stupid enough to fall for Simon Hudson.

"You don't like or respect me at all, do you?" He sounded resigned and slightly dejected.

She turned her body toward him as she scooted to the edge of her seat with her backpack. "I don't know you well enough to like or dislike you. And money doesn't buy respect for me." Her lips turned up in a slight smile as she saw his surprised expression. "But I do respect you a lot for loving your brother."

He stared at her as he answered gruffly, "Who says I love him? He's a pain in the ass and he messed up my face so bad that I couldn't step outside the house for a week."

She gave him a sad smile and placed her hand over his on the table. "I'm sorry. I know you and Simon are close and I would never want to be the cause of any problems in your relationship."

Sam shrugged. "We've been through tough times before. We'll get through it."

She pulled her hand back. "Are you speaking?"

He laughed weakly. "Trading insults. It's a start."

"Do you know what happened to him? How he got scarred?" The words flew from her mouth before she could censor them.

Sam's jaw dropped, his expression shocked. "You've seen his scars? All of them? Is that why you're avoiding him?"

Anger simmered and her palm itched to slap his face all over again. "Jesus, do you think every woman is that superficial?" Trying to get a grip on her irritation, she continued. "Your brother is the most attractive man I have ever met, scars or no scars. He's hot enough to melt glaciers in Antarctica. Obviously, he suffered a severe trauma and I hate that for him. But I don't give a damn about his scars."

"You think he's better looking than I am?" The question was arrogant, but Sam sounded damned delighted by the fact that she was hot for his brother.

"Yes. No contest. Sorry." Her answer came out severe, but she was a little touched by the fond look in Sam's eyes. Chewing her lip, deep in thought, she mused aloud. "I wonder if you could give Simon something for me."

Sam shrugged and looked at her with curiosity. "What?"

"A check. I need to pay him."

Sam snickered, his lips forming into a wicked grin. "That good, was it?"

"He put money in my account. I want him to have most of it back. I intend to pay back the rest later when I get a job." Kara ignored his innuendo. Simon's brother might look like a blond angel, but she already knew that he had a set of devil horns hidden somewhere in those loose, abundant curls.

"*You* want to pay *Simon*? Newsflash…in case you didn't realize it, he's a billionaire. If he wanted you to have the money, I'm not taking it." He put his hands up in the air in a defensive gesture. "He'd really chew my ass up and spit it out. He's in a lousy mood."

Her shoulders sagging, she gave him a flimsy smile. "Yeah. I didn't think about that. I don't want him mad at you. I just wanted to get it back to him."

"Without having to see him?" Sam hit the nail on the head. "Guess you'll just have to do it personally." He sounded pretty happy about that whole idea.

"I'd better get moving. I have studying to do." She stood up.

Sam rose and stared down at her. "Are you living with Maddie Reynolds? Redhead? Beautiful?" He breathed the last two words reverently.

"Yes." She was surprised. Sam didn't sound nearly as hostile toward Maddie as her friend was toward Sam.

"How is she?" He was trying to sound nonchalant, but there was a brief glint of pain in his hooded eyes.

Kara hesitated, not wanting to betray Maddie. "She's good. She has a private practice and does some work in a free children's clinic."

"She made it. She graduated from medical school." Sam's answer was quiet, almost as if he were talking to himself. He sounded like he admired Maddie.

"Yep. One of the best and kindest physicians I've ever met. And an awesome friend." Sam looked like he wanted to ask more questions that Kara didn't care to answer, so she scooted in front of him and headed for the door. "Take care, Sam. Bye." She dropped her empty cup in the trash without breaking her stride and pushed on the heavy glass door.

It was dark as Kara slid outside, heaving a large sigh of relief as the light wind hit her in the face.

Everything and nothing had changed as a result of her conversation with Sam. While she was very glad that Simon hadn't set up a liaison with the woman at the party, it didn't alter the fact that she was just too emotionally involved with a man who didn't do relationships. It was either going to hurt now or destroy her later. Simon was kind and Sam had said that Simon cared about her. Maybe it was true, but it wasn't enough.

Please come home.

That line from Simon's letter echoed in her head as a fist clenched around her heart, making it hard to breathe. Oh God, how she wanted to go home, back to Simon. They had started…something. He had trusted her, let her touch his naked flesh, let her see his scars, fucked her without restraints. How she wished she had the courage to finish it, help Simon find freedom from his past. But her self-preservation instinct was fierce, warning her away from danger, letting her know that in helping Simon, loving Simon, she would destroy herself.

She set her emotionally spent body in motion, heading toward Maddie's house. Lost in thought, her spirits low, she wasn't very aware of her surroundings. That was a mistake that Kara, a woman who had been raised in a less than desirable area, usually didn't make. The lack of concentration bit her in the ass.

Two men approached quickly, one on each side. Her arms were seized and she was being dragged along the sidewalk before she even realized what had happened. She struggled, kicking out at the brutal men who were hauling her forcefully forward, trying to wrench her arms from their grips. With startled horror, she realized that they were pushing her toward a dark vehicle at the curb, the back door open, ready to claim her.

It was dark, but the area was lit just enough to see the faces of the two men who had broken into the clinic.

They'll kill me. I'll die. Have to fight.

She screamed without pause, trying to make her voice carry to anyone who was in the area, as she kicked out, trying to hit vulnerable places on the two hulking males.

"Shut the fuck up, bitch," a menacing, foreboding voice grunted as her foot connected with his kneecap, an action that earned her a punch to the face.

Momentarily stunned from the powerful blow, she faltered as they shoved her forward.

Fight, damn it. Fight.

As the junkies hefted her body to toss her into the car, she raised her legs and planted her feet, one on the door, the other on the body of the car next to the open entrance.

Don't let them get you into the car. If you do, you're dead.

Her feet slipped, sliding lower as one of the men grabbed her by the hair and started slamming her head against the metal top of the open door. She could hear the horrific sound of her skull cracking against steel and her head swam, her vision starting to blur.

I should have told Simon that I loved him.

She was still screaming, but the sound weakened as the men continued their ruthless attempt to render her unconscious.

"Fucking bastards!" Another male voice sounded, one that she recognized.

A muscular arm wrapped around her waist, yanking her away from the two thugs. She was quickly jerked back against a hard chest, her head spinning like she was on a tilt-a-whirl. Looking up, her vision spinning, she could make out Sam Hudson's furious face as he lowered her gently to the sidewalk and sprinted back to the car.

Panic rose as she realized that Sam was going to take on the two men by himself. Amazingly, the men looked unsure of what to do. Sam was slightly larger, but there were two of them.

Gotta help him. Gotta get up.

She couldn't let Sam get killed after he had saved her life. Kara came to her knees, trying desperately to fight her obscured vision. Unable to stand, she started to crawl just as Sam engaged the first man, landing punishing blows to his face.

Pounding feet approached, hitting the pavement beside her. Two men she didn't recognize entered the fray, grabbing Sam's arm and subduing the man who Sam was hammering on.

"Don't hurt Sam," she whimpered, afraid they might injure Sam in the confusion.

"Sorry, sir. Didn't recognize you." The man released Sam's arm.

One bad guy was on his stomach on the sidewalk, with one of the newcomers that had entered the fray on top of him. The other bad guy was scrambling into the driver's seat of the car, a gun waving wildly at Sam and her other rescuer.

"No. No." Tears were flowing down her cheeks, her heart slamming against her chest as she silently pleaded with Sam and the other innocent man not to provoke the junkie with the gun.

Sam lunged, but the man had already hit the gas and the dark vehicle sped into the night, the door yanking closed as he flew down the street, disappearing almost as fast as she could blink.

Her terrified eyes raking over the scene, she saw that the two rescuers and Sam were unharmed, though Sam was releasing a stream of obscenities as he raced to her side.

"Kara! Are you ok? Fuck! Your head is pouring blood. What were you doing?" Sam gently lowered her to the sidewalk to rest on her back. He continued to whisper soothing words as he pushed her hair from her face.

"Wanted to help you," she rasped, her throat dry.

"Crazy woman." Sam shook his head, but his voice was light and sweet. Then, in a harsh, booming voice he ordered, "Get an ambulance. Now. She's hurt."

Darkness started to encroach on her vision and she struggled, determined not to lose consciousness. "Tell Simon…" Her voice trailed off, her mouth so dry that her tongue was sticking to the roof of her mouth. Her eyelids fluttered. She tried to focus on Sam, but he became just a large, unfocused blur.

She sighed as Sam clasped her hand and grumbled. "You can tell him yourself. He's on his way and pissed as hell."

Simon's coming?

Her heart skipped a beat and she gave Sam's hand a feeble squeeze as a humming noise started in her head. It grew louder, so loud that she could barely make out the sound of approaching sirens that were screaming through the night.

"Kara. Are you still with me?" Sam's voice sounded panicked and desperate. And distant.

A blanket of darkness completely consumed her as the low-pitched droning sound in her head reached the very top of its crescendo.

"Simon." She whispered his name, not knowing if it was even audible, as she slid into complete darkness and blessed silence.

~*~ *The End* ~*~

BOOK THREE

The Billionaire's Obsession

Chapter 1

K ara opened her eyes slowly, blinking several times to clear her blurred vision, and feeling like her head was in a vise. Temporarily disoriented, she lifted her hand to her head, poking at it experimentally, only to feel her forehead wrapped with gauze. *What the hell?*

Her memory returned slowly, trickling back in bits and pieces. Sam and his apology. The attack. Sam and two other unknown men saving her life.

She remembered waking briefly several times in the Emergency Room, Simon right next to her, holding her hand, murmuring encouraging words while she...*oh God*...had she really thrown up all over him?

Right after the attack, everything had been so intense: the dizziness, the nausea, the blurred vision, the desire to escape back into the darkness and blissful relief of sleep.

Her surroundings were dim, the only light illuminating what appeared to be a hospital room with a small square and narrow overhead light near the door.

Her eyes scanned the room. It was set up for double occupancy, but the bed beside her was empty and completely undisturbed.

T. A. Scott

Compared to the way she had felt in the Emergency Room, the headache she was experiencing seemed like a major improvement. Her stomach was slightly queasy and she had obviously suffered an open wound to her forehead, but she was still alive. She sucked in a deep, tremulous breath, releasing it slowly as a wave of adrenaline washed over her body; clearly she was experiencing some delayed anxiety from the experience that had happened...uh...when?

Crap...I really need to get my head together!

Squinting at the clock, she could see that it was four a.m. Nine hours had passed since the terrifying experience that had left her alone in a hospital room, thanking the Almighty that she was still among the living.

She flinched as she moved her left arm, stretching the tubing of the I.V. inserted in the back of her hand, causing stress at the insertion site. *Damn, that hurt.* Replacing the limb to its former position, she attempted to cautiously stretch her other arm, finding it trapped, encapsulated inside a large, strong, warm prison.

"Simon," she whispered softly, suddenly realizing that she wasn't alone, her eyes landing on the place where their skin touched, finding his fingers entwined with hers, his head resting next to their joined hands, his eyes closed.

Her heart contracted as her gaze swept over him, taking in every feature of his beloved, handsome face. She drank in the sight of him, feeling as if it had been forever since she had seen that handsome face. Even in sleep, he looked tense and fierce, the lock of wayward hair that slithered over his forehead the only thing that softened his appearance in slumber.

Slowly disentangling their entwined fingers, she stroked his hair back, enjoying the texture of the thick, disheveled strands between her fingers.

Had he been here all night? Had he ever left the hospital?

He was dressed in a pair of light blue hospital scrubs, a sure sign that her memory of tossing her cookies down the front of what was probably a very expensive sweater was probably accurate.

I love you.

The recollection that she had spoken those words between retching violently and feeling like she was about to die made her hand stop pawing his hair and her body tense with trepidation.

Oh God, did I really say those words to him?

Yeah, she had said them-the memory flashed vividly in her mind. Knowing that she had babbled that particular phrase to him, she pulled her hand completely away, wondering how he had taken those words, or if he had even really heard them. At the time, she had been desperate to say them, to let him know how she felt in case she didn't make it through the night. With no idea what her injuries actually were, she hadn't hesitated to say them, didn't want something to happen without him knowing how much she cared.

Now that she knew that she was obviously going to live, she wasn't so sure that she should have confessed, bared her soul.

"Kara!" Simon shot up into a sitting position, his hand reaching reflexively for hers, twining their fingers back together. He was instantly awake, his eyes jerking to her face, scanning it with obvious unease. "You're awake."

Her throat was dry; her tongue felt like it was swollen enough to take up the entire space of her oral cavity. She reached for a cup of water from the bedside table. Simon sprang from his chair, reaching it first, unwrapping a straw and placing it into the plastic cup, before directing it to her mouth. She took slow sips, her hand covering his as she let the moisture slide over her tongue. "Where am I?" she asked quietly, licking the moisture from her lips.

He told her what hospital she was in and explained that her CT scan was normal, but that they were keeping her overnight for observation. "You have several stitches from a cut on your forehead. From what Sam told me, you're damn lucky they didn't crack your skull." Simon's voice was rough and slightly irritated.

"I have a hard head," she answered lightly, remembering the force of the blows, amazed that she had suffered nothing more than a few stitches and a hammering headache.

He shot her an aggravated look. "Like I haven't noticed?" Setting the glass down on the bedside table, his eyes locked with hers, staring intently, his gaze like liquid fire. "You're never leaving me again. Ever."

Her breath hitched as she looked at him, fascinated, unable to break the compelling, silent communication. "Forever is a long time," she answered, unable to come up with a more intelligent response while his eyes were shooting volatile sparks, a clear warning he was about to get stubborn.

"I don't give a fuck. You're going back home with me, and I'm not leaving your safety in the hands of a few green security agents. If Sam hadn't been there..."

"He saved my life, Simon. Your brother risked his life for me," she murmured, silently thanking Sam for being there, for getting to her before those men had gotten her into the car.

I'd be dead if he hadn't.

Running a frustrated hand through his already-tortured hair, he growled, "He damn well should have seen you home. And the security guys were inexperienced. They should have been tailing you so close that they could hear you breathe. Their reaction time was unacceptable."

"I left. I didn't give Sam a chance to offer to take me home. He was asking questions about Maddie and I wanted to leave. And the agents got there fast. These guys were quick. It all happened in seconds." *Even though it seemed like hours.*

"Sam shouldn't have been there at all. You would have been home and safe," he rumbled, his chest vibrating with emotion.

She squeezed his hand. "You don't know that. They might have gotten to me anyway. It would have been worse if Sam hadn't been there. Please don't blame Sam or the agents. I'm grateful to all of them."

"Doesn't matter. You're coming home with me tomorrow. And you'll have better security than the president of the United States. Even Maddie agrees that you're safer at the condo. Although I'm not sure she's thrilled about you being in such close proximity to any Hudson." He sat back down in the chair without releasing his powerful grip on her hand or softening his intense, relentless stare.

"Maddie was here?" she asked curiously, wondering how her friend even knew that she had been injured.

"She just left an hour or two ago. I called her. She was here all evening. You don't remember?"

She shook her head. "Everything that happened after the actual attack is just snippets of memory. Did I really vomit on you?"

"You remember that?" He searched her face, looking for something, as though he were trying to figure out what she did and didn't remember. "Maddie found me a pair of scrubs and a shower after you got settled in a room."

"Oh God. I'm sorry." Was there anything more mortifying than puking all over a man like Simon Hudson?

"Why? You didn't do it on purpose. And I was actually relieved that you were awake."

Kara found it pretty damn amazing that a man had actually stood beside her, holding an emesis basin while she heaved, without being completely grossed out. "Is Sam all right?"

"Fine." He barked a short, humorless laugh. "Except for the fact that he had to be in the same room with Maddie Reynolds. Sam looked uncomfortable as hell and Maddie looked like she wanted to kill him, slowly and painfully."

"I wish I knew what happened between them," she breathed wistfully, wincing as the squeezing sensation in her head increased in intensity, beginning to feel as if she had a huge boa constrictor wrapped around her head.

Simon frowned. "You want some pain medication? I can call the nurse." He reached for the call button.

"No. Wait." She took a deep breath, knowing she had to set Simon straight. Going back to the condo with him wasn't an option. "I can't go home with you, Simon. I'll go back to Maddie's. I'll be fine. They caught one guy and the other one is probably running scared. I doubt his main concern is to come after me."

His body tensed, the pressure on her hand increasing as his fingers clenched and released, his eyes shooting her a dangerous glance.

"The matter isn't up for debate. You. Are. Coming. With. Me," he answered with a growl.

She released a frustrated breath. "You aren't my keeper. I don't need one. I've been alone for a long time." And lonely, missing Simon, although she hadn't known who she was missing at the time.

The pain was horrific when I was away from him. I can't go through another goodbye later. Spending any more time with him is dangerous. It will just hurt twice as much to part from him after spending more time with him, making more memories to torture myself with when I'm alone again.

"Yeah...well...get used to having company, sweetheart," he snorted, his eyes gleaming with possession, his expression raw and feral. "As long as you're in danger, I won't be very far away. And you won't be without protection."

She shuddered, trying to pull her hand from his fierce grip. He wasn't hurting her and his grasp wasn't tight enough to make her uncomfortable. It was actually just the opposite. Simon made her feel safe, and that terrified her. There was no possible way she could let herself get used to being treated like she was actually a woman he cherished. "You can't tell me what to do. We've only known each other for a handful of weeks. Why are you concerning yourself about my safety?" Her voice was rough, emotional, and probably slightly panicky. She needed to distance herself, but it was difficult. Needy and raw after her experience the night before, she wanted nothing more than to throw herself into Simon's arms and let him hold her there, safe in his warm masculine embrace until she recovered her equilibrium.

"Your safety has been my concern for over a fucking year!" he blasted back at her, his voice low and husky. "And there hasn't been a day that has passed in all that time when I haven't been completely obsessed with whether or not you were safe."

"But we just met a few weeks ago..." Her voice was barely audible, confused.

He blew out an uneven breath, his face ravaged with uncertainty as he looked away, staring blankly at the sterile, white wall in front of him. "Mom talked about you all the time. She pointed you out to me over a year ago while you were serving in the restaurant." He sighed, as though resigned to completing his explanation. "I can't really explain it because I don't understand it myself, but from *that* moment on, I felt compelled to look out for you. Fuck, I even followed you home every night just to make sure you got to your apartment safely."

Stunned, she asked in a hesitant voice, "Like I was your friend because I was a friend of your mother's?"

He turned his head and gave her heated, masculine look. "No. Like a goddamn obsession that I couldn't control. Like you're mine to protect." He hit her with his I-want-to-fuck-you-until-you-scream stare, the heat rolling from him in waves.

Should it bother her that Simon had been watching her, following her like a pseudo stalker? Maybe it should, but it didn't. Instead, she felt eerily calm, her heart melting inside her chest as she watched his tortured expression. He had stayed in the background, silently watching over her like a dark guardian angel, never expecting anything in return. Thinking back on her conversation with Helen at the restaurant, she was relieved to see that Simon's protective, rescuer instincts were still intact. "Why me? There must be tons of women who could use your protection."

Simon shrugged, but the intense look on his face was far from nonchalant. "I have no idea. You're the only woman who's ever made me feel this way." He choked out the last few words, obviously damn unhappy about his inability to control his actions.

She shook her head gently, still trying to come to terms with the fact that Simon had been trying to protect her for the last year. Really, what sort of guy did something like that? What gorgeous billionaire took the time to check on the safety of a nobody, a woman who kept a low profile, a woman who should have been far beneath his notice? She didn't think herself beneath anyone simply because she was poor...but reality was reality. Men of Simon's status simply didn't notice women like her. They were too busy accumulating more wealth, being king of their empires. "Looking out for me because I was your mother's friend was very kind of you. But you can't protect me forever."

He got up from his chair slowly and seated himself gently on the bed, facing her. "You don't get it, do you? I'm not the least bit kind." His words belied his actions as he carefully tucked a strand of hair behind her ear, his index finger trailing lightly over her temple and stroking over her cheek, as soft as a feather. "My behavior wasn't magnanimous or unselfish. I wanted to fuck you. I think that's a pretty damn self-serving motivation." His tone was dry, self-mocking.

She bit back a smile, wondering why he always had such an aversion to someone calling him kind. "If that was your motive, then why didn't you? You could have made your presence known, asked your mom to introduce us. I think it's pretty obvious that I'm attracted to you." *More than attracted.*

He jerked his hand away from her face, averting his eyes. "I forgot about your pain medication. I'm sure you're hurting." He slapped the call button for the nurse.

A response came immediately from the small speaker attached to the call button. "Can I help you?" The voice sounded young and female.

"Ms. Foster needs some pain medication." Simon's answer was abrupt; he came to his feet as he spat out the order.

"Someone will be right there," the faceless voice answered as the call light went from red to black.

Kara's head was still spinning from his brusque dismissal-or was it avoidance?-of her question. She tipped her head back to look at his face. He was scowling down at her, his face implacable.

Crossing her arms in front of her, she met his ferocious look with a small smile. "That tactic won't work on me anymore," she told him quietly.

"What tactic?" he rumbled, his arms crossing just like hers, challenging her, his expression unreadable.

"The one where I'm supposed to feel like I'm Little Red Riding Hood and you're the big, bad wolf." She lifted an eyebrow, refusing to look away from his disgruntled face. Simon Hudson could scowl, growl, and snarl all he wanted to, but she had his number. Somewhere beneath his gruff, bossy exterior, there was a layer of compassion and benevolence that he would probably never show to the world. But she saw it; she recognized it. If he had really just wanted to screw her, he could have come forward, met her in person. It would have saved him valuable time.

He leaned down slowly, so slowly that her breath seized, as those molten dark eyes glinted with tiny flames and focused intently on her, making her want to squirm. Her body quivered, the waves of intense masculinity that were pulsating around her making her body react. His mouth lowered to her ear, the heat of his breath heavy against her neck and the side of her face. "Don't be so sure that I'm *not* the big, bad wolf, little girl. I'd gobble you up in a heartbeat." His low, menacing voice sent a shiver down her spine, but not from fear. Longing slammed into her body with hurricane force.

Her pent-up breath escaped in a tremulous sigh as the nurse entered the room, forcing Simon to straighten up and move away from the bed. The efficient, middle-aged woman gave Kara her medication and took her vital signs. After doing a quick assessment, the woman left, only after asking if there was anything else Kara needed and getting a negative reply.

"I'm surprised that I don't have a roommate," she muttered quietly after her nurse had departed. "This hospital is usually pretty busy." She had done clinicals at the facility and at this time of year, the rooms were generally filled as soon as they were vacated.

Simon flipped his chair around and sat in it backwards, his forearms resting casually along the wooden back. For the first time since she'd opened her eyes, he grinned.

"There are some benefits to being a billionaire who just happens to be a generous donor to medical charities." The chair was close to the bed, his teasing eyes close enough to be visible in the muted light.

"So you asked for a private room because you donate?" Her lips twitched, but she tried to make her voice admonishing.

He shrugged. "Not me. Sam took care of it while I was taking a shower. And I doubt he *asked.*"

She rolled her eyes, positive that Sam Hudson rarely asked for anything. He demanded, expecting people to do as he commanded. However, just like Simon, Sam hid a tender heart under layers of ice.

Her eyes grew heavy as the powerful medication started to kick in. Yawning, she felt Simon's hand clasp hers, his thumb running loosely up and down her palm. "Pain medication. I'm not used to it," she murmured, suddenly feeling exhausted.

"Sleep. I'll be here," he replied in a husky, concerned voice.

"You should go home and sleep. You've been here all night. I'm fine."

"I'm not leaving until you can come home with me," he answered, his tone adamant and inflexible.

"Not coming home with you," she grumbled as her eyelids fluttered.

"We'll see. Just sleep." His tone was soothing, pacifying.

And she wasn't fooled for one single second. He'd try to bulldoze over her later.

Not having the strength or the desire to fight with him at that moment, she slept.

Later that morning, Simon tapped every resource he had to convince her that going home with him was the best option.

She received visits from Maddie, Helen, Sam, her attending physician, and Detective Harris, each person stressing the importance of her being in a safe environment, and naming Simon's condo as the most secure place for her to stay. Maddie gave her the advice grudgingly, obviously not very keen on the idea, but trying to consider the best option for Kara's safety.

Wonder how much he had to bully Detective Harris and her attending physician to get them to agree that his home was the safest?

Privately, Simon told her if she didn't intend to go with him, he'd throw her over his shoulder and drag her back to his condo, kicking and screaming if necessary.

It wasn't his threat or the fact that she really had nowhere else to go that convinced her to get into the Mercedes and let James drive them home to the condo. In the end...it was the exhausted, wild, frantic look in his eyes while he made the demand that swayed her.

Honestly, he looked like he hadn't slept in days: his five o'clock shadow dark, his handsome face marked heavily with stress and weariness.

He's scared. Worried about me.

Her chest aching with tenderness, unable to let him go on freaking out about her, she caved in and let him take her home.

She'd worry about her additional pain later, when it came time to leave again. For now, she wanted Simon to relax, sleep, and eat.

Screw her fears of hurting later. The look of despair on Simon's face hurt more than any pain she would suffer in the future.

I'll just have to suck it up!

Really, what other option did she have? She could watch Simon suffer, or she could worry about the pain later.

She chose the second option, the relieved look on his face worth every bit of hurt she would suffer in the future.

Chapter 2

A few nights later found Simon tossing and turning in his massive bed, unable to sleep. Rolling onto his back, frustrated and pissed-off, he stared up at the ceiling, his eyes wide open when they should be closed, catching up on lost sleep. Shit! He hadn't slept more than a few hours every night since the evening that Kara had left him. Now that she was back, he was still restless.

I love you.

Her whispered confession in the Emergency Room haunted him every fucking minute of every day. Had she meant it? Had she even been talking to *him*? She had been confused, disoriented, barely aware of her surroundings. There was no evidence that she even remembered speaking those words, so how did he know who she meant them for? Maybe it was just mindless babble, brought on by her injuries. He didn't even know if he wanted those words to be intended for him.

Oh, hell yeah, I do.

Groaning softly, he shoved another pillow under his head, trying to ignore his swollen cock as it pulsated beneath the sheets, creating a large tent underneath the coverings. Christ, could he ever think about Kara without his balls turning blue?

Actually, yeah, he knew he could. Scared shitless after the attack, his cock hadn't been his primary concern. Seeing her appear so fragile, pale, and helpless in a hospital bed had nearly destroyed him, making him ache in other areas *above* his waist. For several days, his driving need to protect her, to keep her safe, had been his primary motivation.

His lips turned up in a small smile as he remembered her outrage over the fact that he had contacted the college, explaining the situation and getting her absence for the rest of the week approved. He had thought he was being helpful, smoothing things over so she had time to recover. His crazy woman had actually thought she was going to return to classes the day after she was discharged from the hospital, and she had raked him over the coals for interfering in her life. She had gotten right up in his face and ripped him a new asshole. Kara had no problem challenging him, and he found her intelligent mind provocative. Maybe-just maybe-part of him enjoyed it. Had a woman ever opposed him, questioned him, called him out for a behavior she didn't like? The women in his life used him, let him use their bodies. None of them had ever cared enough to get in his face about anything.

She's getting to me. Bad.

He could feel his internal walls beginning to crumble and it wasn't a comfortable sensation.

Fuck. Pay. Move on.

It was the way he had interacted with women his entire adult life, but Kara was changing all that, tempting him to trust her. And fuck, he *was* tempted. It might be excruciatingly painful when her eyes bored into him as though she were peering into his soul, but knowing that she cared enough to do it? *That* was intoxicating, bewitching.

She didn't give a shit about his scars, his money, or elevated social status.

And she thinks I'm hot enough to melt glaciers in Antarctica.

Sam had told him about his conversation with Kara, how she had declared Simon the hottest Hudson. He and his brother had never been competitive. They had always been too busy working together to survive and then to thrive. Although they liked to verbally spar, Simon loved his brother. Fiercely. Yeah, Sam was fucked-up when it came to women, but he could hardly chastise his brother for that when he was just as bad. Probably worse. However, he had gotten perverse satisfaction from knowing that Kara had verbally slapped Sam down during her conversation with him at the fast-food place before the attack.

I love you.

Gritting his teeth, he rolled to his side, punching his pillow and trying to get comfortable. He had to forget, get a grip on his emotions, stop wishing for more than her presence. He had the comfort of knowing she was safe. Wasn't that enough? At least he wasn't going insane from not knowing where she was, if she was okay.

A piercing, terrified female howl made Simon shoot straight up in bed, his muscles clenched, his heart racing.

Kara!

Panic held him in its grip for a few seconds as the screams grew louder, more intense.

His feet hit the floor, protective instinct making adrenaline pump through his body as he raced down the dark hallway to her room. Flipping on the light without even breaking his stride, he halted abruptly at the side of her bed.

Her arms were wrapped protectively around herself, tears flowing like a river down her sweet face. Hair tangled, head down, she was whimpering and gasping for breath.

"Sweetheart, what happened?" He sat next to her on the bed. Her sheets were snarled and twisted, as though she had been fighting World War III on her mattress.

"Dream," she whispered, as though still trying to convince herself. "Just a dream."

She was shivering violently. He scooped her up and placed her in his lap, pulling her unresisting body into his, trying to warm her in his embrace. Heart racing, he enfolded her, pulling her head into his neck.

"What were you dreaming about?" He stroked her silky hair, letting it slide over his fingertips, as he took a deep breath, trying to calm his hammering heart.

"The attack. It was so real," she murmured, shuddering against him.

"It's over. You're safe. You'll always be safe." *Right here. With me.*

Sliding her off his lap, he went to stand, only to have her arms tighten around his neck, holding on for dear life.

"No! Please! Don't go yet." Her vulnerable cry stabbed him straight in the gut.

She needs me.

And he was going to be there for her, insecurities be damned. "It's okay. I'm not leaving you alone." *I'm never leaving you alone.*

He didn't bother trying to pry her fingers apart. Shifting his body, he lifted her into his arms and came to his feet, trying not to notice that she was scantily clad in a silk, pink, lacy garment that barely covered her ass. He suppressed a groan as he adjusted her weight against him, the lace abrading his chest as the silk caressed his skin. He strode out of the room, making his way down the hallway and into his bedroom, with the most precious thing in the world to him held safely in his arms.

Simon lowered her into his massive bed, coming down with her because she still hadn't loosened her death grip around his neck. Her panic abated slowly and Kara relaxed her arms, allowing him to pull the covers and a quilt on top them before he slid in behind her, spooning her body against his, and wrapping his warm, muscular arms around her body protectively. Kara sighed, sinking into his warmth, as she relaxed her head back to rest against his shoulder, relishing the security of his huge, masculine body.

"Okay?" he questioned softly, his breath ruffling her hair.

"Yeah. I'm sorry I woke you. I'll go back to my own bed in a minute." She didn't want to go back. She wanted to stay right where she was, warm and safe in his arms. But she respected the fact that he liked his space when he slept.

"You're not going anywhere," he rumbled against her hair.

"But you won't sleep," she protested, feeling suddenly selfish for wishing she could stay.

"I won't get a fucking minute of sleep unless you're here. I haven't slept worth a shit for two weeks." His arms tightened around her waist.

Her body plastered against his, she could feel a hard protrusion against her ass. "You're naked."

"Yeah. I sleep in the raw, sweetheart. Get used to it," he murmured, his voice husky. "You want to tell me about the nightmare?"

Actually, what she wanted was to forget. But she turned around in the circle of his arms, needing desperately to wrap herself around his warm masculine body. She wasn't a tiny, delicate female, but as she buried her face against his bulky, solid chest, she felt like one. "It was just a dream about what happened. Only in the dream, they got me into the car. They were going to rape me before they shot me in the head. I fought, but they were ripping at my clothes. They were so much stronger. All I could think about was that I wanted to die before they could violate me, but the one who got away was on top of me, the other holding the gun to my head." She shook her head, trying not to get emotional. It was only a dream. It hadn't really happened. "But it was so real. I could smell their body odor, see those evil eyes. I woke up just as they..." Her voice trailed off in a shaken whisper.

Simon rocked her, running a hand over her back as though he were comforting a small child. "Shhh...it's okay, sweetheart. You're safe. They can't get to you anymore."

Her body quaking from the nightmare, all she wanted was to wipe away the bad memories, to bury herself in sensation, to indulge herself in the incredible body of the man comforting her. The one man who could make her forget the last few days, wipe it away with his sensual touch. "Make love to me. Make me forget," she whispered, her voice seductive and tremulous.

She felt his body tense as she pushed him gently, rolling him on his back. Her hands roamed over his chest, savoring the hard, sinewy muscles and taut, hot skin. Unhurried, she traced each muscle from his shoulders to his abdomen, caressing the enticing swirl of hair that led from his navel to his groin.

"Shit! We can't do this!" Simon groaned, catching her wandering hands in his strong grip. "There's no better feeling than having your hands all over me, but you just got out of the hospital."

"Several days ago. And I'm not hurt. I feel fine. I have a little cut on my forehead. There's only one place where I really ache." She pushed his unresisting hand to the heat between her thighs, parting her legs. Maybe she was coming on too strong, begging too much, but she didn't care. She needed Simon's possession, needed him inside her. "Please." Her voice was pleading, desperate. Pulling her hand from his grasp, she slid her hand down, lower, wrapping it around his engorged cock.

"No! Christ! I'll come if you touch me." His voice was strangled as he captured her hand, holding it against his chest. The hand between her thighs breached the elastic of her tiny panties, his fingers slipping easily between her saturated folds. "You're wet. So fucking hot."

"Because I need *you*." She moaned as his large, blunt fingers explored her, moving sensually over her clit and the tender flesh surrounding it. Mindless desire devoured her body whole. Not thinking, only able to react to the relentless need that was pounding at her, she yanked the soaked panties down her legs, kicking them into the sheets, and clambered on top of him, straddling him. Placing a hand on each side of his head, she kissed him.

One minute she was on top of him, her lips covering his, ready to lose herself in the power of his touch, and the next moment...she was flat on her back. He had flipped her, tearing his mouth from hers.

"No. I can't. I fucking can't." His voice was tortured, his torso imprisoning her, his hands gripping each one of her wrists at the side of her head.

His breathing was labored, ragged. She could hear harsh sounds coming from his throat as he attempted to get air in and out of his lungs.

Shaking her head, starting to emerge from her erotic fog, she looked up at the massive figure looming over, a man in obvious torment.

Shit. What did I do? Did I push too hard?

The moon provided some muted light in the room, but it still wasn't enough illumination to see his eyes...but then, she didn't have to. The sound of his voice, his breathing, his trembling body, his tight hold on her wrists told her that she had sent him plummeting into his own personal nightmare.

"Simon. It's me. Kara." She pulled on her wrists, but she couldn't free them. "Talk to me."

"I know who you are. I just can't fucking do it." Chest heaving, he stayed locked in place.

"Kiss me."

Trapped under his body, under his dominance, she still wasn't sure that she could assuage his fear. He wasn't hurting her, but she wanted to bring him back to the *here and now*. Somehow, she had inadvertently hurt him, sent him into a panic.

Her heart was racing and it seemed like forever until he finally lowered his head slowly, fitting his mouth over hers. He kissed her like a man who had come unglued. His tongue speared into her mouth, conquering, lashing, over and over.

His wild, dominant embrace released a primal instinct inside her, as if her body was automatically responding to her mate. She moved her tongue against his, surrendering herself to him, letting him be her master.

"Kara." He breathed her name as he released her mouth, burying his head in the side of her neck.

"Yes. Just you and me, Simon. Just us."

"Need to fuck you." The statement was muffled, his rumbling voice vibrating against her neck.

"Do it. Just like this." Something about her being on top, being in control had flipped his detonation switch. But his lust was still there. She could feel it, rock-hard and hungry, pushing against her thigh.

"I'm sorry, sweetheart. It felt so good, but I just couldn't-"

"No. Don't. It doesn't matter. I just want you inside me." She parted her legs, and pulled at her wrists. "Can you let go of me?"

Slowly, he loosened his powerful grip as he moved between her thighs. "Yeah. I think so," he answered in a tone filled with trepidation.

Her heart stuttered as she pulled her wrists out of his now only slightly resisting hands and wrapped her arms around his shoulders. "I just want to hold you. You have control."

"Around you, I doubt I'll ever really have any control," he muttered quietly, his voice filled with reluctant resignation.

"Make love to me, Simon." Her voice was pleading, but she didn't care. His momentary fear and vulnerability had crushed any self-preservation instincts left in her body. She needed to help set him free, to obliterate whatever was in his past that held him prisoner. He was too good a man, too kind a person to remain trapped, unable to move forward.

Not to mention the fact that I love him and want him so desperately that it's painful.

It was past time to stop being in denial, thinking that she could keep Simon at an emotional distance. She'd been a coward, so afraid of destroying herself that she had selfishly tried to deny the totally amazing connection that she had with him. And it was a two-way connection. She wasn't the only one struggling with it, uncertain how to deal with it. For Christ's sake...he had followed her around, protected her, for over a year. He had literally plucked her off the streets, giving her everything a woman could ever dream about, and not just materially. He comforted her, stayed by her side when she was sick. He listened to her as though her concerns, her thoughts, her dreams, were important to him. Obviously, he felt *something*! The question was, could it be the same fascinating, beguiling, impossible-to-resist coupling that she felt for him? In her case, that incredibly mystical chemistry had turned into a gut-wrenching love, evolving so fast that it had had taken her breath away...along with her common sense.

"Touch me, sweetheart. Please." His voice was ragged and edgy, full of desire and longing, more of a desperate command than a request.

Her hands moved slowly, stroking his wide, strong shoulders, touching every inch of solid muscle, savoring the strength radiating from his powerful body. She traced up his spine, her hands landing on the nape of his neck. Pulling his head down, her lips traced his collarbone lightly as she speared her fingers into his hair. She moaned softly as her mouth moved over the pulse at his neck, the masculine scent of him flooding her body with carnal heat. She breathed deep, letting his fragrance consume her, his galloping pulse beneath her lips letting her know that he was as swamped in erotic need as she was.

He groaned, his massive body starting to move, his hard member finding a warm resting place between her thighs. His velvety cock slid along her tender folds, saturating itself with wet heat.

Every nerve in her body caught fire, and she opened her legs wider, silently begging him to satiate her, to satisfy the violent need that was clawing at her relentlessly.

Suddenly, he reared up, making her whimper as he deprived her of his heat. Reaching for the hem of her short nightie, he pulled it over her head, tossing it onto the floor beside the bed. "Nothing between us," he growled as he lowered himself over her again.

She hissed as his fiery-hot body met hers from breast to groin, savoring the sensation of being skin-to-skin.

"Mine. You're mine. Say it." The demand exploded from him as though he couldn't help himself.

Dominant Simon had returned with a vengeance, and Kara shuddered. He did love control, and that had nothing to do with his past. That was simply, utterly, completely...Simon.

His hand snaked between their bodies, positioning the blunt, silky head of his cock against her tight opening, starting to enter her oh-so-slowly.

"Say it." His tone grew more demanding, more possessive.

Oh God, how she relished his dominance, his strength. "I'm yours. I need you."

He rewarded her by filling her with one smooth stroke, burying his cock completely to the root. The carnality of the action nearly made her climax.

"Fuck! You feel so good." He pulled out slightly and buried himself again, rolling his hips, making her take every inch of him. "I'm not sure I know how to make love. I only know how to fuck."

She clutched his shoulders, trying to find her balance, her sanity. "I'm not sure I do either. I guess we'll learn together," she told him breathlessly.

She wrapped her legs around his waist, needing to get closer. A low, choked, reverberating sound came from his throat as he pulled back and sank into her again. And again.

His head swooped down, capturing her distressed whimper, his mouth seeking, his tongue conquering. Every touch of his tongue, every thrust of his cock was a branding, a claiming. And she could do little else but surrender.

Tearing his mouth from hers so they could both take a much-needed breath, his hips continued to piston into her, as he rasped, "Mine!"

His teeth nipped at her neck, making her shudder with primal desire. Hips lifting, meeting every furious pump of his hips, Kara moaned as her fingers left his hair, sliding lower, clenching at his back. Her short fingernails dug into his flesh as he changed angles, never slowing his heated, frantic pace.

Just when she was ready to scream with frustrated need, he started to grind his groin mercilessly against hers with every deep penetration of his cock, stimulating her sensitive clit. A scream ripped from her throat as she shattered. He swallowed it with his mouth, his groan vibrating in her mouth as her channel pulsated around his silken cock.

He panted harshly as his mouth moved to her shoulder. "Nothing better than feeling you come around me." He buried his shaft deep, connecting their bodies tightly, fusing them together.

Still quivering from her explosive climax, she felt his muscles tighten and his big body tremble as he flooded her womb with scorching heat.

I love you.

Her eyes moist, she tightened her arms around him, never wanting to let go. Emotion welled up inside her, ruthlessly fighting to be freed. She choked it back with an audible gasp, grappling with the overwhelming need to say those words aloud.

"You okay?" he questioned breathlessly and with gruff concern.

He rolled to one side and she mourned the loss as she loosened her hold on him, reluctantly allowing him to rest beside her. "I'm fine." He had obviously thought he was crushing her. Like she was a delicate flower? She was taller than some men, even in her bare feet. Simon was the only one who could make her actually feel petite.

She sighed as he hoisted her easily into his arms, pulling her against his side as he tucked the covers over their entangled bodies. She burrowed into him, her head on his shoulder and one arm flung over his mammoth chest. His muscular arm pulled her closer with a firm grasp around her waist.

"We made love," he grumbled, his voice weary.

Smiling slightly at his disgruntled announcement, she simply answered, "Yes."

Making love wasn't about the mechanics; it was all about emotion, although she had to admit that he was pretty damn incredible with the mechanical portion of the act. It didn't matter how they touched or in what way they came together; it was the emotion and the intensity of the experience that got her. The truth was, the sex tonight had been no different than anything that had happened between them before. It had been just as explosive, just as emotional, and just as earth-shattering. The man rocked her entire world *every single time*. And it was never indifferent or detached. It had been wild, passionate, intense love-making every single time. At least, for her it had been.

I wish he could trust me.

The deep, steady cadence of his breathing told her that he slept.

Small steps.

Simon didn't sleep with anyone, didn't allow himself to be in the same bed with another person when he was vulnerable. The fact that he was sleeping with her plastered against him was bigger than a step; it was more like a huge stride.

Moving a little to get comfortable, her heart flipped over when he grumbled an incoherent protest and yanked her back against him.

Yep. They would need to have a talk about his trust issues tomorrow. She needed to know something about what happened to him, why he had reacted the way he had earlier. It wasn't possible to combat a ghost she couldn't see, couldn't understand.

Never again did she want to see Simon in the grip of panic, lost in an unknown fear. His vulnerability had nearly ripped her heart out.

A fierce protective instinct flowed over her as her eyes fluttered closed, completely spent and exhausted.

He'll dodge and be evasive. He won't want to talk about it.

If he wasn't ready...well...she'd wait until he trusted her enough to discuss it.

Satisfied that things would work out fine, she yawned against Simon's shoulder until her breathing matched his, deep and even, and fell into a dreamless, contented sleep.

Chapter 3

Three days later, Simon scrawled his signature on the last of a stack of mile-high documents that his secretary had dropped on his desk earlier that morning. Slamming the gold pen on the top of the pile with more force than was necessary, he leaned back in his enormous leather chair with a frustrated sigh, wondering how many more days he could take of the tension between him and Kara.

No sex. No touching. No waking up in the morning with her delectable body wrapped around mine like a silken blanket.

God, that morning three days ago had started off as the best morning of his life.

Unfortunately, what happened at breakfast also had it ranking right up there with one of the worst.

She had wanted to talk about the night before.

He didn't.

Oh, he had been more than willing to talk about and repeat what had happened *after* his freak-out. The actual panic attack?... not so much.

Raking his hand through his hair, he leaned back and tried to relax his body, admitting to himself that the distance between the two of them really wasn't really her fault. Much. She had taken his unwillingness to discuss it gracefully, giving him one of her sweet smiles and telling him that she would wait until he was ready. But then...just when he was thinking she might end up waiting until she was old and gray before he wanted to discuss it...she dropped *the bomb.*

I can't make love with you, Simon. Not until you trust me enough to tell me what happened. I just can't.

Then, after turning his world upside down with that comment, she had kissed him on the forehead like he was a child, wished him a good day, and sashayed her sweet little ass out the door. And she had done it all with a smile. What. The. Hell.

To her credit, she hadn't been a bitch to him, hadn't raised her voice or thrown a tantrum. Shit, he wished she would. Maybe he could generate a lot more anger at her to help him through his current torment.

The only thing that really pissed him off was the fact that he *did* trust her. He just didn't want to talk about *that.*

"You look like a man who's ready to attend his own execution. What's the matter, little brother? Getting tired of Kara? 'Cause if you are I would gladly-"

"Touch her and you die." Fists clenched on the desk in front of him, Simon leaned forward, the threat of fratricide on his face, as he watched his brother saunter across his office. "Don't you fucking knock?" He knew Sam was goading him about Kara, trying to push his buttons. In reality, his brother would never come near her again. Sam had made that perfectly clear to Simon when he had apologized for his behavior at the party. However, it didn't stop Sam from trying to irritate the hell out of him.

Sam shot him a cocky grin as he dropped into a chair in front of Simon's desk. "Why would I? I own the company."

Simon decided that the only thing worse than owning Hudson with Sam was the fact that they had both had an office on the same floor. "Last time I checked, so did I," he snapped back at Sam, not in the mood for his older sibling's bullshit.

"I'm older. It gives me seniority." Sam propped his Italian leather-clad feet casually on Simon's desk.

Simon waited, watching his brother relax back into the chair. The bastard. Leaning forward, Simon swept one muscular arm across the desk, knocking Sam's feet into the air. "Get your damn feet off my desk!"

Really, was there anything more amusing than watching a man in an immaculate designer suit flailing his arms like a baby bird, trying to catch his balance before his chair flipped over? Simon didn't think so. Not when it was Sam fluttering his arms while his chair tilted. The only thing that would have made it better was if his brother had tipped the chair over and landed flat on his ass.

Sam's feet found purchase on the floor. He glared at Simon as he opened the buttons on the jacket of his perfectly tailored suit and leaned forward, resting his elbows on his knees. "Was that really necessary?"

It was Simon's turn to grin, his smile evil. "I thought so."

"It's not my fault that you made the mistake of falling in love and now you're miserable. Shit, I thought you'd be happy now that she's living at your place again." Sam sat back and laced his fingers over his stomach, his expression grim.

Simon's head jerked up. "Who said I love her?"

Rolling his eyes, Sam replied, "You didn't have to say a damn thing. I think I figured it out when I ended up practically blind from the swelling when you beat the hell out of me just because I touched her."

"That doesn't mean I love her," Simon grunted. "And it wasn't because you touched her. It was the intent."

"When was the last time you thrashed me because I touched a woman?"

"Never."

"Exactly."

Simon sighed. "Kara and I had a slight disagreement." Okay, for him, it was more than slight, but he didn't mention *that* to his brother.

"About?"

"She wants me to trust her. Tell her about the incident that left me scarred." Simon's voice was hoarse. "She thinks I still have"-he hesitated before choking out-"issues."

Eyes narrowing, Sam asked, "And do you? Still have issues?"

"No! Hell no! For Christ's sake, it happened over sixteen years ago," Simon answered quickly. *Too* quickly and *too* defensively.

"Time doesn't necessarily make everything go away, Simon," Sam answered thoughtfully. "Maybe you should just tell her. Maybe you need to. Is your silence really worth losing her? She obviously loves you, and whether you want to admit it or not, you love her too. Guess you just need to decide if she's worth it." Sam leaned forward, spearing Simon with a sharp glance. "Don't fuck up. You'll regret it for the rest of your life if you do."

Pain? Regret? Sorrow? For a fleeting moment, Simon could see every one of those emotions reflected in his brother's eyes. By the time he took a deep breath and opened his mouth to ask his elder brother about it, Sam's expression had turned indifferent and apathetic. Simon snapped his jaw closed, recognizing the look on Sam's face, the unequivocal signal that meant his sibling didn't want to talk about it.

"She's being unreasonable," Simon grumbled, returning his attention to his current problem. He wouldn't push Sam to share his pain if his brother didn't want to.

"Admit it. You love her." Sam crossed his arms and shot Simon a knowing look.

"She's stubborn."

"You love her."

"I trust her. I tell her everything else."

"You love her."

"Fuck!" Simon slammed his fist down on the desk so hard that the solid oak shook on its foundations. "She makes me crazy. She makes me happy. I think she's so beautiful that I want to just sit and look at her for hours. One minute, I'm perfectly sane, and the next, I'm totally losing it. She couldn't give a shit less about the fact that I'm rich, and I think the woman is blind because I swear she doesn't even notice that I'm scarred. The way she looks at me sometimes makes me feel like I'm ten feet tall. And she's looking at *me*. Not the billionaire, not the wealthy executive. Just the man. She can be as stubborn as a damn mule, but I even like that because she's determined. Smart. Kind. And she puts up with my cranky ass, accepts me exactly as I am." Breathless from his tirade, Simon sucked in a trembling, uneven gulp of air. He slumped forward, his anger spent. "So, yeah. If these wild, lunatic, possessive feelings for her that I have every fucking minute of every day are love...I'm screwed. I can't even imagine having to live my life without her." Voice vibrating with emotion, he looked up at his older brother, his expression tortured.

"Then don't," Sam answered simply, his brow lifting, meeting Simon's questioning glance. "We built this company together. We started in a crappy, one-bedroom apartment, bro. Now we're wealthy beyond our wildest dreams and a major player worldwide. If you can accomplish that, you can handle this." Sam's voice went from serious to teasing as he added, "Pull your head out of your ass and solve the problem."

Simon's lips curved up in a small smile. He hadn't heard Sam say those words in years. It had been a frequent statement back in the days when they were still building Hudson. If one of them got stalled in the business by a roadblock, the other would deliver a swift kick to the rear with those exact words. It had become their mantra, but they hadn't needed it in a very long time. They had plenty of employees who were paid very well to solve those problems before they ever got to Sam or him. "Sometimes I think that I'd rather rebuild a whole business than to have to deal with this."

Sam shrugged. "Business is business. It's not always easy, but the outcome is fairly predictable. Relationships are messy. You have no data, no statistics. Nothing to justify taking the leap, except for emotion." Sam shuddered, as though the thought of jumping into a serious relationship was akin to torture.

"Then why in the hell are you telling me to do it?" Simon pierced his brother with an irritated glare.

"You need her." Sam stood abruptly and buttoned his suit jacket. "But if you ever decide you don't want her-"

"Don't start!" Simon rumbled, his voice lacking venom. If he had realized anything today, it was the fact that his brother had his own secrets, a woman in his past-very likely Maddie, judging by Sam's strange reaction to the curvy redhead-who still haunted him. He suspected that whoever she was, she was the reason that Sam went through women so fast, so unemotionally. Sam was trying to fill a void, trying to forget. Simon shook his head, knowing that his elder brother was smart enough to figure out eventually that it just wouldn't work. If a woman got under your skin, she stayed there. Simon's whole world revolved around Kara now, and no other woman could ever be a substitute, could ever fill the black, huge vacuum she would leave inside him if she ever walked away.

Sam's charming smile was back. "You love me. You know you do."

"Not right now," Simon answered automatically.

Sam swaggered to the door, not a hair out of place, his suit and tie undisturbed. No one would ever know that he had just watched his younger brother practically have a nervous breakdown before his eyes.

Sam placed his hand on Simon's door. Before he could exit, Simon called after him in a husky voice. "Sam?"

Sam turned back with a quizzical expression. "Yeah?"

"Thanks for listening."

The look that passed between them spoke volumes. Simon wanted to tell his brother how much he cared, but a lump formed in his throat. They sparred like brothers often did, but Sam had sacrificed a lot for Simon and his mother. Worked his ass into the ground for all these years.

"Nobody deserves happiness more than you, little brother. It's within your grasp. Take it," Sam answered, his voice full of brotherly support, as he exited without another word.

Blowing out a shaky breath, Simon stood and grabbed his brief-case, looking around the plush, executive office. Other than his desk and chair, everything was decorated in art deco, a design that he really didn't like. How in the hell had that happened?

The office had been done years ago, but he'd never really noticed, never really cared.

Maybe because you told the decorator to do whatever she wanted.

Yeah, that's exactly what he had done years ago. He couldn't have cared less what decor the interior designer chose. He came to work, took care of business, and retreated back to his condo so he could immediately bury himself in his lab at home. Maybe he grunted a greeting to his secretary and personal assistant when he arrived and departed from the high-rise building every weekday morning. Or maybe not. He was usually so hyper-focused on work, so enclosed in that bubble, that he didn't even remember.

He jerked at the knot in his expensive burgundy tie to loosen it and undid the top button of his shirt. Christ, how he hated wearing a suit.

Careful with the tie. It's one of Kara's favorites.

Actually, that might not be true. He wasn't exactly certain that she *had* a favorite. She told him every morning how handsome he looked when he arrived in the kitchen, dressed for work in a business suit and tie. But the very first time she had told him that, he had been wearing this tie. Since that day, he found himself reaching for this particular tie pretty damn often on his workdays.

He snorted softly as he walked toward the door of his office, his stride nearly silent on the plush carpet. Christ, he was going off the deep end.

When had he started caring which tie he wore, how his office was decorated, whether or not he was cordial to his employees every day?

It was definitely time to go home.

Home. Kara makes me think of the condo as home. Her laughter. Her voice. Her smell. Her very presence makes it home, and not just a place where I go when I'm done in the office.

He exited the office, letting the door close softly behind him. He glanced at Nina's desk, halting abruptly in front of it.

"You need something, boss?" Her tone was professional, but she had a genuine smile on her face.

He looked over the top of an abundant bouquet of roses that was placed prominently on her desk, frowning at his gray-haired assistant. Had he forgotten her birthday? No. No, he hadn't. Nina's birthday was in September. And his secretary, Marcie, always reminded him. "Nice flowers. What's the occasion?" he asked curiously.

Nina gave him a puzzled look, peering at him over her reading glasses. "Boss, it's February fourteenth. Valentine's Day. You know... hearts, flowers, romance." The little woman's smile broadened. "My Ralph has sent me two dozen red roses every Valentine's Day for thirty-seven years." She sighed. "He's still so romantic." Her voice vibrated with affection and adoration.

Valentine's Day? Yeah, he knew the holiday; he had just never paid any attention when it came and went every year. It was just another day, a twenty-four-hour period of time when he saw a lot of Cupids and red hearts-when he chose to notice them, which wasn't very often.

He shot a quick glance at his blonde secretary, her desk situated next to Nina's. "Where are your flowers?"

Marcie paused, turning her head toward him and away from the computer on which she had been clicking away on diligently before his question. "Haven't gotten them yet. My hubby will give them to me before we go out to dinner. He always does."

"Uh...is this normal? Dinner? Flowers?" He looked back at Nina with a scowl. Shit, he hadn't planned anything for Kara. She deserved romance, hearts, flowers, and whatever else a man did for a woman on a day for lovers.

"It depends. Most couples make their own traditions," his assistant answered, her eyes questioning. "Are you okay?"

Damn it. He didn't know what to do and he hated that feeling. What else was traditional? What else would make a woman happy, feel cherished? Had Kara gotten flowers from her ex? Had he taken her out for dinner?

Setting his briefcase on the floor, he tried to squash the jealousy and possessiveness that were rising up inside him. It didn't fucking matter what some man had done for her in the past...Simon was determined to do better. She was his woman now. His to protect. His to cherish. He wanted to make her Valentine's Day so memorable that all she could think of was *him* from this day forward. Except he had no idea how to accomplish his goal.

He leaned over Nina's flowers and told her in a hesitant, low voice, "Kara."

Nina grinned. "She's a gem, boss. A wonderful young woman."

Only one woman could make him say three words that he never thought would come out of his mouth. "I need help." Really, when it came to Kara, the words weren't all that difficult. "I'm not sure what to do. Can you help me, Nina?"

His assistant sprang out of her chair with an enthusiasm and speed that really shouldn't be normal for a woman of her age, motioning vigorously to Marcie to join her. The two of them surrounded him, peppering him with questions.

He should have been embarrassed, but strangely enough, he was not. Simon Hudson, billionaire and co-owner of one of the most powerful corporations in the world, in a huddle with two female employees, listening raptly to every word the women spoke, to every bit of advice they gave.

Sam passed by them, smirking as he made his way to the elevator, obviously able to pick up part of the conversation even though they were speaking in low, conspiring voices.

Simon shot his brother a one-finger-salute when he saw Sam's mocking expression, barely taking his eyes away from the two women in front of him who seemed to know the answers to all of the mysteries of women. Right now, to him, they were goddesses.

He completely ignored the snicker he heard from Sam as his brother walked away. The bastard. He couldn't wait until the day that his elder brother needed advice.

Turning his attention back to Nina and Marcie, he listened and learned.

Chapter 4

Kara let out an audible, heartfelt sigh as she sank deeper into Simon's garden bathtub, the hot water and bubbles covering nearly her entire body, leaving only her head bobbing above the water. He had offered her the use of his tub in the master bath any time she wanted it, but she had never taken him up on the offer. She had a perfectly wonderful tub and shower attached to her own room, but it wasn't nearly as elaborate as this one.

Admit it. It isn't the size of the tub. It's the fact that it's his that made you come in here.

Frowning, she grabbed a large loofah sponge from the ledge of the tub and starting scrubbing her arms with enough force to make her skin burn. Damn it. She didn't want to admit that she missed Simon so desperately that she wanted to use the tub *he* used, breathe in *his* scent that lingered in his bathroom.

Refusing to have sex with him was your brilliant idea.

Yeah, it was. But she was seriously re-thinking that decision. It had felt like the right thing to do at the time. She wanted to be with him, secure in the knowledge that he trusted her completely. Not knowing what had happened to him could cause her to make other mistakes, to hurt him inadvertently. She couldn't stand that thought.

She'd hoped he might open up and share his trauma with her, let her help him through it.

But she had been dead wrong.

He had distanced himself, pulled away rather than share his internal torment. He hadn't touched her, hadn't kissed her, since she had told him that she couldn't make love with him unless he told her about *the incident*. What in the hell had happened to him? Had she pushed him too far, too fast? Would it have been better to settle for only what he was able to give?

I could let him tie me to the bed and fuck me senseless. That way, I can't hurt him unintentionally.

She groaned as she stopped scrubbing her arms raw and lifted a leg from the water, resting it on a seat at the edge of the tub. God, the thought was tempting. She might be an independent woman, but she had loved his sexual dominance, his take-charge assault on her senses. In some strange way, it aroused her beyond endurance, and he exercised that alpha side of him every single time he touched her. Mixed with his added tenderness and vulnerability that peeked through on occasion, it was an impossible-to-forget lure that sucked her toward him like a moth to a flame.

Simon made her feel beautiful.

He made her feel safe.

God...she loved her primitive, protective, possessive male who had a heart of gold.

Lifting her leg, she ran the sponge over her calf, slowly toward her knee and gently across her thigh. Images flashed through her mind, making the sensitive flesh between her legs pulsate with need and causing her heart to miss a beat.

Being bound to Simon's bed, at his mercy, his mouth devouring her.

On the couch, her wrists restrained while he rocked her world.

In the elevator, opening to him, him pummeling her until she screamed.

Three nights ago, holding him as he made her come apart.

Oh hell, he was her every erotic fantasy come to life in stunning, glorious color and there wasn't a thing she didn't love about him.

A lone tear streaked down her cheek as she switched legs and worked on the other one with the sponge.

Three days. It had only been three days and she was already a mess. The lonely yearning for him was already pulverizing her, swallowing her whole. Not only was he her erotic fantasy, he was her complete fantasy. The whole damn package. She had never met a man like him, and probably never would again.

He was sweet, although he would deny it.

He was tender, although he would deny that, too.

Kind.

Compassionate.

A freaking genius, a man she learned something from every single day, although she *definitely* knew he would blow that off, too.

Because he was also humble, Simon Hudson didn't *ever* see himself as someone special. But she saw him as he was: a man to grab hold of and never let go.

A second tear flowed down her other cheek as her heart crumbled.

She didn't want to go back to her life before Simon. And not because she cared about being poor. She had always lived in poverty and had never planned to be anything other than comfortable. Secure. Money didn't buy happiness, and having material things couldn't even come close to competing with having love, having that one special person who could make her complete, whole. What good were things and money if a person wasn't emotionally fulfilled, happy with their accomplishments, no matter how big or how small?

I'd feel exactly the same way about Simon even if he wasn't wealthy. As long as he was happy.

Granted, Simon was too intelligent, too ambitious *not* to be successful. But there were times when she wished he wasn't quite so wealthy, didn't work so hard. But his intelligence, his drive to make his products the very best, were parts of him that she loved. She accepted the whole package, freaking adored the sexy, masculine, quirky bundle of testosterone that made him uniquely...Simon.

Taking a seat on a high ledge of the tub, she closed her eyes as she ran the loofah up her stomach slowly, letting her images of Simon take control of her mind, the elusive smell of him on the scrubbing sponge assailing every one of her senses.

Kara bit her lip as the slightly abrasive loofah slid over her breasts, teasing her swollen, hard nipples. She imagined Simon biting them gently, swirling his tongue over the tips, her erotic thoughts and arousal making her let herself go. Giving in to the pounding demands of her body, she opened her thighs and allowed her other hand to slide up her slippery thigh and begin a decadent indulgence, a fantasy.

If she couldn't be with Simon in reality, at least she would be with him in her mind.

Kara has no reason to stay.

Simon's gut clenched as he knocked on the door of Kara's room, waiting for her to answer. Hoffman had called him less than an hour ago, informing him that the police had apprehended the second offender, the other bastard who had tried to abduct Kara.

Cursing under his breath, he pushed the door open, finding her bedroom empty. He breathed a sigh of relief as he saw her cell phone and her backpack sitting on her bed. She was home, still somewhere in the condo. She'd never leave without her pack.

Does she know? Had Detective Harris called her? Knowing very well that he shouldn't, he picked up her phone, thumbing through her missed calls. There was only one that was recent. It had occurred thirty minutes earlier, and it was from Harris. There was a voice-mail, but he drew the line at listening to her messages. He already knew what the message was about. She was safe; the men who had attacked her were both locked up.

The reason for her being here in his home with him...gone.

He had to tell her. He might be a selfish bastard, but he wouldn't let Kara spend another minute fearing that someone was on the loose, trying to kill her.

As far as he knew, she hadn't suffered another nightmare. God knew that he listened closely every night, left his bedroom door open in case she needed him. She hadn't.

Dropping her phone back on the bed, he yanked at his tie, undoing the knot completely, leaving the material to drape around his neck. He had discarded his jacket in the kitchen a few minutes earlier when he had arrived home. Uncertainty settled over him like a dark cloud as he exited her bedroom. Would she stay even though the immediate threat to her was gone? And if she wanted to leave, how in the hell could he ever let her go?

Not happening. She's mine, damn it!

Gritting his teeth, his emotions bouncing between determination and fear, he went in search of her. Most likely, she was in the computer lab. His lips curved upward, wondering if she would badger him for clues in her pursuit of mastering *Myth World II*. She played his game exclusively, declaring that the other games weren't as challenging, alternately praising him for being a genius and nagging him for tips. He knew she didn't really want him to tell her, to spoil the challenge of the game. Hell, if she had really wanted to know, if she had just once turned those baby blue eyes in his direction with a questioning glance, he would have spilled every damn secret she wanted to know about the game and probably some she had never even thought about yet.

He checked the lab, but she wasn't there. She had to be in the gym. Hesitating as he headed in that direction, he started to unbutton his shirt, heading toward his bedroom. He wanted to get out of this irritating, stiff shirt and pants, throw on some workout clothes and pump iron until his body relaxed. How in the hell he could relax when he saw Kara in her skimpy exercise clothing he didn't know, but he wanted to be with her, ached to see her.

He wouldn't blame her if she turned on her heel and left the minute he walked into the room, but he hoped she didn't. Honestly, he would deserve it. The last three days had been tense, and he had been a complete bastard to her, answering her cheerful questions with one-word, terse answers, practically ignoring her presence when she was in the room with him. Slowly, she had become as withdrawn as he was, speaking only when they had to communicate. Still friendly, but distant.

As he made his way down the hall to his room, he promised himself that he would resolve *that* issue. He couldn't take it anymore. Sam was right-for once! He needed Kara, and feeling her move further and further away from him was like cutting off a limb. Fuck! It was more like cutting out his heart with a dull knife.

Ripping the tie from his neck, he dropped it on his bed and finished unbuttoning his shirt. He had just picked both of them up to put in his hamper when he heard her.

Heart pounding, his head tilted to listen. He picked up a whimper, a feminine moan, and then...his name.

"Simon."

The choked, urgent longing in her husky, seductive voice sent shivers down his spine. The garments in his hand dropped to the floor unnoticed. He moved toward the needy sounds, stopping at the door to the master bath. He could no more turn away from that door than he could stop breathing. The door was closed, but it wasn't latched. In a daze, he pushed the door open slowly, light steam greeting him as he silently took a step forward and pushed the door wide open.

Holy Christ!

His heart paused, his breathing halted, as his hungry eyes landed on Kara. She was spread out on a high ledge in the tub, above the mass of bubbles, water licking her ankles, caressing her thighs, lost in erotic ecstasy. Her thighs were spread wide, exposing the mouth-watering, glistening flesh between her thighs. Head thrown back, eyes closed, she wasn't aware of him watching her, his senses mesmerized by the hand between her legs. Her luscious breasts bounced as her hips rose up and down in the water, meeting the furiously moving fingers that were teasing her clit.

He struggled for air, his cock hard enough to split diamonds. Biting back a groan, he knew he should leave her to her privacy, but he couldn't. It wasn't possible. Nothing less than the whole world ending in a cataclysmic catastrophe was ripping him away from one of the most erotic, beautiful things he had ever seen.

"Simon."

She was fantasizing about *him*. Imagining *him*. He wanted desperately to know what he was doing to her in her imagination. Probably exactly what he wanted to be doing right now. *He wanted to bury his head between those silken thighs, fuck her tight channel with his fingers as he pleasured her clit with his mouth and tongue.*

He stripped off his pants and briefs, his eyes never leaving her writhing body as he dropped them silently to the floor, stepping away from them. Part of him wanted to approach her, worship that begging, swollen pink flesh between her thighs, give some attention to those hard, pebbled nipples. But he couldn't move. He was swept up into her arousal, a sight so carnal that it had him palming his engorged cock, stepping closer to the tub.

A low, throaty groan that he couldn't hold back startled her. Her head jerked up, her eyes full of lust and sultry need.

"Don't stop. Please. I need to watch you come." His voice was graveled, raspy with desire and longing.

Her hand quit moving, but she left it on her pussy. "I'm sorry, Simon. I-"

"Make yourself come, Kara. Keep going. Think about me. There's nothing more that I want in this world than to watch you pleasure yourself. It's beautiful." She didn't know how beautiful she looked-skin flushed, wanton, abandoned.

Her eyes roamed his body, hesitating, narrowing in on the cock that he held tightly in his grasp. "No. You're beautiful, Simon. The most beautiful man I've ever seen."

He didn't think it was possible to get more aroused. But her low, come-fuck-me voice nearly sent him over the edge, the fact that she wanted *him* almost his undoing.

Their eyes locked, an invisible thread keeping them focused on each other. He groaned as her hand moved, her eyes growing steamier as he starting pumping his cock.

They watched each other with naked, unbridled passion. She became wild, uninhibited as she licked her lips, watching him jerk on his ready-to-explode cock.

Rivulets of sweat poured down his face as she whispered his name between jerky pants and erotic moans as they stayed connected, completely lost in a web of desire so fierce that he could barely remain standing.

"That's right, baby. Bring yourself off," he demanded as he fisted himself harder, the pure pleasure of feasting his eyes on her unrestrained lust making his balls tighten, the pressure inside him building.

Tendrils of dark silky hair had escaped the clip holding her mane back and they framed her face, brushed over her shoulders. He was intoxicated, bewitched, enthralled with the feast for his eyes spread out in front of him.

Moving her fingers from her clit, Kara pushed two fingers into her tight channel, filling herself, moving them in and out with strong, deep strokes. She gasped every time her fingers slammed into her opening, increasingly deep, faster. Simon increased his pace, keeping time with her.

"Make yourself come for me," he demanded, knowing he couldn't keep this up much longer, however much he'd like to watch her like this forever.

Her fingers moved back to her clit, gliding easily along the swollen nub. Panting, she threw her head back with a long, throaty moan.

She climaxed hard, moaning his name, her back arching, her whole body quivering.

Not able to hold back another second, Simon exploded, putting his hand in front of his cock to capture the stream of hot fluid that probably would have hit the damn wall had he not stopped it.

She leaned back, her breathing heavy and uneven, her eyes glassy. After quickly washing his hands, he crossed the space between them, and stepped into the tub.

He pulled her unresisting body into the water with him, his mouth covering hers in a tender, languorous kiss.

Her face was flushed as she pulled back, her eyes darting away from his. "I can't believe I just did that."

"Don't, Kara." His fingers gripped her chin, gently tilting her face, making her meet his eyes. "Don't ever be embarrassed with me. You're beautiful. The sexiest woman I've ever seen. Watching you come was so fucking hot that it damn near gave me heart failure. There's no shame in something that incredible."

Wishing he could express his desire to share all things intimate with her, his obsession to be close to her, he tugged her back onto a built-in lounge seat. After sitting and leaning back, water lapping at his torso, he pulled her between his legs. Molding her naked body to his, her back to his front, he wrapped his arms tightly around her waist to anchor her. He nearly sighed in ecstasy as she relaxed against him, her head resting against his shoulder. He buried his face in her hair, breathing in her tantalizing smell for the first time in three days, feeling like he was finally where he belonged.

"I've just never done that when someone was watching. I told you I don't have much experience." She sighed. "I missed you. I know I pushed you away. I shouldn't have. I just wanted you to share what happened with me, to help me understand what happened the other night. I'm really sorry, Simon. I-"

"Shhh...stop!" His mouth to her ear, he whispered, "It isn't you, Kara." Hell, it made his chest hurt to hear her apologizing when he should be begging her to forgive him. He'd treated her poorly. Shut her out. He just wasn't used to a woman who actually wanted to be close to *him*, a woman who actually gave a shit enough to try. "It's my problem. Something that I've never told anyone. Shit! I never even told the shrink that Mom made me see after the whole thing happened. Not the whole truth, anyway."

"Helen had you see a counselor?" she questioned in a low, thoughtful voice. Her hands covering his arms that were wrapped around her waist, she squeezed gently in a comforting gesture.

He shivered, even though the water lapping over their skin was still hot. Taking in a deep breath, he exhaled slowly, knowing that at this point...he was *all in*. It was time to risk it all, throw all his cards on the table and pray that he came out the winner, that she cared enough to stay with him. Truth was, he *did* trust Kara. But, did he want to talk about his shame and irrational fears? Oh, hell no...he absolutely fucking didn't want to talk about it. But his obsession was to be close to the woman he was holding in his arms, the woman who was leaning back against him with complete faith and trust, with a gentleness and patience that had him in awe of her.

Nothing between us. Ever.

"Yeah, she did. I saw Dr. Evans for over a year." His voice was hoarse and hesitant as his instincts warred with his emotions. "Mom wanted to make sure I was okay emotionally."

She squirmed back against him, pushing her body tightly against his, getting as close as she possibly could. Her hands slid down his arms, finding his hand under the water, entwining their fingers together.

He breathed in the scent of her as she tilted her head, resting it against his jaw, her fragrance surrounding him.

"Simon?" she whispered softly.

"Yeah?" He gave her fingers a gentle squeeze.

"I love you." Her voice was barely audible. "I love everything that you are, every part of you. Nothing that happened in your distant past is going to change that. I even love you when you're bossy."

"I'm never bossy," he answered automatically, the walls around his heart crumbling, allowing his heart to soar. Holy shit! He had wanted her to say it, but he had never imagined that it would feel this damn amazing to hear it. He wasn't sure what he had ever done to deserve a woman like her, but he wasn't stupid. He was keeping her. "You know that I'll never let you go now, don't you?" It wasn't really a question, but he figured that she should know his intentions.

"I didn't tell you so that you would feel obligated. I just wanted you to know." In a lighter tone, she added, "And you are bossy. Now tell me about Dr. Evans."

Obligated? She wasn't an obligation. She was his whole damn life. His arms tightened around her convulsively.

She loves me!

He relaxed, the tension draining from his body. Suddenly, talking about the past didn't seem quite so difficult. Yeah, he'd much rather take his woman to bed and show her exactly how much he worshipped her, but he wanted to do it with full disclosure. He needed to explain what had happened the other night, and the only way to do it was to talk about the past.

She loves me.

He started to talk.

Chapter 5

"Before I tell you about Dr. Evans, I guess I should start at the beginning."

Kara nodded, not wanting to interrupt the flow of his words with any questions or comments. She hadn't meant to confess her love, but she hadn't been able to help herself, hadn't been able to hold back the words. And she didn't regret it. She was weary from trying to hide it, and no man deserved to be loved more than Simon.

"My father died a month before the incident. Overdose. Drugs and alcohol. He was foolish enough to steal drugs from one of the biggest drug dealers on the West Coast, a guy he ran errands for or distributed drugs for in return for enough drugs and booze to feed his own habit. He rarely got paid in cash, and even if he did, he didn't use it to feed his family or his wife." His voice was low, seething with distain for the man who had fathered him. "Mom tried her best, but she had dropped out of high school and couldn't get anything but minimum-wage jobs. She did whatever she could to feed us and keep dear old dad's business away from our shitty apartment and away from me and Sam. Mostly, she kept us out of trouble, making us see that we could be something more, something better." His voice cracked, his adoration for his mother evident.

Everything that Helen had told her made sense *now*. Helen blamed herself for not being able to give her boys a better childhood. Kara frowned as she remembered the sorrow in Helen's eyes when she had talked about her boys, their crappy childhood. Didn't Helen realize that she had given her boys something to cling to in their childhood, something they desperately needed to survive intact? Helen had given Simon and Sam love...and hope.

Simon's voice strengthened as he continued. "Rose was my childhood friend, really my only friend other than Sam. She grew up in the apartment next to ours. She was a year older than me." He shifted uncomfortably, his foot bouncing in the water as though he were nervous. "We were as close as friends can be until my hormones started to rage and I started to see her as a female. I cared about her a lot and I thought she cared about me."

"So you did have a girlfriend when you were a teenager?" She wasn't sure where he was going with his explanation, but she sensed that it was important to his history.

"Yes and no. I guess. We kissed, we held hands. I had horny, teenage-boy wet dreams about her every night. I wanted to get laid for the first time and I wasn't exactly an attractive teenager. I was quiet and skinny, not much to look at. Clumsy as hell. I read a lot. Mom made sure Sam and I had books from the library or reading programs. But Rose seemed to like me even though I was a gawky, ugly kid."

Kara's heart contracted, trying to picture a young, awkward teenage Simon. She was willing to bet her nursing career that he had been adorable.

"She started changing when she turned seventeen. She dropped out of school, started hanging with my father's crowd, wouldn't talk to me anymore or was so distant that she acted like I was nobody." She squeezed his hands. "That must have hurt."

"It did." He didn't bother to deny it. "I knew she was using, stoned out of her mind most of the time. I begged her to let me help her, but she wouldn't listen. She just laughed in my face, saying that there was nothing I could do because I was as poor as she was. And she was right, damn it! But I wanted to help her get clean. And stop working the streets."

"She became a prostitute?" *Oh God, poor Simon.*

She couldn't see him, but she felt his shoulders lift in a shrug. "She had to pay for her habit somehow and I know she gave some of the money to her mom to help her younger brother."

"You didn't give up, did you?" Kara didn't need an answer. She already knew. Simon was stubborn and tenacious, his rescuer tendencies still alive and well. It wasn't in his nature to stop trying.

"No. I wanted to believe that the Rose I knew was still inside her, waiting to come out again." He snorted. "It didn't matter how many times she tried to avoid me or told me fuck off, I still tried. I was pretty naive, I guess."

No, you weren't. You were good, even though life had dealt you a crappy beginning. You were a dreamer who wanted to believe that everyone could be saved. You must have been as guileless, honest, and direct as you are now. You just didn't hide it as well then.

"Having hope doesn't make you naive, Simon."

He laughed, but it was self-deprecating. "I was gullible. I didn't see her for about a month after my father died. Then one night, she showed up at our apartment, dressed in a short sexy skirt and a friendly smile. For a teenage male virgin...that was all it took for me. Mom was working and Sam had already gone to Florida to start a construction job there. I was getting ready to graduate from high school and Sam had made enough money working construction to bring us to Florida to join him."

"You were graduating from high school at the age of sixteen?"

"I skipped a grade. Twice. School was never difficult for me," he answered in a sheepish voice, like the fact that he was smart embarrassed him.

Why was she *not* surprised that he was a boy genius too? "So, what happened after she came in?"

"She came on to me hot and heavy. I responded like a sixteen-year-old who had never gotten laid. She had me in my bedroom within minutes. She was experienced and I let her take the lead. She opened my fly and had my dick out of my pants and a condom on me before I really knew what was happening." He laughed, but there was no humor in the hollow sound. "Not that I would have objected. I had a beautiful woman above me, ready to fuck me senseless. I was a teenager in complete ecstasy."

Oh. Dear. God.

Kara bit back a horrified gasp. Her suspicions *had* to be wrong. It couldn't have happened *that* way.

"She had the knife hidden in her bra." His voice trembled.

She wasn't wrong, and the nausea started to rise in her throat.

"So there I was, getting my first fuck, drowning in erotic bliss, never once thinking that there was something strange about the whole situation. She grabbed the knife and started stabbing the moment I started to come. It took me by surprise. She had stabbed me so many times before I realized what was happening that I didn't have a chance to defend myself." His chest was heaving, his voice strangled and raw.

Kara's whole body quivering with emotion, she turned in his arms, straddled his thighs and wrapped her arms around his neck. "Why?" she asked, her question coming in a short sob. "Why would she do that?" Burying her face in his neck, she let her tears flow unchecked down her face. All she could think about was the vulnerable teenage Simon, lying in a pool of blood, dying, just because he was a hormonal, typical young man.

Wrapping his arms tightly around her, he answered in a graveled voice, "Revenge. My father died before he could be punished for stealing from a powerful boss in an organized and huge cartel. The organization was sending a message, letting people know what happens to a person or their family if they try to steal from them. They couldn't let my father's bad deed go unpunished. He died before they could send that message. I was just a substitute."

"But why Rose?"

"The boss knew we had been friends since childhood. Her loyalty was being tested. She was pretty deeply involved in the organization.

They threatened to kill her mother and brother if she didn't kill me."
Surprisingly, there was no bitterness in his voice.

Shaken to the depths of her soul, she choked out, "Is she in jail?"
"She's dead." His voice was flat. "She fled as soon as I passed out
from blood loss, obviously convinced that I was a goner. She went
straight to an alley, took a lethal amount of drugs and slit her wrists
with the same knife she used to stab me. They found a suicide note
and her confession in her pocket. She begged forgiveness from both
her mother and mine, saying that she had to protect her family. She
never knew that I survived. Mom came home a few minutes later
and found me. If she hadn't, I would have been dead."

Unable to contain her horror, she sobbed into Simon's neck, crying
for all of the pain that he had suffered, both emotionally and physically. How did one survive a betrayal like that? Especially by a friend,
a woman he had adored. "I'm so sorry."

"Why?" he asked, sounding perplexed. "You didn't stab me." He
rubbed his hand up and down her back. "Don't cry. I don't like it."
His voice was demanding, but he rested his head against hers, his
touch on her back gentle and comforting.

A sad smile crossed her lips as she tried to rein in her emotions.
His comment was so...Simon. He had no idea why she was crying for
him, why she hurt for him. Being loved by anyone other than his
family was completely alien to him. "Tell me about your injuries?"

"I had stab wounds. Lots of them." His voice held a slightly teasing
note. He paused and asked in a more hesitant, gruff voice, "Are you
going to cry again if I tell you?"

*Oh, good Lord. He's telling me about the most traumatic event of
his life and he's worried about whether or not it will make me cry?*

"I'll try to contain myself. Tell me."

"I was in the hospital for a while. Lucky for me, Rose was a lousy
murderer. She managed to miss most of my vital organs and some of
the wounds were shallow. They had to do surgery and repair a few
organs, but I lived through it. As soon as I was well enough, Sam
moved Mom and me to Tampa." He breathed a long, masculine sigh.

"Were you scared?" she whispered against his neck, still visualizing a young, frightened, injured Simon. Her arms tightened around his shoulders, wishing she could have been there to comfort him.

"Honestly, I barely remember any of it." He shook his head slightly. "Sam said Mom was a total wreck. The only thing I remember was being ashamed when I was finally coherent. And sad because Rose was dead."

Her head jerked back abruptly in shock. Searching his eyes, confused, she asked, "Why? You didn't do anything wrong."

"I was duped because I was horny. I was thinking with the head below my waist instead of the one above it. Rose coming on to me wasn't logical. It didn't make any sense. I should have been suspicious. Christ! All she had said to me in months was to go to hell. Should have known something wasn't right. But I didn't think about anything but getting off." His face was dark and tortured. "I was pissed at myself. I put my mom and Sam through hell because I was stupid. I knew better. I grew up in the neighborhood. I sure as hell knew how to watch my own back."

Her palm lifted to his face, stroking over his jaw, realizing that he had been a man in a boy's body when he was injured, expecting himself to make rational decisions even when his hormones were raging. Didn't he realize, although he may have had the intelligence of an older man, his body had still been young, his maturity still that of a sixteen-year-old boy? "Simon...you were sixteen. Still a boy. You may have been a boy genius, but you were still a teenager."

"Yeah, and I didn't grow up to be exactly...uh...normal." He caught her hand that was roaming over the stubble on his face and brought it to his mouth. He kissed her palm gently and entwined their fingers, resting their conjoined hands over his heart.

"No, you didn't. You grew up to be extraordinary. You have reason not to trust easily. What happened with Dr. Evans?" Sure, he needed to have control, but given the circumstances surrounding the traumatic event, she was willing to bet that anyone would have their demons from *that* experience. She knew she would.

"He made me talk. I hated it, but I went every week to make my mom feel better. After a while, it got easier. He helped me through my feelings about Rose's death and about my father. But I never told him what really happened. I couldn't. I couldn't tell anyone. Everyone assumed that Rose came in through an unlocked door and stabbed me while I was sleeping...and I just let them continue to think that. It seemed easier." His body tensed. "It was a coward's way out."

"But there must have been signs at the scene. The condom and–"

"Apparently, Rose had some sort of feelings for me, some guilt. There was no condom and my dick was in my pants. No one ever assumed that it was anything but an attack on me while I was asleep. A revenge hit against my father. You're the only person who knows. I couldn't even tell Sam." His voice trailed off in a husky whisper.

Her heart ached for him, her soul needing to somehow comfort him. Pulling her hand from his, she turned his face to hers, forcing him to meet her eyes. "Listen to me. You were attacked when you were young and vulnerable. You have no reason to feel guilty or ashamed. Not one bit of it was your fault. I understand why you have trust issues. I understand why you panicked the other night." She saw doubt in his eyes and it pissed her off. "But know this...you survived and grew into a gorgeous, sexy, brilliant, successful man in spite of the fact that you got a raw deal when you were younger. You're the most incredible man I've ever known. Do you understand me!?" Her statement was fierce and her eyes were shooting fire. Damn it, he needed to get it through his thick head that he was someone special.

His eyes grew warmer and his lips twitched. "Yeah. I got it. Can we go back to the sexy part?"

She rolled her eyes. Trust Simon to focus in on only the sex part of her statement.

"Is that the only part you heard?" she replied, exasperated.

"No. But it was the most interesting part." He grinned at her unashamedly.

Frustrated, she scooped up a handful of water and dropped it on his head. "I'm trying to explain something to you here."

He grabbed her wrist and pulled her back into his body, creating a ripple in the tub that had water lapping against their skin in a gentle caress. Eyes heated and intense, he speared her with a look that spoke of possession, desire that ran much deeper than lust. "Do you want to know what I understand?"

She shivered as his arms slid tightly around her body, anchoring her against him. Unable to speak, she nodded.

His voice low and raspy, he answered, "I understand that I have to be the luckiest bastard on the planet because you love me, you accept me. Hell, I think you almost understand me-which is a fucking miracle because sometimes I don't even understand myself. I don't really know how to romance you like I should, but it isn't because I don't want to. I just don't know how. I understand that before I met you I was living in a very small world, and somehow you dragged me into the light, made me look around and actually see things that I never saw before. I understand that you make me a better man." He snaked a hand around her neck and planted a fierce, possessive kiss on her lips. Pulling away abruptly, he cupped her chin, his eyes molten and fierce. "Is that enough *understanding* for you?"

Breathless, she peered at him with her heart in her eyes. Maybe he hadn't repeated exactly what she had been trying to convey, but it was a start. He was learning to be loved. Burying her face against his shoulder, she murmured against his skin, "It's enough. For now."

"I need you, Kara. Don't leave me again." His voice hoarse, he rubbed his face against her hair.

He hadn't told her that he loved her, but he had bared his soul, shared his secrets, made incredible leaps in sharing his emotions. And he had done it for her. So yeah, for now, it was more than enough. "I'm not going anywhere."

"Damn right you're not!" he growled.

She smiled, because even as he spoke the demanding words, he was rocking her in his arms, holding her like a tender lover. He was wrong about not knowing how to romance her. He showed her how much he cared in so many little ways that were mind-boggling, seductive, and addictive. It was like a missing piece of her soul had finally found her and clicked into place, making her feel complete.

"Did you love her?" She knew she should drop the subject, but she wanted to know.

"Who?"

"Rose? Did you love her?"

"No." His low voice answered quickly and without hesitation. "I cared about her as a friend and I had a gigantic crush on her. But I didn't love her. I didn't want her to die. The sad part of the whole thing is that she died for nothing. A few days after she killed herself, the whole organization was brought down by the authorities. The boss and everyone associated with the cartel are going to rot in jail."

She could hear the sincerity, the acceptance of the whole situation in his voice. He wasn't angry, wasn't bitter. "Good therapist?"

"Yeah. Dr. Evans was the best. We still have dinner occasionally. I think he's still trying to figure me out." He laughed with genuine humor.

She smirked against his shoulder. "You're a fascinating subject."

"Are you saying that I'm odd?" he growled against her neck.

"Hmmm...I'm not sure." She slid away from him and stood, hating to leave the circle of his arms, but dying for something to drink. She'd been in the steamy room for quite some time and she was parched. Unable to resist looking back at him as she climbed the steps, her hungry eyes roamed his muscular body and handsome face. "I think I need to study you a bit more before I come to any conclusions."

He came to his feet in one graceful motion, muscles flexing, a wicked grin on his face. "Sweetheart, if you keep flashing that sexy body at me, I'm going to be doing my own studying." His grin widened and his eyes grew dark as he prowled after her, his big body cutting through the water easily. "And I examine and test my data very thoroughly."

She scooped up a towel from a pile next to the tub and scrambled out the bathroom door, Simon hot on her trail. Laughing as he caught her around the waist before she could make it out the bedroom door, she squealed, "No. I'm thirsty."

As he pulled her back against his wet, solid chest, she wondered if she really needed water all that badly. God, he felt good. Melting back against him, she could feel his hard, insistent arousal against her ass.

"Are you thirsty?" His voice changed, instantly concerned. "Did you eat?" He took the towel from her hands and started to wipe her body gently, drying her back and turning her around to blot the moisture from her breasts and belly.

She bit her lip as she peeked up at his face, his expression anxious and slightly agitated. "I'm not that hungry." Her appetite was increasing for something other than food.

By the time he was satisfied that she was completely dry, she was certain she was going to die of lust. The man was definitely thorough.

"You need hydration and food." He grunted as he tossed her his black silk robe and quickly dried his own body, going to his closet to rummage for clothing. He pulled on a similar garment in navy blue, putting it on quickly, barely taking the time to yank the tie closed.

She nearly whimpered as he covered that glorious, masculine body. She slipped on the black robe reluctantly, her thirst being overridden by the heat between her thighs. All she wanted at the moment was to get horizontal with Simon. "Seriously, I'm not that hungry."

He grasped her hand and tugged, pulling her along behind him. "You'll eat." He stopped, piercing her with a dark, warning stare. "I plan to fuck you until you beg for mercy later."

Her nipples hardened to pebbles and the smoldering heat between her thighs went up in flames. His heated expression made her shiver with longing, every inch of her skin tingling.

I'll be begging. But not for mercy.

With a frustrated sigh, she let him pull her toward the kitchen. She knew that stubborn, determined look of his. He was determined to satisfy her needs, give her whatever she needed. One casual mention of being thirsty and Simon was a man on a mission, pushing his own needs and wants aside, taking care of her first.

And he wondered why she loved him?

Her heart turned over as he squeezed her hand, leading her with focused determination toward food and water. The man was a tantalizing mixture of sizzling male hormones, intensity, tenderness, vulnerability, and compassion. The perfect male wrapped up in a bossy, handsome, irresistible package.

Why did she love him? Shouldn't the question be...how could she *not* love him?

She smiled as she admitted to herself that she had never stood a chance against falling madly, completely, and totally in love with this man. Something had drawn her to him from the moment they met, something elemental and primal. Maybe she had been afraid to recognize it for what it was, but it had always been there. Simon was like a force of nature-dangerous, yet compelling because of its fierce, wild, and raw power.

She remembered her mom once saying that *true love was not for the faint of heart, but the rewards were worth the risk.* Kara had been young, not even a teenager, and she hadn't understood the meaning of her mom's statement.

Now, with Simon, the meaning of those words was crystal-clear and she understood exactly what her mom had meant. And she had finally found the man who was well worth the risk.

Sending a silent *thank-you* to her mother for the words that it had taken her many years to understand, she allowed Simon to guide her out of the hallway and into the kitchen, a silly grin on her face.

Chapter 6

S imon popped open the door of the refrigerator with a flick of his wrist. "Diet Coke or water?" He reached for the Diet Coke, already knowing how she would answer.

"Diet Coke," she affirmed, her attention distracted.

He flipped the top on the can and handed it to her. Opening a regular Coke for himself, he chugged half of the container down in seconds. Christ, no wonder Kara had been thirsty. He hadn't been in the steamy room as long as her, but he was parched.

Lifting the can to her lips, she drank, but her gaze was fixed on the archway that led to the dining room.

Shit, he had completely forgotten his earlier errands. "Happy Valentine's Day." He gulped the rest of the can of soda and tossed the empty container in the trash.

Following her into the dining room, he scowled. She hadn't said one word. Maybe Nina and Marcie had steered him in the wrong direction. Would she like *any* of it?

He'd tried to be organized about delivering stuff to the dining room: flowers on the table, candies on the chairs, jewelry and perfume gifts on the floor. Yeah, there were teddy bears and other miscellaneous stuff scattered around the room, but he had thought he had arranged things *fairly* well. "You don't like any of it?" Damn it, he was firing his assistant and secretary in the morning. They had specifically told him that these were the things that made women feel good, special, cherished.

"Oh Simon, what did you do?" Kara ran a fingertip along the velvety surface of a red rose and tapped on one of the heart-shaped balloons, watching it sway back and forth through the air.

"Okay. Those two are definitely fired in the morning!" Fuck! He wanted to please her. Instead, she looked like she was traumatized. He knew he should have gotten other things, but the Veyron and the Mercedes had been full.

"Who are you firing?" She turned and looked at him with a puzzled expression.

"Nina and Marcie. They told me that these types of gifts make a woman happy."

Oh hell, he couldn't fire either one of them. They did their jobs too well.

Honestly, it was his fault that he didn't know a damn thing about how to romance his woman. But he was willing to try until he got it right. "We could go shopping. Pick something else," he suggested, hoping she'd let him take her, see what *she* thought was romantic.

"You asked Nina and Marcie for advice?"

"Yeah."

"Simon, this is incredible. I don't know what to say." Her voice was tremulous as she bent down and picked up a fluffy brown teddy bear and held it against her chest in a death grip. "I think Marcie and Nina were giving you suggestions. They didn't mean for you to buy *everything*."

Damn it. She sounded like she was going to cry. He fucking hoped she didn't. "I don't know your favorite flower. Or what kind of candy you like. I don't really know your favorite color. Shouldn't a guy know those things? Shouldn't I know how to please you?" he answered, his voice disgruntled.

Dropping the stuffed bear gently to the floor, she turned to him. "You didn't need to do all this. I've never even gotten flowers before."

What did he do? He went shopping. Big fucking deal! Sure, he'd usually rather have a root canal than go shopping, but for the first time, he'd enjoyed it. "I went shopping. It wasn't exactly a big effort." *At the last minute, because he had only just realized that it was Valentine's Day.* How pathetic was that? Thank God for Nina's thoughtful husband!

"You did all of this for me." Her arm stretched out, motioning toward the full dining room. "The flowers are beautiful. I love them all. I want a piece of that candy so badly that I can taste it already, and everything else is so overwhelming that I'm speechless. I would have been over the moon with a few flowers or a card. You didn't need to do this. It's more gifts than a woman gets in a lifetime. But it isn't the *things* that amaze me. It's *you*. Your desire to make me happy. You're the most incredible man on the planet. That's why I love you." She took a long sip from her can of soda and set it on a small, available area of the table.

He caught her body as it rocketed into his arms, savoring her softness as she pressed against him. Warm lips nuzzled his cheek and the side of his neck. As he wrapped his arms tightly around her waist, her body gliding slowly along his until her feet touched the floor, he decided that maybe he would give Marcie and Nina a raise instead of a lecture in the morning.

"You're insane. You know that, don't you?" Pulling back, she planted a loud, smacking kiss on his lips. "But I love that about you."

Okay. He was willing to be bat-shit crazy if it made her love him more.

Giving him an adoring look, she added, "But one gift next time, okay? Or a card."

Oh, hell no. He wasn't getting roped into that promise. "We'll see." His answer was noncommittal.

"Wait. I have something for you." She pulled away from him and scampered to her room.

She returned with a small gift bag, decorated with hearts and little devils. "The bag was definitely screaming your name." Shooting him a mischievous smile, she handed him the bag. "I don't really have my own money to spend, so I had to improvise."

"You need more money? Why didn't you tell me?" He glowered at her, pissed that she hadn't told him that she needed cash.

"I don't need you to give me anything more. I want you to take some of it back. I have almost a hundred grand in my bank account. I don't need it, Simon." She met his eyes with a stubborn tilt of her chin.

"You haven't spent hardly any of it. How in the hell are you living, taking care of your needs?"

She snorted. "You take care of my needs. What in the hell do I need money for? I don't have one single need or want. I'm living like a spoiled brat right now. All I have to do is mention something and it magically appears. I don't need to buy one single thing."

"Women love to shop. Buy things. Even when they don't need them." Hell, he knew that much from his mom. Her favorite activity was shopping.

"Not me. I'd rather be reading. Or playing Myth World II, if I have time. I have every comfort, every need met." She reached a hand to his face, tracing his lips lightly, running the back of her hand softly over his five o'clock shadow. "The only recurring need I have is you."

She was trying to distract him, and damn him, it was working. "The money was a gift. You're keeping it," he snarled, determined that she wouldn't get her way by getting his cock hard...which it was. Extremely hard. Totally ready.

"I'm not keeping it." She placed a soft kiss at the side of his mouth. "Open the bag."

He had all he could do not to strip that fuck-me robe from her body and devour her whole. His whole body was tense as he opened the gift bag, trying not to think about his pulsating cock and his nearly impossible-to-ignore compulsion to be driving into her body right at the moment.

His head jerked up before he could finish the task, suddenly remembering that he needed to tell Kara that the other asshole who had tried to abduct her was in jail. "They caught the other guy today. He's in jail. You probably have a message from Harris."

"Oh, thank God. You can call off the security. I think they intimidate some of my fellow students. They don't exactly keep a low profile anymore." Her voice was light, but her body visibly relaxed.

He saw the relief on her face. No matter how much she denied that the man had been a threat, he knew it had bothered her, knew that she was still frightened. She'd have to be a fool *not* to be. She had come too damn close to losing her life on the day they had injured her. "Not happening. The security stays."

"I don't need them anymore-"

"No! I can't take the risk of something happening to you. There are too many crazy people out there and I've made enemies over the years." Granted, he hadn't pissed as many people off as his brother Sam had, but you couldn't become a billionaire without having a few people out there who hated your guts. "The security stays."

He pulled on the red tissue paper in the bag, sending pieces of heart-shaped paper fluttering to the carpet. He caught one in his hand, clutching it tightly, before it hit the floor. She dipped a hand into the bag and pulled out the material that lay at the bottom.

She held up the black silk boxer shorts by the elastic. Generally a boxer-briefs type of guy, he stared for a moment before his lips curved upward. The black silk was dotted with little devils and hearts.

"They're so...you, Simon." She wiggled her eyebrows and the underwear at the same time. "You'll look hot. Not that you don't already, but all I could think about was how sexy they'd look on you." She pulled the material to her face, nuzzling the soft silk.

He stared at her with horny fascination, imagining his cock inside those boxer shorts, her lips on the material. Holy fuck! Those particular underwear had just become his very favorite. He didn't give a shit if he didn't usually wear traditional boxers.

"I already took the tags off. Try them on so I can take them off later." She held them out to him with a seductive smile.

He had his robe open in seconds and the shorts over his hips a moment later. He shuddered as he felt the soft brush of her delicate hands on his shoulders as she slipped his robe completely off, leaving him standing before her in his new pair of favorite underwear.

"Hot. Definitely very hot," she whispered.

The needy, breathy sound of her voice nearly made him come undone. Actually, he liked the feel of silk next to his skin, caressing his engorged member. And he positively loved the look of hunger in his woman's eyes as they roamed over his body, narrowing on the bulge at his crotch.

She didn't bother to hide her desire for him and it made him insane. "What's this?" He opened his fist, exposing the tiny cardboard heart. Flipping it over, he saw the handwritten words.

Good For One Wish!

He looked up at her, perplexed. She was worrying her bottom lip, looking anxious.

"It's a heart-wish. I didn't really have my own money-" She held her hand up as he drew in an audible breath to argue. "Don't start that again. Anyway, I made these up. You can cash them in any time. They're good for one wish or favor that you want from me. Anything that you can think of that's in my power to grant you."

"Anything?" His heart pounded as his mind filled with images.

She raised a brow. "Anything I'm capable of doing."

"I wish you would keep the money I put in your bank account and not argue about the security." Feeling a little guilty that he was using his gift against her, he frowned.

She gave him a look that his mother used to give him as a child. It was the dreaded "I'm-so-disappointed-in-you" look. Fuck! That hurt.

She folded her arms in front of her. "That wish interferes with my morals and values. Plus, that's two wishes. Not fair."

"Compromise?" he breathed softly, not liking the disgruntled look on her face.

Her face softened. "I'm open."

"Keep the money in your account. Use it if you need to. I'm not saying you have to keep it forever. Just keep it for now. Until you graduate and get a job. We can renegotiate later." Of course, he'd refuse to take it back later. But this was now, and he wanted her to be safe if anything ever happened to him.

"Wish granted." She let her arms slide down her body and planted them on her hips. "Security?"

"Let me leave the security in place, but I'll make them back off. You'll barely know that they're there. But let me keep security on you." Holding his breath, he watched her expression. "For my peace of mind, Kara. For me."

"I'll do it for you provided they back off and quit scaring my classmates. Wish granted." She snatched the paper heart from his hand and tore it up.

He dropped to the floor, searching frantically for the other heart-wishes. "How many were there?" He'd found two. Seeing another one lying under the table, he crawled forward, totally oblivious of the carpet burns on his knees. He wanted every one of those bad-boys in his hot little hand. They were definitely made of solid gold.

"Five," she choked out with a laugh.

He heaved a sigh of relief as he snagged the last one from the carpet. As he stood, she had her hand out and an expectant look on her face. "What?" No way was she getting another one to tear up.

"You made two wishes. You owe me one of those."

"I compromised," he said heatedly. Compromise should count for something. It wasn't like he did it every day, or for just anybody.

"Gimme," she answered, wriggling her fingers.

Oh, hell. He *had* gotten his way. Mostly. Pulling one of the small hearts from his palm reluctantly, he handed it over with a grunt. "Can I have these every holiday?"

"We'll see," she muttered vaguely, a secret smile on her lips, as she tore up the paper.

"What did you mean when you said you'd never gotten flowers? You had a long-term boyfriend."

She sighed heavily. "He didn't do gifts. Thought they were a waste of money. Especially flowers, because they eventually die."

"No offense, sweetheart, but why in the hell did you stay with him for so long?" His jaw clenched, wishing he could beat the hell out of her ex.

"I honestly don't know. It probably had something to do with the death of my parents. I missed them. I felt so alone after they died. I guess I was pretty young, vulnerable, and stupid." Her voice was forlorn.

Simon hated the bastard even more. She had been young and alone, stunned after losing her parents. He wished he could have been there for her then.

But he was here now. He pulled her unresisting body into his arms, vowing to protect her from this moment on. "Never again, baby. You'll always have me. I'll never let you be lonely."

Neither one of us will ever be lonely again.

He took the clip from her hair and dropped it on the floor. As he ran a soothing hand over the silky strands, he realized that he had been lonely his entire life. He'd just never really recognized it. "I've been waiting for you forever," he whispered to her in a husky voice. Somehow, he had known her from the moment he saw her. Not with his eyes, but with his heart.

And God, how he needed her.

She pulled away from him slightly to see his face. She didn't say anything, but she didn't need to. He could see her love, her heart glittering in her eyes. He traced her lips with his fingers, moving slowly to her cheeks and down her neck, savoring the softness beneath his fingertips. He drew invisible initials on her exposed cleavage, left bare by his too-big robe. *His* initials, tracing over them again and again, needing to stake his claim on this woman who drove him to ecstasy and to the edge of sanity.

"Simon." She whimpered his name, pulling his head down to her lips.

He groaned into her embrace as her hands stroked over his shoulders, loving the feel of her fingers on his heated flesh, a touch so exquisite that his heart was thundering against the wall of his chest.

Needing to make her his, claim her, he thrust his tongue into her mouth with desperation, his need so intense that it was almost painful. The possessive beast in him sighed as she opened for him, letting him in, asking for more. He plundered until they were both breathless, panting. Pulling back, he sucked in a deep breath, nibbling at her lower lip, unable to separate himself from her, but also needing to have her naked.

He moved back, cupping one of her silk-clad breasts, running a finger around the prominent nipple. "Do you remember what I told you about this robe," he rumbled against her lips, tracing them with the tip of his tongue.

"Every word," she answered in a low, sexy voice. "I have very fond memories of this robe."

"Me too," he replied hotly, reluctantly releasing her and pulling one more tiny heart from his other hand. "But right now I wish you would get naked."

With a graceful move, she swept the heart from his fingers and tore it up. Slowly, she opened the front tie of the garment, letting the silk glide effortlessly off her shoulders. He swallowed hard as her perfect breasts appeared and the garment caught at her elbows for a heart-stopping moment, before it slid to the floor in a pool of shimmering black.

He had to force himself to breathe, make the air move in and out of his lungs. She was so fucking beautiful. So very his.

Mine.

"I love these fucking hearts," he rasped, his hand clenched tightly around the remaining two.

Her gorgeous blue eyes danced, but they were also hot with desire. "You wasted that one. I would have done it for nothing. I need you."

I need you.

His soul echoed her desire, his body clamoring, clawing to possess what belonged to him. His cock was as hard as marble, ready to be buried in her wet, hot pussy. At this point, he was afraid he was going to explode the moment he buried himself inside her. He tucked the tiny hearts beneath a placemat on the table for safekeeping.

She took a step forward, bringing her silken skin against his, making him shudder. Her hand fluttered gently against the material of his boxers, stroking his ready-to-explode cock like it was a treasured pet.

He moved her hand and swept her up into his arms, unable to wait a moment longer. "Time for bed."

"About time," she murmured against his shoulder, obviously impatient.

Immediately, his mind shifted from his cock to the wanting woman in his arms. *His woman.* She needed him, wanted him to pleasure her, sate her needs. He'd get his satisfaction, but she came first. She would always come first. Literally.

Chapter 7

Simon dropped her gently on the bed. She rolled and popped open the drawer on the bedside table, jerking out his restraints and handing them to him. "Tie me. I don't mind."

Please. Tie me and fuck me before I die of longing.

She was panting, both her mind and body out of control. If she didn't have his muscular, hot body possessing hers within moments, she was going to scream.

He looked at her with confusion. "You want me to tie you up?"

"I want you. Tie me up. Tie me down. Whatever you want. It's hot. You're hot. I just want you to fuck me. However you're comfortable with it."

Oh God, I'm babbling. He's making me crazy.

"Sweetheart, the possessive caveman in me would love nothing more than to have you at my mercy and make you come until you scream, but I don't need to tie you up." He took the restraints from her hands and dumped them beside the bed. "But now that I know it makes you hot, I'll do it another time. Right now, I just need to watch you come, make love to you until neither of us can move."

Every light was on. They hadn't shut them off earlier. The expression on his face was fierce, tender, and strangely peaceful. She took a deep breath, her whole body quivering, her pussy saturated, ready for him. She became intoxicated as he stretched himself over her, the silk of his new boxers sliding along the tender folds between her thighs. She opened for him, moaning as his rock-hard erection pressed firmly against her mound, stimulating her already-sensitive clit.

She clutched him to her, almost afraid that he would escape, needing some sort of reassurance that he was real, that he was hers. She had never, ever been a possessive or obsessive woman, but Simon was so incredible, so completely amazing, that it seemed almost impossible that he really existed, that he was truly hers. Sometimes he almost seemed like a dream, a lovely dream that took her existence from ordinary to extraordinary.

"Relax, baby," Simon whispered in her ear, his warm breath making her shiver.

Relaxing her arms, she wrapped them around his neck, trying to control her feral instinct to bind him to her, protect herself from ever having to live without him. "I'm sorry. I guess I'm feeling desperate." She hadn't meant to say it; it sounded pathetic, but it was true. Her emotions were on overload and her body was clamoring for more.

He trailed hot, open-mouthed kisses up the side of her neck. "No more desperate than I am. Every time I hear your voice, see you, talk to you, I want to get closer. Hell, all I have to do is think about you." Lightly, his tongue licked her lips, tracing the contours of her mouth. "I want inside of you. I want us to be fused so tightly that you can never get away."

Yes. Yes. That's how she felt.

His mouth came down on hers-no more teasing, no more seduction. He invaded, pillaged, ravished with his lips and tongue, and she opened to him like a flower to the sun. She moaned as he sated a small portion of her desire for cohesion, her hips automatically lifting, wanting other body parts to merge, needing some relief from her hyper-aroused state.

He pulled his mouth from hers, his breathing ragged. "Fuck! You're sweet. So sweet and so damn hot!" Pulling her arms from around his neck, he gripped her wrists and imprisoned them at her side, sliding slowly down her body.

She squirmed, pulling at her wrists that were held tightly, one on each side of her waist. He licked and kissed his way down her chest until he reached her breasts, making her want to scream with frustrated desire.

He wasn't gentle, and she didn't want him to be. His teeth abraded a sensitive nipple, pulling the tip into his scorching mouth, using both his teeth and his tongue.

Pleasure and pain.

"Simon. Oh, God. Please." Her head thrashed as he switched to the other nipple, torturing her, arousing her until she could barely draw breath.

He kept up his erotic assault on her breasts, laving, gently biting, switching from one to the other while he kept her hands clamped firmly at her side. The feeling of being at his tender mercy was maddening, intoxicating, breathtaking.

His mouth dipped lower, moving in circles over her belly, leaving a trail of heat in its wake.

Finally, he let go of her wrists, using his hands to spread her legs wide as he moved between her thighs. "You smell so sweet. Like aroused woman. My woman. Mine to satisfy. My honey to lick up." He growled, taking deep breaths, the hot exhalations caressing the tender folds of her pussy.

Her body nearly exploded just from his possessive, completely aroused, masculine snarl. "Yes, Simon. Please. I need you. I need to come."

"I need to make you come. Satisfy my woman."

He pushed her legs up, bending her knees, opening her for his hungry mouth.

His attack was immediate and totally carnal. Mouth devouring, tongue penetrating, he claimed her pussy with an intensity that made her cry out his name as her body quivered.

He breached the tender folds, delving deep, licking up her cream with a sensual abandon that left her breathless and whimpering. His tongue found and attacked her swollen clit with mindless focus.

Kara speared her hands into his hair, oblivious of anything other than the total ecstasy her body was experiencing from his primal, animalistic mission. He was going to make her climax. Hard.

He laved the tiny bud over and over. Faster and faster. Again and again.

Her body shaking, she fisted his hair, pulling his mouth tightly against the pulsating flesh of her pussy.

Her body wound tightly, her nerve endings sizzling with heat, she detonated with a force so powerful that her back arched and she tried to pull away from his relentless mouth, the pleasure too sharp, too vehement.

Gripping her hips, he held her tightly, making her ride the waves of the volatile pleasure as she screamed his name. He didn't stop until the last spasm subsided, leaving her as limp as a wet dishrag.

Still gasping for breath as he crawled up her body and lay at her side, she rolled into his body and threw her arm over his massive chest, burying her head against his shoulder.

"Feel better?" his voice was raspy, but laced with amusement.

She batted his shoulder weakly. "Were you trying to kill me?"

"Only with pleasure, baby," he whispered, his voice heated.

"Well, then you were successful." She ran her hand down his chest, tracing his scars, wondering why a man as wonderful as this one had suffered such pain. Sometimes life just wasn't fair.

Her hand trailed down his abdomen, tracing every toned muscle. He was sculpted like a Greek statue. And had a cock much bigger than those depicted in any of those marble nudes. "You're so gorgeous," she whispered in awe as she followed the silky trail of hair from his navel downward.

"I'm starting to think we need to take you to an eye doctor," he rumbled, his voice graveled, but adoring.

"My eyesight is perfect and so is my perception. You're so strong. Handsome." Her fingers curled around his engorged cock. "And big."

He sucked in an audible breath as she dipped her hand into his boxers and swiped her fingertip over the head of his cock, spreading the moisture of a drop of pre-cum over the silken tip, rubbing it gently, slowly.

"Fuck! I love feeling your hands on me. It's the best damn feeling in the world."

Gripping his shaft a little tighter, she started to move it sensually, provocatively. *This* was something that Simon had always missed because he couldn't let a woman have her hands free during sex. Until now. Simon would never be tame, but the fact that he felt comfortable with her touch, that he actually wanted it, humbled her. After all he had been through, he trusted her.

He groaned, a tortured sound between pleasure and torment. His larger hand covered hers. "Ride me, sweetheart. Fuck me senseless." He stripped his new, already much-loved favorite underwear off, letting them drop to the floor.

Her head jerked up to look at his face as his arms came around her, lifted her over him. "Are you sure?" She wanted nothing more at that moment than to take that mammoth cock into her body and watch him take his pleasure under her. But she was trembling at the thought, terrified of making him live through another bad memory.

"Yeah. I want to watch you ride me. I want to watch your face as you come from riding my cock," he answered, his expression dark and desperate.

Straddling his hips, she hesitated, her heart racing. Could he do this? He didn't have to. "You don't need to prove anything to me. We don't have to do this."

"Take me inside you, sweetheart. I need you," he grunted, his voice husky with desire.

I need you.

Those three little words had her lifting up, grasping his engorged cock and placing the head at the opening of her slick channel. Need surged through her, an elemental, pure desire to feel him fill her, have him moving inside her, as deeply as she could take him. Her hands on his chest, she maneuvered up and down, taking him slowly, getting used to the angle. She lowered again, taking most of the shaft as his hips lunged up, trying to go deeper.

Big, strong hands gripped her hips, pulling her down to meet him as he surged up, their skin slapping together sharply as she finally had him deeply imbedded inside her, filling her completely. He stretched her, opened her, held her hips tightly as they completely joined, his cock buried to the root.

"Christ! You feel so good. So tight and hot." His voice was wild, feral.

She watched his face, looking for any sign that the position was troubling for him. There was nothing but pleasure. His liquid chocolate eyes met and held hers fast. His hands guided her strokes, his hips moving up with powerful thrusts.

Their eyes stayed locked and a tear trickled down her cheek as she saw no sign of fear in him, no doubt of who he was fucking.

"Only you, Kara. It's only ever been you," he told her, his chest heaving. "You look so beautiful. Let go. Ride me. Come for me."

She let her eyes flutter closed as he pummeled her, holding her hips in his strong hands. Her head fell back as she let herself be consumed by the pounding strokes of his cock, the friction of his furious thrusts, the feel of him owning her again and again.

Her breasts bounced with his powerful entries. She lifted her hands and cupped them, pinching them lightly.

"Yeah. Take what you want, sweetheart. Whatever you need." He panted heavily as his strokes became deeper, harder.

Her fingers plucked at her nipples as his grip on her hips got tighter, more demanding. She rode him hard, grinding, taking him so deep that she shuddered.

Throwing her head back, she imploded. The muscles in the walls of her channel clenched and released, repeatedly squeezing the cock invading her. As her body quivered, she felt his body tense beneath hers.

She watched, their eyes meeting, as he came.

He was hot and wild, masculine and perfect. The low, reverberating sound that ripped from his throat was the most beautiful sound she had ever imagined.

A hot, explosive stream emptied into her womb and they both collapsed. She could feel his body trembling as her body crumpled, covering him like a blanket. "I love you," she murmured with a sigh against his chest.

His arms came around her, holding her tightly against his body. They were both sweaty and spent, but she felt so complete, so content.

It took a while for her breathing to return to normal and her racing heart to quiet. She started to crawl off Simon's body, to move to his side, but he wouldn't let her. He grunted and pulled her back over him. "Stay."

It should have pissed her off that he was giving her a dog obedience order, but the way that he said it, with such longing in his voice, made her smile. She was also so sated that she could barely move.

She snuggled her head back onto his shoulder, determined to get up the energy to move shortly or she would end up crushing the poor guy.

His breathing became deep and even, his arms still locked around her, but relaxed.

He's sleeping. We just had sex in his nightmare position. And he's sleeping with me on top of him.

Her heart flipped and a bone-deep ache penetrated her body. He trusted her so much that he could be at ease when he felt most vulnerable. She turned her head and kissed him lightly, her heart overflowing with love for this man.

This man who put her needs first.

This man who trusted her.

This man who would go to any lengths to please her.

This man she loved.

She'd always treasure his trust, nurture it as though it were precious. Which it was.

Exhaustion made her eyes close, her body relax.

Really, you need to roll off Simon. It can't be a comfortable way to sleep.

Her breathing became deeper, matching the same rhythm as the man beneath her.

They woke the next morning in the same position, completely rested and comfortable.

Epilogue

Simon paced the courtyard of the elegant resort with a frown. Was he about to make a big mistake? What if she wouldn't have him? The last six weeks had been the happiest of his life. Did he really want to screw that up?

He looked out at the water, reliving those memories with a contented sigh.

I don't want to screw it up. But I need her. I want her to be mine. The need to brand her as his, to stake his claim, was nearly overwhelming.

Looking toward the outside door to their suite made him shudder. Fuck! Why was this so hard? He and Kara shared everything. There wasn't a corner of his heart and soul that she didn't know.

His phone vibrated in the pocket of his suit jacket. He was in a suit and tie, and it wasn't even a damn workday. He was currently in Orlando, to visit Disneyworld of all places, to realize one of Kara's dreams. Incredible that a woman born and raised in Tampa had never been to Disneyworld!

Of course, neither had he. But, then again, he had come to Florida as an almost-adult.

He clenched his last heart-wish in his palm, squeezing it until his hand was white, his blood circulation nearly cut off.

He had saved one wish. The other one had been used to get her to come on a vacation trip during her spring break. He had given her the heart a month ago and told her he wished that he could take her someplace that she wanted to visit during her spring break.

Okay. Yeah. He expected Paris, London, the Orient, or even Africa. Instead, she had mumbled quietly that she had always wanted to go to Disneyworld. Barely more than an hour's drive from Tampa, and with a private jet available for travel anywhere in the world, he hadn't expected *this* to be her dream vacation.

Granted, it had actually been fun. He especially liked it when she got scared on a ride and threw herself in his arms with a shriek and a delighted laugh. Tonight was their last night at the resort, and he was taking her to dinner in one of the best restaurants in Orlando. He just hoped that they had something big to celebrate.

Fishing his phone from his jacket, he looked at the caller ID. *Hudson, Samuel.*

"What?" he snarled into the phone.

"Did you ask her yet?"

Simon nearly laughed at the slightly nervous voice on the other end of the phone. Sam acted like this event was just as important to him as it was to Simon. "No. She's getting ready for dinner."

"You've had a week. What the hell?"

"What do you care?" Actually, Simon knew very well why Sam cared. He'd let it slip that if Kara said yes, Sam would very likely be seeing Maddie Reynolds again.

"She's good for you. You need her. Plus, I don't want to put up with your shitty mood if she says no."

She wasn't going to say no. She couldn't say no. He would just have to convince her. Anything else was *not* an option.

The door of their suite opened, and Simon lost all interest in his conversation with Sam. "I'll call you later."

"Ask her."

Simon clicked off the call and pocketed his phone, his eyes never leaving the beautiful woman in red, framed in the door of their suite.

God, she's incredible. Will I ever get used to the sight of her?

Most likely...not. It didn't matter where she was, or what she was wearing, he started having palpitations the moment he saw her.

Tonight, dressed in a red cocktail dress that flirted with her knees, and a pair of matching heels, she took his breath away. Her hair was down, tiny strands ruffling from the slight ocean breeze.

"You look beautiful," he told her truthfully as he reached her side, planting a light kiss on her lips. *You look like a fucking goddess.*

Every day. Every single time he saw her.

"Thanks. You're looking very handsome yourself, Mr. Hudson. Are we ready?" she asked, shooting him a happy smile.

I'm ready. Ready to strip off that sexy dress and see what kind of underwear you're wearing. Then I'll strip them off with my teeth and fuck you until you scream.

His cock was rock-hard, but that was nothing new. It happened every day, every time she smiled at him. Or when she didn't smile at him. When she frowned. When she argued. Fuck! Her mere presence was all that was required to give him an erection.

Or her voice. Or just the thought of her. Damn...he was easy when it came to Kara.

"In just a minute." He guided her back in the door, closing it behind him. "I need to talk to you."

Her smile faded and he wanted to kick himself.

"Is something wrong?" she asked, her voice suddenly concerned.

"No." He sat on a leather couch in the opulent suite and pulled her down into his lap. "I need to ask you something."

Do it. Just do it. Before you go crazy.

He opened his clenched fist, showing her his final heart-wish.

"Don't waste it on asking for sex, 'cause I'm pretty much a sure thing," she answered, laughing softly.

He slid her off his lap and seated her beside him. Reaching into his pocket, he handed her a small box.

She looked at him, then the heart, and then the box. Taking the box in her hand, she lifted the lid slowly.

"I wish that you would marry me." His voice was husky and filled with part hope, part fear.

"Oh, my God. Simon, I didn't expect this." She pulled the huge, sparkling diamond ring, housed in a platinum setting, from its velvet home, her fingers trembling. "I don't know what to say."

"Say yes. Please." *Say yes or I'm gonna lose it.*

She looked at him with a stunned expression. "You want to marry me? Simon, you haven't even told me that you love me. I assumed you just weren't ready. I didn't expect this."

How in the hell could she *not* have suspected? She'd owned his heart, body, and soul for what seemed like forever. "I love you. I love you. I love you." Surely he had said that to her before? "I do. I can't believe I've never said it, but you had to have known."

She smiled up at him. "I know. I just wasn't sure if you were ready to say it."

"I'm more than fucking ready. You're mine and I want it official." His eyes were intense, his body tight. "I should have told you that I loved you. I'll make sure you hear it so often from now on that you'll be tired of hearing me say it. You deserve to hear it every fucking day. Maybe I haven't verbalized it because there aren't really words to explain how I feel about you. Love seems lukewarm, not enough. But I love hearing it coming from *your* lips. I should have known that you wanted to hear it." He sighed. "You're my life, sweetheart. Please be mine. Mine forever."

She threw herself into his arms. He wrapped his arms around her and closed his eyes tightly, knowing he held his whole world in his arms at that very moment.

"Mine forever," she breathed, close to his ear, her voice incredulous.

He pulled back to look at her face. She was crying, tears spilling from her eyes in an endless stream.

"Don't cry. I don't like it."

"I know. But they're happy tears."

Fuck! Crying was crying, and he hated to see her cry. He plucked the ring from her trembling fingers and grasped her hand gently, sliding the ring on her finger. His heart raced as he stated, "You're marrying me."

"I thought you were asking." She shot him an amused look. "I haven't said yes."

"You will," he warned, his expression dark. "Say that you will." *Say it. Before I have a damn heart attack. Say it. Now. Right fucking now!*

She pried his fist open and pick up the heart gently. She tore it up, letting the tiny pieces scatter over the couch. "Wish granted."

He blew out a relieved breath, his heart hammering. "Yes?"

"Yes. I'll marry you. I love you, too."

"Soon," he demanded.

"We'll see. Compromise?"

"No!" He took her hand in his and gently kissed the ring he had placed on her finger. "No compromise this time."

She wrapped her arms around his neck, dropping a soft kiss on his lips as she caressed the nape of his neck. "A small compromise?"

"No."

He groaned as she pulled his head down and gave him a toe-curling, hot embrace that had him panting in the aftermath.

"You can give a little," she told him in a low, persuasive voice.

He growled as her hand moved down his chest and palmed his erection through his pants. "Are you trying to seduce me into compromise?"

"Maybe. Is it working?" she answered in her irresistible "fuck-me" voice.

"Hell yes, it's working," he growled, pulling her into his arms. "Fine. We'll talk terms. Later." He stood and pulled her to her feet.

Fuck! He *was* easy.

"Later," she agreed. "Much later." She grabbed his tie and tugged, leading him willingly toward the bedroom.

Maybe being easy wasn't *always* a bad thing.

They missed dinner and ordered room service hours later. In the hours preceding their celebratory engagement dinner in the suite, Simon learned that compromise wasn't bad at all and that being easy could be a very, very good thing.

~*~*The End*~*~*~

Mine Completely

VALENTINE'S DAY ROMANCE

The Billionaire's Obsession

This one is for the wonderful readers of The Billionaire's Obsession series who loved Simon and Kara as much as I do and wanted to see more of them. Thank you for following the series and looking forward to each new book with enthusiasm.

Also, many thanks to Karma for the selfless things you do for me as a friend and a critique buddy. Please get well soon.

~J.S.~

Chapter 1

"**C**an we talk?"

Simon Hudson flinched as he glanced up from his computer screen to see his fiancée, Kara, standing at the entrance to his home computer lab, as she uttered the three little words that he swore every man in America probably dreaded hearing from the woman he loved. After living with the gorgeous brunette for over a year, seeing that familiar crinkle of concentration between her beautiful blue eyes, Simon knew exactly what was about to happen. *Can we talk?* Those words murmured in that husky, low, and seductive voice of hers was actually a warning, a sign that she was about to broach a topic of conversation that he absolutely, positively did not agree with or didn't want to talk about.

He grabbed the mug beside his computer, taking a slug of coffee and wishing it were something a little stronger, even though it was barely eight o'clock in the morning. The last time Kara had wanted to *talk*, she'd badgered him about her personal security, wanting him to decrease it. *That* was so not happening. She already had far less security than he would like to see tailing her luscious ass every day. Swallowing hard, trying to get the coffee down around the huge lump in his throat, he tried not to notice how adorable Kara looked in a pair of baby pink medical scrubs as she sashayed into his office. Even after a year, just the sight of her, the sound of her voice, the thought of her, her enticing scent-anything that even *reminded* him of Kara-had him completely enthralled and his cock instantly standing at attention. Simon had convinced himself that his obsession with Kara would calm down after some time had passed, settling into a more rational love, one that didn't make him completely insane. It hadn't, and he had been seriously deluding himself to think that he could feel anything other than completely irrational thoughts when it came to all things Kara. If anything, his fixation had gotten worse.

I'm a goddamn billionaire, co-owner of one of the most powerful corporations in the world, sensible in every other area of my life. How can one woman make me so crazy?

Kara smiled at him as she stopped in front his desk, making his raging erection strain against the zipper of his jeans and his chest ache with happiness. Every fucking time he looked at her, Simon was constantly amazed that this incredible woman was his, had accepted him completely, with all of his faults.

Mine.

Simon wanted to reach across the desk and free that silken mane from its confining ponytail, pull her into his lap and kiss those smiling ripe lips until she made those needy little noises, abandoned moans that...

"Simon?" Kara's questioning voice jerked him out of his erotic fantasies. *Damn it.*

Can we talk?

Oh, hell. Did he have a choice? He smiled up at her, but answered cautiously, "What did you want to talk about?"

"I need you to read something and sign it. It's no big deal." She dropped several papers on his desk, fastened together with a paper clip.

Scanning the top document quickly, his eyes flying over the printed words, he answered in a bewildered voice. "This is a contract. A prenuptial agreement." He flipped the pages quickly, no stranger to contracts and legal documents. It didn't take long for him to search out the pertinent information. "What in the hell is this?"

She sighed. "I had an attorney draw it up. We're getting married in a month. You're a billionaire and I'm a brand new registered nurse without a penny to her name. It's hardly an equal arrangement. I think it's only fair that you're protected. I've already signed it. I just need your signature. Please."

Eyes narrowing into a dangerous look, he raised his head and shot her a mulish glance. "Not happening, sweetheart. Christ, you aren't allowing yourself anything. What attorney would even agree to this for their client? You're never leaving me and I'm sure as hell never leaving you. Till death do us part, what's mine is yours, etc. etc."

Kara propped her hands on her hips and met his ferocious stare with one of her own.

Uh oh. Simon was well acquainted with *that look*, that ornery tilt of her chin, but he'd be damned if he was losing this disagreement. No prenuptial agreement, no divorce. Ever. He'd never survive it. The stubborn woman standing before him had become his entire world, holding his happiness in her delicate hands; she'd yanked him out of his previously lonely, empty existence, forcing him to face his issues head-on, changing his whole life from dysfunctional to extraordinary. Losing her was *not* an option.

"Things happen, Simon. You saved my life. We aren't equals financially. I owe you this." Her voice was frustrated.

The wheels on Simon's computer chair screeched as he stood, stalking Kara as he moved around the desk. "Things don't happen to *us*. And you don't owe me a damn thing. You don't let me buy you anything without a major argument; you won't take a penny of my money. I'm willing to bet everything that I have that you've barely touched the money I put in your account over a year ago." Taking a deep breath, Simon tried to contain his emotions, pushing down ruthlessly on the hurt and possessiveness that were trying to claw to the surface. There was nothing he wanted more than to give Kara everything, things she had never had before she met him, but she wouldn't allow him to do much more than put a roof over her head and feed her, and it was killing him. Damn it, Kara's life should be easier now that she was going to be his wife. Spending her entire life in poverty, working her ass into the ground-Simon wanted things to be different for her now; needed to give her a worry-free, happy life after the hell she had been through just to survive. God knew he had the resources.

Kara blew out a shaky breath before answering, "You rescued me from the streets, Simon. You sheltered me, cared for me, made me fall madly in love with you and loved me in return. You've given me every single thing a woman could ever want. Let me give you this."

Bullshit. Not enough. Not enough. She deserves more. Probably a better man than I am, but I can't give her up.

Shuddering as he breathed in her unique, feminine scent, Simon turned her around, slapping a hand on each side of the desk, imprisoning her. Denying this woman anything she wanted was hell since she asked for so little except his love, but he refused to give in this time. She had his love, his body, his mind, his fucking soul. Obviously, his woman hadn't yet realized that she had him by the balls every minute of every day.

Mine.

His mouth nuzzled her ear, crowding her against the desk, shoving his body into hers just to feel those lush curves molded against him. God, how he loved the way her body surrendered to him, yielded to him, melding them together with her willingness to accept him as though his flesh was part of her.

Kara's arms snaked around his body, her hands wandering beneath his t-shirt, her touch setting fire to his already hot skin. He groaned as she plastered her body against him, stroking his back, rotating her hips against his swollen cock.

His mouth next to her ear, Simon growled. "No contracts. Nothing between us. Not now. Not in the future. You're mine. You'll always be mine."

Her irresistible fragrance surrounded him, drowning him in desire, his body begging his mind to take her. Feral need engulfed him and he pulled her head back gently by her ponytail, covering her mouth with his as she parted her deliciously tempting lips to argue.

Kara whimpered a sweet little sound of need as his mouth devoured hers, Simon swallowed the noise with hungry lips, desperate to claim his woman, to brand her with his touch until she could think of nothing but him, needed nothing but him. She tasted like coffee, peppermint, and pure carnal desire, and it nearly drove him mad. He plundered, taking her mouth, groaning as her tongue slid along his, claiming *him*. His heart thundered against his chest wall, wanting to tell her that she had owned him forever, since the first moment he saw her. Probably, if he was honest, long before that. He had waited a lifetime for the woman he held in his arms, and he would never let her go.

Releasing her lips reluctantly, Simon buried his face in the side of Kara's neck, panting for air and struggling for control over his rampant, covetous emotions. His hands slid down to her shapely ass, cupping it, pulling the heat of her core against his swollen cock.

"Simon," Kara moaned in her husky *fuck-me* voice, her warm breath wafting over his ear.

Animal instinct slammed him in the gut, uncontrolled and wild. Nothing, absolutely nothing, was important at that moment except the driving desire to satisfy his needy mate.

"I love you," she panted restlessly, her teeth biting gently at his neck.

This time, her words went straight to Simon's heart, the pleasurable pain striking him directly in the chest. "I love you too, sweetheart." Resting his forehead against her shoulder, he closed his eyes, floored by the strength of her emotions, humbled by the fact that this woman truly loved him. Him. The man. Not the billionaire or the material things he could give her. He bore the scars of his past, inside and out, but Kara never seemed to see anything except a man worth loving. She was a miracle, his miracle. "No more talk about prenuptial agreements, okay?"

He felt her silky hair brush against his jaw as she shook her head, pulling back slightly to meet his eyes. Frowning at him, she answered, "We have to talk about it."

Nope. They sure as hell did *not* have to talk about it. She could drop the whole ridiculous idea and just kiss him again. And again. Simon wasn't about to make the most incredible, happiest event of his life into a fucking contract. "You know I already revised my will. We went over it." He'd made damn sure Kara would always be taken care of, no matter what happened to him.

She nodded slowly. "It's one thing if you leave me unwillingly by death. But what if..."

"Not happening," he replied swiftly, his jaw tightening at the thought of losing Kara. "This is forever. I'm not signing a damn prenuptial agreement. You and I are not a fucking business deal. This is about you and me. Together. For the rest of our lives." Simon's green-eyed monster was clutching at him, irritated at the possibility that anything could take this woman away from him. *Not happening.*

Pushing against his chest, she wriggled out of his hold. "I want you to know that I'm not marrying you because of your money." Her voice wobbled and her lower lip trembled.

Oh, fuck. No. "Don't cry. I don't like it." Actually, he hated it. Seeing her cry practically brought him to his knees, made him want to give in to just about anything she wanted. Luckily, she rarely cried unless it was tears of joy and Kara never used his weakness at seeing her cry as a weapon. "And it's always been quite obvious that you aren't after my money." *More than obvious.*

Giving him a wide-eyed, astonished glance, she replied hotly, "How can you know that? You supported me while I finished nursing school, paid my expenses, buy me outrageously expensive gifts. I want you to be able to trust me completely."

Shit! Seriously? The woman knew every one of his dirty little secrets, things that he had never revealed to another soul, not even his brother, Sam. "I've trusted you with every detail of my life, Kara. I trust you. I wouldn't be marrying you if I didn't. I don't need a prenuptial agreement. I don't want one," he rasped, trying to squelch his anger, his hurt over the fact that as much as he had poured out his soul to her, she still didn't completely trust *him* or the fact that their relationship would never come to an end. "If you had enough faith in me, you wouldn't need it either."

It took Simon about a nanosecond to regret the words, wanting to take them back the moment that they left his stupid mouth. Kara's beautiful face fell, every ounce of hurt showing in her expressive eyes that were filling with tears. *Shit. What kind of dumbass statement was that?* Instead of appreciating the fact that Kara wanted him so much that she was willing to give up any financial gain from their marriage just to show him how much she cared, Simon had slung the hurtful words at her out of frustration and more than a little fear. And the words weren't the least bit true. Kara had always had faith in him, even when she probably shouldn't have had any, even when he hadn't had faith in himself. Problem was, he wanted more, needed her to believe in *them* as a couple. Although she balked whenever he bought her something because of her past financial situation, Kara had never seemed to question the fact that they were soul mates, destined to be together forever...until the last few weeks. Her recent hesitance scared him, terrified him into starting to consider that maybe it was *she* who might want out some day. Her notion that she *owed* him and didn't want to share everything, especially his wealth, bothered the shit out of him. It made every lingering insecurity he had jump up to bite him in the ass.

Spearing a hand through his hair with a remorseful sigh, he told her softly, "I'm sorry. I shouldn't have said that."

He watched her carefully, his heart breaking as Kara angrily swiped away a tear that escaped from her liquid blue eyes as she answered, "You wouldn't have said it if there wasn't some truth to it. Maybe you're right. Maybe this is all a mistake."

His eyes turned dark and turbulent. "What kind of mistake?"

"Us." She gestured at him and then at herself. "Maybe we shouldn't be considering marriage right now. Maybe there's just too big a difference in our circumstances." Hands shaking nervously, she swiped at both her eyes, the tears coming so fast she couldn't keep up with them.

What. The. Hell. He'd waited, fighting against every instinct he had to make her his wife immediately, for nearly a year. And now she was questioning their upcoming marriage? Because he was wealthy? It wasn't like his money was something new, something unknown. He'd been a billionaire long before they met. Cursing under his breath, Simon stepped forward, reaching for Kara, but she pulled free, backing away from him with a strangled sob. Dropping his hands, he fisted them at his side. Jaw clenched, he forced himself not to reach for her again. In the year that they had been together, he and Kara rarely fought, and he had never seen her look this fragile...except for the time she had been attacked and nearly killed by two violent junkies. Even then, she hadn't looked this freaked out. When his woman was really angry, she got in his face and told him off. Their arguments fired hot and blew over quickly, usually resolved with a compromise and earth- shattering make-up sex.

Did we wait too long? Is she getting cold feet?

Wishing he had just thrown her over his shoulder nearly a year ago and swept her away to Vegas on his private jet, Simon answered, "We are getting married and you need to tell me what's really going on." Trying to keep his temper and his voice level, Simon clenched his fists harder, nearly cutting off all the blood circulation to his fingers. Kara had never backed away from him, rebuffed his attempts to comfort her. What had happened to the woman who would throw herself into his arms whenever she needed him? And, damn it, he wanted her to need him. Her rejection was killing him.

"I don't know if I can marry you." Her statement was released with a mournful sob.

Screw it. Simon couldn't watch her tears another damn moment and he didn't for the life of him understand what she was trying to say. All he knew was panic, desperation, and pain. Panic at the thought of losing her, desperation to fix whatever was wrong, and an unholy agony from hearing her say that she wasn't going to marry him. To hell with that. "You're marrying me. No fucking prenuptial. I need you, Kara. I'll always need you. Please don't do this." His statement was low, dangerous, spoken like he was barely able to contain his caveman instincts…which he was. Right now, he wanted to pin her to the wall and get inside her so deeply, take her so thoroughly, that she never again considered saying that she couldn't marry him. Hell, if she needed a reminder of how they fit together, how much he wanted and needed her, he'd be glad to give it to her. Right here. Right now.

Eyes wild, Kara backed up as he followed slowly, stalking her until he had her pinned to the wall beside the door. Her eyes shot to his face, then the door, and back to his face.

"Don't even think about it," he rumbled, slamming a hand beside each of her arms, boxing her in, cutting off any hope of her escape. "Talk to me," he demanded roughly, needing to soothe her pain…and his own. After spending the last year blissfully happy with a woman he loved more than life itself, Kara's sudden irrational behavior was out in left field. He was usually the one who was a controlling, dominant asshole and Kara was his voice of reason. "Are you okay?" he asked gruffly, his eyes searching her face. If something was wrong, he'd fix it. There was nothing he wouldn't do at the moment to make her smile again, take away the confusion and pain he saw reflected in her eyes.

As long as she doesn't say she can't marry me. If she says it again…I'll lose it.

Kara nodded hesitantly and then shook her head. "Yes. No. I don't know." She put her forehead on his shoulder and started to sob like her whole world was ending. Lifting her hands, she clenched at his t-shirt, fisting large portions of the cotton at his waist while she saturated the top half of the garment with her tears.

Holy Christ! Completely baffled, Simon wrapped his arms around her, his grip so tight she squeaked.

"Can't breathe," she mumbled as she sucked in a labored breath.

"Shit. I'm sorry. Kara, I don't understand." Simon loosened his hold immediately, keeping her pliant body against his, feeling completely helpless and hating every moment of it.

She twisted in his arms as a series of sharp raps sounded on the wood frame of the door and his older brother Sam strolled, uninvited, into the room.

Using the distraction to her advantage, Kara slipped from Simon's arms and made her escape. "I have to go. Maddie is expecting me at the clinic." Her explanation was rushed and breathless; as she hurried out of the open door like her ass was on fire, skirting around his brother as she went.

"No! Kara. We aren't finished. Don't you dare leave right now," Simon bellowed loudly after her retreating figure. Angry and completely desperate, he plowed after her, determined to track her ass down until she explained what was going on.

Simon never made it out the door, his brother jerking him back into the room with a strong grip on the back of his shirt. "Whoa, bro. Let her go. It doesn't look like you were resolving much of anything."

Simon turned to face his brother, absolutely livid. "Take your fucking hands off me. She's going to listen."

Sam let his brother turn, but firmly gripped Simon's shirt in the front, pulling his younger brother closer. Nose to nose, Sam drilled Simon with an icy stare, his voice as cold as his eyes as he replied, "Oh yeah, you both looked like you were totally ready to have a rational conversation." Sam shook Simon lightly. "Calm the hell down and think about what you're doing. The woman was dissolving in a puddle of tears. You love her. Is this really the mood you need to be in when you talk? You'll say stupid things that you'll regret later. Trust me."

Deflated, Simon's body relaxed, allowing Sam to loosen his grip. "Fuck. I already did." He flinched as he heard the door to the condo slam closed, his heart sinking to his feet at the realization that Kara had left their home. Left *him*.

Sam stepped back and grabbed Simon by the shoulders, asking quietly, "You good now?" His older brother was really asking if Simon had a grip on himself.

"Yeah. Yeah, I think so." Shrugging off Sam's light hold, Simon dragged himself back to his desk, slumping into his computer chair.

Burying his face in his hands, he groaned. "I really need to talk to Kara. Work things out. Something's wrong."

Sauntering to the circle of computers, Sam grabbed up a chair, swinging it around and seating his large body in the chair backwards. Resting his forearms on the back of the chair, Sam locked his fingers together and shook his head, causing the curly blond locks of his hair to ruffle lightly as he told Simon in a grave voice, "Bro, you really need to work on your communication skills. If that was working things out, I'd really hate to see what happens when you two are having an argument."

Chapter 2

"**Y**ou're not sick. You're pregnant."

Kara cringed, her head shooting up to give the vivacious redheaded physician walking through the door of the exam room an alarmed stare. Her jaw dropped and she shook her head. "How is that possible?"

Dr. Madeline Reynolds came to a stop in front of the exam table Kara was seated on and folded her arms in front of her. "You're a nurse. Do we really need a refresher on anatomy and physiology?" Maddie lifted her arms and made a circle with the middle finger and thumb of her left hand while inserting her index finger of her right into the circle. "Part A is inserted into part B, which may result in pregnancy." She shrugged, smiling at Kara as she dropped her hands to her side. "You know the other details."

"I'm on the pill, Maddie. It's not possible."

"You know it can still happen. And I think it's entirely possible that you conceived soon after you had that stomach virus between Christmas and New Years," Maddie answered, her voice contemplative. "You missed your period recently, didn't you?"

Kara nodded reluctantly. "But I still took my pill every day when I was sick. I didn't forget. And I didn't take any antibiotics that would interfere with the effectiveness of my pill," Kara answered, her voice panicked.

Maddie gave her a wry look. "But you were vomiting every day for a week. I suspect most of your pill came right back up and was never dissolved in your bloodstream."

"Shit, shit, shit." Maddie was probably right and Kara was experiencing some serious denial. All of the symptoms had been there. She just hadn't wanted to acknowledge them. Cursing herself for not thinking about the possibility that Maddie had just mentioned and using an alternative method of birth control, Kara's eyes dropped to the floor.

"You were sick. Don't blame yourself because your brain was scrambled." Maddie handed Kara the paper in her hand. "Here's the result of your HCG. It's positive. You know the test is pretty damn accurate, but we can repeat it in a week if you want to."

Kara took the test results from Maddie, staring down at the positive result in shock, her eyes flooding with tears. Again. "I can't believe it. Oh God, how am I going to tell Simon?"

Maddie plopped her ass on a rolling stool, wheeling herself between Kara's feet, which were dangling from the exam table. Snatching the test results from Kara's trembling fingers, Maddie dropped the sheet of paper on the table and grasped both of Kara's hands, staring up at her with a concerned expression. "You think Simon will be upset? Kara...I don't think he will. You're getting married in a month. It's a little soon, but I think he'll be delighted. And I know you want kids."

Kara looked down at Maddie, her expression grim. "I do want children. I'm thirty years old and I'd like to have more than one. But any time I bring up the subject with Simon, he shuts it down immediately. He wants to wait." She covered her flat stomach reflexively, sighing at the thought that she was carrying Simon's child. She wanted this baby desperately, already loved it. "I don't think he'll be happy. His expression looks pained every time I talk about it. And we fought this morning."

"About?" Maddie prompted gently.

"I was being a raving bitch. I haven't been myself for the last few weeks. That's why I wanted you to run a few blood tests. I think I knew I could be pregnant, but didn't want to admit it. I feel so emotional all the time, so scared. I had a premarital agreement drawn up by an attorney to protect Simon and he wouldn't sign."

Maddie squeezed Kara's hands lightly. "You know, I like that man more and more every day. Good for him. He trusts you enough to know that you would never screw him." Maddie smirked. "Not financially anyway. Any other billionaire with Simon's money would have already had your signature on a prenup the moment he put that gorgeous ring on your finger. Why would you argue about that?"

"I insisted he sign. He refused. Told me I didn't have enough faith in him. Then I told him that maybe we should reconsider this marriage because we were just too different. God, I don't even know why I said that. Simon is like a missing piece of my soul, my other half. I don't know what I'd do without him. We fit in every way except for the money. I guess I panicked."

Kara shuddered as she remembered the shattered look of pain on Simon's handsome, beloved face and wanted to start crying all over again. Why had she said that? Simon was her world, and she knew he felt the same. The man had suffered enough pain in his past. He shouldn't have to receive it from the woman he loved, the woman he wanted to marry and spend the rest of his life with.

"You're pregnant, girlfriend, and your hormones are raging out of control. It's normal to be a little touchy, do and say irrational things, and to have mood swings. Tell Simon. Let him understand and be there for you. You need him right now," Maddie told her in a persuasive tone.

Kara smiled at her friend weakly. "It's hard to believe that you once hated him."

"I never hated Simon. I didn't know him. I was just afraid he'd end up being a snake like his brother, Sam." Maddie's voice was soft, but it held a trace of bitterness. "It's pretty clear that he's not. He adores you, makes you happy. For that alone...I love the guy. But he's also a very good person. He's helped me keep this free clinic afloat with his donations."

The money that was donated belonged to Sam too, a charitable gift from the Hudson Corporation, but Kara wasn't about to mention that fact to Maddie. Sam Hudson and Maddie had a past--and things obviously hadn't ended well. Maddie never wanted to discuss it, but Kara knew that neither one of them were exactly over it, even though Kara surmised it was an incident in the distant past. "Sam's a good man, Maddie. He saved my life."

"Yeah. After he insulted you," Maddie snapped, irritated.

"He's not perfect, but he has a good heart," Kara argued. Sam *had* been an ass the first time she'd met him, but over the last year, Simon's brother had become dear to her, like a big brother she had never had. And he had saved her from two deranged criminals, risking his own life for hers. She'd forgiven Sam a long time ago for his actions at Simon's birthday party. He'd been a perfect angel since that incident.

"He's a man-whore," Maddie muttered fiercely.

Okay. Kara couldn't really argue *that* point. But Kara suspected Sam went through women like a surgeon went through rubber gloves because he'd never met the *right woman*. Or, he had met the right one...and she had gotten away. Sam never dated a woman worth keeping; he went out with superficial women who only cared about his status and money. They were all stunning to look at, but there was never any genuine warmth in a single one of them. Scanning Maddie's flushed face and volatile expression, Kara had a feeling that Maddie was definitely a factor in Sam's dysfunctional relationships with women. "Something happened between you two. Are you ever going to tell me what?"

"No. It was a long time ago and it's not important." Maddie released Kara's hands and rose to her feet, sending her stool backward with a practiced flick of her foot. "You need to start taking prenatal vitamins and see an OB doc."

"I'll make an appointment with Dr. Shapiro." Kara rubbed her tummy, still incredulous that she was actually carrying Simon's baby.

Boy or girl? She didn't really care as long as the baby was healthy. However…she *would* love to have a little Simon.

No doubt he'd be bossy and demanding like his daddy. And hand-some, with dark eyes and raven hair, just like Simon. Kara smiled, her eyes dreamy, hoping her son or daughter also inherited Simon's kindness, his generosity, his freaking off-the-charts IQ. Yeah, an adorable little replica of Simon would be incredible, and Kara knew Simon would be a wonderful father. *If he wants to be a father.* Strangely enough, she knew he would fall in love with the baby, even if he was initially reluctant. He'd spoil the baby shamelessly, the same way he spoiled her. Problem was, Kara didn't want to force Simon into fatherhood if he wasn't ready for it. Not that she had much of a choice now.

Maddie nodded her head. "Katherine Shapiro is an excellent OB. Good choice." Seeing the distant look in Kara's eyes, Maddie snapped her fingers in front of her face. "Hey, where are you?"

Kara's head jerked up, meeting Maddie's eyes with a guilty look. "Um…sorry. I was just thinking about the baby." *And Simon. Always Simon.*

"Are you okay? I know this was a shock." Gently, Maddie rested a comforting hand on Kara's shoulder. "Don't worry about the moodi-ness and being emotional. It's hormones. Tell Simon and let him help you. He'll understand your emotional behavior once he understands that it's caused by your hormones and pregnancy."

Kara gulped, wondering if he *would* understand. Dear God, she loved him more than anything or anybody else on earth. What if he didn't understand? Hopping off the exam table, not really wanting to think about Simon's reaction, Kara muttered, "I'd better get back to work," She was here in the clinic for her weekly volunteer shift and Maddie had patients to see. "Thanks for taking the time out to check me over. I thought I was losing my mind."

"You're pregnant. Pretty much the same thing," Maddie answered with a touch of dry humor. "Go home. The schedule is light for the rest of the day. I can handle it alone. Go and talk to Simon. You both need time to get used to this." She pulled Kara's unresisting body close and hugged her fiercely. "Everything will be okay. Simon loves you and you love him. You're getting married in a month and you can't cancel the wedding-I already have my dress!"

Kara hugged Maddie back, clinging to the petite woman for an extra moment. After Simon, there was nobody she loved more than Maddie. "Thank you, Maddie," she whispered softly, tears welling up in her eyes.

Oh, Lord, not again. How many times could one woman cry in a single day? I can count the number of times I've cried in the last five years on one hand, most of them because of something sweet that Simon did for me. I'm turning into a damn broken faucet that's constantly dripping water.

Emotionally, Kara knew she was a mess, her emotions swinging radically from one extreme to the other. Not even her damn body was her own anymore. She craved Simon's hot body every moment of the day. Sure, she'd always been like a female in heat whenever he was near, but now, she wanted to jump his bones every other second. Simon was insatiable, but Kara was betting she could easily surpass him in the carnal need department right now. And then, there was her growing urgency for food, cravings so strong they compelled her to seek out the strangest foods like a crazy woman. One day it was a hamburger, the next day it was chocolate. Today, it was ice cream. She'd do just about anything for a large bowl of the chocolate sundae gourmet ice cream in the fridge at home. Or maybe a gallon or two. Her stomach rumbled aloud at the thought.

Maddie's laughter flowed lightly over the room. "No morning sickness, I take it? Cravings?"

"Food and sex. Sex and food. Which one is more important, changes frequently. I'm a little queasy in the morning, but it doesn't last long and then I'm eating like a horse for the rest of the day. Sometimes I crave things that I don't even like. How could I have not suspected that I might be pregnant?" Kara answered, annoyed that her brain wasn't in control of her actions anymore. "If you're sure you don't mind, I think I'll go home. I have to tell Simon, so I might as well get it over with." Honestly, she wanted to tell Simon as soon as possible and hope he forgave her for treating him so poorly that morning. The look on his face earlier was nagging at her, tugging at her heart.

Maddie snorted as she turned Kara around and pushed her gently toward the door. "You volunteer your time here, Kara. Every damn week, even though you have a full-time job at the hospital. I'm grateful for your help, but you don't have to ask permission to leave. I'll be fine." Maddie hesitated before asking softly "You said you were scared? Do you mind if I ask why?"

Kara shook her head slightly. With her hand on the doorknob, she stopped, and turned her head to look at Maddie. She didn't mind her friend asking, but she wasn't quite sure she could even explain. "Have you ever had something happen to you, something so good that it's hard to believe that it's even real?"

Maddie hesitated before nodding slightly. "Yeah. Once."

Kara had a feeling her friend truly did understand. "It's like that with Simon. Sometimes I need to pinch myself to make sure that I'm not dreaming, that he's real, that he loves me. I guess I'm afraid that something this good will somehow be taken away, that it isn't forever."

"You lost your parents at the age of eighteen and didn't have any other family. Maybe it's the memory of that loss that makes all of this so scary, so terrifying to feel the way you do. Everything seems amplified when you're pregnant and you're running on emotions," Maddie answered thoughtfully.

Kara's eyes widened as she thought about her friend's statement. Had the death of her parents made her afraid of loss? "That's possible. I guess I just want Simon to know how much I love him and that it's not about his wealth. I've been scared lately, afraid that he won't understand that I love him for the man he is and not his money."

"The problem is, he already knows that." Maddie let out an exasperated sigh. "He isn't seeing your gestures to protect him or prove your love for him as reassurance, Kara. He's seeing it as rejection, a refusal to accept all that he is. Simon might have grown up poor, but he and Sam busted their asses to become successful. It's a major accomplishment in his life and you want no part of it." In a gentler voice, Maddie continued, "I understand what you're trying to do and I get that you've always been independent, but if your positions were reversed and you had more money than Fort Knox, wouldn't you want to share it with Simon, make his life easier after living a life of poverty?" Maddie waited until Kara nodded before continuing. "In his own screwed-up way, he's trying to take care of you. Sometimes men connect their own self-worth with their ability to take care of the woman they love. Yeah, it's old-fashioned and ridiculous, but true. Believe me; Simon has never had any question about you being a gold-digger. That's your hang-up, not his."

"I do accept him. I don't reject any part of Simon. I admire the way he and Sam pulled themselves up from poverty and..."

"Then for God's sake, drop the prenup idea and let the guy buy you stuff. If it makes him happy, what does it matter if he spends his money to give you something? You deserve it and he knows you aren't after him for his money. But you need to accept that he's richer than God and anything he gives you won't make even a tiny dent in his net worth." Maddie put her hands on her hips as she finished, giving Kara an admonishing stare.

"He already buys me things. More things than I need."

"Yeah. And you fight him over it. I understand that you've lived with almost nothing your entire life, so you think you don't need anything. You're going to have to deal with the fact that you're marrying one of the richest men in the world. If he were trying to buy your love or could only show his affection through material things, *that* would be a problem. But that's not true in Simon's case. He's just trying to be thoughtful, trying to take care of you. I say...let him do it and enjoy the things he gives you without feeling guilty. If you really want him to be happy, let him spend his money on you. Compromise. You're still living in survival mode, counting every penny you spend. I get that. But you don't need to do that anymore and Simon doesn't see his spending as extravagant. He sees it as normal because he's become accustomed to being wealthy. Understand?"

Kara stared at Maddie, comprehension dawning slowly. Compromise? Wasn't that what she had always *thought* she was doing? But was she really? Had she ever really tried to understand Simon's side of the money issue? Groaning inwardly, Kara realized that she *still* never bought anything that wasn't vital to her survival and she chastised Simon whenever he spent any money on her. For Simon, his gifts had been normal, equivalent to his lifestyle. They may have seemed over the top to her because she had always lived in poverty, but she was starting to see how Simon could interpret her behavior as a rejection.

"How did you ever become so wise when it comes to men?" Kara asked Maddie, knowing her friend rarely dated and had been raised in several foster homes.

Maddie shrugged. "It's easy to see as an observer. Harder to recognize when you're actually emotionally involved. I've watched you and Simon for a year now, seen your reaction on your birthday, Christmas, and any other time he gives you something nice. Instead of accepting his gifts with a smile, you chew him out for spending money on you. And I've seen his injured looks. He thinks he's giving you something that will please you and it doesn't. I think it's hard on his ego."

"Oh, God. I'm such a bitch. I didn't know. I didn't think about it that way." Tears sprung to her eyes. *Oh shit, don't start crying again.*

"Hey, don't beat yourself up over it. You're a survivor. Your attitude has gotten you through a lot of challenges in your life. There's no shame in that. I'm just saying that it's time to let go of that particular defense mechanism and relax a little. Let Simon give you some nice stuff, take a nice honeymoon. The man has a private jet. Use it." Maddie scooped up Kara's test results from the exam table. "Try to go somewhere other than Disneyworld this time."

Kara smiled at Maddie weakly. Disneyworld on her spring break was the only vacation Kara had ever allowed Simon to give her. "Hey, I wanted to go to the Magic Kingdom. I'd never been there before. It was wonderful."

"Save Mickey Mouse for after you have the kid. Let Simon fire up that jet and whisk you away to someplace romantic. There's plenty of time for family vacations later."

Kara grinned. "London? Paris? Italy?" They were all places she'd love to visit, but didn't think she could ever afford.

Maddie smiled back at her and winked. "Now you're talking. Think big. Very big. I have a sneaking suspicion that Simon wouldn't mind a very long honeymoon."

Kara opened the door and stepped through it, making her way to the front of the clinic with Maddie close behind. Scooping up her jacket from a hook near the reception area, she asked Maddie quietly, "You're going to have to deal with Sam for my wedding. Are you okay with that?"

Maddie's spine stiffened visibly as she reached for a file on the reception desk in preparation for her next patient. "Of course, He's nothing to me."

Hmm…Kara doubted that. "If you spend some time together, you might discover that he isn't quite the ogre that you think he is. Maybe he's matured since you knew him."

Maddie shot her a doubtful look. "Pleeeze! I do read the newspaper and magazines. The man still has a set of horns underneath those golden curls of his. Don't hold your breath on that assumption. You might pass out, and it wouldn't be good for the baby." She followed Kara out the door and into the reception area. "Headed for home?"

Kara slipped her arms into her jacket and zipped the front, a mysterious smile on her face. "Shortly. I have some shopping to do first. It is Valentine's Day. I need to pick something up and hit a few other stores. I had my lucky penny made into a medallion with a men's gold chain for Simon so he can't give it back. The jeweler was able to do it without ruining the integrity of the coin." The coin collector in Simon would have flinched had she made the rare penny into a piece of jewelry that would destroy the rare coin. "I need to pick it up at the jewelry store."

"I guess it is Valentine's Day. I actually forgot," Maddie answered, her expression distant and slightly sad.

Kara said her goodbyes and slipped out the front door, sending a silent Valentine wish to Cupid for Maddie to find the extraordinary man that her friend deserved.

Chapter 3

S imon paced his computer lab like a caged tiger, knowing the thoughts he was having about Kara leaving him were probably irrational, but he wasn't exactly feeling levelheaded at the moment. He'd felt better after Sam had left-his brother had talked some sense into his thick head-but after getting a text from Kara telling him that she would be home later than normal, he'd gotten anxious all over again, expecting the worst. He hadn't been reassured by her responses to his text messages, which had been incredibly vague. The only positive had been the fact that she had sent him a message telling him she loved him.

I love you so much. I'll be home soon.

Simon stopped pacing long enough to trace the words she had typed in her text message, hoping they would lighten his mood, give him hope. And maybe they would have, but he spotted that damn premarital agreement on his desk out of the corner of his eye, making him grunt with irritation.

Maybe I should have just signed it if it would make her happy. What does it matter? Is a stupid piece of paper really that important? He'd always take care of Kara, regardless of whatever agreement was signed.

Simon snatched up the contract from his desk and flipped the pages. Gritting his teeth, he picked up a pen and signed his name with angry strokes. Slamming the pen on top of the papers, he muttered, "Fine. It's done. The world isn't going to end because I signed the stupid thing." He was never leaving her, and he'd move heaven and earth to keep her at his side. The damn papers could just rot, collecting dust in some quack attorney's office, while Simon lived his life with the woman he loved. "I just want her to be happy," he whispered fiercely, hoping his signature would end her sadness. Kara's behavior the last few weeks was making him crazy. His woman was usually so serene, so upbeat and positive, even though life had thrown her a very rough deal. It was hell seeing her beautiful face with anything less than a smile. If the prenup was what she needed to bring her peace, he'd sign a hundred of them. Sure, he might not like the fact that Kara had doubts about them, had thoughts about them someday separating, but he'd do whatever it took to convince her otherwise. Maybe she just needed more time. Kara had given him so much, most importantly her unconditional love and support over the last year. If she could put up with his cranky, irritated, scarred self-most of the time without complaint-he could sign a damn paper for her. "I should have done it before," he said quietly, cursing himself for being so argumenta- tive about something so trivial. He knew Kara was sensitive about their differences in financial positions. He'd hoped she would get over it, begin to consider the fact that what was his also belonged to her, but he guessed she just wasn't there yet.

"Should have done what?" The husky, feminine voice flowed over him like fine silk, lilting softly behind him.

Simon turned, drinking in the sight of the woman he loved, his heart accelerating. "Should have signed the fucking papers when you wanted me to sign instead of fighting over it," he told her in a husky voice, needing desperately to have her in his arms, feel her warm softness against him.

Still in her soft pink scrubs, her sneaker-clad feet padded softly around the desk and picked up the papers, sending the pen that Simon had used to sign the documents rolling across the desk. "You signed them?" Kara sounded shocked, surprised.

"Yes. I'm sorry for what I said." And Simon *was* sorry. More sorry than he could convey in words, because he'd never been very good with flowery speeches or finding the right words to say to Kara. Honestly, most of the time he was obsessed with his need to possess her, protect her. Tender emotions and sweet words weren't exactly his forte.

Kara's gaze flew to his face, scanning his features as though she were looking for something. "Why? I thought you didn't want this."

"I don't." He shrugged. "But I want you to be happy. I know the money issue bothers you." He speared her with a dark look. "I signed them for you. But you're still not leaving me. Ever." And the papers would never be used or important. They were just a damn poor use of trees as far as Simon was concerned.

Kara's lips turned up in a small smile. Her eyes never left his as she picked up the agreement and tore the papers in two. And then ripped them again. And again. "You're right. I'm not leaving you. Not as long as you love me."

His heart racing, he replied, "That would be as long as I'm still breathing. Why are you doing that?" he asked, watching her scatter the little pieces of the contract across the desk.

"Because I never should have let money be an issue between us. I'm so sorry, Simon. So very sorry." Her voice cracked as she moved quickly around the desk, throwing herself into his arms.

Simon savored the contact, wrapping his arms around her, closing his eyes with relief. He kissed her temple, her cheek, holding her as closely as he could without crushing her. "I shouldn't have said what I said."

"I hurt you because of my own insecurities. You've never let money be a problem in our relationship, and I shouldn't have either. You were right. I was wrong," she murmured quietly against his chest.

Gently, Simon brought Kara's head to his shoulder, letting her rest comfortably against him. *Where she belongs. Where she'll always belong.* "I love you. I just want you to be happy again. You seem so sad. I don't like it."

Kara pulled back, but only far enough to look into his eyes. "I'm not sad, Simon. I'm emotional."

"I'd rather see you be happy emotional than sad emotional," he grumbled, kissing the tip of her nose gently.

Cupping his cheek softly in her hand, she answered, "You're an incredible man, Simon Hudson. Always so worried about my happiness, my safety, so willing to sacrifice for me. I love you so much it scares me sometimes."

Simon caught her hand and brought it to his lips, kissing her palm gently. "I never sacrifice anything for you. I love you. And feel free to love me as much as you want to. You won't hear me complaining." Simon couldn't hide his grin, knowing he would never get tired of hearing how much she loved him, even if she told him a hundred times a day.

Kara smiled softly. "I spent money today. Your money. Um…I mean our money. And I've decided that I need a car. Or maybe an SUV. Something…uh…with more space. And I want a long honeymoon. Can we use the jet?"

"Absolutely. Any place you want to go." *Thank God.* Simon's grin broadened as he asked her playfully, "Was it painful?"

Kara didn't even need to ask what he meant. Simon understood her. "Horribly. I started out on the clearance racks, but I couldn't find anything I wanted there so I had to move to the regular - priced stuff."

"Ouch." God, he loved this woman. "And how did that go?"

"Okay. My hand only shook a tiny bit as I ran my debit card," she admitted with chagrin. "I even went to get a manicure and pedicure. I've never done that before. It felt…weird…but I wanted to try it."

Simon laughed as he hugged Kara closer, reminded of just how few luxuries this woman had ever had in her life, how few things she had done that many women did on a regular basis and took for granted. "What did you buy?"

"A few things. And um…a new wardrobe. Bigger clothes." Her voice was hushed, nervous.

"Are you planning on gaining weight?" Not that he cared. She could wear whatever size she wanted, put more meat on her bones. Her curves would be lusher, softer.

"For a while. Oh…hell! I might as well just say it." She pulled back and put a hand on each side of his head, Kara's pensive eyes meeting his still-teasing look. "I'm pregnant. We're going to have a baby. That's the reason I'm so emotional. I feel like my hormones are taking over my brain."

Simon's jaw dropped and his face took on an astonished expression as he looked at Kara, his mouth moving, but no sound escaping. *Pregnant? She was going to have his baby?*

Emotions rolled through him, one after the other.

Fear.

Happiness.

Anxiety.

And a healthy dose of fierce possessiveness.

"How? Why?" Stupid questions, but they popped out of his mouth anyway, his brain still trying to catch up with his emotions.

Kara burst into tears, large drops rolling down her cheeks as her face contorted with remorse. "I'm sorry. It probably happened when I was sick. I didn't get enough of the pill in my system because I was vomiting. I should have been more careful. I know you don't want to be a father right now. But I already love our baby so much."

Our baby. Our. Baby. His heart slamming against his chest, he pulled her completely against him, rocking her gently. "Shhhh…it will be okay. I…I…oh holy shit. I'm going to be a father." Intense joy spiraled through him, making his heart swell until he swore it was going to explode.

"I'm sorry," she wailed against his shoulder.

"Please don't be sorry, sweetheart. It isn't your fault. Are you ready to be a mother?" He tripped over the last word, still incredulous that Kara was carrying their child; a baby conceived with so much love that he was ready to burst with pride.

"Yes. I want it so desperately. But I know you don't. You've never wanted to talk about it before except to say you wanted to wait." She sniffed and snuggled against him.

"It isn't that I don't want our child. I just can't fucking stand the thought of you being in that much pain, that something might happen to you. It's dangerous. Women can die in childbirth." Hell, he couldn't stand the thought of Kara being in pain for any reason. He hadn't realized that he had actually cut her off, unable to cope with the thought of her going through what she would have to suffer to bear his child. He shuddered, still fucking hating those thoughts.

His emotions warred inside his body. He wanted Kara to have his child with a longing so painful that it nearly knocked him on his ass. However, the thought of anything happening to her was making him demented, maniacal. Simon wanted to wrap her in his protection, never let her out of his sight for a moment. Maybe he wouldn't. Not for a very long time.

"It's not dangerous, Simon. Women do it every day. Most women say the pain is soon forgotten once they have their child in their arms." Her voice was breathless, hopeful. "You don't mind?"

"I mind, but not in the way that you're concerned about." It bothered him because he couldn't stop thinking about Kara hurting. And he was going to triple her damn security, whether she liked it or not. His woman was pregnant, which made her even more vulnerable. "I want a girl." A beautiful, sweet replica of her mother. "We need to move. Buy a place outside of downtown where she can have a yard. Maybe a dog. Oh hell, whatever makes her happy. And we need to be in a good area with good schools. She'll be beautiful just like you, so no dating until she's at least thirty." He scowled as he thought about some bastard laying a hand on his daughter.

His heart lifted as Kara laughed, pulling back to smile at him. "I want a boy. A sweet little boy like his daddy."

"Girl."

"Boy."

"Girl," he growled.

Kara sighed. "Healthy. I'll be happy if our baby is just healthy and happy. I don't really care. He or she will be dearly loved."

Simon felt his eyes moisten, his happiness almost too much to bear, even though he was fucking losing it about Kara's safety. "Me, too, baby. I'd love to have either one. I just hope the baby looks like you. I'll love our child so much and give the baby everything I never had." *A stable, happy childhood, security, love.* "Are you feeling okay? You said you were emotional. Are you sick? We should see the doctor. What else do we need to do? What do you need? Tell me and I'll get it for you." He sounded anxious, desperate. His gut clenched, his protective instincts gnawing at his insides. Kara was pregnant. Simon needed to research the condition immediately, find out what Kara needed to do to stay healthy. Didn't women need things when they were pregnant, special things? Oh hell, he didn't know a damn thing about pregnant women, but he needed to change that situation immediately. How could he safeguard Kara when he didn't have a clue what to do to protect her?

"I need your hot body and some ice cream," she answered in a sultry voice. "But first I need a shower."

"Me? You need me? Should we be doing that?" Sex was safe when a woman was pregnant, right? Shit, he really had to look *that* information up immediately.

"Oh yeah. We should be doing it a lot. I'm horny all the time. Hormones," she whispered as she gently took his earlobe between her teeth and nibbled.

Christ. He had no control when it came to Kara. His cock throbbed with the need to bury himself inside her welcoming heat. "We should be careful," he answered, his mind already filled with erotic thoughts, his caveman wanting to take control. *My woman. Pregnant. My baby.*

Mine. Fucking completely mine.

"I need sex. Lots and lots of sex. Hot, sweaty, crazy sex," Kara told him emphatically. "And I expect you to meet my needs since you knocked me up."

Yeah. He had. He'd planted his seed inside her and it had taken root. An animalistic, male satisfaction slammed into him. "How crazy exactly?" Simon shifted, his cock ready to explode inside his jeans. "What's safe?"

"Any way I want you to fuck me. I'm only at about five weeks pregnant right now. Some women get tired, sick or lose their sex drive during their first trimester, but not me. I want to get laid at least five times a day." Kara rubbed against him sensually with a small, breathy moan. "Don't be afraid to make love to me. It's safe. And I need you. In every way."

At that moment, Simon wanted to meet any needs Kara had, give her whatever she wanted. "I'll take care of you, baby. Always. And you'll tell me how you feel?" If she just wanted him to hold her, cherish her, be close to her, he'd do it quite happily. His inner beast might be snarling because of the way Kara was rubbing against him, but Kara's needs would always come first.

"Right now I want a shower. I want to orgasm. And I want ice cream," she answered insistently, moving out of his arms, walking toward the door, her hips swaying sensually.

Shit. How was he supposed to *not* act like a possessive maniac when he was marrying the sexiest pregnant woman on the planet? "I'm up for that." *Literally.* His cock was as hard as granite.

Simon followed in Kara's wake, catching up to her at the bottom of the stairs and wrapping his arms around her from behind. Hands stroking her still-flat belly, he whispered, "I love you. Ask me for anything and I'll do it. No questions asked, no negative replies."

She relaxed, letting her body rest against him. "I thought I just did." Laughing, she entwined his fingers with hers, both of them covering her stomach protectively. "I just...need you. I feel needy as hell. I'm not myself right now. Please try not to take anything I do or say personally. It's not you. It's hormones right now. I think they're eating my brain."

"Be needy. Be grouchy. I won't even tell you not to cry." Well... he'd *try* not to anyway. Shit, Simon hoped she didn't cry a lot. He'd be a wreck by the time the baby was born. "Just don't ask me not to worry, or be protective, or be concerned about your happiness and safety. I can't do that," he growled, his fingers clenching hers.

"You won't be bossy?"

Simon gulped. "No." Okay…maybe not *quite* so often.

"Or demanding?"

Uh…he could manage to tone it down, couldn't he? "Nope."

"Domineering? Controlling?"

Well, crap. She was hitting him where it hurt. "I'll try," he told her sincerely.

Kara burst out laughing, a full belly laugh that he hadn't heard in more than two weeks, a delighted sound that made his heart soar. She laughed so hard she snorted. "I give you twenty-four hours. Those traits are so deeply embedded in your DNA that you'll never make it more than a day." She continued to chortle as she went toward their bedroom, making his mouth go dry as she lifted her scrub top over her head, revealing an abundance of smooth, silky skin.

He chuckled, knowing she was probably right. But it wouldn't keep him from giving it his best. "A week at least," he called after her in an arrogant tone.

Her laughter rang out louder, stronger, drifting through the hallway and echoing back to him, making him grin ever broader. Damn it. She knew him too well.

Shaking his head, he walked to the kitchen to get his woman her ice cream.

Chapter 4

Maddie Reynolds chewed on her thumbnail, a look of total concentration on her face, as she flipped the pages of a medical file on one of her five-year-old patients at the clinic. It was seven p.m., way past time for her to get home and try to get some rest, but something about the case was nagging at her. She had to be missing something, something important. Timmy was tired, listless, having occasional vomiting and diarrhea, and it had to be more than a virus. The poor tyke had been that way for weeks.

Sighing, she leaned back in the chair of her office in the clinic, grimacing as she bit a little too hard on her fingernail. She'd need to consult a pediatrician, run more tests. Sending up a silent prayer that Timmy's mother would show up at her next appointment with her son, Maddie closed the file. The poor kid didn't have an easy life, and his mother wasn't exactly consistent.

"Hello, Madeline."

A husky baritone sounded from the doorway of her office, causing her to leap to her feet, ready to push the alarm button on the side of her desk. The free clinic wasn't in a good neighborhood and poor Kara had already come close to getting shot here.

"I didn't mean to scare you."

A cold chill ran down Maddie's spine, but not from fear. She recognized the voice. Eyes narrowing, she focused on the body and face behind that smooth-as-velvet masculine tone and the man standing right in front of her. "How did you get by Simon's security? And what in the hell are you doing here?"

Sam Hudson shrugged and stepped into the room as though he owned it. Even dressed casually in a pair of jeans and a burgundy cable-knit sweater, the man oozed power and arrogance, carried it on those wide shoulders like an elegant mantle. "They're my security too, Sunshine. They work for Hudson. Do you think they would do anything other than let me by them with a polite good evening?"

Arrogant bastard. Maddie's heart raced and her palms grew sweaty. She wiped them over her denim-clad thighs, wishing she hadn't showered and changed in the tiny shower in the back of the clinic before coming into her office. Maybe it would have been easier to face Sam in her professional attire, her hair confined in a conservative knot. Trying to push a flaming corkscrew spiral behind one ear, she stiffened her spine, trying to make herself appear taller than her five-foot-three height. "What do you want, Sam? This is hardly your neighborhood. And I don't think you need the services of a hooker?" Her voice was hard, brittle. Damn it. Why couldn't she act nonchalant? So many years had come and gone since that heart-shattering event with Sam. He was a stranger to her now. Why couldn't she treat him like one?

Moving closer, he answered darkly, "Would you care, Sunshine? Would it matter to you if I fucked every woman in the city?"

"Ha! Like you haven't already? And stop calling me by that ridiculous pet name," Maddie answered sarcastically, but her heart was racing and her breath caught as Sam moved close enough for her to catch a whiff of his enticing scent of musk and man, a spicy aroma that made her slightly dizzy. His scent hadn't changed, and it was still as tempting as it had been all those years ago.

"Why are you still here? My security alerted me that you were here after dark. You should be home. This neighborhood isn't safe during the day, much less at night," he growled softly.

"Simon's security." Somehow, she couldn't associate the two men, even if they were brothers. Simon was nice and had a heart of gold underneath his gruff exterior. Sam was the devil himself, Satan disguised as a GQ model, with more money and power than any man had the right to have. Especially a man like Samuel Hudson.

"What if some thug got through security, found you here alone and vulnerable?" He moved closer, so close she could feel his warm breath caressing her temple.

God, he was so tall, so broad and muscular. Sam had worked construction when she had known him years ago, hard physical labor that had given him a sculpted, perfect body. Strangely, it hadn't changed one single bit. How in the hell did a man maintain that awesome body sitting behind a desk? Backing away from his intimidating presence, her ass bumped against the desk, leaving her no space to move away farther.

"A man could take advantage of a woman alone in an empty office," he continued, his voice low, dangerous.

Maddie pushed against Sam's chest, trying to get free of her wedged-in position between him and the desk. "Move. Back off, Hudson, before I'm forced to send your balls into your throat."

His muscular thigh moved over hers, immobilizing the possibility of kneeing him in the groin. "I taught you that move, remember. And never tell your attacker your intentions, Madeline."

She craned her neck and looked at him, his emerald green eyes watching her carefully. Just as it had years ago, his handsome face took her breath away. He'd always reminded her of some ancient blond god, so damn perfect that his body and features should be carved in marble. However, at the moment, he might be as hard as marble, but he was far from cold. Heat emanated from his body in waves, his eyes just as fiery and molten. "Go fuck yourself, Hudson."

Sam's lips turned up, twitching precariously like he was trying not to grin. His hands splayed over her back, pulling her body completely into his as he whispered into her ear, "I'd rather fuck you, Sunshine. Much more satisfying. You're still the most beautiful woman I've ever seen. Even more beautiful than you were years ago."

Liar. He's such a damn liar. If I had been so desirable he wouldn't have done what he did. "Let go and get the hell out of my office." The bastard was playing her, and it was intolerable. She wasn't beautiful and she was nothing like the twiggy blonde models that he sported on his arm and took to his bed.

"Kiss me first. Prove to me that there isn't something left unfinished between us," Sam answered, his dark green eyes lit with sparks of fire, his voice hard and demanding.

"The only thing left unfinished is the fact that you never even said you were sorry for what you did. You didn't give a damn. You didn't-"

Maddie never got a chance to finish. Sam's hot, hard mouth smothered her bitter words, never asking, only demanding her response. His large, agile hands moved down her back, grasping her ass and lifting her to a sitting position on the desk, making it easier for him to devour her mouth.

Sam never just kissed: he branded, he claimed. Maddie moaned into his mouth as his tongue entered and retreated, entered and retreated, until she was breathless. Surrendering, her arms wound around his neck, her hands fisting his silken wavy locks of hair, savoring the fall of softness over her fingertips.

Wrapping her legs around his hips, needing to somehow find an anchor to keep her from drifting away in a tidal wave of lust, she allowed her tongue to duel with his, feeling his arousal against her heated core. Her hips surged against his erection with every hard thrust of his tongue.

Sam groaned, his hands delving under her sweatshirt, his fingertips stroking over the bare skin of her back, making her shiver with longing.

Maddie was drowning, lost in a sea of desire and need, slowly being pulled under the surface by a force stronger than her will.

I have to stop. This has to end before I'm completely lost.

Yanking her head back, her mouth disconnected from Sam's, leaving her panting for oxygen and completely shaken. Sam pulled her head forward to rest against his heaving chest.

"Shit. Maddie. Maddie," he choked out, one hand spearing into her curls, stroking her hair reverently.

Oh, God. No. She couldn't be sucked in by Sam Hudson again. Not in any way. She shoved hard against his chest, twisting away and lowering her legs until her feet hit the floor. "Get off me."

Fury built to a raging inferno inside her. How dare he use her, play with her because he was bored and she was the only available female in the building? Sam Hudson was a playboy, a man who took women to his bed and discarded them, finding another plaything soon after he was done with the last one. Did the man have a conscience? Did he care about no one but himself?

Maddie wanted to curl up into a little ball to protect herself, shamed by the way she had responded to Sam even though he was a complete dog. What kind of a person did that make her?

She shrugged away from him, turning to sprint for the door.

"Maddie. Wait." Sam's voice was husky, pleading, demanding.

He grasped her arm, swinging her to face him before she was able to get to the door. Maddie glared at him, her fury and fear battling for dominance. "Don't touch me again. Ever. I'm not the stupid, naïve woman you once knew. I trusted you once, and I forgave myself because I was young. I won't do it again. I don't have the excuse of youth to even justify being that stupid."

"You still want me," Sam answered vehemently, his eyes raking over her body, settling on her face.

Looking him straight in the eye, she answered angrily, "No, I don't. My body might respond to a gorgeous man, but it's just physiological, a sexual reaction. You," she poked a hand to his chest as she spat out, "mean absolutely nothing to me anymore."

"You want me to fuck you until you scream. I can still make you purr, Kitten," he told her arrogantly, a satisfied smirk on his face.

She shrugged, trying to force down her violent desire to slap the conceited look from his handsome face. "I wouldn't know. You've never fucked me. And you never will."

Wrenching her arm from his hold, Maddie vaulted through the office door, scooping her jacket from the hook by the reception desk and bolting through the lobby and out the front door of the clinic. Maddie didn't look back. She couldn't. One of Hudson's security officers escorted her to her car and Maddie drove away like she was a convicted criminal with the law on her tail, wanting nothing more than to get as far away from Sam as she could possibly get.

Maddie drove in a daze, two words playing through her hazy brain like a broken record.

Never again.

Never again.

Sam Hudson walked slowly through the reception area of the clinic, lost in his own thoughts. What the hell had just happened? He'd stopped to see if Maddie was okay, concerned that she was still at the clinic so late, a quick stop to make sure all was okay. Damn. Could he ever see the woman and not want to possess her, make her want him as much as he wanted her.

You've never gotten over her. You probably never will. She's haunted you for years. She got under your skin like a sliver of wood that's always a little bit raw and irritated, never working its way out again.

Stepping outside, Sam closed the outside door behind him. He glanced at one of his security officers. "Can you lock up?"

The man nodded. "Yes sir. Hope your meeting with Dr. Reynolds went okay."

Sam barked a humorless, self-mocking laugh. "Yeah. It was very informative." He lifted a hand to the other guards as he departed, making his way to his vehicle.

Yep. That meeting had gone really well, he thought darkly as he stepped into his Bugatti and started the engine.

You never even said you were sorry.

Her words tormented him, would probably always torture him now. "Fuck!" Sam slammed his fist against the steering wheel in frustration. Nope. He hadn't ever said he was sorry. Then again, Maddie had never given him the chance. Still, he should have said it, found a way to apologize. He hadn't had a chance back then, and he had just blown his second chance a few minutes ago.

What was it about Maddie that made him lose his reason?

You're acting like an asshole because she doesn't really care about you anymore and it's eating you alive. You might be able to have her body if you seduce her...but never her heart. Never again.

Once, years ago, Maddie had looked at him with eyes that sparkled with admiration, adoration. One stupid action, one idiotic incident, and he had washed that look from her beautiful eyes forever.

Leaning his forehead against the steering wheel, he closed his eyes, still able to picture the Maddie who had looked at him with respect and affection even when he hadn't had two pennies to rub together. It was ironic: now that he was one of the wealthiest men in the world, that she eyed him like a bug that needed to be squashed, a rodent that needed to be exterminated.

You'll see her again. She'll be forced to talk to you for Simon and Kara's wedding. The wedding was being held in his home, so Maddie wouldn't have a choice. He was the best man and she was the maid of honor. Maddie would have to at least be civil, and Sam knew she would. She was considerate and loyal to anyone she considered a friend. Her own feelings would take a back seat to making sure Kara had a happy wedding, one with no hassles or ugliness.

And no matter how Maddie treats me, no matter how she looks at me, I won't be a dick to her.

Sam sat back in his seat with a heavy sigh and put his car in gear, wondering if *that* were even possible anymore. Truth was, the years had changed him, made him into a man that he wasn't at all certain *he* liked anymore.

Find a woman, someone to take your mind off Maddie.

Snapping his seatbelt on as he backed out of the parking space, Sam took a deep breath and ran through a mental list of willing females...until he caught a tantalizing smell, an elusive scent that clung tenaciously to his sweater. *Her* fragrance. A reminder of what had just occurred in her office.

"Fuck! I can't do it. I can't be with another woman. Not now," he whispered to himself, pissed off that he had kissed her, felt her lush curves against his body. Now, thinking about spending the night in the bed of any other woman but Maddie left him cold.

Sam braked his vehicle at the exit of the parking lot, glancing quickly at his watch, grinning as he turned left instead of right, headed toward Simon's condo.

It was time.

Simon had called him earlier, informing Sam that he was going to be an uncle, and asking for a favor, which was a complete rarity for Simon. Honestly, there was nothing Sam wouldn't do for his little brother. He had failed to protect Simon once, and it wasn't happening ever again. Whatever Simon needed, he'd be there for him.

Thank God Simon had found Kara. Sam adored his brother's fiancée, wanting to kiss the ground she walked on because she loved his little brother unconditionally, made Simon happier than Sam had ever seen him. And Simon deserved that happiness, that kind of devotion from a woman. Unfortunately, watching Simon and Kara together made Sam realize just how empty his own life was, how desolate and superficial his existence had become.

Kissing Maddie, holding her again after all those years, had made things even worse. It was like something was awakening deep inside him, a sensation that was familiar, yet not. Certainly, it wasn't comfortable.

Forget her. Forget what it felt like to lose yourself in Maddie's softness, her scent, the feel of her lush curves and deliciously eager mouth.

Sam cursed, knowing he'd be sleeping alone tonight, taking himself in hand as he fantasized about Maddie. And this time, those memories would be much more vivid, newer, more real than ever before.

Fuck! He was so completely screwed...and definitely *not* in a good way.

Chapter 5

"Yes!"

Kara punched her fist in the air, ecstatic that she had finally conquered the first level of Simon's new game. Actually, her new game, the computer game Simon had designed especially for her, named after her. *The Adventures Of Kara* was awesome, not that she was surprised. Her fiancé was a freaking genius, and every game that he designed was unique. It was no wonder that she was completely addicted to anything Simon created.

Running a hand over the computer screen, she sighed. What man would spend countless hours on a game designed especially for her, a game that he never intended to reveal to the world?

Only Simon.

Kara swung the computer chair slightly, glancing at the clock. *Oops.* She had spent more time than she had intended in the computer lab once she had gotten involved in the game. But it was so incredible, so damn addictive.

The new computer game had been a Valentine gift from Simon, one of many, a present that she would always cherish because Simon had done this himself, probably spent weeks of his nearly nonexistent spare time designing it just to amuse her. Simon had led her up here over an hour ago to surprise her. He had left, grinning broadly, when she had sat down in the computer chair, unable to wait before trying to master one of his creations.

Kara shut the computer down eagerly, ready to find Simon and thank him properly. The diamond on her left hand caught the abundant light in the room, glittering brightly, making her heart contract painfully.

Simon's mine. We're going to be married. Have a child together.

Her sadness and hesitation had dissolved like they had never existed. Kara felt like herself again with Simon. She realized that her irrational fears had to do with the fact that she had suspected she was pregnant and hadn't wanted to acknowledge it, afraid of Simon's reaction to the news. She should have known better. Really, when had the man she loved ever disappointed her? If anything, he was way more protective than he needed to be. But that was Simon, and Kara loved everything about him, even when his high-handed dominance pissed her off.

Kara smirked, thinking about his promise to try not to be so domineering and controlling. He'd been good all afternoon and evening, taking care of her, making love to her gently, as though she would break because she was pregnant. The intimacy and tenderness had been comforting, something she had needed after the turbulent emotions she had experienced the last few weeks. However...she was about to tweak her alpha. Simon's sexual dominance was something she not only enjoyed, but reveled in. He was one half tenderness and the other half complete testosterone. It was time for her caveman to come out and play.

She stood, pulling the red silk robe she was wearing tighter around her body. It was strange that she hadn't seen Simon in over an hour. Usually, he would sit with her, work on one of his games while she played on the usage computer in the lab.

Her bare feet didn't make a sound on the plush carpet as she padded down the stairs, her freshly painted toenails peeking out from under the robe as she went. Looking down at her feet as she took the last step, she decided that maybe she would go for a pedicure again in the future. Her feet were smooth and it had been really relaxing. Maybe she and Maddie could go right before her wedding.

Her wedding. Simon was going to be her husband. Kara Hudson was a name she'd always carry proudly, knowing the sacrifice that both brothers had made to achieve their status.

"Simon?" Kara called to him as she entered the kitchen, perplexed when she didn't find him there. Surely he wasn't asleep. He never went to bed without her.

"In the bedroom, come here," Simon called hoarsely, demandingly.

A small smile formed on her lips as she moved toward their bedroom. Simon rarely asked; he instructed. Kara complied when she wanted to, and right now she felt compelled to follow his instructions. Curious, she wandered down the hallway. The door to the bedroom was partially closed, swinging open soundlessly as she placed her palm on the wood and pushed gently.

She gasped as her eyes landed on Simon, clad in nothing but her lucky penny on a gold chain and a pair of silk Valentine boxer shorts decorated with hearts and devils, completely bound to the bed. Heart racing, she rushed to the bed. "Simon, what are you doing?"

Kara had been in the restraints herself several times, once because it was the only way that Simon could have sex, and later just because it was erotic and sexy. Considering Simon's history, she couldn't believe what she was seeing. She blinked, and blinked again.

Both of his hands were restrained, but he opened one of his fists, revealing one of the heart-wishes she gave him every holiday, a tiny paper heart, good for one wish, one thing that he wanted from her. The tiny paper fluttered in his hand. "I wish you would believe that I trust you completely."

"No, Simon. No." Kara climbed onto the bed, tearing at the restraints in a frenzy of fear and panic, but the bindings held fast. Frustrated, realizing that she wasn't completely sure how to get them loose, she begged him, "Tell me how to release these." Desperate, she jerked hard on one of the arm restraints, needing to free him, not able to see him helpless. This had to be killing him. *Damn him.*

Was there nothing he wouldn't suffer just to prove himself to her? "You didn't need to do this. I do trust you completely."

"Kara, stop. Now. Before you hurt yourself." His voice was stern, rigid in a way that she had never heard from him before. And it stopped her in her tracks. In a more relaxed tone he added, "I'm not uncomfortable. Well...except for some minor swelling."

Kara slapped a hand over her racing heart and looked at Simon's face for the first time since she had entered the room. He was... smiling. A complete shit-eating grin that made her relax slightly and examine the situation. Holy hotness, the man was sexy as sin. All four of his limbs were bound and there was nothing on the bed except his body and the black silk fitted sheet beneath him. The black boxers were new, one of her many Valentine gifts to him this year, and they molded over his erection perfectly.

His erection? Simon was actually aroused? How was that possible? With his history, the things that had happened to him, how could he do this without emotional pain and distress? Searching Simon's face for any sign of discomfort, she found...none. His eyes were hot, devouring her, without a trace of unease.

"How did you do this? How is it possible to put yourself into these things?" All four of his limbs were bound snugly, judging by the lack of give when she had been yanking on them.

"Sam," Simon answered in a disgruntled voice. "I think the bastard enjoyed making them as tight as possible."

Slapping a hand over her mouth, Kara tried to stop a delighted giggle from escaping her lips...and failed. "Your brother did this?"

"I'm sure I'll never hear the end of it. I wanted to be naked, but he insisted that I cover my family jewels so he wouldn't go blind," Simon answered, unhappy.

Oh God, Kara would have given anything to see *that* event while it was taking place. She could only imagine Sam tying his brother to a bed, insisting that he cover his privates. Sam didn't know all of Simon's secrets, so he had probably just considered the situation odd, something he could tease his little brother about eternally, rather than finding it alarming. "I can't believe you did this." She plucked the heart from his palm and tore it up, throwing the tiny pieces over her shoulder. "Wish granted. But I already trust you completely, Simon. I told you it was hormones. And I've done some thinking. I realize now how my actions could have seemed like rejection or doubt to you, but it was my issue, not yours."

"I wanted to make sure you trusted me. Now touch me before I go insane," he insisted, his dark eyes demanding.

Kara looked at him, her breath catching as she drank in the sight of him, completely laid out for her pleasure. Simon was like a leashed tiger ready to pounce. Having him bound was heady, erotic. He was all rippling muscle and dark pleasure. And she was dying to touch him, and stroke that golden skin. "You are the sexiest man on the planet." Her voice was husky, aching with desire.

"I think you need your eyes examined. I've always thought so. I have scars, sweetheart. Ugly scars."

Yes. Simon had scars, a testament of his strength and courage. Kara would never find them unappealing or ugly. "Like a dark warrior, the hero of my dreams."

She reached out and ran her palm down his chest, tracing each scar with her finger and bending to lave them with her tongue.

"You're crazy," he groaned, straining against the arm restraints.

"You make me that way," she retorted with a laugh, continuing to tongue his chest, nibbling lightly at one nipple, cupping his silk-clad cock with her other hand.

Having Simon at her mercy was novel, and completely enticing. Coming to her knees, she shrugged out of her robe, nearly forgetting her hidden gift to Simon in her eagerness to touch him.

"Holy shit. What are you wearing?" Simon's voice was tortured, and she smiled at him, a naughty, seductive smile.

"Another Valentine gift for you." It was the raciest item she had ever worn for Simon, and that was saying something, because he loved sexy lingerie. Simon usually appreciated it briefly before he tore it from her body. The red babydoll dress was nothing but wisps of fabric with spaghetti straps. The top barely covered her nipples and the tiny strips of fabric surrounding her belly were transparent.

The panties were barely-there, leaving her ass exposed and her pussy only partially covered. "Of course, I had to shave. Completely. These panties don't cover much."

Simon gulped, his eyes hot and wild as they raked her body possessively. "Completely...bare?" He choked out the last word, his voice hoarse. "You weren't earlier."

Tossing the robe on the floor, she turned to him, running a finger over the outline of his engorged cock. "I had to do it when I put it on. Right before you took me upstairs to play my new game. It's wonderful, Simon. I think you should release it."

"For Christ sake, release it. I'm ready to explode," he grumbled, his breath becoming heavy.

"I wasn't talking about your cock, silly. I was referring to the game." She chuckled as she liberated him, watching his length spring free as she lowered the elastic of the boxers.

"Don't give a shit about the game right now," he huffed.

The computer game left Kara's mind completely as she touched him. Her hand wrapped around his silken member as she bent to kiss him, rubbing her sensitive breasts against his chest. His tongue thrust into her mouth as his hips lifted in response to her firm grip on his rod. Simon kissed her like a man possessed and she answered him with an equal passion, while her hand caressed the part of him that she was dying to have inside her. But that could wait. Simon had done this for her and she was determined to make it pleasurable for him. Extremely pleasurable. She meant to prod her caveman before she gave into her own urges.

Releasing his mouth, she knelt beside him, still stroking his velvet cock, taking her time to run her hands over every inch of his body. She might never get this opportunity again and she wanted to touch. "I'm having a craving," she told him in a sultry voice as she released him and slid from the bed.

"Kara. Get back here." His voice was both pleading and insistent.

Kara dashed to the kitchen, returning with a can of whipped cream. Shaking it sensually, she tipped her head back and opened her lips, squirting a stream of sweet cream into her mouth. "Mmmm...

delicious," She licked her lips, swallowing the frothy confection. Simon's dark, dangerous look as he watched her, mesmerized, nearly broke her. "There's only one thing that would taste better exploding into my mouth right now. Something I crave." She crawled across the bed, between Simon's bound legs.

"Kara." His voice was a warning, one that she didn't heed.

She dabbed the white fluff onto his ripped abdomen, his thighs, and finally all over his bulging cock.

She lapped at his abdomen first, enjoying the sweet taste of whipped cream, tracing every hard, vigorously contracting muscle.

Simon jerked on his restraints, groaning, "Kara. I'll make you pay for this."

She smiled as she licked his thigh. "I'm counting on it, big guy. And I do mean…big." His cock was straining, pulsating.

Moving to his other thigh, she nibbled and sucked, leaving a small mark with her teeth as she devoured the sweet treat.

Her pussy contracted as she moved to his groin. The panties of her outrageous lingerie were already saturated.

She purred softly as her tongue snaked over his groin, licking away the whipped cream softly, thoroughly.

"Fuck. I won't last. Goddamn it, Kara. Free me." Simon's voice was frustrated, and completely aroused.

She looked up at him, met his liquid brown eyes filled with desire, searching for any sign that he was uncomfortable in any other way but passionately. He wasn't. He was completely consumed with erotic pleasure, watching her, his only frustration the fact that he wasn't pleasuring her in return. "I thought you wanted to satisfy all my cravings," she whispered to him softly. "I crave tasting you."

Simon growled, his head dropping back onto the pillow as Kara took his cock into her mouth, her tongue circling the bulbous head.

"You're going to kill me," he panted heavily as her mouth consumed him completely.

Only with pleasure, big guy.

She took as much of his substantial length as she possibly could, tightening her lips around him, sucking hard, her head bobbing as she devoured him.

His hips rose, thrusting himself into her mouth as she came down for every stroke. Glancing up, she could see his muscles straining, his fists clenching the restraints. In that moment, Simon looked beautiful in his passion, his complete loss of control, his face harsh with ecstasy.

"Fuck. Kara. Sweetheart. Ahhhh...God. Yessss."

He shouted incoherent words continuously as she moved faster, harder. He exploded, his body glistening with sweat, his hot release flowing into her mouth so satisfying that she moaned around his cock as she swallowed. After licking every drop, she crawled up his body and kissed him, letting him taste himself and a hint of sweet cream in her embrace.

He tasted her mouth, finally ripping his lips from hers. "Bare pussy. Now." He strained at his bindings, looking desperate to be released.

Yep. It was time to release her caveman. "Help me." She had no clue how to get him free.

Simon gave her clipped instructions and she finally got his hands free. He sat up and deftly removed the restraints on his legs himself.

He was on her in a heartbeat, his sweaty, still-panting self completely out of control. God, how she loved him. Alpha Simon was on the prowl and sexy as hell.

He ripped her lingerie, shredding the top and bottom in a few hard tugs, completely destroying the ensemble. She sighed, admiring his brute strength, the ease with which he could get her naked. The desire to chastise him for shredding her lingerie had left her long ago. He would replace it later. And seeing him go completely insane with passion was well worth it. As usual, he was rough on the garment without hurting her.

"God, you're so fucking beautiful," he breathed heavily as he uncovered her shaven pussy. "Time for revenge. You want to play, little girl, you have to pay up."

Kara was more than ready for Simon's type of punishment, the type that would leave her breathless, begging and moaning. As his fingers traced her swollen, sensitive nipples, she moaned. She was so, so ready.

"Please, Simon."

"Please, what? What do you want?" he asked her harshly.

"Fuck me. Please."

"I think not. I'm having a craving of my own. My mouth is watering for some cream. Are you wet for me, sweetheart?"

Wet? Hell…she was beyond wet. "Yes."

She bucked her hips, but she couldn't budge his rock solid body. His moist skin plastered against her, but he was keeping most of his weight from her with his arms. Looking up, she met his wild, intense dark eyes, her body clamoring for his possession. "You're going to come for me while I taste *you*." His voice was raspy, and he buried his face in her hair, biting gently at her neck, before he licked his way down to her breasts.

She gasped as he tongued her breasts, moving from one to the other, as though he had all the time in the world to worship each sensitive nipple. Her core clenched as he moved to her belly, stopping to flick his tongue into her bellybutton, laying moist, hot kisses to her stomach.

Finally, right before she was ready to scream with frustration, he spread her thighs. She shivered as he blew a warm breath on her naked pussy.

"I can already smell your arousal, see how wet you are," he growled, his fingers trailing over the bare flesh.

She thrashed her head, needing desperately to feel his mouth on her. "Please, Simon. I need you."

His finger delved along her saturated folds, slowly meandering deeper. "Like this?" he asked, his tone demanding.

"More," she begged, ready to lose her mind if he didn't make her come immediately.

"Like this?" He circled her clit, his finger gliding through her slick flesh.

"More. Damn it. More." She was losing it, her body begging for him.

"Like this?" His mouth closed over her tender flesh, his tongue lapping, licking her arousal, consuming her.

Oh, God. Yes. Yes. Yes. Her hips lifted, trying to get his tongue deeper, faster. He parted her folds with his thumbs and buried his face in her pussy with a tortured reverberating sound, devouring her like a starving man, relentlessly flicking her clit as he completely consumed her.

"Yes. Please, Simon. I need to come." She grasped his head, threading her fingers into his hair, moaning as she pulled him against her, rocking her hips as he pleasured her with his scorching hot mouth.

He groaned against her flesh, the vibrations pushing her slowly toward insanity. Her climax engulfed her, consumed her, her body catching fire as Simon laved her over the edge.

Nearly ready to sob with relief, Kara cried his name as wave after wave of pleasure crashed over her body.

After he had wrung every ounce of pleasure from her that he could with his amazing mouth, Simon shed his boxers and crawled up her body. Kara opened her eyes, and saw the man she loved, raw and edgy, just the way she liked him. Just the way she loved him.

Kara's body was sated, but her need to have him join with her was almost unbearable. "Fuck me, Simon. Now." His erection jutted against the still-quivering flesh of her core.

"Mine," he told her roughly. "You'll always be mine."

"Yes. Always."

Simon positioned his hard cock at the entrance to Kara's begging channel, entering her with one hard thrust, taking her breath away. He filled her, completed her. She wrapped her legs around his waist and her arms around his neck, wanting to be as close to him as she could get.

Simon's mouth covered hers, suffusing her entire body with heat, taking her away to a place where only she and Simon existed. His cock pummeled her, Simon pulling almost completely out before entering her again, and Kara embraced the volatile mating. He was claiming her, and she wanted to be claimed by him.

Yanking his mouth from hers, he panted, "Tell me you're mine. I need you. I love you. You're never fucking leaving me."

"I'll always be yours, Simon. Nothing will tear us apart. I love you." Her gasping admission was barely out of her mouth before she felt her orgasm building. Wrapping her legs tighter around Simon's waist, she met his powerful strokes, their sweat-soaked bodies melding together seamlessly.

Kara flew apart, her body trembling and her channel contracting, nails biting into the skin of Simon's back. She cried out his name, rocking her fiery body into his, milking his cock as her orgasm crested and then let her come back to earth slowly.

"Fuck. Kara. Kara." Simon came, his explosive orgasm flooding her womb.

He rolled off her immediately, clutching her against him, pulling her into the protective shelter of his arms.

His chest still heaving, he choked out, "Did I hurt you?"

She shook her head, her body still quivering. "No," she whispered, still short of breath. "You gave me exactly what I needed."

Her need satiated, Kara kissed his forehead before burying her face in his neck, still trying to recover.

Somehow, Simon always seemed to know what she needed. Tonight, on their second Valentine's Day together, he had given her his unbridled passion and his deep unconditional love. Certainly, he hadn't needed to put himself in restraints to prove anything to her. But just the fact that he had been willing, had put himself completely at her mercy, humbled her beyond belief.

Kara sighed, wondering how she had ever been so lucky, how she had ever stumbled across a man like Simon, a man to whom she could surrender everything, a man who would always hold her love, her trust and her soul safely in his care.

"I love you. Happy Valentine's Day," she breathed softly against his neck.

"Happy Valentine's Day, sweetheart. I'll love you forever," Simon murmured against her shoulder, his arms tightening protectively, possessively around her.

Whatever challenges she and Simon might face, they would deal with them together.

"You'll always have me," she told him softly, sleepily.

"I know, baby. I'm the luckiest bastard in the world," he rumbled.

Kara fell asleep with a smile on her lips, and the contentment of knowing that she had found a love that would last forever. For a woman who had once been so alone in the world, it was the best Valentine's gift she could ever receive.

Epilogue

Maddie turned the page of the book on her lap, wondering why she just didn't give up and go to bed. It wasn't like she was really absorbing any of the written words.

"Damn it," she whispered, slamming the book closed and dropping it on the table beside the sofa. Honestly, she didn't want to go to bed. If she did, she would just keep remembering her encounter with Sam, torturing herself with memories of that scorching hot kiss earlier in the evening.

Swiping the remote control from the table, she pushed the button to activate the television, hoping she could drown out her thoughts with the ten o'clock news.

Her doorbell rang just as the news anchor started recounting the top stories of the day.

Who the hell could it be? She had no real family to speak of and none of her friends would come to her door at this time of night unless it was an emergency. She sprang to her feet and sprinted to the door, her heart racing. Looking through the peephole, she saw a man in uniform, a Hudson security uniform.

"Who is it and what do you want?" she called loudly through the door.

"Special Valentine's Day delivery for Dr. Reynolds," the man called back.

"Leave it and go." There was no way she was opening her door, even if the guy was apparently from Hudson.

"I understand, ma'am. I'll just leave it here on the doorstep." The uniformed man bent over briefly, then straightened again and left.

Maddie opened the door a crack, leaving the security chain in place. She watched the man get into his truck and drive away. Closing the door, she lifted the chain and opened the door, her eyes widening.

On her doorstep was the most incredible bouquet of red roses she had ever seen. There were several dozen, too many for her to count in her stunned condition. Lifting the heavy, sturdy vase that appeared to be crystal, Maddie lugged the roses to her dining room table. Placing them in the middle of the circular oak surface, she plucked the card from the middle of the arrangement.

She sat, her shaky knees barely able to support her legs. The card was small, the outside of the tiny envelope decorated with hearts and a cute little Cupid in the corner. The only thing on the front was her name. She opened it with trembling fingers, yanking the cardboard notecard from its surrounding paper. There, in handwriting she still recognized, were only two words.

I'm Sorry.

There was no signature, no other identifying markings.

Dropping both the envelope and card on the table, Maddie buried her face in her hands and wept.

~*~ *The End* ~*~

Mine For Christmas

A SIMON AND KARA NOVELLA

The Billionaire's Obsession

Chapter 1

"**N**o. I don't want to have another baby. Ginny is enough," Simon Hudson insisted gruffly to his wife.

Kara Hudson gave her husband of two years an obstinate look. But really, it was difficult to get truly angry at Simon. Her eyes roamed over his fierce expression as he held their sleeping baby closely against his chest. How did a woman get irritated with the man who was holding their child in his arms as if she was the most precious thing in his life?

She and Simon had had this discussion about having another baby several times over the last few months. Kara didn't want Ginny to be an only child. She knew what that was like; the loneliness had been almost unbearable when she'd lost her parents in a car accident right after she graduated from high school.

Kara hadn't always been rich, married to one of the wealthiest men on the planet. Simon had rescued her from homelessness, and then proceeded to turn her inside out with a fierce, protective, all-consuming love that had changed her entire existence. Her husband might be one of the most stubborn men on the planet, but she loved him with every fiber of her being.

That's why I hurt so much right now. I need him to want me the way he used to, to consider having another baby together so Ginny isn't an only child like I was.

It wasn't like she wanted another child immediately. Ginny was only sixteen months old. But Kara at least wanted to *discuss* it. She couldn't figure out Simon's reasoning for being so adamant about not having another baby someday. He was an incredible daddy, and he loved their daughter so much, but he seemed almost terrified of having another child. Crossing her arms in front of her, she asked him calmly, "So this is going to be all your decision?"

"Fuck," was Simon's grumbling response. "I can't win. I want you to be happy, but I don't want you to have another baby."

The frustration on his face made Kara's heart melt. He always wanted her happiness. Most of the time they compromised when they didn't agree, but this wasn't really a situation where any give-and-take was possible. They either had a baby…or they didn't. Moving forward, she gently traced the scar on Simon's whiskered cheek, her heart skittering as his eyes flared with heat. "I want you to be happy, too. You adore Ginny. I don't understand."

Things had changed since their daughter was born, Simon's previously fierce desire for her body seemingly diminishing. At five-foot-eight, Kara could carry some extra baby weight that she hadn't managed to take off, no matter how hard she tried. But the additional pounds definitely showed, her figure more rounded, and probably not as attractive. Simon now treated her with gentle tenderness, like she was as fragile as blown glass. Every time they had sex, he used a condom, even though she was on birth control.

No more spontaneous, carnal sexual interludes.

No more uncontrollable passion, both of them unable to wait until they had torn each other's clothing off to satiate themselves.

No more caveman possessiveness, when her husband had been a dominant beast, demanding her surrender.

And she missed all of those things. Badly. Simon could still drench her panties with one look from those dark eyes of his, make her want to grasp his coarse, dark hair and kiss him until he lost control. The problem was, he didn't lose control. Not anymore. The condom usage and the lack of passion had made her afraid to even try to test his boundaries. She was too afraid that she couldn't cross them anymore, and it would crush her heart to have verification that he didn't feel the same way about her as he had when they were first married.

He was giving her one of his dark stares, stroking a gentle hand down Ginny's back in an unconsciously protective manner as he answered hoarsely, "I can't do it again, Kara. I can't."

She took her hand away from his face, dropping it to her side. "Okay," she relented. "I'm going to work out. Can you put Ginny down for her nap?" Kara needed a good, hard run on the treadmill. It was obvious that Simon wasn't in the mood to talk, and this wasn't a situation where they could negotiate.

Not waiting for him to answer, she bit her lip to keep her tears from falling as she turned and walked toward their home gym.

"Kara?" Simon called after her in an urgent, yet strangely hesitant tone.

She stopped, but didn't turn around. "Yes?"

"You and Ginny make me happy. I don't need anything more," he answered in a low, serious voice. "But if you really won't be happy without having another baby, I'll think about it," he grumbled unhappily.

She turned and gaped at him, astonished that he was backtracking.

He's doing it for me, even though I can see it's killing him to even think about it.

Nodding slowly, she swallowed hard as she looked at the heart-wrenching sight of Simon and Ginny together. Dressed in jeans and a tan fisherman's sweater, her husband was the hottest man on the planet to her. Although Kara was fairly certain that Simon had gotten over being self-conscious about his scars, she could never really explain to him that there had never been another man who moved her like he did—not even close. Her husband and child were her entire life now. "I'll think about it, too," she agreed huskily. "Maybe it wouldn't be so horrible for Ginny to be an only child. It was just hard for me because my parents died when I was so young."

"Ginny will never be in the position you were in, sweetheart," Simon promised. "Even if she's an only child, I'll give her enough love to make up for not having siblings. And she'll never be alone and penniless," he vowed fiercely.

"I know." Kara's response was gentle, knowing Simon had already made sure Ginny's future was secure. And her daughter would always have Simon's mother and her Uncle Sam and Aunt Maddie. Ginny adored her cousins, Noah and Brianna. She probably wouldn't really feel the lack of family in the future.

"I'll take care of Ginny right now. Relax," Simon demanded.

Kara smiled at him weakly, loving to hear him being his usual bossy self. She'd learned a long time ago that he wasn't really arrogant; his sometimes overbearing dominance was manifested by protectiveness and not selfishness. "I'm going to torture myself on the treadmill. It's hardly relaxing." Turning again, she made her way to her workout, pondering Simon's comments.

Maybe I'm overreacting because of my own history. I love my daughter, and I don't really feel a desperate need to have another child. But Simon's such a good father. Why doesn't he want another baby?

As she entered their home gym, her blue eyes caught her own image in the mirror, and she frowned. Her dark brown hair pulled back in a ponytail, her rounded curves covered by a pair of gray yoga pants and a matching t-shirt, Kara knew she looked frumpy. She'd never been anything more than acceptable in the looks department, but Simon had always salivated over her like she was a goddess – at least he had, before Ginny was born. She'd never understood what he saw in her that was so irresistible, but she'd loved it. Not that he treated her badly now—he spoiled her and Ginny rotten—and he was still the same bossy, ultra-possessive alpha male she'd fallen in love with, but sometimes he was....emotionally distant. Especially since she'd brought up having another child a few months ago.

Mounting the treadmill with determination, she started off slow, increasing the speed quickly as she warmed up, her sneakered feet pounding on the moving surface the only sound in the room.

She and Simon used to exercise together, but they couldn't do that anymore. Usually they had to trade off, each watching Ginny for the other so they could do their daily workouts. Simon worked himself hard every single day, and he had a hot, muscular body as a result. Personally, she'd been slacking, working out sporadically when she wasn't working at her job as a nurse in her best friend's clinic or taking care of Ginny. Okay…Maddie wasn't *just* her best friend anymore. Maddie was also her sister-in-law now, since she'd married Simon's older brother, Sam. Kara had cut way down on her work hours since Ginny's birth, only working one or two days a week. Since Maddie had given birth to twins, she'd become more of a medical director at the clinic rather than a practicing physician. The overprotective Sam made sure she had plenty of time at home with their babies.

Panting as she pushed her body harder, Kara tried not to remember all of the sexy times she and Simon had had in this gym. When she'd first gotten pregnant, Simon had wanted to move out of their penthouse, find a home outside the city somewhere. Eventually, she'd convinced him to stay—the last thing she had wanted to do when she was sick and pregnant had been to move. Besides, they'd made an adorable nursery for Ginny in a room close to the master bedroom, and the penthouse was so enormous that they could probably build an entire playground in one of the bonus rooms. Simon's computer lab was on the second floor, taking up one of the extra spaces, but there were plenty more bedrooms and spaces that they weren't even using.

Kara was startled out of her thoughts as the treadmill slowed down quickly, a large masculine hand slamming down on the controls to reduce her pace down to a walk. "What the hell are you doing?" Simon's annoyed bellow echoed through the gym. "Are you trying to kill yourself?"

Coming out of her daze, her chest heaving, Kara glanced down and was surprised at the distance and speed she'd been doing. Unable to speak, she simply shook her head at Simon, struggling for air, her heart racing inside her chest wall. Grasping the bars on the treadmill, she walked slowly, her muscles screaming with pain.

"You weren't doing those speeds and that distance even before you were pregnant and worked out every day. It's too damn much. You'll hurt yourself." Simon's voice held irritation.

She knew she'd been pushing too hard, determined to lose her baby weight.

"Five more minutes of that shit and you'd have keeled over," he stated angrily, watching her carefully as he stopped the treadmill completely.

His muscular arm wrapped around her waist and bodily lifted her off the treadmill, and then scooped her up and strode toward the living room.

"I need to shower," she told him, breathless, as she wrapped her arms around his neck. Inhaling his intoxicating scent, she smiled as she realized it included a hint of baby powder, which she found incredibly appealing. Simon could change a diaper expertly, but he still hadn't managed to not make the powder fly everywhere when he was using it.

"We need to talk." Simon was unyielding. "You were starting to cry earlier. I don't like it." He dropped onto the sofa in the living room, taking her with him and situated her on his lap. "I want to know why."

Simon never liked it when she cried—under any circumstances. Even if she cried happy tears, he didn't like it.

"I'm fine," she assured him, wanting to cry because of the way he cared about how she was feeling. She hated feeling even slightly disconnected from him, and since she'd started keeping her negative images of herself quiet, she'd thrown up a wall between them that was hurting her heart.

"If this is about having another baby—"

"It's not." She tried to wiggle off his lap because she knew she was heavy and she was stinky, but he wrapped his steely arms around her waist, keeping her exactly where she was. She relented with a sigh, knowing exactly how stubborn Simon could be. If he'd decided she was staying…she wasn't going anywhere. "I'm beginning to realize how selfish I was being. My maternal instinct is satisfied.

I don't *need* another baby to make my life complete. I was already ecstatic because I had you, and Ginny is a miracle to me. I guess I worried because I was so alone after my parents died. But you're right. It will never be like that for Ginny." Kara's parents had been dirt poor, but they'd been happy. Unfortunately, they'd been her only living relatives, and when they'd been killed so suddenly and traumatically, she had been lost without them.

"I'm being selfish, too," Simon rasped. "But I can't watch you go through that kind of pain again. I barely lived through Ginny's birth. I was caught between the miracle of you struggling to bring our child into this world, and the fucking agony you were in. It has nothing to do with not wanting another child with you, but I can't do it." He released a masculine sigh. "And then there was the endless colic and teething. Jesus, you looked like you were going to drop over at any moment during those months. I don't want to see you look that tired and worn out again."

"You were just as tired, and you were always right there with me," Kara argued, acknowledging that those had been difficult months, endless nights with little or no sleep for both of them.

"That's different," Simon said belligerently.

Kara pulled back, only to meet his ferocious expression. "That's why you don't want another child? Because you think it will be painful and difficult for me?" Her eyes filled with tears, the enormity of the reasons for Simon's hesitance slapping her in the face.

It's all for me, because of me. He's trying to protect me...as usual. Had she not been so wrapped up in her negative imaginations, she might have realized why he was being hesitant earlier.

He looked back at her, their gazes clashing together and holding. "Why the hell else would I object?" Simon asked, perplexed.

She reached out and stroked his cheek with her palm. "Oh, Simon," she sighed, hating herself for never asking him exactly *why* he didn't want a child when they'd discussed it before. She'd been too busy wondering if he was losing his passion for her, if she was less attractive to him now. Her damn post-pregnancy insecurities were getting to her. "I love you."

His grip tightened convulsively around her waist. "I love you, too. That's why I don't want you to hurt anymore."

Kara's heart ached as she glanced at his agonized expression. With Simon, everything was black and white: if something would hurt her, he'd do whatever it took to avoid it. "The pain was quickly forgotten as soon as I held Ginny for the first time," she told him softly.

Simon shook his head, the movements stubborn. "Not for me. Fuck. I still have nightmares about you screaming, of being terrified something bad was going to happen to you. That was the longest day I've ever had to live through, and I think that one damn day took years off my life."

Kara bit her lip to keep from smiling. She'd told Simon many times that if he didn't stop saying *bad* words, Ginny was one day going to add them to her limited vocabulary. She hadn't seen him curse in front of Ginny since she'd told him that, but Simon would never be an angel. He'd been through too much, lived his early life so tough that he was lucky he'd survived, much less become a self-made billionaire along with Sam. The fact that he could still be so sensitive to her needs constantly amazed her. He'd never been able to stand to see her unhappy or in pain. She knew it, but it still astounded her. "You're an amazing man, Simon Hudson." Leaning forward, she kissed him softly and backed away again, aware that she was still sweaty and smelly. "I forgot all about the pain very quickly. And those colicky days, the teething and sleepless nights are all part of being a new parent. It's over. Let it go." She wanted him to stop tormenting himself. He'd been there with her every step of the way—except for the actual labor pains, and he'd been up whenever she was up with Ginny, even though he'd needed to work the next day.

"It can't happen again. Not if we have a choice and it doesn't matter to you if we have another child," he said gruffly.

"It doesn't matter. And it won't happen again. I'm okay with not having another child." Watching the agony in Simon's expression had convinced her having just Ginny would be fine. In reality, she *could* end up pregnant again someday. Birth control was amazingly effective, but there was always a tiny, tiny chance that she could still get pregnant. However, she wasn't about to remind Simon of that little fact. He'd never get rid of the condoms.

His muscles relaxed, and he shot her a relieved grin. "Thank Christ!"

Her heart lighter, she asked him teasingly. "Are you going to let me take a shower before Ginny wakes up? I smell."

"It's not like I haven't had your sweaty body in my arms before, sweetheart. Except those times were a lot more satisfying," he reminded her in a graveled voice.

"We were both sweaty." Kara wanted to remind him that they hadn't had hot, sweaty sex in a long time, but she didn't. Did it matter if their sex life had mellowed out when they both loved each other? Having a child was wonderful, but exhausting. Wasn't it natural for things to change?

"Don't work out like that again. It's dangerous," Simon warned ominously.

"I know."

"And Ginny isn't here. Mom and Michael took her for the night."

Kara gave Simon a shocked look. He rarely let their daughter out of his sight. "Surrounded by security?" Knowing Simon, he'd likely sent an entire army of his security detail to watch over Ginny while she was with his mother and her new husband. Ginny's grandparents adored her, but Kara was surprised that Simon had relented to an overnight visit.

"There are so many agents with them that their cupboards will be bare tomorrow just from feeding them all," Simon agreed without remorse.

Kara chuckled. "She won't like it." She moved off his lap, and he finally let her go. Helen Hudson was an independent woman who ran her own restaurant and had never allowed her sons to put their security anywhere near her. Even though she'd finally relented and married her live-in boyfriend, Michael, she was still the same kind, feisty woman Kara had always known. And Helen had no problem taking her sons down a peg or two when they deserved it, billionaires or not.

"She'll have to get used to it if she wants to take her granddaughter overnight. I don't compromise on security for you and Ginny," he replied ruthlessly.

Don't I know it!

She and Simon used to argue endlessly about the legions of security he'd put on her ass. Now, she didn't bother. She usually had Ginny with her, and she wanted her daughter protected just as much as Simon did. "So we're alone tonight?" she asked, heat beginning to bloom in her at the thought, realizing they hadn't had any time together without Ginny since their daughter was born.

"We are," Simon answered, his eyes smoldering, looking up at her as she stood. "I plan to take my wife out to dinner and spend some time alone with her."

Kara shivered at the flash of fire in his gaze. "I'll shower quickly. It will be nice to have a night alone." Ginny was her heart, but she and Simon hadn't spent a night with just the two of them together since their daughter had been born.

"Nice? It will be much better than nice, sweetheart," he growled.

"I hope so," she whispered to herself as she scurried off to the bathroom, happy that she and Simon had talked about one of the things standing between them right now. They spent so much time talking about Ginny, scurrying from one task to another, that they'd forgotten how to talk about themselves as a couple.

Somehow, I have to tell Simon how I feel about our love life.

Had she really been afraid of how he'd respond, or had she just been too busy being a mother?

I'd trust him with my life. I've always trusted him with my feelings, and he's never let me down yet.

Hopefully they could resolve all of the issues they'd put aside for so long…tonight.

Chapter 2

Kara entered the kitchen nervously, knowing that what she was wearing now hugged her curvier body tighter than it had before she'd given birth. Her little black dress seemed even smaller than before, the skirt flirting with her knees and the silky material clinging to her fuller hips and breasts. Leaving her hair down, she'd done her makeup carefully, feeling more feminine than she'd felt for a long time. Digging into the drawer, she'd donned her sexiest lingerie set, another item of clothing she hadn't bothered with for a while. She'd slipped on her three inch stiletto heels with no worries. They might make her taller than some men, but Simon would still tower above her. Her husband was so muscular and tall that he'd been the first man to actually make her feel petite.

Her jacket on her arm and her small clutch purse in hand, she looked around the large room, spotting Simon leaning against the counter, his back to her, talking on his cell phone.

Kara moved into the kitchen, the clicking of her heels on the tile floor causing Simon to turn around.

"I'll call you later, Mom." Simon switched the phone off and dropped it into the pocket of his suit, his gaze never leaving her as it roamed over her body possessively.

"Is everything okay at your Mom's?"

"Everyone's fine," Simon answered distractedly, his covetous stare never wavering.

Kara sighed, eyeing her gorgeous husband in a dark gray suit and burgundy tie. "You're looking very handsome, Mr. Hudson," she teased, trying to get her racing heart under control. Even after two years of marriage, Simon got to her, especially when he was looking at her like he wanted to devour her whole.

He stalked toward her like a predator, his eyes flaring with hunger. "You look beautiful, but I'm not sure I like that dress," he growled.

Kara's heart sank. "It looks too tight?"

"It makes you look like every man's goddamn fantasy, and I don't want you to be any man's fantasy except mine," he grumbled unhappily as he stopped in front of her.

Kara let out a startled laugh. "You're the only one crazy enough to think I look good." She was letting her own insecurities get to her. Simon had never, ever criticized the way she looked. In fact, he'd always made her feel like the most desirable woman in the world. Even when she'd been at her frumpiest since she'd given birth, he'd told her she was beautiful. She just hadn't believed it.

"You don't just look good. You look hot and too damn sexy." He speared a hand through her hair and tilted her head up.

Her breath hitched as she heard a possessive, feral tone in his voice that she hadn't heard in a long time, the sound of a man who was about to lose control. She exhaled into his mouth as he gave her a warm, gentle, tender kiss on the lips before releasing her to help her put on her jacket.

Did I really think he was going to tear my clothes off right here in the kitchen and take me?

Kara loved the tender side of Simon, but she missed her out-of-control husband who had to have her, needed to possess her and know that she was his.

He guided her out the door and to the private elevator for the penthouse without saying another word. Breaking the silence as they stood by the doors, she asked curiously, "Where are we going?"

Letting her into the elevator first before following her, he answered, "I made a reservation at your favorite Italian restaurant."

"Oh, God," she moaned. "The pasta will go right to my hips. I'm trying to lose weight."

"Why?" Simon asked, sounding perplexed as he pushed the button for them to go down to the ground floor.

Her head snapped up and she gaped at the confused look on his face. "You know I've gained weight since I had Ginny. I haven't lost my baby weight. I don't feel...sexy anymore," she confessed, knowing she never *had* felt sexy until she met Simon.

It's time to step up to the plate and tell him about my insecurities. I don't want to hide my emotions from him anymore.

Simon's face grew stormy and he reached out and punched the emergency stop button with an angry grunt. "Is that the reason why you were nearly killing yourself on the treadmill? And why you're barely eating?"

"I'm eating," she argued.

"Not enough," he grumbled, crowding her against the wall of the elevator. "You think you're not sexy?" He pinned her to the wall of the plush elevator with his muscular body, a hand on both sides of her head, his body an impenetrable wall against her.

"We don't have sex the way we used to, and I know I'm carrying extra weight," she blurted out without censoring herself, letting Simon know exactly how she was feeling.

"Jesus Christ," Simon hissed irritably. "You're the mother of my child now. I can't be the same selfish bastard that I used to be. You're exhausted taking care of our child."

"I'm also a woman," she reminded him hesitantly. "I need you."

"You are *my* woman," his forceful voice informed her. "*My* wife. But you never seemed to want me. I knew you were tired, and you fucking shied away from being naked in front of me all the time. I thought you were sending me signals that you were either too tired or not in the mood, and I didn't blame you. I tried to help as much as I could with Ginny, but it wasn't enough."

Kara froze as she gazed up at his face. She *hadn't* wanted to be naked in front of him, and she'd breastfed Ginny until she was a year old. The first months had been rough, her daughter waking during the night wanting feeding. Then came the colic, and lastly the teething. Kara's priority had been taking care of her daughter, and she probably *hadn't* been in the mood. "I was tired until Ginny got past the colic and teething," she admitted. "After that, the exhaustion got better. But I didn't want you to see my body because of the extra weight and my stretch marks. I feel...unattractive, Simon." She wondered if this was how all women felt after having a baby. She hadn't been herself, barely taking time to shower in those early months when Ginny needed her constantly.

Simon pinned her hands over her head with a husky, tortured groan. "You're the most beautiful woman I've ever seen, and you're even more beautiful because you've borne a child, our daughter. I was trying to be respectful of what you needed. I felt like a selfish bastard every time I had to have you, but I tried to be quick and gentle with you."

Kara's eyes filled with tears. "You were gentle. And I wanted you, too. I just didn't feel sexy. I want to feel like your woman again."

"Fuck!" Simon's curse exploded, the sound booming in the small space. Stepping back, he released her wrists and held her face between his hands, forcing her to look at him. "You *are* my woman. You never stopped being mine, and you'll always be mine. Don't you know that I can't live without you, that you'll always look beautiful to me? Christ. You accepted my damn scars. I don't think you even see them when you look at me. Do you think it was easy for me not to lose it every time I was inside you? No matter how tired I am, every time I see you, my cock is hard. Every time I look at you, I want you. Every. Single. Fucking. Time." His voice was low and vibrating with emotion.

Seeing the fierce possessiveness and adoration in his dark eyes, Kara's tears started to fall.

I'm an idiot. Simon loves me. He's always loved me. If I'd just talked to him, he would have reassured me.

Kara *hadn't* ever seen Simon's scars as something that made him unattractive. She'd only seen the pain they'd caused him, and it made her heart ache. To her, he was perfect. His strength, his capacity to still love after all he'd been through had been what made her fall in love with him in the first place. He never did anything on a small scale, and his single-minded goal of making her happy had touched her soul. He'd always said he was clueless when it came to romance, but the way he went way over the top with everything just to please her was one of his most endearing qualities. "You're absolutely perfect," she whispered, stroking back a lock of wayward hair on his forehead. "Beautiful."

Simon shot her a wicked grin. "What happened to stubborn, bossy, and domineering?"

Oh, yeah. Her husband was a dominant, hardheaded alpha male, but she loved even those qualities. Most of the time! "I like that sometimes," she told him in a *fuck-me* voice that made it abundantly clear where she really adored his bossiness.

"Don't push me, woman. My patience is about shot," he warned her.

Kara visibly flinched as the emergency phone rang in the elevator. It wasn't the first time that had happened. She had fond memories of this particular elevator.

Simon snatched the phone, grumbling into the mouthpiece, "We're fine. I'm looking for something. It could be a while. Don't call again." He hung up the phone with an audible *slam*, not even waiting for a response.

Kara moaned and slumped against the wall. "I can't believe you just did that. Security will think we're having crazy sex in the elevator." She raised an eyebrow at him, her heart beginning to pulse heavily. "What could you be looking for that takes this long?"

Simon's eyes turned dark and liquid. "My wife," he replied dangerously, opening her jacket and tugging it down her arms. "It seems like I've waited forever to see her beautiful body again, to hear her scream my name while she's coming around me. I can't wait any longer," he growled.

"Simon, we can't do this here." Her words held no conviction, her legs growing weak as her core clenched with need. Bossy, demanding Simon was back, and all she wanted to do was let him manhandle her, take her over with the passion she could see firing in his eyes.

"We are doing it here. Now," he demanded.

The insistent command in his voice told her he was nearing the end of his control. *Thank God!*

He unzipped the back of her dress and pulled it over her head, and she heard him release a tortured groan as she lifted her arms so he could free her from the garment. It dropped to the floor, unnoticed.

"Jesus, woman. Are you trying to kill me?" he grunted, his eyes roaming covetously over her scantily clad body.

She was wearing red lingerie, with miniscule panties, thigh high stockings, and a lacy bra that was so thin, she knew he could see her hard, sensitive nipples. "I thought you liked my sexy lingerie," she teased, feeling more comfortable as she saw the expression of rampant desire on his face.

"I fucking love it. But you know what it does to me." Simon shot her a feral, carnal look.

Kara shivered as he ran his hands over her body, teasing her nipples through the flimsy fabric of her bra, and stroking his hands over her abdomen and hips. The desperate, rough touch of his fingers set her body on fire.

"You look even sexier now than you did before our daughter was born, and I didn't think it was possible for me to want to fuck you any worse than I did then. But I do. It was hell trying to be quick and gentle all the time. I thought it was what you wanted. But I think you want it the same way I do right now. I think you need it to understand exactly how I feel." His hands stroked over her hips and then cupped her ass, his fingers squeezing her flesh, and then using his grip to pull her body flush against his. "Your body still fits against mine like you were made for me. It's mine, sweetheart. You're mine," he whispered in a graveled voice, his hot breath wafting over her ear. "You're a fucking goddess. Don't ever hide yourself from me again," he demanded as he pulled her tighter against him.

Kara bit back a moan as she felt his engorged cock against her core through the material of his dress pants. "Never," she agreed. She was ready to capitulate on anything he wanted if he'd just fuck her senseless. He was right. She did need it. She needed her Simon exactly as he was: raw, untamed, and completely out of control.

Taking his hands from her ass, he buried them in her hair and held her head in place as he covered her mouth with his in a kiss that was far from gentle. Kara relished it, fisting his hair as he devoured her mouth, branding her with the fire of his desperate embrace. He demanded, and she gave, opening to him as he explored the recesses of her mouth with his tongue boldly, greedily.

They both came out of the kiss panting and needy.

"Mine." Simon's tone was carnal, snapping her flimsy bra easily and letting it fall to the plush carpet soundlessly.

He cupped her breasts, teasing her nipples with his thumbs mercilessly. "These are so full and beautiful." Simon lowered his head and latched onto one of the sensitive peaks, sucking it in, and then biting down hard enough to make the pleasure/pain sensation nearly unbearable.

Kara gripped the metal bar at her back to keep from falling, letting her head slump against the wall. "Oh, God. Simon. Please."

He lifted his head. "Please what, baby?"

"Fuck me," she insisted, her pussy quivering in anticipation.

"I plan on it. Eventually. I need to make you come first." He dropped to his knees, placing open-mouthed kisses to her abdomen, over the stretch marks. "I love these marks. They make me crazy. They remind me that you got them from having our child."

Kara let her tears flow as he kissed every scar, the sincerity and heat in his voice making her realize what a fool she'd been. "I love you," she gasped.

"I love you, too, sweetheart." His voice, low and husky, was muffled against her belly. "Are you ready for me, Kara?" he rumbled. "I think I need to find out," he told her fiercely, his fingers delving beneath her fragile panties. "Christ. You're so hot and so wet. Do you know what it does to me when your body responds to me this way?"

Kara moaned as Simon ran one finger through her folds, the digit greeted by the liquid proof of her longing for him. "Please. I want you so much."

"Then you'll have me." He gripped the delicate material of her panties and tore them from her body. "Jesus. I need to taste you." He groaned as he grasped her ass and buried his face in her pussy.

"Simon," she whimpered, quivering as he ran his tongue the entire length of her pussy, from her sheath to her pulsating clit. She removed one of her hands from the bar behind her and thrust it into his hair, bringing his face closer, harder against her.

He didn't tease her; he consumed her in his own dominant, voracious way that had her body begging for release. His lips, teeth, and tongue were urgent. Wild. Ferocious. Zeroing in on her engorged, sensitive clit, he was a man on a mission with only one goal, one objective. He was determined to make her come. Hard.

The heat in her belly started to unfurl, shooting straight to her core. Her entire body started to tremble, and Kara felt like she was being incinerated. *"Yes. Yes. Yes."* She chanted the word like a mantra as she imploded, her climax washing over her with a force that made her come unraveled. *"Simon!"* She screamed his name as her core clenched and released, the spasms hitting her so hard that she had to take her hand from his head and clutch at the bar behind her just to stay on her feet.

He wrung every bit of pleasure he could from her, lapping at the liquid fire of her orgasm.

Finally, he rose to his feet, tearing at his belt and the zipper of his pants. "I need to fuck you, baby."

Slumped against the wall, still trying to catch her breath, Kara reveled in the out-of-control, feral expression on his face. She loved his dirty talk when he lost all restraint. It fueled an answering wildness in her, a need that was not only physical but soul deep to have Simon claim her in the most elemental way. "Do it. I'm beyond ready for you. Fuck me."

Expecting him to wrap her legs around him and take her against the wall, she was surprised when he growled, "Wall sex isn't going to cut it. I need you under me. All mine." He wrapped his arms around her waist and brought her gently to the plush carpet.

The elevator compartment was enormous and private. They were the only ones who used it and it was incredibly clean. But Kara was so desperate she wouldn't have given a crap if it wasn't. She wanted, needed the same things as Simon did right now. "Yes." She sighed as Simon pinned her wrists over her head, his ripped, solid, almost completely clothed body coming on top of her, trapping her beneath him. "Fuck me, Simon. Now."

He'd only taken the time to release his rock-hard cock, and Kara could feel it probing at her folds, sliding sensually against her hyper-sensitive clit. Their eyes locked and held for an endless moment, communicating their mutual need without words.

"Mine," he stated possessively before his mouth crashed down on hers.

He kissed her with a carnal force that left her breathless and squirming beneath him. When he released her mouth, she begged, "Please. I need you."

"Tell me that you want me as much as I want you," he ordered, his mouth buried in her neck, nipping her flesh, and then stroking his tongue along the sensitive skin.

Sweet baby Jesus. Kara was about to lose her mind, wanting nothing more than for Simon to take control of her body and claim her. His probing cock made her squirm beneath him, and lift her hips to try to get him inside her. "I need you more than you need me. Now fuck me."

"Baby, you could *never* need me more than I need you," he rumbled huskily into her ear. "Wrap those sexy long legs around me and hold on."

She responded immediately, knowing her heels were digging into his ass, but she still urged him forward with her legs, tightening them around his waist.

Kara knew the moment Simon snapped completely. Positioning himself against the entrance of her channel, he buried himself to the balls inside her with one forceful thrust, releasing a low, carnal groan as he filled her.

She moaned in response, the merging of their bodies rough and elemental. "Yes. Yes. I need you so much." She urged him on, knowing how much he loved to hear that she needed him, wanted him. And she loved being able to say the words to him, because they were true.

"You'll come for me, again. I need to make you come," he rasped.

She tried to pull her wrists free, wanting to touch him, but he held her immobile, completely at his mercy. He didn't start slow, and she didn't want him to. She'd waited too long to feel Simon raw and untamed again. Every stroke of his cock filled her, fulfilled her longing for him to remind her just how hot and wild their passion could burn.

She met his every entry into her sheath, raising her hips as he slammed into her over and over with a ferocity that had her thrashing her head in ecstasy. "Simon. Yes. Harder." Greedily, she wanted everything he had.

"Come for me, baby. I won't last long," he warned her darkly, his chest heaving, his big body shuddering like he was fighting to hold back.

Kara lost herself to Simon the moment he covered her mouth with his, every sensation amplified. Her sensitive nipples abraded against the coarse fabric of his jacket, his tongue mimicked his cock with deep, fast thrusts into her mouth, and his cock pummeled her, his hips grinding against her pussy every time he buried himself inside her.

Her climax hit hard and explosively, rocking her body as her channel clenched around his cock, milking him to his own release.

"Fuck!" Simon bellowed loudly, his body shuddering as his hot release flooded her womb. Releasing her wrists, but remaining inside her, he rolled and held her body on top of his, both of them breathless and spent.

Still dazed, Kara smiled as she realized she finally felt like a woman again. Simon's woman. She wished the transition back to herself hadn't taken so long, that she and Simon had talked about this before. But maybe she hadn't been ready. Maybe being a mommy had needed to come first before she could find her way back to being a woman again.

"I missed you," she whispered. "I missed you so much."

Simon stroked a hand over her back comfortingly. "I've always been here, baby. And I always will be." He paused before adding, "I missed you, too. But Ginny needed you first. I just wish I could have been there for you more, helped more. I knew you were exhausted, and I felt so fucking helpless sometimes." His voice was filled with remorse and frustration.

Kara's mind flashed back to nighttime feedings, being up with Ginny when she was fussy with colic and teething, diaper changes, and all of the other responsibilities and worries of new parents. Maybe there were some things that Simon couldn't do, but he'd always been there, right beside her. "You're a very good daddy," she told him gently.

"I love you more every day that we're together, sweetheart. I don't ever want you to forget that," Simon's words were a vow. "And you can always talk to me. I'm always ready and willing to show you exactly how beautiful you are to me."

Kara sighed, knowing her insecurities and lack of feeling sexy were probably just part of the process of being a new mom. "I know. It wasn't you. I guess it was just a part of being a new mother that I needed to go through. But we should have talked more instead of guessing about how the other was thinking. Thank you for helping me get my sexy back," she told him with a smile.

"Baby, you never lost it in my eyes," he answered, his tone protective and fierce. "But I'd be happy to help you keep finding it."

Kara sighed, realizing that he'd been constant, his love and his desire always there. It had been she who had had doubts and insecurities. "I'm ready." Her heart swelled with happiness. "Are we done with the condoms now?"

"Hell, yes. Having anything between us drove me fucking crazy. But I was so worried about you getting pregnant again that I used them for extra protection. It was my own paranoia, and I'm over it. You're on birth control, and I'd rather be as close to you as I can possibly be. I'm ruined. I just reminded myself of how good you felt," he said, disgruntled.

"I'd be happy to reinforce the reminder," Kara teased.

"I'm taking you out for dinner first," he demanded. "I want some time with my wife. And you're going to eat. Your body is perfect."

"I'm starving," she admitted, her stomach grumbling. She knew her post-pregnancy body was far from perfect, but she had no doubt that Simon believed it was.

Simon rose and helped her to her feet. He tucked himself back into his pants, watching her as she slipped her dress over her head. "I guess I need to start buying you more lingerie," he noted with a naughty grin, scooping up her ruined panties and bra and shoving them into his pocket.

"I do have an underwear problem. If we don't go back upstairs, I'll be sitting through dinner with no bra and no panties." Kara smiled. It wasn't the first time they'd had that dilemma.

Simon seemed to consider that problem for a moment before he finally slapped the buttons on the elevator to release it from the emergency stop to move upward again. "It's a tempting idea, but I can't stand the thought of any other man getting a look at what's mine," he told her possessively.

Leaning forward, she grasped his tie and pulled him close to her. "You can rip the new ones off later."

His eyes flared with dark desire. "Count on it."

Kara's core clenched tightly. She could hardly wait.

Chapter 3

"**S**imon, you have to stop buying Christmas gifts for me and Ginny. We still have three weeks until Christmas and all of the space under the tree is full," Kara told her husband gently, taking a sip of her wine while she watched Simon demolish his tiramisu.

Dinner had been delicious, but she was stuffed full of pasta and rich cream sauce. While Simon ate his dessert, she carefully broached the subject of his habit of going way over the top when it came to gifts. Every single day, he brought home more presents for Ginny and her. At his current rate of adding to the collection under the tree, their enormous living room would be full to the ceiling by Christmas. It certainly wasn't like he couldn't afford it, but she'd tried unsuccessfully to make him realize that she and Ginny didn't need any more gifts. Their greatest gift was Simon.

Simon shrugged. "I love you. I want to give you everything you need."

A tremulous sigh left Kara's mouth, and she looked at her husband adoringly. "We have everything we need. We have you. Ginny and I want for absolutely nothing already." It wasn't only on holidays that Simon gave. Kara had a collection of jewelry that could probably rival the Crown Jewels.

Simon had grown up with nothing, and he was trying to make sure the ones he loved never wanted for anything. Ginny was already growing up with a golden spoon in her mouth. Literally. Simon had bought his daughter a solid gold feeding spoon, for God's sake. Kara didn't want her daughter spoiled rotten. She and Simon had both grown up poor and knew the value of money. She wanted to spoil Ginny, but she also wanted her to understand the value of money.

"My wife and child deserve to be taken care of." The words were obstinate.

Kara rolled her eyes with exasperation. He was so damn adorable when he was trying to defend his right to give them things. "We *are* taken care of. We're both spoiled rotten."

Simon nodded his head sharply as he dropped his fork and napkin on his empty dessert plate. "Good. That's the way I like it."

Damn. It's so hard to argue with him. I never win.

"Your daughter is going to end up being a spoiled brat," she warned him ominously, but she was biting back a smile.

His dark eyes met hers, and his words were adamant, "No, she won't. She's going to be as sweet as her mother. She's your daughter, and she'll grow up to be just like you."

Oh, hell. How can I argue when he says things like that?

"Can you slow it down a little so we can get into the living room on Christmas morning?" Truthfully, she didn't want to change Simon, she just wanted him to realize that they loved *him* and not the *things* he gave them.

"Maybe. No promises." He grinned at her shamelessly. "Maybe if I knew I was getting some heart-wishes for Christmas, it might slow me down a little."

Kara smiled back at him, unable to resist his mischievous grin. He still loved those silly little handmade paper hearts she'd given him when she hadn't had the money to buy him an actual gift for Valentine's Day. He got one thing he wanted from her for each heart she gave him. Sadly, she realized she hadn't given him any of the heart-wishes on any holiday since Ginny was born, probably because he usually used them to get her naked. "If you slow it down, you might get some heart-wishes this year," she bantered cheekily.

"I'll stop for the rest of the week," he promised.

Kara snickered. "That'll work. I think you'll get some in your stocking, if you're a good boy for the rest of the week." Honestly, it amazed her that he loved those little pieces of paper so much. He was a billionaire, but nothing had ever made him as happy as getting those little hearts that he could turn in whenever he wanted her to grant his wish.

"We're only talking about not bringing home presents this week, right?" he asked carefully, folding his arms in front of him.

She leaned across the table, speaking in a low voice that only Simon could hear. "Oh, yeah. Just about the gifts. Otherwise, I'd be happy if you'd be very, very bad."

His eyes flared, desire swirling furiously in his heated gaze. "Thank God. Being good is really hard," he answered in a relieved voice.

"How hard is it?" she asked sultrily. "And I never really wanted you to be that good."

"Right now, it's about as hard as it can get," he rasped.

Liquid heat pooled between her thighs and her core clenched with violent need. She'd been deprived of her raw and hungry husband for too long. "Well, I'm ready to leave," she squeaked eagerly, reaching for her jacket. Holy hell! She couldn't wait to get home now.

Simon's grin was wicked as he rose and helped her put on her jacket. Her cell phone startled her, the muffled ring coming from her small purse. She fumbled with the clutch and pulled out her phone. "It's Maddie," she told Simon as she looked at the caller ID.

She stepped outside to answer the call while Simon took care of the bill. By the time she'd finished, he was just walking out of the restaurant.

"You're frowning. What's wrong?" Simon asked in a concerned voice.

"One of the patients from the clinic is in the hospital. It's serious, and he's all alone. Maddie can't leave the babies right now. I have to go," Kara told Simon anxiously. "Can you drive me?"

He scowled at her. "You care about this guy," he observed unhappily. "I know you get attached to all of your patients, but you look freaked out."

She'd just finished stowing her phone back in her purse, and her head jerked up to look at him, worried about the jealousy and hurt she heard in his voice. She reached out her hand and grasped his forearm. "He's not a guy really. He's seven years old and his name is Timmy Madden. Maddie diagnosed him with type 1 diabetes, and he was supposed to be seeing a specialist, getting a team of professionals to help him. His mother was a prostitute and was never sure who his father was. She evidently never got him the medical care he needed. They found her dead in her apartment near the clinic, and Timmy was in a coma. He's sick and he's just a child, Simon. And he doesn't have anyone there with him," she told him desperately.

"Shit," Simon's frustration was evident. "I'm sorry, baby." He pulled her into his arms and hugged her tightly. "I'll go with you."

"Thank you." She squeezed him back, her sadness for Timmy making her heart break. "He's always been such a good little boy. He doesn't deserve any of this."

"No kid deserves something like that, sweetheart," Simon answered huskily, wrapping an arm around her and leading her to the car.

After he settled her into the Bugatti, Simon drove carefully but way too fast to get to the hospital.

For once, Kara didn't tease him about the possibility of getting a speeding ticket in his expensive sports car.

In fact, she never said a word.

Simon watched as Kara fussed over the small child in a bed in the pediatric ICU, one that looked way too big for him. The kid had woken up, but he was disoriented and clinging to Kara like he never wanted to let her go.

He knew the feeling.

Nobody had to tell him that his wife was special. He'd known that from the moment he'd seen her. Her compassion was endless and her ability to love incredible. Hell, she put up with his cranky ass, and he thought *that* was a damn miracle. The fact that she actually loved him was almost unbelievable. But he believed it. He experienced it every damn day, and he was more grateful for that love than she could ever rationally understand.

Simon eyed the boy from his seat next to Kara. He was dark-haired, and his brown eyes looked too big for his face because he was so thin. As the kid looked at him, Simon saw the weight of the world reflected back at him in the eyes of a seven year old who had seen too much, experienced too much sadness in his short life.

Fuck! Why is nobody protecting him, taking care of him? How is it that he has nobody in this world who gives a damn about him except Kara and Maddie?

"Who's that?" Timmy asked Kara as he clung to her hand, his voice weak, and his words slurred.

"That's my husband, sweetie. His name is Simon," Kara responded in a sweet, gentle voice.

"Is he the guy who made you your own computer game?" Timmy asked groggily, but his voice was more animated. He looked at Simon with a slightly awed expression.

Simon designed some of the most popular computer games in the world, and Kara loved to play them. He *had* actually made Kara her own game and named it *The Adventures of Kara*. He'd never intended to release it to the general public, but she'd badgered him to do it because she wanted other people to enjoy it. He finally had, and it had been enormously successful.

"Yep. My husband is a genius," she told Timmy. "He makes all kinds of games."

"I wish I knew how to play." Timmy's answer was wistful.

"You don't know how to use a computer?" Simon was incredulous. What kid in this day and age didn't know how to use a computer?

"I learned some when I went to school, but we weren't allowed to play games. But some of my friends talked about the Myth World games and they sound fun," Timmy said longingly.

Those were *his* games, *his* designs, and the hottest games on the market. "I make the Myth World games," Simon confessed in a more gentle voice. "I'll teach you how to play when you're feeling better."

Of course the kid didn't have a computer of his own. He was poor, and Simon knew what it was like to grow up in severe poverty.

"For real?" Timmy answered, looking like he wasn't quite sure he could believe Simon.

Simon's heart clenched as he answered, "I promise, and promises are important to me. I never break them."

They were interrupted as the nurse came into the room. Even as sleepy as Timmy was, he obligingly held out his finger to be poked, never even flinching as the nurse stuck him for blood to test his sugar level.

Brave kid. Life is so fucking unfair sometimes. Not only does the poor little guy have nobody in this world who cares about him, but he's poor and sick. What the hell? I might have grown up in poverty, and in a tough neighborhood, but at least I had Sam and my mother, and I was relatively healthy.

Kara and Timmy's nurse conferred for a few minutes before the latter left the room. Simon didn't catch exactly what they were talking about, but judging by the relieved look on his wife's face, Timmy must be getting better.

"Does that hurt?" he asked Timmy. Simon was genuinely curious and concerned for the little boy who had endured so much.

"Naw. The shots don't hurt neither, and they make me feel better," Timmy answered nonchalantly. "I just don't like the hospital."

"I don't blame you," Simon muttered, amazed by how the child seemed to take everything in stride. It was damn sad when a boy his age didn't kick up a fuss about anything. Probably because no one would care if he did.

Timmy looked back at Kara and asked solemnly, "My mom is dead, isn't she?"

Simon looked at the torn look on Kara's face before she answered sadly, "Yes, Timmy. She is. I'm sorry, sweetie."

The boy nervously plucked at the blanket on his bed. "She hated me. She told me so. It was my fault because she drank, and I was a big problem because I was sick. But I still didn't want her to die."

"It wasn't your fault," Simon answered huskily. "Drinking is a sickness, too. She was sick, and she wasn't happy. But it wasn't your fault. She didn't mean it when she said she hated you. It was the sickness."

Kara shot him a grateful look, her eyes shining with unshed tears. "Simon's right. It wasn't your fault, Timmy."

"I think she really did hate me. Because I'm sick and I need so many doctors, I was too much trouble for her," he answered, sounding resigned.

Simon clenched his fists, trying to restrain himself. He was angry, pissed at a woman who was already dead. "No child should ever be a problem to their parents. Did you ask to be born?"

Timmy shook his head slowly.

"She gave you life, and she should have taken better care of you, but she couldn't because she was sick herself. It's not your fault that you need doctors. It's not your fault that you're sick. You can get better, Timmy. You just need to get the care you need. Your mom couldn't handle that, but somebody else will." Maybe his conversation was a little too adult for the kid, but Timmy seemed to be an old soul, and Simon seemed to know instinctively what to say. Maybe it was because he could emphasize with some portions of the kid's childhood.

"Do you really think so, Simon? I've always been sick." Timmy's voice was cautiously hopeful.

"I know so," Simon rasped, still angry that this child had never gotten the care he needed.

"You really can, Timmy," Kara reinforced. "When they get you stabilized and stronger, you can do all the things you've wanted to do." Kara stroked his hair tenderly. "You'll get better."

J. A. Scott

"I want to learn to play Myth World," Timmy said with a huge yawn. "Simon's going to teach me when I get better."

Simon decided at just that moment that he'd buy the kid a whole damn system and be his tutor so Timmy could kick everybody else's ass at his games. "Get better fast," Simon demanded. "It takes a while to get the hang of it and kick some butt."

Kara sent him a reproving glance at his language, but Timmy just grinned at him, a little hesitantly, but with dawning hope.

"I'll get better by tomorrow," the child said emphatically as his eyes started to droop.

"I'll be ready," Simon answered, his heart swelling that the boy believed in him when he'd had so few adults who gave him reason to believe.

Simon was silent after that, watching Timmy closely as he drifted off to sleep, Kara still grasping his hand and stroking his hair.

Mine.

Christ, he loved his kindhearted wife. Very few women would take the time to comfort a small boy who had nobody else in the world. No wonder he fucking worshipped her.

And she doesn't understand why she's so damn beautiful to me?

Kara was sexy as hell because she was…Kara. Her fuller figure and the love that she gave their baby girl just made his cock even harder every time he looked at her. She was perfect in his eyes, and always would be. Thank fuck he could finally love her the way he wanted to, the way he needed to. Time hadn't dampened his crazy, possessive love for her; it had just made it more intense.

They stayed until Timmy fell asleep, and Simon walked silently to the car, clinging to the same hand that Timmy had had in his grasp a short time ago.

It wasn't often that his thirty-five-year-old self could be completely humbled by his thirty-year-old wife and a seven-year-old kid from the streets. But as Simon struggled for the words to tell Kara how he felt, he knew there was no way to convey to her how much he loved her.

"I love you," he simply told her fiercely, right before he closed the passenger door.

Unable to express himself with more eloquent words, it would have to be enough.

Kara hopped into the shower, just as she always did whenever she arrived home from the clinic or the hospital, thinking about just how lucky she was to have such an extraordinary husband.

"How many billionaires would care about one of the many street kids out there who have nobody to really love them?" she whispered silently to herself while she washed shampoo from her hair.

She and Simon had talked about Timmy all the way home, Kara explaining his painful and sad history. She'd always adored the sweet little boy, and her heart had ached every time he left the clinic, she and Maddie both hoping that this time, his mother would follow up with Timmy's care. Maddie had reported what she suspected was neglect to the authorities several times, but nothing had ever come of it. After Timmy was diagnosed with type 1 diabetes, Kara had made the appointment herself with a specialist for him. Yes, his mother had been a scattered emotional mess and a raging alcoholic, but it never occurred to Kara that she wouldn't follow through on Timmy's care when she knew damn well how serious her son's condition was.

"It's so unfair," she whispered fiercely, scrubbing her skin with a sponge.

"Talking to yourself again, sweetheart?" Simon asked, his voice teasing as he opened the door and entered the large shower.

Sputtering as she rinsed the soap from her eyes, Kara finally cleared her vision to see the perfectly splendid form of her husband in front of her. Her breath caught as her eyes roamed up and down his body, taking in every defined muscle of his six-pack abs and rippling biceps. Simon wasn't handsome in a conventional way, but the entire package of the man was irresistible, dark, seductive, and incredibly hot.

Sweet Jesus, he's beautiful.

She reached out and traced the scars on his chest, a testament to just how strong Simon really was, and the power of his will to survive. Every single thing about him had always drawn her to him, lured her closer to him until they were completely entwined.

Dropping the sponge and adding soap to her hand, she offered huskily, "Would you like me to scrub your back for you?" *Dear God, she needed to touch his masculine, strong, naked body. It had been way too long.*

He turned obligingly without a word, and Kara stroked her soapy hands over his shoulders and back, lingering over each tense, flexing muscle. "You're tense." She kneaded at the contracting muscles, forcing them to relax. "What's wrong?"

"I guess I'm still thinking about the kid. The whole situation really pisses me off. Do you know he didn't once ask about my scars, and he wasn't afraid of me?" he told her in a puzzled, low voice.

Kara sighed softly, loving her husband even more because he was still troubled by Timmy's situation. While it was true that Simon could be formidable, it wasn't intentional on his part. He was a big man, dark, and the scars on his face were intimidating, even though Kara just saw them as being part of who he was. He was also blunt, gruff, and often anti-social, although he'd changed a great deal in the last two years. "Children have good instincts," she told him matter-of-factly. "He knew he could trust you." She glided her palms over his rock-hard ass, feeling the muscles flex in response. Simon had the tightest, hottest butt, and she loved the feel of it under her adoring hands. "Turn," she requested.

He swung around, and Kara was confronted with his powerful chest, and one very hard cock. Heat shot straight between her thighs, her core clenching to have his impressive length inside her. Moving her hands down his chest, she wrapped her fingers around the shaft, loving that she could make him this way.

"Kara," Simon grunted in a warning voice.

She ignored him, lowering her body until she was on her knees, and removing her hand to let the water wash away the soap. "My turn," she muttered greedily, grasping his ass with her hands and taking the sensitive tip of him into her mouth. Simon had missed out on any woman giving him oral sex for the first thirty-three years of his life, and she loved knowing she was the only woman who'd ever given him this kind of pleasure. And yeah, she knew it drove him completely insane.

"Fuck. Baby, I'll come." His desperate growl reverberated in the small, contained space.

She smiled as she took as much as she could of his length into her mouth and sucked as she pulled back.

"Christ." Simon fisted her wet hair and took control, guiding her mouth over him faster and faster with a long, tortured groan. Kara tilted her head and watched Simon as his face contorted, water spraying onto his chest, startled when he rasped, "Not. Like. This."

He grasped her around the shoulders and pulled her up easily, pinning her against the wall of the shower in less than a heartbeat. His chest heaved as he stood with his hands braced on each side of her head.

"I wanted to make you come," Kara said indignantly.

"I want to come inside you, Kara. I need it right now. Jesus, woman…do you know how much I love you?" he groaned, his liquid brown eyes fixed on her face. He was still panting heavily as he added, "I don't know how I got so damn lucky or what I ever did to have you fall in love with me and become mine forever, but I'm never letting you go, and I swear I'll never take what we have for granted." His voice was awed and sincere.

Kara's eyes locked with Simon's desperate gaze. "And here I am thinking I'm the one who's lucky." Kara felt damn blessed. There wasn't a better man in the world than Simon, and he filled her heart and soul completely. "I was so alone until you came into my life."

He speared one hand through her hair and said hoarsely, empathetically, "You'll never be lonely again, baby." He swallowed hard. "Promise you'll always stay with me."

Kara wanted to weep when she saw the flash of vulnerability in Simon's eyes. For some reason, he'd always been afraid of losing her, and it was the last thing he needed to worry about. "We're meant to be together, Simon. I think it was fated." She was very rational and realistic, but she'd always felt like she and Simon had been meant to find each other. They simply…fit.

"Then destiny was real fucking good to me," Simon replied, placing both of his hands under her ass and lifting her up against him.

Kara wrapped her legs instinctively around his hips, enraptured by how strong he was, how easily he lifted her body. She was no dainty woman, but he pinned her easily between the shower wall and his enormous body, his eyes never leaving hers.

The water was pounding forcefully against their upper bodies, but neither one of them cared. Kara wrapped her arms around his shoulders and begged, "Take me. Please. I need you."

Simon's eyes flared as he heard her urgency, her desperation for him. He surged into her in one powerful thrust. "Fuck, baby, you feel so damn good."

Her head fell back against the wall of the shower, breaking their eye contact, her body already clamoring for release. "Yes. Please fuck me, Simon." Her fingernails dug into the skin of his back, her senses whirling as she began to drown in pleasure.

"Mine," he declared possessively, as he reared and thrust back into her again.

"Yours," Kara moaned, her senses overwhelmed by her husband's possessive claiming. This was what she wanted, what she needed.

"Tell me what you want," Simon demanded.

"You," she whimpered obligingly, loving the way Simon wanted to be reassured that she belonged to him, that she was satisfied. "Just like this. Hard. Fast. Forever."

He gave her exactly what she wanted, his cock pummeling into her as he grasped her ass tightly, holding her still to accept him over and over again.

"I love you, Kara. I wouldn't be worth a shit without you anymore," he told her passionately.

"You'll never be without me," she assured him, her body tightening with each powerful stroke of his cock.

"Come for me, sweetheart. Come with me," he commanded, grinding his hips against hers with every strong, surging entry, stimulating her throbbing clit.

She started to scream his name as her powerful climax rolled over her, but Simon captured her lips with his, claiming her pleasure as his tongue filled her mouth. He consumed her with his embrace, his large body shuddering, his groan vibrating against her lips as he found his own release.

"Oh, my God..." Kara panted the moment Simon moved his mouth from hers. She dropped her head on his shoulder, completely spent. She'd missed him, missed *this* so much, the raw passion that caught fire whenever they were together.

Slowly, he lowered her feet to the ground, keeping an arm around her waist as he picked up the sponge and cleaned both of them, taking his time with her. His actions were sweet, tender, and completely different from the obsessed lover he'd been just a few minutes ago. He loved her in so many ways that it made Kara want to cry tears of happiness. "I love you," she murmured softly as he turned off the water, and grabbed a large, fluffy towel to dry her.

Simon was silent as he roughly dried his own body and tossed the towel into the hamper. She squealed as he picked her up and cuddled her against him.

"If you love me, then I really am a lucky bastard," he said gruffly, taking her into their bedroom to prove how much he loved her back.

F or the next week, Simon was true to his word, not bringing a
single present home to put under the tree. He went into the
office for a while almost every day, trying to help cover for
Sam. Usually, Simon worked a lot at home in the computer lab, preferring to be out of the public eye. But with Sam and Maddie now
having twins who were younger than Ginny, Simon picked up the
slack at all of the divisions of Hudson Corporation, going into the
office daily to give his brother a break.

Blond and gorgeous, Sam was the public face of Hudson, the work-
aholic who was almost always in the office. Since he'd reconnected
with Maddie, his priorities had changed, and he spent as much time
at home as possible with his wife and children, trying to relieve
Maddie of some of the stresses of having twins.

Surprisingly, Simon stopped at the hospital every afternoon to
visit Timmy, much to Kara's relief. She didn't want the little boy
to be alone, but she didn't want to take Ginny into the hospital and
expose her to viruses and bacteria at such a vulnerable age. Maddie
fretted about him too, but she had her hands full with the clinic
and her babies. Luckily, the twins were getting easier for Sam and
Maddie to handle as they approached their first birthday.

Kara had been relieved when Simon told her that Timmy was out of the ICU and had been pronounced stable. Eager to see the little boy she adored, she let Helen and Michael babysit one afternoon so she could dash up and see him.

She drove herself, completely aware of Simon's agents following her. She smiled, thinking about all the times in the past where she'd hated being followed. Now, not so much. It was Simon's way of making sure she was safe, and she'd learned to tolerate it because it put her husband's mind at ease.

Finding Timmy's room once she reached the hospital, she froze when she walked through the door.

"Holy shit," she whispered to herself, taking in the multitude of items filling the private room. Colorful balloons floated on the ceiling, and every space was full of toys that most seven-year-old boys only dreamed about.

And there, on the pristine hospital bed, was her husband, with Timmy watching him with focused fascination as he demonstrated something on the laptop resting on his thighs. Simon had his back propped up against the wall, his shoes next to the bed, as he handed the computer to the boy sitting comfortably next to him, who was giving Simon adoring looks as he accepted the electronic device and placed it on his lap.

"You can do it, Tim," Simon said gruffly, watching the boy carefully as his small brows narrowed in concentration, trying to do something on the laptop.

Kara watched, her heart swelling as her husband continued to bark encouraging words at Timmy, trying to help him get through one of his computer games. Simon looked so comfortable, even though the bed was small. He'd shed the jacket of his suit and removed his tie. His white shirt sleeves were rolled up to his elbows and his legs were crossed, his tan socks poking out from beneath his pants.

Now I know why he was content not to bring presents home. He bought them for Timmy instead.

She smiled as she looked around the room. Her husband had gone overboard...as usual. As it was, the nurses couldn't get to Timmy without skirting skateboards, a new bicycle, games, and even stuffed animals. Kara nearly burst out laughing as she saw the enormous teddy bear sitting in one of the chairs, its furry body bigger than its owner's.

Oh, Simon.

He was being so patient with the child, gently correcting him when he made a wrong move on the computer. Their two dark heads were lowered to view the computer screen, looking so natural and sweet together that Kara wanted to weep.

"Aw, I died," Timmy squealed tragically, falling back on the bed.

"You did good," Simon argued. "You made it through two levels this time."

"I'll keep trying," the boy replied determinedly. "Do you think I'll be able to take my stuff with me when I go to a home? They said I can go home soon, but I don't have a home anymore." Timmy looked at Simon and scrambled back into a sitting position, fear creeping into his dark eyes.

Kara's body slumped against the wall.

Oh, God.

She hoped they had found him a good foster home.

"You'll be taking it all," Simon growled. "It's your stuff."

Timmy clambered onto Simon's lap, giving him an earnest look. "Do you think the people who take me will be nice?" His voice quivered with anxiety, his eyes apprehensive.

"They'll be good," Simon reassured him.

"I'm scared," Timmy admitted, throwing his thin arms around Simon's neck.

Kara's heart nearly broke as she watched Simon swallow hard before he wrapped his muscular, protective arms around Timmy's small body.

"I think it's natural to be worried," Simon told him. "But just think about getting well right now, Tim. I won't let anything bad happen to you," he told the boy roughly, protectively.

"Promise?"

"I promise," Simon answered in a graveled, tormented voice.

Kara blinked back her tears as she moved into the room, unable to bear watching Timmy's fear and Simon's anguish a moment longer. "Hey, little man," she said loudly, cheerfully. "You look better." Timmy untangled himself from Simon and threw himself into her arms.

"Kara," Timmy exclaimed breathlessly. "Look what Simon did." He gestured around the room as he clung to her. "And he's teaching me to play Myth World on my very own computer."

"Is he now?" Kara raised an eyebrow at her husband. "I see you got an awful lot of stuff in here, Timmy."

"I don't like that name." Timmy scowled. "It's a baby name. I'm a guy," he added, puffing out his tiny chest, sounding like he was parroting something that a certain someone she knew had told him.

"She's okay to use it," Simon grumbled. "It's just us men who have to use guy names."

The little boy nodded. "Okay then. I guess you can still call me Timmy. But Simon calls me Tim."

Kara hugged the child, smirking at Simon. "Thank you. I think I'd have a hard time changing names now."

Simon shrugged. "It's a guy thing," he mumbled somewhat sheepishly.

She sat on the edge of the bed, watching man and child as they practiced more on the computer games, Timmy's face lit up like she'd never seen before. He'd been so sick when she'd seen him in the clinic, so lethargic. He'd always been sweet, but so incredibly weak. The little boy needed a haircut; she'd try to remember to bring a comb and scissors tomorrow. Otherwise, he looked like a normal, happy child.

The nurse came in with a snack and Timmy's insulin, and Kara and Simon finally left. She found herself feeling depressed as she walked to the parking lot with her husband, even though Timmy was doing well.

"What's wrong?" Simon asked anxiously. "Don't you think he's doing okay? He looks so much better. And he has a lot of energy now."

"Nothing's wrong really. And he's doing fine," she reassured him, threading her fingers through his as they entered the parking lot. "I'm just worried about where he'll go from here. He has special needs. A diabetic child needs special care, and I'm not certain how easy he'll be to place in foster care. He needs a good family, somebody patient. He's such a good boy, and he's had it so hard," she answered tearfully.

"A nurse would make a handy foster parent," Simon said casually. "And somebody who didn't care about money, somebody who maybe has...billions of dollars to make sure he has the best care?"

Kara's head jerked to the side to meet her husband's gaze. Was he thinking...?

"Us?" she asked excitedly. "But we'd have to get approval for foster care," she warned him, not wanting to get his hopes up.

"I found out a few days ago that they were having a hard time placing him. He'll probably have to go to a group home until they can find a permanent place for him." Simon's voice vibrated with frustration and concern. "Baby, I can get us approved. Sam knows the right people. But I think it would be too much for you—"

"It wouldn't. I swear. I know exactly what to do, and a team of professionals will be on Timmy's case. He can get an insulin pump eventually to make things a little easier." She hesitated, running out of breath. Kara stopped and turned to him as they reached his vehicle. "Please, Simon. I don't want him to be alone or with strangers for Christmas. He's had such a hard life. He deserves to be happy for a while." The thought of Timmy going to a strange group home made her heart clench. She couldn't stand the image of that happening.

"Fuck. I can't let it happen, either," Simon rasped. "You should have seen his face whenever I brought him something. Every single time, he thought it was for someone else. I don't think the kid thinks he deserves anything."

"So, we can do it?" Kara asked tremulously, holding her breath.

"We'll sign the papers, and they'll come over to check out the penthouse. Then we can take him when he's discharged," Simon agreed. "Sam's ready to push all the paperwork through. I had a feeling

you'd want to take him when you found out what was happening.
I just worried about putting anything else on your plate right now.
Ginny keeps you busy."

Kara threw herself into Simon's arms with a sob. "Thank you.
Thank you." She peppered tiny kisses all over his face.

"I'll help as much as I possibly can. Are you sure this won't be too
much?" His voice was concerned and gentle.

She pulled back to look at him as his arms tightened around her
waist. "It won't. I'll take a leave of absence from the clinic and stay
home. Now that Sam is funding the clinic with donations, we have
plenty of staff. Timmy will need constant monitoring for a while."

"I like the kid," Simon admitted gruffly.

Kara considered that Timmy might remind Simon a bit of
himself at that age. They'd been raised in similar circumstances.
Unfortunately, there had been no rescue for Simon. "I know," she
answered with a smile, knowing the child was more likely to follow
Simon around with hero-worship on his face than spending a lot of
time with her. It was obvious that man and boy adored each other.
"Will you have time to spend with him? You're pretty busy."

"I'll make time," Simon vowed.

Simon gave his agents instructions to bring Kara's car home and
helped her into his own vehicle.

They talked about Timmy and their upcoming Christmas all the
way home.

Chapter 5

"I feel like the most unattractive woman in the world. Please explain to me why Sam still pants after me like I'm some sexy goddess," Maddie Hudson asked her sister-in-law wryly. "I'm constantly exhausted, and I'm carrying even more extra weight than before I had the twins. I haven't used any makeup in over a year, and I barely have time to shower, so I'm pretty sure I smell like baby poop and formula most of the time."

Kara turned her head and smirked at Maddie as they walked slowly through the mall. The guys were at the penthouse watching the kids so the girls could do some Christmas shopping. Maddie did look tired, but she glowed, even without makeup, and she certainly didn't stink. Her curly red hair was pulled back in a ponytail, and she was dressed in a pair of jeans, and a colorful Christmas sweater. She looked... happy. "Sam doesn't see anything except you, no matter what your weight might be or how you look. Simon finally...um...convinced me of that a while ago. I think I had a very long case of the baby blues, and we weren't communicating well," Kara informed Maddie as they both stopped in front of Starbucks. She thought back for a moment, wishing she'd approached Simon with her feelings earlier.

Her husband was insatiable now that he understood how she'd felt, and she loved it.

"Shall we?" Maddie asked, nodding her head toward the coffee shop.

"Absolutely," Kara replied. "I'm addicted to their cookie crumble coffees. I could use a fix. I'll try not to think about the calories."

Maddie snorted as she walked ahead of her. "Like you need to worry?"

"I did worry," Kara admitted, ordering her coffee at the counter before replying. "I've gained weight, Maddie, and I felt like a hag. I finally told Simon how I felt and he showed me rather convincingly that it didn't matter." She handed the cashier a twenty after Maddie ordered her coffee, dumping the change into the tip cup.

"Sam's the same damn way, and I know I need to lose weight. But then he kisses me like I'm the only woman in the world for him, and I forget all about it," Maddie answered, sounding exasperated.

They picked up their coffees and found a seat in a small booth.

"Can you believe how different our lives are now from how they were a few years ago?" Kara said with a sigh after taking a long swig of her icy drink. "Sometimes I swear that I'm dreaming, and I'm afraid I'm going to wake up to find I'm still alone and homeless."

"And then?" Maddie asked in an amused voice, proceeding to answer the question herself. "And then Simon gets demanding, bossy, and stubborn, so you know it's not a dream. Let's face it, if we were going to make our men dreamy and perfect, we'd never get annoyed at them." Maddie stirred her coffee around with a straw, mixing the whipped cream into her drink.

Kara chortled. "Okay. But Simon's almost perfect."

Maddie sighed. "So is Sam. He's so good with the kids. I don't know how I would have coped in those early days with the twins if not for him. Kade, Asha, Max and Mia were a big help, too."

Asha, Maddie's half-sister, had married into the wealthy Harrison family, and their brother, Max, was a billionaire in his own right.

"How's Asha doing with her new little one?" Kara asked, remembering she'd recently given birth to an adorable baby boy.

Maddie's face softened. "She's good. Kade is an incredible father." She paused for moment before she asked, "How's Simon coping with Timmy? God, I'm so relieved that you two fostered him. Sam and I considered it, and we probably would have done it had you two not decided to take him. After all he's been through, he needs a little bit of happiness," she said wistfully.

Kara shook her head. "We're in a better position to do it. The twins are a handful, and Ginny is getting easier as she gets older. Timmy adores her, and she babbles to him constantly. Simon's great with Timmy, but I think he's getting really attached. If they find him a family, I'm afraid Simon's heart will be broken." *And so will mine.* They'd only had Timmy with them for a week, but he was quickly becoming part of their family.

"So, look into adopting him."

Oh, how Kara wanted to do that. "I think it's too soon. They're still searching to make sure that Timmy doesn't have any blood family who wants him."

"I never had any record of anybody except his mother, and she's dead," Maddie said flatly. "I doubt anyone will pop up and want a diabetic child that they've never given a damn about before." In a milder voice, she asked, "Is he stable?"

Kara swallowed a sip of her drink, nodding her head. "He's doing great. He even tests his own sugar with supervision. He's amazing. Simon's trying to help him catch up on his studies. He was behind in school because his mother stopped sending him after he was di-agnosed. Timmy said she didn't want to be bothered if he got sick at school," she replied, annoyed with the dead woman who had expired from a lethal level of alcohol. Kara still didn't know if she'd died before Timmy went into a coma, but she was glad the boy couldn't really remember much.

Maddie shot Kara a knowing look. "It sounds like Simon isn't the only one getting attached."

"He's not. Timmy's hard not to love," Kara admitted. "He's so starved for attention and affection that he's grateful for every bit of it that he can get. He's happy, and we love having him with us."

Both women finished their drinks at the same time.

"I guess we should get shopping," Maddie said, rising to her feet.

"The only things I really have to buy are for Simon," Kara answered, standing up, feeling tall—like she always did—next to the petite redhead beside her. "He was good for a week because he promised he would be, but then all promises were done. He's been buying gifts for Timmy and Ginny like a maniac."

"Same here," Maddie admitted as she walked out of the Starbucks next to Kara. "It's crazy. The twins won't even remember this Christmas, but they have an enormous pile of presents underneath the tree."

"You know this all stems from their childhood, Maddie," Kara said thoughtfully. "They had nothing, so now that they can afford it, they want to give everything to the people they love."

"I know," Maddie answered softly. "It breaks my heart to think of the Christmases they had as boys."

Kara stopped abruptly, grabbing Maddie's arm so she didn't lose her in the congested mass of holiday shoppers. "Do you have credit cards?"

"Sure. Lots of them. I'm married to Sam Hudson, remember. They have limits so high it's terrifying. Did you forget yours?" Maddie asked, perplexed.

"Nope," Kara answered with a devious look. "But I'm thinking about doing a lot of frivolous buying right now."

"You're up to something." Maddie's expression was playful. "Spill it."

Kara explained her idea and her reasoning to Maddie before both women pulled out their credit cards with obscene credit limits and nearly shopped until they both dropped.

A few nights later, Simon was doing a nighttime check on Timmy's blood sugar when the boy asked him, "Do you think there's really a Santa Clause, Simon? Kara says there is, but he's never shown up for me before."

Simon looked at the bleary-eyed boy, his chest aching. Santa had never found him and Sam when they were kids either, but he wanted Tim to believe in Santa Claus for the rest of his damn life. The kid had gotten majorly screwed throughout his early life, and he needed some magical time. All kids did.

Honestly, Simon had found his magical time with Kara, so he no longer thought much about his unfortunate early life. What he shared with her more than made up for having a crappy childhood. But Tim deserved more. "Kara's pretty smart." Simon swallowed a lump in his throat as he looked at Timmy's sugar level, relieved when it looked fine. "And yeah, I know Santa exists. I think he brought me Kara because he accidentally missed me a few times when I was a kid," he explained carefully. "Santa isn't perfect, but he generally makes up for it later if he misses your house a few times." He disposed of the strip and the trash from checking Timmy's sugar and sat down on the boy's bed.

Tim's face scrunched up in concentration. "So, maybe being with you and Kara for Christmas is my big gift for Santa missing me before." He looked satisfied with that explanation.

Jesus. It sucked when a kid was just grateful to be taken care of and have a roof over his head.

"Santa will find you this year. He knows where I live," Simon told the child gruffly.

"Do you think so?" Tim's face lit up like a lantern.

"I know so," Simon told him adamantly, ruffling the boy's dark hair.

Maybe he shouldn't be encouraging a lie, but hell, the boy had done plenty of living in cold, hard reality. Some fantasy wouldn't hurt. Tim deserved at least one damn extraordinary Christmas, and Simon was determined to see him happy.

"You don't think I'll get taken away before then?" Tim asked anxiously.

Fuck. Simon hated seeing that uncertain look in the little boy's eyes. "No. I won't let anybody take you away. Do you trust me?"

Tim nodded and flung his small body toward Simon. He caught the child as Tim slammed against his chest, hugging him tightly, protectively, settling him on his lap.

"I don't need nothin', Simon. You already gave me more than I need. I just want to stay here with you, Kara and Ginny for Christmas," Tim mumbled, his voice full of longing.

Simon gulped and held Tim tighter as he vowed, "You're not going anywhere. You'll be here." They'd have to go through him to get to this child in his grasp. "Now, get some sleep before Kara gets mad at us."

Tim giggled as he flopped back onto his pillow. "She never gets mad. She just gives me this look sometimes when she isn't very happy about something I did or said."

Simon nodded in agreement. "Tell me about it. I've seen that look a lot more times than you have." He knew all about 'the look' and he hated it. When Kara wasn't happy, he wasn't happy.

"Night, Simon," Tim said sleepily.

Simon stroked a hand over the boy's neatly trimmed hair, a cut that Kara had done herself. "Sleep tight, Tim," he answered in a shaky voice. The kid was getting to him, making him feel protective, as though the boy were his own child.

Getting up, Simon clicked off the overhead light, leaving only a nightlight to illuminate the room.

"Simon?" Tim called tentatively.

Simon turned around. "Yeah?"

"I don't have nothin' to give anybody this year. It's only a week until Christmas, and I want to give something to you, Ginny, and Kara," Tim murmured, his tone upset. "Can you help me make something?"

Simon smiled in the darkness. "We'll go shopping tomorrow if you go to sleep right now," he muttered happily. "I like to Christmas shop." Kara would kill him, but hell, he had to let the kid buy some stuff.

"I'm sleeping," Tim vowed adamantly.

"Good." Simon left the door open a crack and made his way back to his bed to snuggle with his warm, sleeping wife.

Personally, he felt he never needed to receive another gift for the rest of his life. Kara was the best damn gift he'd ever gotten.

But hell, it was great to be a billionaire, and he was damn good at buying stuff. Smirking deviously, Simon was happy because he could buy more stuff for Kara and Ginny. His wife couldn't get irritated if the presents were from Tim.

Chapter 6

"Da-da," little Ginny Hudson said happily as Simon spread a mashed banana and some cheerios on the plate of her high chair.

Kara watched as he grinned hugely, right before his daughter threw her arm out and accidentally smacked him in the face. He completely ignored it as he straightened, boasting to Kara, "See how smart she is? Who is mama, Ginny?"

She moved over to her daughter as Ginny babbled, "Ma-ma," waving her arm toward Kara.

Simon had a silly grin on his face that said he thought he had the smartest daughter in the universe.

She leaned over and kissed her darling daughter on the head, Ginny's face already covered in mashed banana. "That's right, my sweet girl," she cooed, watching as Ginny flung Cheerios, only a few of them ending up in her mouth.

"Damn," the toddler muttered clearly.

Kara folded her arms in front of her and gave Simon an irritated glance.

"What? I didn't teach her that!" he protested.

"Then where did she hear it?" Kara asked curiously. Really, it was rather hard to keep a straight face, the sound of that word coming out of her daughter's mouth startling. "Little ears have to learn from somebody."

"I'm sure it was just baby talk," Simon argued, but he didn't meet Kara's eyes. "It only sounded like she was saying da—" He halted quickly and finished, "Um…a bad four letter word."

"It might be my fault," Timmy said unhappily as he joined them in the kitchen for breakfast. "I used to say it sometimes until Simon said it wasn't a nice word," he confessed, looking at Kara warily. "I'm sorry."

Kara's heart melted because Timmy looked so sad. She bent over and kissed the top of his head. He'd been raised in an environment where he'd constantly heard that word and probably many other four letter words that were much worse. It wasn't his fault. "It's all right, sweetheart. But it *is* a bad word, and we don't want you to say them or for Ginny to pick them up."

"I won't say it again. I promise."

Kara beamed at him. "I know you won't."

"Tim," Ginny squealed excitedly, obviously happy to see him.

Kara watched as Timmy went to Ginny and patiently helped her eat her cheerios.

"How come she doesn't use a spoon?" he asked curiously.

Kara smiled at him. "She isn't quite grown up enough to coordinate a spoon yet, but she will eventually."

"I'll teach her someday," Timmy offered.

Kara looked at her husband. Her heart clenched and they exchanged a melancholy glance. Would Timmy still be here to teach Ginny anything? She felt teary-eyed at the thought that he wouldn't. He was so good with their daughter, and Kara already loved the little boy. She was pretty certain Simon was getting attached to him, too.

All four of them together in one room, they just seemed to…fit. They felt like a…family.

Simon grabbed Timmy around the waist and sat him down at the table, putting his breakfast in front of him. Kara watched as Simon mentally calculated the carbs in the food, and got the appropriate amount of insulin for Timmy's meal. Her husband did it with such ease and such a lack of fuss that it had become part of their morning routine. Amazingly, he didn't shy away from what the diabetic child needed, even though it would have been far easier to leave it for her since she was a nurse. Nope. Not Simon. He attacked everything with gusto, learning everything he needed to know from books and from Timmy's team of medical consultants, which he himself had chosen. Her hubby already handled everything like a seasoned professional.

Kara went over to Ginny, her bare feet crunching down on fallen Cheerios. Her daughter was a complete mess, banana smeared all over her cherubic face. She grinned up at her mother with an innocent look in her dark brown eyes.

She looks so much like Simon.

Ginny had been born with blue eyes and dark hair, but her eyes had started turning brown months ago, and her resemblance to Simon had become even more defined. Her daughter had a generally sunny disposition, but when she got obstinate, Kara swore that Ginny had inherited every one of Simon's ornery, stubborn expressions.

"You're going to be a handful, baby girl, if you get as stubborn as your daddy," Kara said adoringly as she scooped her messy child out of the high chair to clean her up.

"I heard that," Simon called from the dining room table. "I'm not stubborn," he refuted in an obstinate voice.

Kara sniggered as she cleaned up her daughter and then the mess she'd made of her breakfast, while Ginny toddled over to see what her daddy and Timmy were doing. Simon *was* pigheaded, but he was also heartbreakingly sweet, and his gruff, bossy demeanor all revolved around protecting the people he loved.

It was funny now to think back to the days when he'd intimidated the bejesus out of her.

Grabbing her bowl of cereal and her coffee, she joined her family at the table. Finished with his breakfast, Timmy had Ginny cuddled on his lap and he was listening to her babble as though he understood every word she said.

Simon had his tablet on the table, flipping through some documents and finishing off his coffee. He was dressed casually, looking damn handsome in jeans and a forest green, long-sleeved, button-down shirt. He was expecting Sam, Max, Kade, and Travis any moment now, the four of them getting together to discuss the programs and investments for their charity for abused women. All four billionaires were heavy donors to the cause, and Kade and Travis wanted to keep everyone involved and informed. The charity had been the brainchild of the Harrison brothers because Kade's wife, Asha, had been badly abused, but Sam and Simon raised and donated money, too, and were one hundred percent supportive.

Kara was happy. The men were all bringing their wives and children, so she'd be together again with Maddie, Mia, Asha, and Ally. Their hectic lives made it pretty difficult for them to meet up as often as they liked.

She heard her cell phone ringing a few minutes later, and she jumped up and scrambled to the kitchen, thinking it might be someone who was going to be late dropping by.

It wasn't. And the news that the unwelcome caller relayed was information Kara definitely didn't want to hear.

Hanging up the phone, she walked back toward the kitchen, having stepped into the living room so Timmy wouldn't overhear her conversation. Her husband was just greeting all four men and their families in the hall right inside the door. "Simon. We have a problem," Kara told him loudly enough so he could hear her over the greeting taking place in the hallway.

His dark gaze landed on her with concern. "What is it, sweetheart?"

"That was the Department of Children and Families. They found a distant relative of Timmy's—somebody who might want to take him in." Kara's voice was anxious and tremulous, her knees shaking as she filled him in on the phone call.

"Bullshit," Simon exploded. "This apparent distant uncle never gave a shit about Tim before. I doubt they've ever met."

"They haven't," Kara admitted. "And I don't think they're going to turn him over anytime soon because this person has had some problems with the law in the past. It was the only family of Timmy's that they were able to find."

"Fuck. Tim is not going away with a goddamn criminal he doesn't know. The kid has been through hell. They'll have to go through me to get to him." Simon's voice was protective and rough, his hands clenching at his sides.

"They'll have to go through me, too," Sam offered his support.

"You can add my name to that list," Kade stepped forward.

"And mine," was the short, sharp response from Travis.

"I'm in," Max Hamilton said angrily.

"I'll call right now to have the papers drawn up for the bastard to sign." Sam handed Noah over to Asha, who was holding her arms out for her nephew since Maddie was already holding Brianna. Sam pulled his cell phone out of his pocket and stepped outside the door to talk.

Despite her anxiety, Kara's heart melted as she saw all five powerful men ready to do whatever it took to make sure one small child wasn't mistreated. "How will Sam know who the relative is?" Kara queried softly, laying a hand on Simon's muscular forearm.

His body was tense, his jaw clenched tight, but his expression morphed into one of reassurance and tenderness as he looked down at her. "He'll find out. There aren't many people who don't owe Sam a favor. Important people. I'll protect our boy, whatever it takes."

Our boy.

If Kara hadn't been so uptight, she would have smiled at Simon's slip of the tongue. Judging by the look on his face, Timmy was already his to protect, and he was taking it damn seriously.

She knew from experience that once Simon claimed someone, his protectiveness and affections never wavered.

Stroking her hand over his tight jaw, she answered softly, "I know you will."

Sam got all of the information he needed, and the men all filed out the door, their faces stony and determined.

Kara closed the door behind them and sighed heavily, hoping they could make things right. She didn't want Timmy to be afraid again, worried that he'd be taken away by somebody he didn't know, even if that person was distant family.

"Love is thicker than blood," Maddie called over her shoulder at Kara as all of the ladies and the kids gathered together in the living room. "And can you really doubt that anybody could stand up to all of our men?"

"No," Kara admitted with a weak smile. "One of them is fearsome. Together, they're completely terrifying."

She busied herself with getting something to drink for all of the ladies, a confident smile finally appearing on her face.

Simon had never, ever let her down, and she knew he wasn't about to start now.

Our boy.

She passed by a joyful Timmy on her way to the kitchen, who was happily carrying Ginny with him toward the living room so they could play with Noah and Brianna. Asha's baby did very little except sleep since he was a newborn, not even a month old, but Kara knew Timmy would keep the twins and Ginny busy.

Our boy.

Kara was mollified by Simon's words, knowing that Timmy really *did* belong with them, and her husband would never let him go without a fight.

Fortunately, he wasn't afraid of conflict, and he'd never lost a battle since she'd known him.

He's too damn stubborn to lose.

Kara was comforted by that thought the rest of the day.

Chapter 7

"What happened?" Kara murmured softly from their massive bed, watching her husband as he started to shed his button-down shirt.

Simon had called earlier and asked Kara to arrange for all the women and their children to be sent home amidst tight security since the men were going to be tied up. She'd agreed, and hadn't gotten any word from him since, except for his texts that all was going well.

It was late, but Kara hadn't been able to sleep. She'd waited up for him, every moment seeming like an eternity, slumber eluding her because of her overactive brain.

The bedside lamp was lit, and she could see her husband's enormous grin. "Mission accomplished. We took an attorney with us to draw up the papers for this asshole to sign off any rights to Tim. He lived in a shithole in Georgia, a drunk just like Tim's mother. He was so fucked up that he was barely coherent. We had to sober him up just to get him to sign."

She shuddered at the thought of Timmy being in almost the same situation again. Kara's eyes narrowed. "Did you pay him off, or beat him up?"

"Neither," Simon answered neutrally as he shrugged out of his shirt and tossed it onto a chair. He started working on his jeans before he answered, "Let's just say we confronted him with a little bit of dirt about his criminal activities we found on him, and he decided he didn't want to fight against us. He didn't really want Tim when he found out he had health issues and he'd need special care. I guess he thought he could take the check he got for fostering him and get some slave labor out of him. Bastard. Tim is only seven years old." He stepped out of his boxers and jeans, leaving him completely nude.

Kara sighed as she surveyed Simon's gloriously naked body. He was strong, so muscular and incredibly beautiful. "You're so handsome," she murmured softly, her eyes roaming over his six-pack abs and muscular chest. He bore the scars of his childhood, but they made him even stronger, more powerful, and completely irresistible.

Simon crawled onto his hands and knees on the bed, stalking her. "Woman, if I didn't love to hear you say that so much, I'd swear that you're blind." He tossed back the comforter and the sheets. "Holy hell, you're naked," he croaked.

She smiled at him seductively. "I was waiting for you." After she'd had Ginny, she'd starting wearing a nightgown because she had to get out of bed so many times every night. But she'd missed the intimacy of being skin-to-skin with him.

"Fuck. If I'd known I was going to get this kind of welcome, I would have tortured the bastard to get things done sooner," he said gruffly, his gaze caressing his wife lovingly.

"My hero," Kara whispered as she wrapped her arms around his neck. "Kiss me, handsome."

Simon wasted no time. He flipped her onto her back and pinned her wrists over her head. "Mine, dammit. Mine," he growled as his mouth came down over hers.

Kara reveled in his embrace as Simon's tongue swept into her mouth demandingly, an act of total possession that sent heat shooting straight between her thighs. Their tongues tangled with urgent need, Kara giving way to Simon's dominant insistence.

This is how I like him. Demanding and greedy.

When he broke off the kiss, she was panting, desperate to get him inside her. "Fuck me, Simon. Please."

"Mine," he rasped, kissing and nibbling at the skin on her neck. "Mine." His lips trailed down to her breasts, taking one of the tight peaks into his mouth and worshipping it before he switched to the other. "Mine," he repeated, biting gently on her nipple before soothing it with his tongue.

Kara whimpered and managed to yank one of her wrists free, and she put her hand between their bodies and grasped his cock. "Does that mean this is mine?" she asked breathlessly.

"Baby, my dick has been yours to command since the moment I saw you, and that's never changed. It'll never change. All I have to do is think about you and I'm fucking hard." He let go of her other wrist and slid down her body, forcing her to release his cock.

Kara's breath hitched as he pushed her legs apart with a palm to the inside of each of her thighs. Her heart thundered as she felt his hot breath on her core, her body trembling with need. "Simon. Please," she begged. "I need you."

"Mine," he groaned before he buried his face in her pussy.

She moaned and arched her back as he devoured her, licking her from her anus to her clit, his nose sliding over the throbbing bundle of nerves as he put everything he had into the task of making her come. Hard.

Spearing her hands into his dark hair, she fisted the locks hard, urging him onward. "Harder," she pleaded, needing more. With Simon, she always craved his total possession.

His tongue rolled over and over her clit, each motion harder, rougher. Kara felt the rush of liquid heat between her thighs, her body beginning to quiver. "Yes," she moaned with complete abandon, her head thrashing, and her hands holding Simon's hair in a death grip as he gave her exactly what she needed. He thrust two fingers into her channel, filling her as he bit down gently on her clit and used his tongue to vibrate against the nub.

She flew apart, her climax rolling over her. "Oh, God. Simon." Her sheath pulsated around his fingers, clenching and relaxing as she found her release.

He crawled up her body after he'd wrung every bit of pleasure he could from her orgasm, and lapped up every last drop of her liquid heat. "You taste so damn sweet," he grunted as he covered her body with his own. "I could taste you all fucking night."

"I couldn't take it," Kara answered breathlessly, wrapping her arms around his neck, wallowing in the feel of his warm skin against hers. "Fuck me. Please." She needed him so badly she wanted to weep.

He rolled her over, pulling her on top of him. "You take me, baby. Show me exactly what you want. Touch me."

As Simon lay in a position that he once hadn't been able to tolerate, Kara's eyes grew teary as she looked down at the man who'd learned to trust her completely. The man who actually wanted her touch instead of fearing it.

Boldly, she straddled him, feeling his cock bumping up against her clit as she moved her hips, sliding his long, thick length along her wet folds. "I don't feel like being gentle," she warned him, half serious and half joking, throwing back a comment to him that he'd made to her many times before.

Simon grinned, understanding her tender mocking. "Rough me up, sweetheart. I think I can take it."

She took his head between her hands and leaned down to kiss him, the taste of herself on his lips fuel to her already fiery body. "Hmmm," she hummed as she removed her mouth from his. "You taste like me. Mine," she murmured softly, watching Simon's eyes flare with possessive heat. She knew he loved it when she claimed him like he claimed her.

"Fuck me, Kara," Simon demanded. "Now."

She bit her lip to keep from smiling. She might be on top, but her being in control was an illusion. Other than the few times he'd trusted her by being bound, and the times when he'd misunderstood her hesitance to get naked, he was always a demanding, possessive, bossy lover. And she loved it. Simon made her feel loved, and he satiated her in a way that no man had ever satisfied her. "Bossy," she accused, swiveling her hips against his rock-hard cock.

"You want bossy?" he asked in a threatening voice before he bodily lifted her from him and placed her on her hands and knees in front of him. "Teasing time is over, baby," he growled. "I want you too damn much."

Gripping her hips forcefully, he seated himself inside her completely, groaning as he buried himself to the balls. "Mine," he rasped, his cock filling her, his hands moving from her hips to her belly and sliding up to cup her breasts. "You feel so fucking good."

She quivered from the feel of his cock stretching her, his fingers pinching her sensitive nipples just hard enough for the pleasure/pain sensation to drive her nearly insane.

Panting, Kara thrust her hips back, taking every inch of Simon that she could get.

"Fuck," he grunted. "I'm not going to be gentle," he warned her gravely as his hands gripped her hips tightly again, pulling his cock almost completely out before he thrust back in with one smooth stroke.

"*Aaah*," Kara breathed, needing Simon so much, her entire being shuddering from his possession.

He wasn't gentle. He began with a fast, hard rhythm of pounding into her that just got harder, faster, their skin slapping together with every powerful thrust.

"Harder," she pleaded, needing this rough reassurance of how much her husband wanted her.

"Come for me, sweetheart," he commanded as he slipped one hand to her belly and then down between her thighs.

As she pushed back into each stroke of his cock, she imploded when he ran rough fingers over her clit, her body rocking with her explosive climax. "Oh, God. Simon. I love you!" she screamed as she came apart.

"Love you," Simon groaned loudly as he found his own release, her sex milking him as she spasmed around him in a long, volatile orgasm.

Collapsing onto his back on the bed, he pulled her on top of him, his chest heaving. "I love you so goddamn much it scares the hell out of me," he grumbled, his arms coming around her protectively as he threaded his hands through her hair. He stroked over it soothingly and kissed the top of her head.

Kara burrowed further into his chest, resting her ear against his heart, feeling the rush of her heartbeat matching his own racing rhythm. "Me, too. I thought maybe I'd get over the craziness, but it never seems to stop. I love you more today than I did yesterday. And I think I'll love you more tomorrow than I do today." she sighed. "I guess this is how a good marriage should be. I think I'll spend a lifetime discovering something else about you every day, another thing to make me love you even more."

"Then I hate the days I piss you off," Simon said earnestly. "I want you to love me more *every* day."

Kara chortled. "Even when you piss me off, I still love you more every day."

The things that Simon did that annoyed her were far outweighed by his incredible capacity to love and protect the ones he cherished.

"Good. Then I have a confession to make," he said gruffly.

"What?"

"I took Tim out Christmas shopping. I know you said I was over-doing the gifts, but he really wanted to buy something for you and Ginny," Simon confessed.

Kara laughed. "I took him, too. He wanted to buy something for you."

"He played us. Smart kid" Simon's tone was proud.

"But he wasn't playing. It was really important to him. I don't think he did it intentionally," she answered, absently running her hand over the hard muscles of his chest, tracing each one of his scars lovingly.

"He didn't," Simon agreed. "But he figured out a way to do what he thought was right. He doesn't want anything for himself. He just wants to be with us."

Kara swallowed the lump in her throat. Lifting her head, she looked into Simon's eyes. "I want him to be with us, too. I love him, Simon. I love him just like he was my own child. I really would like to look into adopting him. You said you didn't want another child, but I really—"

He put his fingers to her lips to stop her. "I want that too, baby. More than anything. You know why I didn't want another child. It was all about you. But now that we have Tim, I don't want to let him go," he said hoarsely. "I want him to be able to live a normal life. I want him to be ours. He's damn easy to love."

She leaned down and kissed her husband tenderly before telling him, "You're an amazing man, Simon Hudson. I don't know why I never thought about adopting. I don't need to have a child with my DNA to love him like he was my own. There are so many kids out there who need a good home. I almost feel selfish for not thinking about it before."

"You. Are. Not. Selfish." Simon annunciated each word irritably. "It takes a special woman to adopt a child with special needs."

"Not really," she denied. "He's bringing me more happiness than problems. I know that he could become unstable at any time, that he could have complications, but I'm willing to be there for him. I want to be there."

Simon hugged her tighter. "Me, too, baby. Me, too."

Kara felt her eyes well up with tears, and they started plopping freely onto Simon's chest.

"Hey. Don't cry." He tilted her head up to look into her eyes. "I don't like it."

"They're happy tears," she sniffled.

"I don't care. I hate to see you cry," he grumbled.

"I know," she admitted, wiping the tears from her face. "I love you so much, Simon. That's why I'm crying."

Brushing the hair back from her face, he commented dryly, "Hell, if I was in love with somebody like me, I'd cry, too."

Kara giggled and punched him playfully in the biceps. "Loving you, having you as a husband makes me ecstatically happy," she answered fervently.

"Thank Christ," he retorted in a relieved, graveled voice, grabbing the sheets and comforter to cover their nude, entwined bodies.

Kara smiled against his chest, her heart light. After so many years of being alone, she didn't take having a wonderful family lightly.

After everything Simon had been through in his life, *he* was damn easy to love. Behind his gruff, intimidating exterior, he had a tender heart, One that she should have known was true from the minute he rescued her from homelessness a few years ago.

I'm lucky, so very fortunate to have Simon, Ginny, and now Timmy.

Christmas was coming, but Kara knew she already had everything she needed. She had Simon and the family they'd made together.

Still grinning and with Simon running a comforting hand up and down her bare back, she slept.

Chapter 8

Maddie Hudson plopped onto her couch late on Christmas Eve with a relieved sigh. "I'm exhausted, and I didn't even have to clean up the mess."

Sitting on the other end of the couch, the two women finally alone after the wonderful Christmas party Sam had arranged, Kara admitted, "Sometimes it's nice to have catering. Being married to a billionaire does have its advantages at times."

Maddie's eyes narrowed as she watched Kara consume another Christmas cookie, and then reached for the plate herself, taking a green frosted sugar cookie with a grimace. "Oh hell, I'll diet after the holidays."

"I'm stuffed," Kara admitted. "The food was fantastic and I'm beyond full, but I just keep eating."

"Too much temptation around," Maddie mumbled as she consumed her cookie.

The Christmas party had been wonderful. It hadn't been large, and had included only family, but Sam had made it extravagant and magical. Kara stared at the enormous Christmas tree that towered at least fifteen feet tall, and was entirely decorated with white lights, making all the bows and ornaments look absolutely beautiful.

Luckily, Sam and Maddie could accommodate the tree, their house really a mansion with towering cathedral ceilings. Even though their guests had already exchanged and opened all their presents for each other earlier in the evening, the space underneath the tree was still bursting with more to be opened in the morning, presents Maddie and Sam had bought for each other and the twins. "Your pile doesn't look any smaller than ours at the penthouse," Kara mentioned humorously, taking a big swig of her hot chocolate.

"Mostly from Sam," Maddie replied, her voice vibrating with amusement. "After our little shopping trip, I only left a few under the tree for him."

Both of the women had changed into comfortable clothes, jeans and festive Christmas sweatshirts. Sam and Simon had gone upstairs to check on all of the kids. The twins, Ginny and Timmy had all nodded off after the presents had been opened and they'd all eaten.

The caterers had cleaned up the party mess, and everyone had gone home, but Maddie's house was still splendidly decorated and very Christmassy. Kara had decorated the penthouse with Timmy a few days ago, pinning up mistletoe, and putting up greenery, bows and ornaments all over the house to go with the Christmas tree. Timmy even had a tiny tree in his room, one he swore he didn't ever want to take down. Unfortunately, since the small tree was real, it would have to come down, and he'd understand once the needles started to drop. But she'd wait until after Christmas to break the bad news to him. He was so delighted and so happy.

"Are we ready for the show? It's almost time," Kara reminded Maddie.

"I'm ready. We must be mad," Maddie giggled.

"Simon never even asked about the charges, and they were enormous," Kara told Maddie excitedly.

Maddie shrugged. "Sam didn't either. He never does."

"Why did we never think about doing this before? Our guys take care of us all the time, but we never go overboard for them," Kara mused. "And they really do deserve it."

"Because it wasn't that long ago that we were poor," Maddie answered. "And our husbands are billionaires who need or want for nothing."

"Now," Kara added quietly. "But there were so many Christmases when that wasn't the case. Neither one of them really had a childhood. Yet, Simon still tries to convince Timmy that Santa really exists."

Maddie shot Kara a mischievous grin. "He does? How sweet"

"I guess I just want to make up for every hurt that Simon has ever had, every Christmas that wasn't good when he was a child," Kara said thoughtfully.

"You realize that's exactly what they're trying to do for us," was Maddie's insightful response, as she nodded toward all the gifts under her tree.

"I know," Kara said with a smile, glancing at her watch as she rose. Walking over to a large picture window, she gasped as she pulled back the curtain and saw exactly what she and Maddie had been waiting for. "Wow."

Sitting her hot chocolate on the coffee table, Maddie rose. "What?"

"This guy is incredible." The light was dim, but the man who had promised to deliver all the gifts to Sam's pool house at midnight looked incredibly authentic. He was slinging another bag of presents onto his back, and was dressed up as Santa Claus. He was even driving what looked like a sleigh. Since they were in Florida and there was no snow, the vehicle had to have wheels, but they were obviously well concealed because Kara couldn't see them. "Holy crap. Those even look like…reindeer. Where did you find this delivery service?"

Maddie pushed up beside her and peeked out the window. "I didn't. I asked one of Sam's security team to find me a Santa to deliver gifts and gave him the details. He checked out the service and said it was legit, and I swore him to secrecy about the whole thing."

Kara squinted as she tried to figure out how what had to be horses had been disguised so well as reindeer. "We need to ask the agent where in the heck he came from. This guy is perfect."

"Come to think of it, that agent quit just yesterday. Said he had a family emergency and didn't know if he was coming back."

"We need to get the guys," Kara said excitedly, her whole body quivering with excitement.

She dashed up the stairs and sought them out, finding them in one of the guest rooms. It appeared that they'd just done a nighttime sugar check on Timmy, who was lying down trying to get to sleep. It wasn't difficult for her to muster up excitement as she told all three of them, "Santa's here, hurry!"

Timmy sat up in bed, his expression excited but wary. "Aren't I supposed to be sleeping? What if he's mad?"

Kara felt Maddie push in bedside her and said, "He won't be mad. I just asked him."

Timmy shot out of bed and raced past the two perplexed men. Simon shot Kara a confused looked, but she simply took his hand in hers and led him after Timmy, Maddie doing the same with Sam.

"Out in the pool house," Kara called to Timmy. "Santa said there wasn't enough room under the Christmas tree for everything."

"What are you up to?" Simon whispered loudly in her ear as he let her lead him outside and into the pool house, Maddie and Sam following close behind.

"It's Christmas," she told him. "You're allowed to act like a child and be surprised."

"I was never a child," Simon retorted nonchalantly.

Isn't that the truth!

The fact that Simon and Sam had never really had a childhood was one of the reasons she and Maddie were giving them this night. Simon had told her more than once that he'd been an adult his entire life. Just once, she wanted to take care of *his* needs, let him enjoy getting something for himself at Christmas.

"Be one tonight. Please," she told him softly, turning her head until their eyes met and held.

"Okay. Is Santa really here for Timmy?" Simon asked playfully, picking up on her mood.

"He's here for all of you. I told him you've been a good boy this year, too." She hesitated before she added, "Mostly."

They entered the pool house before Simon could reply, both of their gazes suddenly riveted to the massive piles of presents in the gazebo and bar portion of the pool house.

There was a small tree with twinkling lights set up and the room was decorated in red and green, something that Kara assumed Maddie must have arranged.

Santa was squatting next to Timmy, talking to the boy in a low, soft voice.

Ruffling his hair, Santa stood up and said in a booming voice, "Time for me to go. I have a lot of houses to visit tonight."

"Is all of this for us?" Timmy asked in an astonished voice.

Kara blinked as Santa stroked his very authentic looking white beard and winked at Timmy. "They're for every one of you who has been very good this year." His jolly, red face became sober for a moment as he added, "Some things that you should have had years ago."

Timmy was down on his knees, looking through the gifts. "Some are for me," he exclaimed excitedly.

Kara smiled at the pseudo Santa. "Thank you," she said in a voice low enough that Timmy couldn't hear.

"You're very welcome, Kara," he answered with a beaming smile.

How does he know that I'm Kara and not Maddie?

She'd never met the man before, and Maddie had arranged the delivery.

Santa looked at her and Simon's conjoined hands, and then his eyes moved to Sam and Maddie, specifically at their clasped hands before he said solemnly, "Love each other well. You all deserve that." In a louder voice, he bellowed, "Ho, Ho, Ho. Merry Christmas." Lifting a black gloved hand, he strode confidently out the door.

"There's a present here for you, too, Kara. And for Simon, Sam and Maddie," Timmy squealed happily.

Maddie and Kara exchanged a startled look. "Oh, no. He must have made a mistake," Kara muttered, distressed. She let go of Simon's hand and ran after the delivery guy, Maddie on her heels.

Both of them stopped abruptly as they reached the area of the circular drive where the sleigh had been parked.

"He's gone. How could he have left that quickly?" Kara asked Maddie breathlessly. She looked down the drive, seeing no sign of life.

All was quiet.

"I don't know," Maddie answered, sounding as confounded as Kara. "There shouldn't be any gifts for us in there, but we'll act cool. Timmy's so excited. I'll try to figure it out later."

Kara nodded to her, and the women made their way back to the pool house, only to find the "boys" already opening their gifts.

To Kara's relief, it was everything she and Maddie had bought for them. Both women knelt beside the tree and watched as the men and boy plowed through the mound of gifts, all of them grinning like children.

Maddie said she found a collection of tattered baseball cards in the back of the closet after she and Sam had gotten married. When she'd asked him why he no longer collected them, Sam told her the cards she'd found were a few common ones that he'd been able to get cheaply or for free as a kid, and he'd given up the hobby when he was a young boy. Sam loved baseball, and most of her gifts to him were related to the sport, including an incredible collection of cards and memorabilia that he was now eyeing like an enraptured kid.

Kara already knew about Simon's coin collecting, but she noticed he very seldom bought himself any, though he could very well afford it. Honestly, she was pretty certain it was because he was too busy thinking about her and had put the hobby on the back burner. She'd bought him a ton of hard-to-find coins and a bunch of other totally useless gifts that he might never use, but had probably coveted as a child.

Currently, all three "boys" were trying to put together a massive train set that had been a gift with all three of their names on it.

"If we're careful, we can give it to Noah someday," Timmy offered generously as Simon helped him put together a few of the railroad cars.

Sam ran a hand over the top of Timmy's head as he answered, "An excellent idea and very generous of you, Tim. But we get to play with it first." He shot Tim a mischievous grin.

Kara and Maddie sat back and let the men and Timmy have the space to play with their train set.

"They look so happy," Maddie said softly, as she stretched her legs out beside Kara's.

"Aren't you going to open your gifts?" Timmy asked, looking up from his train set to wave at the packages still under the tree.

The two women looked at each other and nodded slowly. Really, what choice did they have? Kara knew it would be weird if they didn't.

Thankfully, there was only one for each of them, and she took the packages that Timmy brought over to them before returning to his task.

Kara tore off the paper on the gift and gasped as she revealed exactly what the contents were. Inside the paper was a gift she'd coveted when she was a young girl: a beautiful holiday Barbie in a pure white, lace and fur gown. She'd wanted it desperately as a girl, but knew it was too pricey to ask her parents to buy that Christmas. They'd been dirt poor, and Kara had been happy to get a normal Barbie from a discount store. But oh, how she'd wanted this one. And it was the very same doll from that very same year, brand new in the package. She clutched the box to her chest reflexively.

"Please don't tell me that you just got a gift that you wanted the most during your childhood," Maddie whispered to her desperately.

Kara turned her head and looked at Maddie. "I did," she told her tremulously, holding out the now collectible Barbie for Maddie to see. "It's even the same year."

"Oh, God," Maddie whispered. "I got the thing I wanted most as a child, too. I wanted this Easy Bake Oven so badly, but I was in foster care. We got practical stuff. This is even the same model – it isn't even in production anymore. It hasn't been for years."

Kara watched as Maddie closed her eyes and clutched the box to her chest. "How can this be a coincidence?" she asked, stunned. Just how had these two presents with their names on them happened to get into this bunch?

"Santa?" Maddie asked hesitantly.

Kara looked around her, glancing at the three males, heads together, all of them grinning as they finally made the train go around the track. She looked down at the beautiful Barbie that she'd wanted so desperately so very long ago and held it to her chest, noticing that Maddie was still clutching her Easy Bake Oven. "I don't care how it happened," Kara finally admitted. "Maybe it was a wakeup call to make me start believing in Christmas miracles."

Maddie nodded slowly. "We have so much to be thankful for," she conceded.

"Like the fact that we both have daughters who we can pass these gifts down to?" Kara murmured, knowing she'd cherish the doll and give it to Ginny one day, and that she'd tell her the story of how it had come into her possession.

"Yes," Maddie sighed. "And sons we can be proud of and husbands who we love so much it's almost painful. Maybe our childhoods were all crap, but Santa's certainly making up for it now." She winked at Kara.

"So much has changed in the last few years," Kara said, watching her husband and Timmy adoringly.

"Thank God," Maddie added, her voice overflowing with happiness and gratitude. "Because our old lives really sucked."

Kara laughed and put the doll carefully on the floor, holding her arms out for a big hug. Maddie stowed her precious gift on the floor and hugged her back.

"Merry Christmas," they said in unison.

"Hey. Can we get into this action?" Simon asked gruffly.

Kara let go of Maddie and looked up at her husband, smiling broadly as she noticed he was holding a sprig of mistletoe over her head.

Next to her, Sam was standing in the same position, doing the same thing to Maddie.

Kara stood and curled her hand around Simon's neck and pulled his mouth to hers, giving him a slow, deep kiss full of emotion, trying to express without words how she was feeling.

As he raised his head, he gazed at her tenderly, his heart in his eyes. "I love you, baby."

"I can't reach," Timmy said unhappily, a piece of mistletoe in his hand.

Kara ruffled his hair and bent down to kiss his cheek. "You don't even need the mistletoe, little man."

Simon hoisted Timmy up and into his arms, bussing the boy on the forehead. "Time to sleep, buddy. We can play with more toys tomorrow," he said with a grin.

Kara got Ginny ready to go while Simon gathered up all of their stuff and loaded it into the car with the help of their driver. Finally, the four of them were situated in the back seat of Simon's limo, all of them very tired but happy.

She rested her head against Simon's shoulder, her heart completely full of joy and contentment. Not so long ago, she'd been homeless, alone in the world without a single person who cared about her, except Maddie. "I'm so happy I could cry," she whispered to Simon.

"Don't cry. I don't like it," he grumbled. "Just be happy."

"I already am." She stretched and kissed his sexy, whiskered jaw. Her husband had never quite grasped the concept of happy tears.

"I bet I could make you happier, once we get the kids to sleep," Simon drawled in a low, wicked voice.

Kara's core clenched and heat flared between her thighs. She smiled into the darkness as she agreed, "I'm sure you can."

"I have a heart-wish saved for a special occasion," Simon answered in a low, hopeful voice.

She leaned into him and flicked her tongue over his ear. "You won't need it tonight or any night that you want me."

"I always want you. You're mine, Kara, and you always will be," he answered in a harsh whisper, both of them keeping their voice down, even though Timmy was fast asleep, his head leaning sweetly against Ginny's car seat.

"And you'll always be mine," Kara retorted, running her palm down the side of his face.

"Damn right," he grumbled, his voice starting to sound lusty and bossy. "You're the best damn present I've ever gotten. You always will be."

Kara bit back a smile, thinking that being loved by and loving the man beside her was the best gift she'd ever had, too.

At one time, Kara hadn't believed in miracles. Nothing miraculous had ever happened to her in her life, and she'd struggled through heartache and poverty, just trying to survive. But just like the Barbie she'd gotten tonight, sometimes marvelous and rare things did come in time. Simon was living proof.

She sent up a silent *thank you* to Santa for reminding her that something as precious and rare as the love that she and Simon shared was worth the waiting and the pain.

Just like Santa had advised them, she'd love him well. Men like Simon Hudson were rare, and as soon as the kids were settled and asleep, she'd show him just how much she loved him.

Epilogue

"**D**o you think I'll get to take all this stuff with me, Simon?" Timmy asked anxiously on Christmas day, surrounded by a mound of presents that was taller than he was.

Simon looked at the apprehension in the child's eyes and scowled. Kara was in the kitchen making Christmas dinner, so he was holding a sleeping Ginny against his chest as he lounged on the couch and wondered if he'd bought enough presents for everyone. Yeah. Okay. Kara thought he'd gone way overboard, but the way he saw it, more was always better. As much as he loved his wife, Ginny, and Tim, he could buy several semi-trucks full of presents for them and it wouldn't be enough to even try to show them how much they meant to him.

Hesitating, Simon wasn't sure what to tell Tim. Hell, yeah, the boy was keeping his stuff. And Simon was keeping the kid.

Mine.

As far as Simon was concerned, Tim was his to protect now, and over his dead body would anyone take his son away. The boy had been through enough, had spent enough of his young life feeling like nobody wanted him. He and Kara wanted Tim, and they were keeping him.

"Come here," he told the frightened boy in the gentlest voice possible, as he thought about someone —anyone—pulling the vulnerable seven-year-old away from his new home.

Bullshit. Not. Happening.

Tim stood up immediately from his place near the tree and scrambled onto the couch right next to Simon, wrapping a protective little arm around Ginny.

Simon swallowed hard as he looked down at Tim and Ginny, the two of them already bonded. Tim was already a protective older brother to his daughter. "Don't tell Kara I told you, but we want you to stay with us forever," Simon said hoarsely. He wasn't certain how Kara would feel about Simon telling Tim about their plans to adopt him so soon and without her present, but he couldn't help himself. He couldn't stand to watch the boy so damn miserable.

Tim looked up at him with a stunned expression. "Forever? You want me to stay?"

Christ! Was it that hard for Tim to believe somebody actually wanted him? That just made Simon even more pissed off at the world. "Yeah. We want to adopt you, Tim. What do you think about that?"

"Why?" Tim asked, his eyes full of wary hopefulness. "I'm sick. I'm a lot of work."

Simon nearly growled, but he restrained himself. "Do you feel sick right now?"

Tim shook his head slowly. "No. I feel good. But I'll feel sick sometimes."

Simon couldn't argue with that. There probably would be times when Tim had problems, but handling it was part of being a parent. He was more than willing to deal with it. "You're not sick. You have a disease that will cause you problems sometimes," Simon answered honestly. "But that doesn't matter to Kara and me. We love you, buddy. And we want you to be our son and Ginny's brother. I'm hoping you want that, too," he told Tim gruffly.

He nearly groaned when large tears formed in the little boy's eyes and started running down his cheeks as he looked up at Simon with an awed expression. "For real?" Tim asked, his expression still cautiously optimistic.

Jesus. The kid was killing him. Where the hell was Kara? She dealt with this stuff better than he did. Maybe he shouldn't have mentioned it. "Yeah. For real. And don't cry. I don't like it," he grumbled, swiping the tears from Tim's face with gentle fingers.

Tim lifted his own palm and scrubbed at the tears. "Because it's not manly, right?"

Simon could have easily lied and agreed, but he answered honestly. "No, Tim. I don't like it because when somebody I care about cries, it makes me sad, too."

"What about happy tears?" Tim sniffled.

"I never saw happy tears when I was young. I don't think I've quite figured them out yet," Simon replied, smiling at him. "Kara does that happy tears thing, but for me, crying means sadness."

"I'm not sad, Simon. I'm just scared," Tim said hesitantly.

Simon frowned. "Why?"

"I want to stay with you, Kara, and Ginny so much. But I'm afraid something bad will happen. It usually does."

"It won't," Simon vowed. "I promise. You trust me, right?"

Tim nodded eagerly.

"You remember what I said about keeping my promises?"

Tim inclined his head solemnly.

"You'll be my son, just like Ginny is my daughter," Simon promised, a lump forming in his throat.

Kara had been right. A child didn't have to have his own DNA to steal his heart. This boy had burrowed himself into that stubborn organ the moment he'd accepted Simon exactly the way he was, scars and all.

"If you adopt me, will I be able to call you dad?" Tim asked hopefully. "And will Kara be my mom? And I'll be able to call Ginny my sister?"

"Yes, yes, and yes. You don't have to wait until the adoption is final. You're our boy," Simon answered protectively.

Finally, a broad smile appeared on Tim's face and Simon relaxed. *Holy hell.* He hoped he never had to see this child cry ever again, happy tears or not.

"What's going on in here?" Kara asked curiously as she stepped into the living room.

"You're going to be my mom," Timmy chattered excitedly.

Simon's heart accelerated as his wife looked at him questioningly. He nodded, unable to get anything past the lump in his throat.

Dressed casually like the rest of them, Kara's body was being lovingly hugged by a worn pair of jeans and Christmas sweatshirt. Her face was flushed from being in the kitchen, and her bright blue eyes were smiling at him.

Mine.

As usual, he wanted her the moment he saw her, but his love went so much deeper than the physical. She was the missing part of his soul, and he was finally whole. Ginny and Tim were a huge bonus, making everything so fucking perfect, it was frightening.

Kara thought he had saved her, but really, she'd been the one to rescue him from a profound loneliness he'd never even acknowledged until he'd met her, a loneliness that no longer existed.

I have a family of my own now.

He grinned at her as Tim threw himself into her arms and hugged her like he never wanted to let go.

Simon understood exactly how the kid felt.

"You're really going to be my mom?" Timmy questioned enthusiastically.

Kara hefted the boy up and sat down beside Simon, holding Tim on her lap. "I really am. I want to be your mom," she told the boy softly.

"Then Santa was right. He said not to worry, that you'd be my mom and dad someday. I should have believed in him," Tim said worriedly.

"Santa said that?" Kara whispered quietly into the boy's ear, looking startled.

Timmy nodded at her.

Simon looked at his wife and she shot him an alarmed look. He wondered if she was upset because he'd already mentioned adoption to Tim. "What's the matter?"

Tim gave Kara a final hug and slid off her lap to go organize and play with his Christmas gifts.

Kara smiled at him and shook her head. "Nothing important. I'll tell you later. But I think I should start believing in Santa."

"I'm sorry I told Tim without you being here, but he was worried," Simon told her quietly, keeping his voice down so the child didn't overhear them.

"It's okay," Kara whispered, resting her head against his biceps with a yawn.

"Tired?" he asked with a grin.

"Yes. Somebody has been keeping me up late," she answered in a sleepy voice.

"Just trying to remind you how much I appreciate your body," Simon replied. *Shit.* He already had a boner the size of Texas just from thinking about the night before, and the night before that.

"I'm beyond convinced," she replied wickedly, turning her head to look at him. "But I might need nightly reminders."

"Want a nap? I'll watch the kids." He didn't want her to be tired. More convincing was definitely going to happen later that night.

"And miss Christmas?" Kara exclaimed. "No way. Besides, I have one more gift for you." She dug into the pocket of her jeans and pulled out a plain, white envelope.

Simon's lips turned up into a broad smile. He already knew what the envelope contained…his heart-wishes. Snatching the envelope up with a covetous glance, he rasped, "How many?"

"Five," Kara replied. "But I promise you'll get some every holiday from now on."

He'd hoped for more, but he'd take whatever he could get. Those tiny pieces of paper were like gold for him. His wife was the sweetest woman in the world, but damn, she could be stubborn sometimes.

Those little hearts came in handy. They were his best gift this Christmas.

Simon shoved them into the front pocket of his jeans as Kara took Ginny from his arms. "Time for her nap," she said in a motherly voice.

Tim ran over and clambered back into Simon's lap. Kara ruffled his hair and gave him an adoring look.

"I can put Ginny down," Simon told his wife, wrapping an arm around Tim.

Kara sighed. "I think I'd just like to sit here for a minute and look at the tree."

"Did you like your gifts?" Simon asked anxiously.

"Yes. Everything was wonderful, but unnecessary. I have everything I need right here with me on this couch." She reached up and stroked Simon's cheek.

God, Simon loved it when she said things like that. And Kara wasn't just *saying* it. He knew it was coming from her heart.

"Merry Christmas, my love," Kara said wistfully, her voice quivering with emotion.

"Merry Christmas, baby," he answered, wrapping an arm around her and pulling her closer him.

Simon knew they'd face challenges in their lives, but right now he knew Kara was right. Everything he needed was right here on this couch, and he was never going to let any of them go.

The family of four sat on the couch for a very long time, savoring the feel of being a family.

After some time had passed, Tim murmured quietly, "I have a mom, dad, and sister now. I won't be alone anymore." The boy let out a quiet, contented sigh.

Simon's arm tightened reflexively around Tim. He didn't truly know what it was like to be alone because he'd always had his mother and Sam. But he'd known loneliness and emptiness before he'd met Kara, and they were a bitch.

Turning his head, he found his wife watching him quietly, her blue eyes shining with happiness. She was smiling and Simon's chest started to ache. How had a scarred street kid like him scored a woman as sweet and beautiful as his wife? "I *am* a lucky bastard," he rasped.

Kara glanced down at Tim and said in an urgent, harsh whisper, "Simon. Little ears." She nodded her head at the boy on Simon's lap.

Timmy grinned at both of them. "Don't worry. I've heard that before, and Simon already told me it's a bad word. He told me not to say a bunch of other words, too."

Kara glared at Simon, but her lips were twitching. "Such as?"

Tim looked at her with boyish smile. "How can I tell you if I'm not allowed to say those words?"

"Smart boy," Simon praised him with a smirk.

Kara shot them both a reproving look. "I can see you two are going to be keeping secrets." Her gaze landed on Tim. "You're starting to sound like a miniature Simon already."

Clearly, Tim was pleased with Kara's comment because his grin got even bigger.

Simon could tell Kara was about to start laughing because she was having a hard time keeping her "disapproving mother" expression on her face.

Tim shrugged, mimicking the expression of nonchalance that Simon had perfected over his years in business. "It's a guy thing," Tim told Kara solemnly.

Even Simon had to admit that Tim did a perfect imitation of him when he was being an asshole. *Damn.* It was good to have a little more testosterone around the house.

Giving up, Kara burst into laughter, and Simon's smirk turned into a chuckle as Tim looked at them both curiously, wondering what they were laughing about.

"It's a man and wife thing," Simon told him, laughter still ringing in his deep, happy tone. "You'll understand it someday when you're older."

Ginny started to fuss, and Kara let her little girl slide down to the floor, Tim already on his feet to catch his new sister protectively.

"Tim," Ginny squealed happily. "Tim. Tim. Tim." She toddled after her new brother as he took her near the tree to play with their gifts.

"They already look so much like siblings," Kara said wistfully.

Simon glanced over to his wife and pulled her easily into his lap. "They are," he answered simply. The two children had bonded almost immediately, blood related or not.

Kara drew a palm down Simon's rough jaw. "Thank you for talking to him about being adopted. I think he needed to know. He's been so afraid." She sighed and wrapped her arms around her husband's neck. "You make me so happy."

Simon's heart began to race as he looked into Kara's eyes and saw the woman who had changed his whole existence, the woman who made his future look better than it ever had before. "I know how to make you a lot...happier." And yeah, it involved a bed...or maybe just a wall, or even the shower.

"Show me later," Kara whispered to him seductively. "Right now, just kiss me."

"Mine," Simon growled as he wrapped a hand around the back of her neck and brought her lips close to his. "And you can count on being shown *everything* later."

He stayed just like that for a brief moment, their eyes locked together, Kara's warm breath caressing his mouth. "Merry Christmas, Simon," Kara whispered softly.

Simon shuddered and covered her mouth with his, unable to have Kara so close and not kiss her.

The rest of their private party came later that night, the two of them celebrating the merriest Christmas they'd ever had.

~The End~

Please visit me at:
http://www.authorjsscott.com
http://www.facebook.com/authorjsscott

You can write to me at
jsscott_author@hotmail.com

You can also tweet
@AuthorJSScott

Please sign up for my Newsletter for updates,
new releases and exclusive excerpts.

❦————————————————————————❧

Books by J. S. Scott:

Billionaire Obsession Series
The Billionaire's Obsession~Simon
Heart of the Billionaire
The Billionaire's Salvation
The Billionaire's Game
Billionaire Undone~Travis
Billionaire Unmasked~Jason
Billionaire Untamed~Tate
Billionaire Unbound~Chloe
Billionaire Undaunted~Zane
Billionaire Unknown~Blake
Billionaire Unveiled~Marcus

Billionaire Unloved~Jett
Billionaire Unchallenged~Carter
Billionaire Unattainable~Mason
Billionaire Undercover~Hudson
Billionaire Uexpected~Jax

The British Billionaires
Tell Me You're Mine

Accidental Billionaires
Ensnared
Entangled
Enamored
Enchanted
Endeared

Sinclair Series
The Billionaire's Christmas
No Ordinary Billionaire
The Forbidden Billionaire
The Billionaire's Touch
The Billionaire's Voice
The Billionaire Takes All
The Billionaire's Secret
Only A Millionaire

The Pleasures of His Punishment

The Pleasures of His Punishment: The Complete Collection

The Billionaire Next Door

The Millionaire and the Librarian

Riding with the Cop

Secret Desires of the Counselor

In Trouble with the Boss

Rough Ride with a Cowboy

Rough Day for the Teacher

A Forfeit for a Cowboy

Just what the Doctor Ordered

Wicked Romance of a Vampire

The Curve Collection: Big Girls and Bad Boys Series

The Curve Collection: The Complete Collection

The Curve Ball

The Beast Loves Curves

Curves by Design

Writing as Lane Parker

Dearest Stalker: Part 1

Dearest Stalker: A Complete Collection

A Christmas Dream

A Valentine's Dream

Lost: A Mountain Man Rescue Romance

A Dark Horse Novel w/ Cali MacKay
Bound
Hacked

Taken By A Trillionaire Series
Virgin for the Trillionaire by Ruth Cardello
Virgin for the Prince by J.S. Scott
Virgin to Conquer by Melody Anne
Prince Bryan: Taken By A Trillionaire

Other Titles
Well Played w/Ruth Cardello